I would like to thank my loving and supportive family for believing in my ability to write this novel and for tolerating the extended stay of my characters, Stellanova and Chase Osborn, with us during the years it took me to bring this project to fruition.

"To Stella Osborn

from Robert Frost

who was brought to Ann Arbor

by Gov. Osborn in 1921

where so much happened."

"Always"

By Irving Berlin

Not for just sixty minutes, not for twenty-four hours,

Not even for a whole darned year,
three hundred and sixty-five days,

But I mean always!

To Pam,

Ward, Wife, Widow

by

A. Arbour

Best Wishes on Your Reading Journey!

A. Arbour

Chapbook Press

Schuler Books
2660 28th Street SE
Grand Rapids, MI 49512
(616) 942-7330
www.schulerbooks.com

Ward, Wife, Widow

ISBN 13: 9781957169071

Library of Congress Control Number: 2022907846

Printed in the United States by Chapbook Press.

Introduction

Dear Reader,

I have enjoyed giving Chase Salmon Osborn (1860-1949) and Stellanova Osborn (née Stella Lee Brunt, 1894-1988) a life in the 21st century by writing this novel. Their legacies warrant renewed attention. Their colorful lives are either forgotten by the vast majority of Michiganders or, if they are remembered, what is remembered would be fodder, in today's world, for tabloid news. I began with a strong impulse to rescue Stellanova's reputation from the tabloid treatment of the trajectory of her life to which she could so easily have been consigned. Anyone would deserve better, and certainly, her scholarly collaborations, her poetry, her lifelong pursuits (including volunteering for several international world peace organizations), and her devotion to Chase Osborn would justify a more in-depth look at her life and her choices.

I hope you will become as enthralled with the real Chase and Stellanova Osborn as I have come to be. However, this book is a novelization of their lives, which has given me the opportunity to imagine the complexities of their unique situation. I have researched their lives and taken great liberties with some of the facts and timelines.

With an appetite for more substantive information about the Osborns, it is easy to find out a good deal of information about Governor Chase Osborn's life on the internet and in his autobiography of the first two-thirds of his life, *The Iron Hunter,* or the biography lovingly written about the last chapter of his life, *Eighty and On* by Stellanova Osborn. There is not, however, much information to be readily accessed about the last third of Chase Osborn's life and even less information about Stellanova's life in general. She was a poet and co-authored many books with Chase Osborn. However, I was not satisfied to relegate Stellanova's life to mere nodes on a timeline of Chase Osborn's life. She should be more than a footnote in history as a helpmate to an important and influential man.

Chase Osborn led a larger-than-life existence, but he is unfairly diminished by death because recent generations have never heard of him or his ward, wife, and widow, Stellanova Osborn. We have Chase's profile, Stellanova's poetry, but not the prose in between about their life together—the dynamics of their relationship and the issues that may have animated their conversations. Their correspondence included in this novel are the actual words that they exchanged between 1921 and 1931, with the exception of the very first letter that Stellanova wrote to Chase in 1921. She did indeed write to him in 1921 to thank him for funding Robert Frost's residency at the University of Michigan. Unfortunately, this letter has been lost to posterity, but it was the spark that lit the flame.

The letters are extraordinary, but I also went in search of the Stellanova who was more than Chase Osborn's adopted (as a 37-year-old) daughter and co-author. Surely, Stellanova had ordinary feelings about an extraordinary life. The search for this Stellanova started when I was given the gift of silence and the absence of modern-day distractions while kayaking on an inland lake in northern Michigan. It was at that moment that a more mature Stellanova—rather than the stars-in-her-eyes letter writer—started "speaking" to me. Stellanova has not stopped speaking to me, and if I am very quiet, she even whispers her deepest, darkest secrets to me.

I hope that my novel will spark a renewed interest in both the Osborns. I believe that getting some things wrong about this unusual pair is a fair exchange for their resurrection.

A. Arbour

Prologue
Burnished Memory

The warm glow of lights through the windows of a library never fails to captivate me. The darkest nights provide the greatest contrast, and there is no darker place than just above the 45th parallel and just below the "tip of the mitt" in northern Michigan. It is there where I have spent nearly all the summers of my life, at the University of Michigan Biological Station along the quiet shores of Douglas Lake. The Station's library was erected in the mid-20th century. A former director of the Biological Station was not an architect or an engineer, but he designed the prototype of this library with his son's building blocks. It is as perfect in form and function as any building I have ever known, entered, or dwelt.

This was my first library. Although I have visited many since, it remains my favorite— from the outside looking in and from the inside looking out. I love everything about this library, from the big black and maroon linoleum tiles to the cement block walls, painted a warm French vanilla-yellow, to the high ceiling supported by exposed wooden rafters from local pine.

I love the creaky and slightly listing loft-like second story where the most coveted study spot is located—a low-slung shell-shaped wicker chair in front of the large double-sashed window overlooking the lakeshore. I love the heady smell of binder's glue, and pine bookcases, intermingled with the faintest scent of Eau de Mouse fermented over many decades—the wafting of incense in a cathedral of learning.

This story begins in my youth, when there was a figure who sat in the library in the same place evening after evening, summer after summer. It was a bust of a man. His head was not bent over a book like those of the students I saw as I walked past the library nightly on the way back to my cabin. This man's profile gave me the "willies," as we used to say—like a prop from a campy "Twilight Zone" episode. His stern visage and his constant vigil may have discouraged anyone from taking books out of the library. The library was open 24/7 and the librarian could not always be there, so no one was allowed to take volumes out of the building. The bust remained there all through the 1960s and 1970s of my childhood, and then it disappeared. It either fell victim to a sophomoric prank or someone with enough reverence for the man's legacy saved it from such a fate and removed it to a safer location on the main campus. In any case, the bust's presence, and then its absence made an indelible impression on me. Even if I could never find out what happened to it, I could at least find out about the man who inspired its creation.

Little did I know this eerie and unsettling sentinel's identity would become clear to me while a student at the storied University of Michigan. I learned that this presence in my childhood library was a copy of a bust of Chase S. Osborn, the Governor of Michigan (1911-1913). And the bust was my muse inspiring this story about Chase S. Osborn and his ward, wife, and widow, Stellanova Osborn. Much of it took place only a few scant miles from where I first saw that strange apparition, though the beginnings go back many years and are revealed in the personal correspondence I discovered in the archives of the Bentley Historical Library on the campus of the University of Michigan.

"All Alone"

March 5, 1921

I wonder, mother, why it was I could never be young when I was young and giddy when most girls are giddy, and getting married when that is the usual thing to do? Sometimes I get to feeling very sorry for myself, mother, for I am quite sure I wasn't "born to be an old maid" at all. But I guess I wasn't born to be unhappily married either. Don't you think, if I had tried, once upon a time when I was so young that I should have made a good housekeeper and a good mother? But now I am growing too old—I am ever so much older than my years inside! And I am growing deep into my books. I shall grow peculiar in spite of myself, and young people will poke fun at me as a funny creature that didn't know what to do with life. But mother, who would want to marry at all unless one could feel that there was to be a home where one and one's children could really care for "dad." I believe in a half-happy loneliness rather than a spoiled home. I didn't mean to make this a confessional, but there is so much of me you have never learned of, mother, it ought to do us both good even to exchange each other's spells of the "blues."

Your Loving Daughter,

Stella

On a Whim

Dear Governor Osborn,   March 12, 1921

I wish to thank you for funding the Frost
Residency. I am a student at the University of
Michigan, and I have had the good fortune of
attending lectures, readings, and discussions led
by Mr. Robert Frost. As a poet and an especial
admirer of Mr. Frost's work, this has been the most
consequential experience of my life. I fear that
everything in my future may pale in comparison.

Since I am from Hamilton, Ontario, I was not
familiar with your name and reputation. I found
your newly published biography *The Iron Hunter* at
the library and was most impressed with your life
and work.

Permit me to elaborate upon what Mr. Frost's
residency has meant to me, and, I venture, to
others. I first encountered Mr. Frost when I was
invited to the home of Professor Cowden, of
the English Department, with a small group of
young ladies, all students, in fact, the founders
and editors of "whimsies" (a literary magazine
published by university students). The Cowdens
set out a big chair, front and center, for Mr. Frost,
but he preferred to sit in an unpretentious, dim
corner. Apparently, he asked the Cowdens not to
bother serving any refreshments, but Mrs. Cowden
insisted, and the poet partook of the cookies
and punch as gratefully as any other guest. As
Professor Cowden introduced us one by one, we
found Mr. Frost to be very kind and unassuming. If
you have never met Mr. Frost, I would describe him
as being a not-at-all-trim man of medium stature
in a not-too-well-pressed grey suit, with fair and
not-too-tidy hair. He speaks lightly enough, with a
whimsical, skipping surface over his comments, yet

there is a lasting tang of significance in the stuff of them. The conversation of Frost sparkles, more elusively, and is at its best, in the pauses—when it is in his eyes, between words.

No other student group has met more with Mr. Frost than our little lot of the "Whimsies." We were thrilled when he wrote a poem entitled "Evening in a Sugar Orchard" for our magazine. He even asked us to address him as 'Robert' or 'Frost.' Would it surprise you to know that he is also an excellent gossip? I can assure you, however, that our interactions were not purely social in nature. He had all sorts of time to critique our poems. He could be both humorous and ruthless. It was a harrowing experience for me when Frost kept scolding me over the same old faults—not making my meaning clear and using old phrases. My nerves were all on edge, to begin with, and that about unsettled me. I didn't sleep all night.

You may hear some criticism of Frost, but not from this corner. Mr. Frost's arrangement to teach no regular classes irked some cranks in the off-campus community. An anonymous writer in *"The Washtenaw Post"* questioned the suitability of funds provided to Frost "not to even twirl his thumbs if he does not so desire." This is utterly unfair because Mr. Frost has kept up a strenuous schedule of public events and meetings with faculty and students. It is a wonder that he has had any time to write, yet he has been very productive. Your generosity in providing the funds for Mr. Frost's fellowship has been well spent.

After sharing the sour sentiments above, I must share with you the lighter side. A local drug store created an ice cream confection covered in chocolate and called it the "Frost-Bite." President Burton jested that Frost might be more popular than football coach Fielding Yost. Frost said that if he were to schedule a poetry reading in Hill Auditorium during a home game, not a single person would be in the auditorium because he, too, would attend the home game.

If there is anything that I can ever do to repay your generosity, I would gladly do it. Humbly, I cannot imagine what that might be, unless you ever needed the services of a personal secretary.

Miss Stella Lee Brunt

Toll

September 1980

To Whom It May Concern,

I will "let time tell the story more plainly," as Chase told me to do in his stinging rebuke in that letter from 50 years ago. I will not censor the story by telling it myself. I will leave all our correspondence to our beloved University of Michigan. That is where it all began, and it is there it should all end, unless someone comes looking —not looking for me or for him—but for us.

Chase started to return my letters because he thought they might also serve as diary entries. That is how the archives were seeded with six hundred pages of correspondence between us in the decade from 1921-1931. Chase also blue-penciled my letters in his scrawling penmanship, almost as inscrutable as a set of hieroglyphs with no Rosetta Stone to help decipher them. He told me in one of his letters, "Write your diary; also put yourself in a novel." He told me to include "your love, your doubts, your spirit, your devil self, your average self, your most intimate experiences physical, intellectual, spiritual." And here is the best part of his directive, "Tell of the men you have known—the two beasts." He also encouraged me to add "a touch of Frost." Chase even suggested a title, "The Damn Heart," or "Wrecked in Ether." As it turned out, I never had the time or the courage, even though he said he would be proud of me if I were to write a novel.

I hope that this long-awaited person who finds herself wading through our correspondence is not a biographer, but a novelist because otherwise I may be only a footnote in the illustrious life of the late great Michigan Governor Chase Salmon Osborn. A biographer would only report the stranger facts about my life, burying me *again* under the shovelfuls of gossip and the weight of Chase's legacy.

A novelist will write with more boldness and honesty about my life than I dared to reveal during my lifetime. So, if the desired novelist is reading this, I welcome you to flesh out my life from the dry bones found amongst the brittle and water-stained sheaves I gave to the Bentley Historical Library. Make me blush like a schoolgirl with the honesty and the grittiness of what you write and reveal. Give me the words that I did not dare to put down on paper for public consumption. I wrote about Chase's life, but not about our lives together. I also wrote poetry about loving the perfection I found in nature, but I did not write about loving an imperfect man.

Find us, Chase and me, on the path where the timelines of our lives intersected. Now, my novelist friend (I shall think of you in advance as a friend), whoever you may be, follow the trail to find us in the woods of Northern Michigan, on a remote island in the St. Mary's River. One day Chase and I will be buried together there under a rock left by the retreating glaciers. We both believed in eternal life with our Heavenly Father, but I want one more go 'round on this planet with Chase Salmon Osborn. Exhume us. Otherwise, our paths in this life will disappear.

Sincerely,

Stellanova Osborn

(née Stella Lee Brunt)

Toll

You must hold a trail down with your foot

If you want it to stay—

It will not lie quiet and wait

while you are away.

The bracken will hide it, the hazel

in no time at all

will fence up with the blueberry patch.

A popple will fall

straight in the center and stretch

and make believe it's a wall.

You can't wander off and expect

to re-find it some haphazard day—

You must hold a trail down with your foot

if you want it to stay.

-Stellanova Osborn

Spring Cleaning
May 1980

Stellanova Osborn, an octogenarian (yet always an ingénue in the public's imagination), was packing up boxes and going through papers in a small log home. The old cabin had its own climate—dust moats with a small chance of sunlight mixed with a haze of soot. Whatever beauty the cabin had, was in the eye of the beholder, as was the present appearance of Stellanova herself. The elderly woman with the sly smile, unnerving gaze, and gray, blunt cut hair was decades away from the younger woman in her 20s with that enigmatic smile, sultry eyes, and the bob of a flapper. Yet if you were to look more closely, you could translate her features into those of decades ago. Be kind and give her that simple gift of your imagination, so she does not feel washed out, and worse yet, invisible. After all, she had already spent so much of her life invisible as a stepchild and then playing the role of a spinster daughter. Equally painful was her feeling out of step with her peers, the memory of which came flooding back while reading that old letter to her mother.

She was not making steady progress on the task of moving. The sluggishness of resisting the move was making the task more difficult. Moving from the secluded island lapped by the capricious waves of the St. Mary's River to an apartment on the mainland, or in The Soo, as the locals called Sault Ste. Marie, would make life more convenient, but that was about all the attraction the move had for her. In truth, there had been times when she felt a bit isolated living on Duck Island—an island within an island—for it was a bit like living with a laird in his fortress surrounded by a moat. But at other times, she had wanted to pull up the drawbridge to interrupt the steady stream of courtiers and have the laird all to herself.

Resisting the move was not the only thing slowing down the process. Reflection was proving to be the greatest obstacle to boxing things up. Memories were not fitting neatly into square or rectangular boxes.

She could so easily lose herself in rereading the letters stored in the trunk. The smell of the cedar flooded her senses. The pivotal decisions of her life were in those cedar-infused letters. Maybe she should burn them like incense, but then she thought, "Why deprive some work-study student at the U of M from getting to read something *truly* interesting?" Although she had been an archivist of her own life, saving every scrap of correspondence for future researchers, she had never had any interest in being an autobiographer. Yes, some of her poems were autobiographical, but only obliquely so. She was more interested in being Chase's biographer.

Yet, if someone were to write a biography, such a person could do so by starting with the guest book from their Sugar Island camp, but then that did not reveal much about their personal lives. What it did reveal was that Chase had a great many visitors who signed the worn leather-bound book. Chase never used the bookmark ribbon. He wanted his guests to thumb through all the names of academics and politicians who had come to pay court to him before they added their own names to the guestbook. Stellanova could calmly weather most of the guests who beat a path to Chase's door because she understood that his distinguished guests made him feel relevant long after his days in politics were behind him.

Stellanova could not begin to remember all of the visitors who had come, but she would never forget those visitors who *stayed for six weeks—six weeks—* in August and September of 1937. Any visit of that length would certainly try the closest of friendships or strain the most amicable of family ties. These visitors were neither. The visitation by the Angells, Carleton and Gladys, that is, upset the Osborn's tenuous equilibrium that summer of 1937. Stellanova thought, "Hell. It would be as good a starting point as any other for a novel about my life."

The Proposal

May 1937

May 9, 1937

Dear Governor Chase S. Osborn,

I write to raise the subject of officially commissioning a portrait bust in your image. This idea arose at a recent dinner party in Ann Arbor when Professor Louis Hopkins, Associate Professor of Mathematics and Director of the Summer Session, others, and I discussed that a likeness of you would be a fitting tribute to your contribution to the State of Michigan, as Governor, and to the University, as a highly esteemed regent and a generous benefactor of the institution. Your generosity to the school is legendary, particularly but not limited to your leading financial support of Robert Frost's residencies.

Taking the liberty of moving forward with this idea, I have given Professor Carleton Angell, Professor of Art and Museums' Artist, an assistantship in Anthropology for the summer session to create the proposed bust. It was Professor Hopkins who suggested Angell as a suitable artist. While Angell is perhaps best known as a specialist in the rendering of prehistoric animals, his sculptural and representation skills are diverse, and he assures me of his interest in this portrait commission. Indeed, he is excited by the prospect of turning his talents to the subject of an esteemed citizen such as yourself. To this end I have also included the Tribute Resolution from the Board of Regents.

If convenient, Professor Angell would be available to travel to your residence on Sugar Island at the beginning of August to begin work on the commission. Professor Angell will soon write by separate cover about the particulars of the schedule and the logistics necessary for embarking on this project. My fervent wish is that you would not decline this proposal based on humility or, God forbid, declining health.

Assuming you are able to establish mutually satisfying arrangements with Professor Angell, Professor Hopkins and I would like to come up to your camp shortly before the Labor Day weekend to see the progress on the bust. We would also be most interested in perusing the collection in your library, and enjoying the celebrated hospitality of the Osborns. Until then, my best wishes to you and daughter Stellanova.

Your friend,

Mortimer

Mortimer E. Cooley

Dean, Department of Engineering

University of Michigan

A Tribute Resolution Honoring
Governor Chase Salmon Osborn

Whereas Governor Chase S. Osborn has been a dedicated public servant of the State of Michigan his entire career, serving as Postmaster for the City of Sault Ste. Marie from 1889-1893, a Game and Fish Warden of the State of Michigan from 1895-1899, and a Railroad Commissioner for the State of Michigan from 1899-1903;

Whereas, in his highest position, Governor Chase S. Osborn served with accomplishment as the Governor of the State of Michigan from 1911-1913, resulting in the elimination of the State's deficit; the passage of a workmen's compensation bill; and the passage of a presidential primary law;

Whereas Governor Chase S. Osborn served with distinction as a member of the Board of Regents of the University of Michigan from 1908-1911 and has continued to exhibit and act upon a broad sense of responsibility and commitment to the University in a manner that has enriched the institution and its reputation;

It is resolved, by this Board of Regents on this Ninth Day of the Month of May, Nineteen Hundred and Thirty-Seven that a bust in his likeness be commissioned, designed, and cast in bronze for the significant adornment of the University of Michigan campus and for the lasting edification of its faculty, staff, and students.

Reservations

August 1937

The Dean's letter was the catalyst that threatened to unspool the Osborns' ruse of their unusual domestic arrangement like a ball of yarn at the mercy of a curious paw.

The former Governor, Chase S. Osborn, now a distinguished septuagenarian and in appearance to a cross between the handsome statesman Warren G. Harding and the arresting presence of actor Lionel Barrymore, was perched on the second step of the library ladder. There he was gesticulating with a pencil and dictating his thoughts on his latest adventure in Madagascar to his scribe and co-author, the thirty-something and subtly stunning Stellanova Brunt Osborn. She was typing rapidly, punching the typewriter keys with heavy strikes as her dark shingle bob of hair shivered like a flapper's dress. The Governor left his rostrum-like perch on the ladder, pointed his pencil baton with a cueing motion, and addressed "the percussion section."

"You've been flinty with me ever since I received that envelope from Dean Cooley. I noticed that you held that letter in your possession for several days."

Stellanova took the pencil from the Governor, placed it behind her ear and crossed her arms. "What are you implying?"

Chase pulled an envelope from the University out of a cubbyhole in his cherry wood desk, placing it on the platen of the typewriter before Stellanova. "I was a postmaster, remember, so I've long had the habit of noticing postmarks. You could say that I am 'post due,' as it were, for an explanation."

"You're speaking to me as if my sole purpose is to be your secretary. I happen to have an eye on your legacy, too."

Chase sighed. He knew that he had to tread carefully. "Isn't it possible that you are making too much of this commission, Stellanova?"

The rasp of Chase rubbing his calloused hands against his two-day beard sounded surprisingly loud and was irritating to her at the moment. "You're making too *little* of it."

Chase stretched his spine—becoming closer to his height in his prime. "I am not making too little of it. It's an honor to have the University consider my contributions worthy of recognition."

Stellanova realized that her concerns did not have the pull with Chase that the University of Michigan did. "The siren call of the University of Michigan!"

"I won't deny it," Chase admitted. "I do envy that you actually attended the University of Michigan. I was in the first class of Purdue University—and only then because they needed to fill the seats."

Stellanova pointed to a plaque on the library wall above the desk. "Not many men can say they were once a Regent of the University."

"True, but being an actual student at Michigan had loomed large in my imagination since I was a boy. Do you know that there was a man from my hometown in Indiana whose house was a famous landmark simply because he was an alumnus of the University of Michigan?" Chase asked this question as if it were the first time he had ever told this anecdote in Stellanova's presence.

"But you have to consider the implications of agreeing to participate in this bust commission," Stellanova pleaded.

"It's an honor to be asked." Chase used unusual restraint in not adding, "Case closed," which he would sometimes punctuate by rapping his fist like a gavel on the table.

"It would have been prudent to refuse," Stellanova scolded. "It's true that I delayed giving you the letter. I have reservations about the proposal. Six weeks is an awfully long time to host strangers. It will be difficult to draw boundaries."

"Boundaries? We have 3,000 acres here. I'm not concerned about bumping up against these people too often."

Chase looked out of the window at the view of the river framed by pines and maples. He seemed to take in the scene through his pores.

"I'm talking about personal boundaries being breached with prying questions. Curiosity doesn't observe boundaries," Stellanova warned. "And I will chafe under having to make small talk with the sculptor's wife for that many weeks."

Chase turned to Stellanova, tilting his head at a more sympathetic angle than usual. "What is really eating away at you?"

"Shouldn't a bust be of someone's likeness...in his prime?"

He struck a pensive pose with his hand to his prodigious chin. "That is an issue of vanity, from which I do not suffer."

"I beg to differ!"

The Governor laughed so heartily that his belt-buckle went up and down as only an old man's physique makes oddly possible. The geriatric version of wiggling one's ears. "You know me well, Stellanova, but I still do not know why you are so opposed to this project."

Stellanova hesitated to play her last card, but she decided to lay it face up. "Your...eccentricities may work on the sculptor's imagination, and the result could be that the bust could look like...a caricature."

"More likely, a dinosaur!" Chase roared. The Governor slapped his bare knee like a rim shot punctuates a joke. "The sculptor's experience is in making dinosaur models for the University's exhibit museum!" The Governor had a bit of fun giving Stellanova ammunition for her argument against the bust commission.

"Listen to me. Your image will bear the sculptor's critique and will also be limited by the skill of that sculptor. Why not just get another professional photograph made and be done with it?" Stellanova offered. She stared over the Governor's shoulder to the opposite wall of the library at a black and white portrait of the Governor. It was taken when he assumed the State's highest office, more than a decade before she had met him. The younger version of the man stared back at her. A bust could never capture the dynamism of the photographic images of Chase. Those images were arresting. He stared unapologetically into the camera lens with that "I dare you to cross me" chin and the dark eyes that were at once penetrating and dismissive. The stern gaze from the photograph worked like truth serum on Stellanova.

She had not buried the letter about the bust commission under a mountain of miscellaneous mail. She was in the habit of sorting Chase's bags of mail and doling it out to him according to how she knew he would want to prioritize his responses. But in this case, she withheld the letter that would have been of the most interest to him.

Chase often spoke in such an emphatic way that if his comments were being dictated, there would be capitalized words and exclamation marks peppering the text. Now, however, he sensed that he needed gently to draw Stellanova out. "Why are you attaching so much significance to this bust commission business? It's not like you to lose your perspective."

"When this bust is completed…" Stellanova opened her eyes wide so as not to let the bead of a tear on her lower lid give her vulnerability away. "When this bust is completed, I will be forced to come face-to-face with your mortality."

"Ah, so that's it." Chase picked up her shawl from her chair and gently draped it around her shoulders and rested his hands there. "Stellanova, my new star. I will be right here for a long time to come, and soon this commission will be behind us, and that bust will be headed downstate to the campus."

"That will not be soon enough for me." Stellanova crossed her arms, placing her hands over Chase's on her shoulders, and rested her head on his hand.

Chase whispered in her ear, "Well then, let's relish our solitude before the Angells arrive." But Stellanova still felt the need to take her frustrations out by doing battle with the alphabet, so she stayed at the typewriter to transcribe another few pages of the Madagascar manuscript.

Chase heard the staccato notes of a motif that he suspected would be a recurring theme as he left the library and traveled the path to the Gander with the most recent issue of the *Sault Ste. Marie Evening News* tucked under his arm. He headed for the screened-in porch that stretched the length of the Gander, a double-sided cabin on a wooded rise above the river with the best view from the Osborn property of the international waters between the US and Canadian shores. The view never disappointed, but there were distractions. The pesky blackflies served as the border patrol in June, but in July, there was a changing of the guard; the mosquitoes, sentinels of the worst sort, were on duty for the rest of the summer.

Reaching the cabin and the sanctuary of the porch, Chase looked forward to reading the paper cover-to-cover, especially his letter to the editor about his recent stay at the regional hospital. As a former newspaperman, he read the newspaper with the eye of an editor and a publisher, but today he had the added anticipation of reading his own words in the very paper he used to own. He read his letter like it was the first time he had seen these words, chuckling and enjoying the offbeat and unusually candid account of his recent illness. He was especially pleased that the newspaper had printed his letter in full.

After about an hour of working on Chase's manuscript, Stellanova had arrived, slowly at a feeling of equanimity, however temporary, about the commission. She left the library and made her way on the path that led to the Gander. In her thoughts, she had made a reservation for a seat in the screened-in porch. It was a big enough porch to accommodate several people, but she needed the space to herself before their visitors would discover her favorite roost. She noticed that Chase had left his newspaper on the roughhewn end table near the chair that was still in the swatch of sunlight near the southwest end of the porch. If she had read the title of the article that was face-up on the table, she would have been able to anticipate the topic Chase would be primed to discuss at dinner. Sometimes both dinner and the conversations were a little too filling when what Stellanova really wanted to do was to think about the next few phrases of her poem she was mulling over in her mind. Soon Stellanova decided she would glance at the headline of the article in preparation for the evening's dinner conversation, and then she would sit in the screen-hatched sunlight, close her eyes, and think about almost nothing. But that was not to be because the item was not an article that she could glance at and think about later in Chase's company. It was a letter to the editor, and the author was none other than Governor Chase S. Osborn.

Stellanova was so accustomed to co-authoring with Chase that finding a letter that she had not edited or typed felt a bit like a betrayal. That feeling of equanimity that she had brought with her from the library quickly evaporated when she read what Chase had written for public consumption without her knowledge. Dinner conversation (or its absence) was going to be altogether of a different order.

The Patient
August 1937

Gib, the handsome young Ojibwe man in their employ on whom they depended for much, had taken the Governor's gas-powered cabin cruiser, christened *The Zheshebe Minis,* to the old settlement of Payment on the northeast shore of Sugar Island to collect the week's accumulation of mail. It was a long but pleasant trip at this time of year. Not as it had been last November when the last trip of the season had begun with having to break the boat out of the ice before embarking on the last journey of the season from Duck Island to Sault Ste. Marie.

Just a few buildings of Payment remained clinging haphazardly to the shore. It looked like the Great Spirit "Gitchie Manitou" had thrown a handful of dice onto the shore to see which buildings would survive the cruel, cold winter winds and the fickle winds of prosperity. The post office and Holy Angels Church, and a few other indifferent structures still stood.

Gib always exchanged pleasantries with Mrs. Edwards, the postmistress, but was careful not to share personal information about the Governor with her. She was well-informed about the regulations of the US postal service, and she could always be depended upon to see that the proofs of the Osborn manuscripts were duly packaged, stamped, and sent on their way to the publishers. Otherwise, Gib would have traveled only as far as the lighthouse station three miles from the Osborn camp to collect the mail. Mrs. Edwards was also well-informed about local news and the business of the residents of Sugar Island. Stellanova thanked her lucky stars that Mrs. Edwards was not the postmistress handling and, no doubt, examining the mail when the courtship correspondence between Stellanova and Chase accounted for some of the voluminous correspondence to and from the Governor's summer residence on Sugar Island for most of the 1920's.

Gib had undertaken another task for the Governor in Payment that week. The second one more personal even than retrieving his mail. Gib had taken the time to light a candle and pray in the old Holy Angels Church to stand vigil over the Governor's recovery from pneumonia after his recent trip to the hospital in Sault Ste. Marie.

Gib had delivered to Stellanova the most recent issue of the *Sault Ste. Marie News* and, perhaps, the miracle of recovery for which both Stellanova and Gib had prayed.

Stellanova had not, however, prayed for Chase to make such a public spectacle of his recovery. She was aghast as she read Chase's unbridled and somewhat unhinged letter to the editor about his illness.

Sault Ste. Marie News: "*Gov. Osborn tells how it feels to be seriously ill; lauds Sault hospital. Experiences in delirium of pneumonia described by former Governor, now recuperating at his camp. By Chase S. Osborn.*

"*My work has urged me over the entire earth. It remained, however, for me to have made just about my most pleasant discovery right here in Sault Ste. Marie: That the Sault has one of the best-managed hospitals in the world, with talented physicians and surgeons adequate for any need, and the tenderest of nurses.*

I reached Detroit on my way to my summer camp in the Sault, early in June. At Detroit, I was on the program for a major address at the three-day Michigan-Ontario Historical Convention. I was expected to be equal to it.

My strength was not sufficient to permit me to attend any meetings except the one at which I spoke. There I was in a feverish state and had little idea whether I had made a satisfactory address or not until I was surprised by being called to my feet a half dozen times by continuous applause. It was a thing to thank God for because I really had thought that I might drop dead while speaking. At Battle Creek, a few days later, an infection of some kind seized me. I traveled on to Grand Rapids and went down again. After a few days' illness there, the final windup came. I had promised to deliver the zero hour address for Kiwanis at the Sault June 27. I got through that and then snapped. I was stricken suddenly with a breakdown illness that finally took the form of pneumonia.

My condition assumed a grave form on Duck Island, where I was resting on a balsam bough bed on the ground in a tent. Without my knowledge, my daughter sent a courier to the government station at Rains to telephone the Sault. My beloved son George came at once with Dr. Husband. The next thing I knew, I was being carried to the river shore on a stretcher, and I did not know much about that except that it was all-enjoyable. Then the wind fanned my fevered face as Coast Guard picket boat No. 2208 sped to the Sault at twenty miles an hour.

The burning fever sent my mind off on trackless pursuits of figments and phantasms. For example, I was back in the jungles of Africa hunting lions. A wounded lion just about had me down and was starting to maul me. Right when things were at their blackest, I got hold of a stove lid lifter. I quietly lifted off the top of the lion's head. Then I took a spoon and ladled out the lion's brains, which I put on the fire to boil. While it was cooking, I counted the lion's respirations, took his blood pressure, put a thermometer in his mouth and read his temperature, felt his pulse, took a blood test and X-ray pictures, and rubbed his back vigorously with alcohol.

At this juncture, the brains having been cooked to a turn, I proceeded to eat them. Wishing to be decent to the beast, I offered him a portion of his own broiled brains, whereupon he walked away contemptuously, and I have not seen him since.

Excruciating pains seized my body from the sole of my feet to the crown of my head. I had been so much without pain during my life that I ought to enjoy these manifestations of vitality. Also, I concluded that a corpse never has pains. During the complete or partial deliriums caused by my high temperature while in the hospital, I had some of the most interesting journeys of my life. One of them took me on a white-winged glider toward the land "From Which No Traveler Returns." I saw pearly clouds with pink linings. Just beyond, there were smiling faces and open, welcoming arms. But I could not pass the cloud just ahead of me. I remember being surprised to see no angels with harps and wings, no gates of chrysoprase, and no golden streets. This life appears to be as probationary as it is ephemeral. We are here to be tested. If we are found suitable, we may be advanced to a higher plane of perfection, there to do a work of the new life just as we have tried to perform here, however crudely. It seems to me to be incompetent for one to break down until his time comes.

I had never been in a hospital before as a guest but had gone to the bigger and better ones all over the earth, to take members of my family or friends, or see them. Within a short time, I began to improve enough to take notice of things about me. Everything at the hospital moved with disciplined precision. There were no disagreeable noises. The nurses came and went on the minute. My medicines were given on the second. The doctor came quite often at first and always twice a day. As soon as I could note things, I comprehended how completely clean and without unpleasant odors, and in what perfect condition the hospital is. Another thing I discovered is the high class of physicians and *surgeons available in Sault Ste. Marie. They are as good as any to be found anywhere.*

Another major discovery I made at the Memorial Hospital was that the earth is filled with the most lovable people. Everyone was so kind. Pastors, priests, rectors, bishops, and the Immaculate Ladies of the Noble Loretto called. Undertakers also were kind because they remained off stage, but all in readiness in the wings.

All the lodges in town sent fragrant flowers. York Masonic Lodge of Grand Rapids remembered me. My old Masonic Lodge in Florence, Wisconsin, did not forget. I was particularly touched by the remembrance of the Trades and Labor Council of the Sault. These men have always known of my sympathetic friendship, even if we do not contact each other as often as would be pleasant. The first lodge I ever joined was the Odd Fellows. They have always been steadfast in their fraternal relationships. During the terrible typhoid epidemic that devastated the Sault a half-century ago, the Odd Fellows took care of me night and day. All these years, that has been a fragrant memory. Among the delicacies sent me while I was convalescing were brook trout, just the right size to be most enjoyable.

I wish I could thank personally all the countless friends who performed precious acts of affection during my illness. These things speeded me on to strength enough to return again to the simple, primitive surroundings of my camp at Duck Island, where it looks now as if I would regain my strength and be able to know the joy of work again. Although I am omitting many things I would like to say, I cannot forego a reference to the kindness, promptness, and efficiency of the Coast Guard. May I conclude with a restatement of my major discoveries: That the Sault has one of the best-managed hospitals in the world, with talented physicians and surgeons adequate for any need, and the tenderest of nurses, and perfect healthful attention to diet and cuisine."

Chase believed that the earth was filled with "the most lovable people." That may have been simply the largesse of a lifelong politician. Or maybe it meant something more? The adoration of the masses registered with Chase, yet the love that was manifest in every small thing Stellanova did for him—from the most mundane tasks to the scholarly collaborations—he did not acknowledge with the effusiveness demonstrated in that public letter. Chase thanked everyone, yet only acknowledged that "his daughter" had sent a courier to phone the Sault for help "without his knowledge." However, he did not fail to mention that his "beloved son George" rushed to his side. Yes, George did come to his side, but from offstage, while *she* remained always onstage by his side and attentive to his every need. She was the main character in this drama, but she felt as if her name had been left off the playbill. Again.

Stellanova wondered what had possessed Chase to give such a full recounting of his feverish dreams, likely exposing himself to public ridicule. He might as well have walked around the town square in the altogether. Frankly, his letter gave off a whiff of senility. Not something one can easily wash off. Stellanova thought that he was possibly striving to be relevant, no matter what the cost might be to his reputation. Yet, he seemed to fear for his reputation when it came to...Well, it was best not to think about that now.

Truly no one was more relieved than Stellanova when Chase turned a corner and started to take notice of things around him. Still, that letter to the paper underscored that he did not actually take note of everything or rather everyone—namely her. Was she more present to him years ago when they were corresponding through letters even before they had met in person? When she existed for him only on paper, she seemed to leap off the page in his imagination. Now his imagination was being exercised in his feverish dreams—and for *all* to read.

The extended stay of the Angells, forty-two days in all, might also expose Chase's eccentricity. Stellanova dreaded playing the part of the dutiful daughter and hostess for the Angells. Not the angels of the type Chase had been disappointed to find absent in his dream at the pearly gates to greet him, but the Angells from Ann Arbor. Furthermore, Chase was still fatigued from his recent illness, and Stellanova felt protective of him. He was looking particularly haggard after his bout with pneumonia. Certainly his was far from the best visage at present to have sculpted for posterity.

Her thoughts continued to circle back to Chase's very public "love letter" to the hospital employees. Perhaps this was all the more aggravating since she had not received a letter from him in over seven years. As the years passed without any written correspondence between the two, the letters she saved were bittersweet memories of a much more ardent, shared, and secret time in their lives.

Stellanova had not intended to re-read their love letters that summer, but circumstances conspired to compel her to re-visit their relationship and to search anew for Chase's affection. For Stellanova, re-reading their correspondence served as a stand-in of sorts for Chase's absent attentions that summer. Anytime that she could steal a few moments for this she did so because the act of reading the letters, as solitary an activity as that was, made her feel somehow less alone, especially in Chase's distancing presence.

As she read, song lyrics would come to her mind unbidden—almost before she consciously acknowledged her mood. As a poet, Stellanova had memorized the lyrics to many songs over the years. When she delved into the letters, emotions were dredged up, and lyrics often rose to the surface and she would begin to sing. The songs she sang, never above a sotto voce volume, were a barometer for the emotions the letters elicited. How she envied the birds that could send out a call to a mate with an instinctive certainty of an answer. Instead, the answers she received were only the thread of her melodies that their cook Lee overheard and would sometimes pick up and weave into her workaday chores.

The number of visitors and the length of their stays during the summer of '37 put a strain on the Osborn's relationship; above all, those visits starved Stellanova of the attention she craved from Chase. What doubly wounded Stellanova about her distant Chase was his insatiable appetite for the attention from others. But that appetite was satisfied only for the time being. Thankfully, she comforted herself in acknowledging that he had had an insatiable appetite once for her, which the passionate letters between them would one day attest.

The Arrival of Angells

August 1937

Sculptor Carleton Angell documented his six-week residency by writing of his first impression of the camp and creating a bust of Governor Osborn as a lasting impression of the man. His first impression was published in an article he wrote for a University publication.

"Arriving at 'The Soo,' we found the city a veritable beehive; it is that way in summer. We purchased a few provisions, inquired for the ferry, drove ten minutes or so on US-2, and found ourselves at the dock. Since the ferry was on the opposite side, I blew our horns as instructed, and soon a great turtle plowed its way through the swift channel water toward us—an ungainly homemade scow, with a hump through the middle. The skill with which the two boys take it day after day across the river never ceased to amaze us.

The road from the dock is of well-packed gravel and winds its way through acres of farmlands, small trees, brush and heavy forest, and over hills on which cattle graze. From the crests of these hills, one may glimpse the Island topography in its relation to the waters of Lake Nicolet and Lake George and may obtain views beyond to the gray-blue hills of Michigan and Canada, where they roll on and on into the distant haze—a beautiful, expansive panorama.

Between two tar paper houses, a rough road strikes off into the woods [about fifteen miles from the ferry], which leads to the Osborn camp. Despite the fact that it is the roughest road I have ever traveled, all who have taken it feel perfectly recompensed for any discomforts because, as it winds its way toward the river, the forest grows dense and cool, and the variety of trees and shrubs and flowering plants increases, until one forgets himself in the beauty of the place. The road ends in a large opening sprinkled with blueberry bushes, June plum, and pin-cherry trees, all guarded by giant white pines and Norway pines."

A welcoming committee of three greeted Carleton and Gladys Angell. They looked at first to be three generations of one family—a grandfather, a daughter, and a grandson, yet on closer examination, the relationships among those in the trio did not appear to be familial. They stood as apart from one another as telephone wire insulators. The lanky young man raised one of his sinewy bronze arms to take off his sweat-stained trilby to swat at the ardent mosquitoes. He ran his fingers through his dark blue-black hair and it stood on end like the ruffled crest feathers on a raven. The woman had appeared older from a distance because of her frumpy attire, but she actually looked much younger and more attractive close up. Her arresting gaze was periodically broken when she cast her dark wide-set eyes at the Governor. Osborn looked more like a caretaker than a squire of Sugar Island in his worn cut-off khaki pants and open short-sleeved work shirt.

Even so, Carleton was a bit star-struck at seeing the Governor, who was waving to them enthusiastically or perhaps impatiently. Gladys actually took more notice of the camp than of the inhabitants and realized that she had packed all the wrong clothes for six weeks in this remote and rustic place.

"Professor and Mrs. Angell, welcome to Duck Island!" The Governor brushed off his palms on his pants and extended his arm while he bridged the gap between the hosts and the guests with a few bounding strides. The Governor's handshake was a politician's power play. His grip, however, could end a sculptor's career. Carleton pretended to warm his hands in an effort to conceal the fact that he was actually kneading his hands to regain feeling.

"Thank you so much for hosting my wife Gladys and me for our extended stay."

"At your service is my young man Gib, and my girl Friday, my daughter Miss Osborn."

Stellanova had never before heard Chase refer to her as his girl Friday, and she was mulling over the significance of that when Mrs. Angell slipped her hand between the curtains of Stellanova's thoughts and offered her hand. Stellanova noticed that Mrs. Angell was a well-preserved woman in her early 50s who was so pretty and fair that she wondered if Mrs. Angell's best features would fade with time more easily than would her darker and more handsome features. Stellanova also noticed Mrs. Angell's smart chocolate brown cloche hat finished with a sheeny brown hat band ribbon. Camp attire was practical, but a part of her missed dressing up for a wider audience than Chase, their loyal worker Gib, and their full-time cook and housekeeper, the ever-industrious Lee.

The Governor directed Gib to take the Angells' luggage to the sleeping side of the Gander cabin.

Now that the Angells had arrived, dreading the visit was behind Stellanova, and surviving the visit was ahead. While she and Gib got Mrs. Angell settled in, the sculptor and the subject got better acquainted.

The Governor directed Professor Angell to follow him to his favorite conference room of sorts, the porch of the Gander, which was attached to the kitchen and dining side of the double-winged cabin.

"We're headed to the Gander, which is the best built-built log cabin in the world," the Governor boasted. He gave him a bracken fern frond to wave in the air to provide him with a fighting chance against the mosquitos.

The Osborn camp proper consisted of four cabins and various outbuildings, a workshop, boathouse, and a concrete fortress-like structure with a steel door and iron shutters that served as the Governor's library for his extensive collection. The cabins all had good fireplaces and funny names. In addition to the Gander, there were two more domiciles, Little Duck and Big Duck. The Gander was really two cabins connected by a wide breezeway with a roof that bridged the two sides of the 70-foot long twin cabins. The best feature of the Gander was the screened-in porch overlooking the St. Mary's River. On either end of the porch hung a Nantucket hammock. Sometimes the Governor slept in the hammock on the west end.

Big Duck had electricity and indoor plumbing and was built as the primary residence. However, by the early 1920's, the Governor had moved into Little Duck, which did not have electricity or his wife, Lillian. Here he had been comfortable in exile, after Lillian, as he had said, "discharged" him. The 14 by 16-foot candle-lit log cabin had two windows to the east and one window facing north, and a swinging ladder to a loft. The Governor was pleased to show off his domiciles, but not the domestic strife that had necessitated the need for multiple cabins. Now, however, the extra space accommodated the many guests who visited Duck Island every season.

"So, you think you're a sculptor, Professor Angell?" Osborn asked.

"I do the best I know."

"I admire your honesty. Well, some men are sculptors in stone and bronze, while others are sculptors of men!"

Carleton realized that he had just had the briefest job interview ever, but he did not feel like he had gotten the job. He wondered if this would turn out to be a six-week-long probationary period?

"How was your trip, Professor Angell?"

"That depends on whom you ask...my wife, or me?"

"It was a rough journey, then?" Osborn asked, knowing full well that it would have been.

"Travel over water is challenging for my wife. And for my part, those roads constructed of perpendicular logs made my spine vibrate like a tuning fork," Angell said, putting his hand to his lower back. A sculptor's work did not involve only small motor muscles.

"Corduroy roads!" Osborn exclaimed as if they were a modern invention. The dirt roads to the Osborn camp were periodically striped with logs placed parallel across the low-lying portions of the road that were often muddy after a period of rain. It was a torte cake of logs, crushed rock, gravel, and dirt. "They will also knock the fillings out of your teeth!" Angell realized that his teeth felt gritty. During dry periods, travel left a patina of fine dust on vehicles, face, hair, clothes, and even scoured the teeth with a grittier application than brushing with baking soda.

"I sympathize with you and your wife. To be honest though, I don't really mind if travel to my remote Duck Island is prohibitive for privacy sake, but I am a strong advocate for a bridge to be built across the Straits so at least that leg of the trip would be easier and safer. The wait for the ferry to cross the Straits can be as long as 24 hours at the start of hunting season."

"Even so, a bridge across the Straits doesn't seem very practical," Angell ventured.

"Not practical? Then you do not have the confidence in the ingenuity of man as I do!"

"I'm sorry. I seem to have struck a chord with my skepticism."

"Yes, and a discordant one. I'll have you know that I have the ear of President Franklin D. Roosevelt himself on this matter, and he has promised his support for the project," Osborn said proudly.

"I suppose the President sees the project as something the WPA can achieve? Artwork, music, buildings, and roads are certainly feasible, but a bridge across that wide an expanse?" Angell pressed.

For Osborn, an argument was simply an opportunity to continue to make his case. "Do not forget that both the newly constructed Hoover Dam and the Golden Gate Bridge are proof that we can achieve great things. Why did I hunt iron ore all my life, if I did not believe that we could achieve great things with the right materials and the right mindset?" The Governor was absolutely poetic about the role of iron ore. "Our span of life is ticked off by springs of iron ore in clock and watch. Let those who produce it hold up their heads with dignity."

Angell made one more attempt to cross the verbal divide. "I'll grant you that there's a need for a bridge. I just don't think it will happen in our lifetimes."

"If I were not morally opposed to betting, I'd wager that I'll yet travel across a bridge over the Straits of Mackinac."

"I hope that you will, sir."

"And iron ore from the iron country of the Upper Peninsula will be used to build it!"

Eager to change the subject, Angell pivotted, "I understand that you were recently hospitalized."

"Ah, you heard."

"Your daughter informed me that you have been quite ill and that I should not tire you today."

The Governor made a dismissive, or possibly a surrendering motion with his hands. "My daughter is very protective of my health. In general, I do not tire so much as I get restless—a chronic condition. Sitting without a purpose has always made me irritable. And when I'm bored, I can be boorish, or so I have been told," Osborn warned as he simultaneously flashed a knowing wink to the professor.

Angell had no doubt that he would have a front-row seat to the bored and perhaps, boorish, Governor at some point in the process. "I will try then to make the sitting for this bust as pleasant as possible."

The Governor raised his hand like he was taking the oath of office. "And I will try to be as patient as possible."

"I hope to be as unobtrusive as I can, but the bust process is as much a study of the subject as it is a sculpture of the subject. I like to observe the physical and emotional sides of the person. Then I have the best chance of creating a faithful likeness."

Osborn leaned forward and said, "Rest assured: Your six-week residency will give you ample time to see all sides of me. I hope you find my best side, if possible. Oh, good. Stellanova and Mrs. Angell have joined us," Chase announced. "I know that it was a dusty trip from the Soo. So, let's have a refreshing drink by the river."

"Thank you, Governor. My throat is parched from the trip," Angell said.

"I owe my strong constitution to my daily intake of fluids. I stay hydrated by drinking eight quarts of water per day. At breakfast, I boil water flavored with grape juice and sugar. At lunch, I imbibe lemonade. And later, I ingest my daily inner bath of orange juice. No need for medicine on such a regimen!" He sounded like he was spouting an advertiser's slogan.

The thirsty Angells were slowly being tortured by the detailed description of all the ways the Governor hydrated himself. Angell came to his own rescue, and said, "On the way up, we stopped in Frankenmuth at the Cass River Brewery and bought some Bavarian beer to share with you."

"Ah, the Geyer Brothers kept their business going even during Prohibition by maintaining that they were producing malt extract solely for the purpose of bread baking. Of course, the extract was used almost exclusively for private stills in Frankenmuth."

"I'm pleased that I chose a brew with which you are familiar."

"That was considerate of you, Professor Angell, but this is a dry camp. I supported Prohibition at one time. I made my views on the subject known during my inaugural address and that doomed my candidacy for a second term. But that's all water under the bridge at this point. That being said, we serve two kinds of ale here. Stellanova, will you please ask Lee to serve the ales we have on tap at the Osborn Camp?"

"No need. Here she is," Stellanova said as she opened the door from the kitchen to the porch to help Lee with the tray of beverages. "We have Canada ginger ale and Vernors ginger ale," Stellanova announced as if on cue.

Never one to let an opportunity pass to educate guests about Michigan products, the Governor continued, "Ginger ale is not a part of my regimen, but ginger does have some medicinal properties. The history of this drink is quite interesting. Vernor, a pharmacist in Detroit, was in the process of concocting a highly carbonated gingery drink for indigestion when he left Detroit to fight in the Civil War. When he returned a few years later, he opened up the oak cask in which he had stored his ginger tonic, of sorts, only to discover that it had aged to an unexpected perfection."

Carleton felt Gladys's hand on his sleeve, which was a signal that he needed to save them both from dehydration. "I'll take a glass of that Vernors, please, Miss Osborn," Angell said.

"I would love a glass of Canada ginger ale, please," Gladys said, trying not to sound too desperate.

"And you can also be refreshed by the view of the international boundary waters. Canada's shore is almost a stone's throw from here," Osborn added.

Angell sputtered and coughed when he brought the glass of Vernors to his lips. The carbonation was almost toxic. The Governor was always amused by watching someone drink their first Vernors. "You can't say I didn't warn you that it's highly carbonated. Sip it slowly." Osborn then took this chance to make a broader point and said, "I was not always a 'teetotaler.' I think I may have walked farther than any man for a drink. I walked across Siberia once to quench my thirst for the stuff! I am rather ashamed of that anecdote, actually, but I have better examples of my character to share with you."

I'm looking forward to it."

"I predict that you will not have to wait long," Stellanova interjected ruefully.

"I rarely have the opportunity to converse with my subjects," Angell said.

"My understanding is that you usually work with stuffed specimens from the museum's collection?" Osborn asked.

Angell heard a bit of a challenge to his artistic credentials in the Governor's question, but he did not need to jump to conclusions just yet. "Sometimes, but the method that works best for me is to build up my sculptures by looking at the bone structure; and then I make a wire armature from that."

Having an anecdote for every occasion, Osborn said, "That reminds me of an amusing story from my freshman year at Purdue."

"You have my undivided attention."

The Governor clapped his large hands and created a tremendous reverberation. "That's my kind of audience!" Then he opened his hands like the opening of a stage curtain. "I made enough money as a chore boy and cookie in a lumber camp to pay for my tuition at Purdue."

Stellanova interjected, "He entered Purdue at age 14." Angell got the distinct impression from the Governor's daughter that he was not only supposed to admire the Governor, but be intimidated by him as well.

The Governor was not at all disturbed by the interruption, since it added a flattering piece of information from his biography. "I was enrolled in a zoology class taught by Professor Hussey, who asked each student to provide a specimen for class. I was quite ambitious as a young man."

"As you are to this day," Stellanova added.

"I endeavored to collect all the bones of a horse skeleton in the river bottom near my home and make a heap of them in the classroom."

Angell underscored the feat by saying, "That would be like trying to assemble a dinosaur skeleton!"

"That was essentially the scope of the task, yes, but there was one important difference."

Osborn stopped for a long pause, and Angell was waiting for the Governor's daughter to interject, but then he realized that the next line in this performance was his. "Oh? What was the important difference?"

"The specimen was too new! Professor Hussey lost his temper, and coming near to where I sat, he growled, 'Osborn, do you know how near a fool you are?' I replied, 'Two feet.' It was not an original retort, I am certain, but the psychology of it was that its very boldness gave me a greater confidence in myself."

The Governor slapped both knees, rose out of his chair, and inhaled deeply. "I have to admit that my stamina is not entirely restored since my hospital stay. I am rather tired now. A nap in the out-of-doors will restore me. Make yourself at home. Dinner is served promptly at 6 p.m. He left abruptly and did not seem fatigued at all, but he did seem energized by making his exit.

"You might want to reset your watches so that you don't miss dinner. Osborn camp time is two hours ahead of your watches," Stellanova advised.

Carleton and Gladys looked at one another. Neither one of them could form the simplest of questions about this apparent private time zone of the Osborns in Stellanova's presence, but thought to themselves, "Why the devil would that be?"

A Gothic Romance
August 1937

Each day Carleton and Gladys resigned themselves to their respective assignments of cajoling both the Governor and his daughter into being a bit more tolerant of their presence at their island sanctuary. Then, in the evenings, they would compare notes on the Osborns. They agreed the Osborns were rare birds, indeed, migrating between the outside world and this retreat with mixed feelings about the intrusion of the outside world. Carleton was making more progress, like a falconer training the hawk-like Governor to land on his glove, than Gladys was with the peckish Governor's daughter.

As Gladys searched for topics, she employed the common conversation icebreaker of noticing the photos in someone's home and asking questions about their subjects. She saw a formal portrait of Stellanova and the Governor, perhaps taken a decade before. Gladys ventured a comment, "This photograph must have been taken after Mrs. Osborn..."

Stellanova quickly and curtly provided the answer. "Left us be."

"Left you be?" Gladys asked. It registered with Gladys that this was a strange way to refer to the death of one's mother.

Stellanova saw that she had just let her guard down because she was not prepared for Mrs. Angell's seemingly guileless line of questioning. "I meant to say...when she left us that final time."

Stellanova realized that the absence of any photos of Lillian Osborn could *raise* more questions than *quell* them. It was Chase who had removed them. He had said, "Just because I am still married to her, does not mean that I have to look at the woman who dispensed with me." Stellanova had to elaborate on her answer to conform to what Gladys expected her to say. Expected her to feel. Stellanova *could* honestly say, "It is still difficult for me to talk about her."

"Of course. I'm so sorry," Gladys offered sincerely.

Gladys picked up another photograph, unable to abandon this topic that had served her well over the years, but hoped for a way out. "This is a really wonderful photograph of you and your father. It's so iconic. It occurs to me that it's really quite similar to the painting *American Gothic*. Do you know the painting?"

"*American Gothic*?" Stellanova asked. Even though she knew of the image, it was more enjoyable for her to let Mrs. Angell paint herself into a corner.

"The Grant Wood painting of a father and daughter standing in front of their homestead?" Gladys pictured herself being skewered by the farmer's pitchfork.

"Interesting comparison," Stellanova said flatly. Some people thought that *American Gothic* was a painting of a husband and wife. At least, thought Stellanova, Gladys was not going down *that* road.

Gladys was worried that she had made an awkward comparison with the photo, so she started to babble. "Being married to an artist has made me a sort of amateur art critic with the informal training I have received by listening to Carleton for so many years. And we often visit the Chicago Art Institute in Chicago."

Again, Stellanova could not help assuming the role of a cat playing with a mouse. "What exactly about this photograph of the Governor and me makes you think of that painting?"

Gladys assumed the docent's role, not knowing that she had already been assigned the part of the mouse. "The pair stares out of the picture frame with those unflinching gazes, and the artist seemed to be making a statement about midwestern stoicism, perhaps." Then, she stepped into it again, to her peril. "Maybe they're grieving the loss of the wife and mother, like you and the Governor, or maybe they have a more complicated relationship?" Gladys found herself comparing the younger woman in the picture with the more mature woman in front of her. She now saw Stellanova as less of a Mother Superior and more of a shy seductress, but why, she scolded herself, hadn't she left well enough alone? Yet she continued, "It is difficult to know if the subjects in Woods' painting are happy, actually."

Stellanova put her verbal trap in the form of a question. "The Governor and I do not look happy in this picture?"

Gladys's neck quickly reddened, and she felt the heat like the proverbial frog in the pot of boiling water that does not try to escape because the water temperature seemed fine just a few moments earlier. "Oh," she tried to recover. "I didn't mean that you and the Governor don't look happy in the photograph. I was just describing what I remember about the pair in the painting at the Art Institute."

"At least you didn't compare us to something you saw at the Natural History Museum," Stellanova said, attempting to lighten the mood.

When Chase had first suggested that they have a formal portrait taken shortly after the adoption was finalized, Stellanova thought that it was such a romantic gesture. When the photograph was printed, however, she noticed that their pose was so stiff. They sat shoulder-to-shoulder, not touching. There was enough distance between them to have allowed someone else to be wedged between the two. Mrs. Lillian Jones Osborn, to be exact. Chase still would not risk having an image taken that would identify them as a couple. Instead, the image that Stellanova preferred, really two, was in a hinged frame containing a separate portrait of each of them. Chase's photograph had been taken in 1898 when he was thirty-eight years old, and her portrait was from 1922 when she was just twenty-eight. There was a mere decade between their ages in those portraits, instead of the thirty-four years that dogged them for the entirety of their relationship. She could imagine that Chase was staring ardently at her as she was looking slyly over her shoulder at him.

God's Country
August 1937

Even though Angell was a guest, he had already developed a proprietary feeling about the porch in the solitude of the early morning, but there sat the Governor staring out at the water as still as a portrait bust.

"I imagine that you must be quite eager to begin our project, but I would like to keep to my routines as much as possible, if you don't mind," Osborn said.

Angell was not surprised that Osborn would initiate the ground rules. "Not at all. Just as long as we can take advantage of the natural light for the sittings."

"Certainly," Osborn agreed. "After my morning devotionals, however, it's my habit to stalk about God's country."

"I can't deny that this place is special, but I suppose everyone thinks that his special safe haven is a slice of heaven," Angell ventured.

"Then they would be mistaken. I don't *think* this is God's country. I *know* it is. I have walked around the inland ocean of Lake Superior on foot, and I have paddled and sailed a canoe completely around its shores. It is my assertion that no one has finished seeing the earth with satisfaction until he has circled Lake Superior both by land and water. The name 'Superior' could not be more apt."

"Ah," said Angell, knowing that the oxygen he had given this topic had just been snuffed out.

The Governor rose from his chair and strode across the floorboards of the porch already launching into the long strides of the vigorous walk on which he intended to include Angell. He didn't hold the screen door for Angell, but pushed it open wide like he was entering the stage with the minor character expected to follow in his wake. The sculptor did so.

Whether the Governor could concede that there might be other areas of the world that could be deemed "God's Country," the name had been coveted by many different people from regions with sparse populations and pristine natural areas. Angell mused that paradise was pretty much a subjective notion. Admittedly, Osborn's place was a kind of paradise with its stark beauty, but it certainly had its harsh realities that presented numerous ways to test those who explored it. Angell's hand reflexively nailed a mosquito on the back of his neck putting an exclamation point on that thought.

God's country. That expression triggered something in Angell that made him want to goad the Governor into justifying his claim. Angell played devil's advocate because he felt personally acquainted with the devil after the tragedy in Bath. One place that would certainly not be called God's Country was Bath, Michigan. How could a just God have allowed a madman to infiltrate that quiet town? Angell did not lose anyone in that massacre, but he lost something of himself there when working on a particular commission. Before the Bath commission, Angell had enjoyed his craft for its own sake, but ever since then he needed something more—a purpose for creating and a sense that what he made had, to a degree, some life of its own. To be sure, everything he had created before Bath had been lifeless, but that had never bothered him before. "Why would he create a likeness when it could not raise the dead? What comfort could his works really bring? What message could his works really convey?" Gladys said the work itself was enough of a purpose. She counseled him to take commission after commission to put as much distance between the Bath commission and the present as possible. He did so, and she seemed satisfied that her husband was safely at that distance in his work, from that event, but something, somehow, was just different with this Osborn commission. For some reason she wanted—needed—to keep an eye on him this time.

Angell sensed that he should always let the Governor have the last word whenever possible. "Since I won't be walking or paddling around Lake Superior, I'll have to take your word for it."

"It isn't just what you can see, but what you cannot see that clinches my argument."

"What you cannot see?"

"The winds that blow from the northwest, even today, are never breathed by man until they get to where the Indians lived and where the whites now have taken their place. The air is the clearest and most vitalizing on earth, for it is as invigorating as that of the Alps without the danger and discomfort attendant on high altitudes. With the lowest pollen count in the State, it is a respite from hay fever as well."

"And that's nothing to sneeze about," Angell quipped.

"I wish that I had said that!"

From his position behind this broad-backed man, Angell found it difficult to see where the path led. Soon, however, that actually worked to Angell's advantage. As the Governor continued, he approached a colossal rock that suddenly appeared to Angell as a fitting backdrop to the figure he struggled to follow. No less than Michelangelo might have seen Osborn's image emerge from such a monolith, even though Angell knew that he would be building up his initial model with clay on a wire frame instead of carving the finished work out of an existing rock. His own method required a completely different technique, not to mention mindset; nonetheless, the rock's craggy face was working on Angell's imagination.

Angell noticed that the Governor was wiping his brow with a crumpled handkerchief he had retrieved from the back pocket of his khaki shorts. One would hope that the handkerchief got laundered with more regularity than the shorts apparently did.

"There's a large rock just up ahead. We could lean against it and take a rest if you like?"

The Governor brushed off Angell's concern by waving his handkerchief like a truce flag, yet he was not giving in to a rest. Unbeknownst to Angell, even if he needed the rest, the Governor would not take it *there*, not by that rock, because it was the one he had selected as his *final* resting place. The younger man's concern for his stamina frankly deflated him. "The only reason that I am winded is that I am trying to be the Scout of Superior and talk at the same time," Osborn huffed. "I will stop talking about the air and give us a chance to breathe some of it while we keep walking to a more interesting place to examine on the river side of the Gander. Now, however, I should allow you to listen to nature's music, instead of listening to me."

Osborn thought that walking in the woods and talking was a bit like the annoying concertgoer whispering during a performance. He had written about the virtues of the area in the manuscript that he had been writing with Stellanova about Longfellow's epic poem *Hiawatha*. The inspiration for the manuscript was an editorial Osborn had written to the Detroit newspaper defending the originality of Longfellow's epic poem after a critic had accused Longfellow of plagiarism. The manuscript was becoming more than a defense of Longfellow. It was becoming an open love letter to the region. The Governor was clearly accustomed to being by himself on his morning walks and was soon lost in his appreciative trance induced by his beloved surroundings. He seemed to forget that Angell had accompanied him.

Angell was aware that his presence had been forgotten or pointedly ignored. This left him with time to think about the enigma that was his subject. Yet, the Governor seemed like an open book on some topics, especially when he was on his soapbox about this topic or that, but there was often an undercurrent of something colder, deeper, and more guarded about this man, especially in his long silences between pronouncements. Angell thought that the expression "still waters run deep" did not exactly apply to the Governor. Turbulent waters, with dark depths like Lake Superior, did though.

Coincidentally, but remarkably, their next exchange went directly to the subject of Superior's depth. "Did you know that the greatest depth of Lake Superior is eight hundred feet deeper than the Atlantic Ocean?" Osborn startled Angell with this sudden revelation; it was as if Osborn could read Angell's mind.

"That reminds me of an expression I've heard about Lake Superior—that she never gives up her dead? Do I have that right?" Angell asked.

"Bodies lost at sea do not come to the surface because the water is too cold to permit fermentation of the bodies."

"That expression seemed more poetic before you explained it."

"That is because *I* am a scientist and *you* are an artist."

Angell could hear the rebuke, but maybe he was overly sensitive from too many years of exposure to the pecking order of campus politics. "I couldn't do my artistic work without also being a naturalist. I like to think that that's one of the small ways that *my* art informs *your* science."

Osborn, ignoring the retort, continued, "That rock there is quite a conversation piece for our visitors." He pointed to an unusual rock within throwing distance from the porch of the Gander where they had now returned and were at work, on the Governor's recommendation, checking for chiggers.

Was Osborn changing the subject or challenging Angell to make observations about the rock as an artist or a naturalist? Angell stood up to take a closer look at the natural sculpture. Angell examined the surface of the rock like an apprentice learning from the master's work. He touched every plane, nook, and cranny of the rock, being careful not to rub off any of the lichen layer. It didn't look like it had been cracked open as much as it looked like it had been scooped out on one side while still molten. Angell thought that the rain would create a dynamic image of rills spilling off the rock and pooling at the bottom of the smooth cavity. There was a temptation to assign a familiar shape to this unique rock formation, but to name it would destroy it. Then you could never approach it anew again. For whatever reason, this rock was "speaking to him," perhaps in some way related to or useful for his commission to sculpt the Governor.

"It looks like a petrified wave, don't you think?" Osborn said.

So much for the imagination remaining fluid, thought Angell. He would rather have the scientific properties of the rock described than having the shape erroneously labeled, in a sense petrifying his imagination.

"It's a glacial erratic dropped off here on this shore thousands of years ago," Osborn said. "I was not originally from this area, so you could say that I too was dropped off here years ago, and I have never found it easy to be able to leave either. Unfortunately, I find it necessary to be away from the island much too often for speaking engagements. I am glad that this project of yours has brought you here, instead of me traveling to your studio on campus. Artists need to see the natural world. It is humbling for them. For instance, natural circumstances have created such an unusual rock formation here. A sculptor could do no better."

"I am tasked with creating a likeness of you, and that's where my skills will come in handy." Angell thought that the Governor's bust should have an immutable quality, like the many rough surfaces of the pieces of granite they had just seen on the trail. The Governor's likeness and his personality would be fused as one into the texture and substance of the clay under Angell's skilled hands. He even started to rub an imaginary piece of modeling clay between his thumb and index finger as he thought. He was now itching to start. "Shall we get down to work then?"

"I wasn't aware I was delaying you. The library is up ahead. That's where I would like you to set up. Let's go. Keep up!" Angell followed the Governor like a scout following the leader on a survival trek along a narrow footpath between flaming sumac bushes that swallowed the view of the Governor at every turn.

This man could erode Angell's confidence if it were not already at a low ebb. Why didn't the University simply decide to haul a rock onto campus and slap a plaque on it with the Governor's name and be done with it? That's exactly what the supervisor of parks in Ann Arbor did just a few years ago when they wanted to commemorate George Washington's 200th birthday. In his wavering confidence of the moment, Angell was reminded of that WPA project that gave rise to the Washington commemoration. The plan, witnessed by him and many others, was to unearth this massive stone from a local quarry and move it onto campus with the horsepower of two trucks that were attached to one another like railroad cars to put it in place. Angell made the plaque for the rock, but how could a plaque ever "improve" on the stone itself? For that commission, he didn't have to coach anyone to sit still for a portrait. This job was starting to feel to Carleton like he was pushing a boulder uphill without the powerful aid of two trucks.

As the men headed down the trail toward what would be Angell's studio, the library came into view. It was a humble but sturdy fortress. It did not appear to be a library so much as a berm-like vault perched on the bluff above the river. Someone boating along the shore would assume either nothing of value was stored in such an uninspired looking building or that something of great value was stored in a structure that had no aesthetic value, but had iron shutters that would serve a jailhouse well. The Governor unlocked the large padlock on the hasp. He eased open the heavy ironclad door that groaned, and the cool interior air released a sigh that met the men as they stood in the doorway. The Governor motioned for Angell to precede him into the library and there he saw thousands of spines standing guard against ignorance and he was awed. The Governor leaning against the doorjamb, announced, "7,000 volumes!"

"Your library will be a good setting for posing," Angell noted as he circled the interior. "It will be like observing you in your natural habitat."

Osborn took a deep breath that swelled his chest as if he were engaging in a preening ritual. "I am equally at home in the out-of-doors. In my day I could walk as many as sixty miles over rough terrain in a single day. It wasn't boasting when I told my good friend Theodore Roosevelt that if we trekked together into the wilds of Canada, that I could walk off his feet up to the knees!"

"You certainly proved that on our walk this morning. I saw a few good benches off the trails to take a rest, but you obviously didn't need to use them."

"Those benches are not used to relieve legs. They are used to relieve the bowels!" Osborn laughed. "Those porta pots are an elegant design made by Gib of a simple plank with a hole in the center and supported on each end with large rocks. The plumbing for my wiki-up! Oh, I forgot to show you my 'wiki-up.'"

Angell had noticed that the Governor had a singular way of referring to dwellings and features on his property. "Your wiki-up?" Angell found the Governor to be the quintessential Boy Scout and, admittedly, that made him feel a bit effete in his presence.

"A wiki-up," Osborn repeated. "I'll show you. It's just above my library here higher on the bluff." As they drew closer, Chase pointed to the structure before Carleton could really distinguish what he was supposed to see against the dense backdrop of the woods: Slowly, however, with the Governor's additional pointing, Angell was able to see a simple post and bark structure.

"There, now you see my wiki-up. I will explain. The Indians made a shelter against the frosts of autumn out of limbs and branches to house a rectangular bed of boughs." The log border was roughly in the shape of a bed frame. It also, quite morbidly, reminded Angell of those marble cemetery borders that outline the plots of old gravesites. Neither the natural construction before him nor its resemblance to a burial plot suggested to Angell that it would be a comfortable or desirable place to rest.

"Gib prepares my wiki-up with balsam boughs and replenishes them as needed throughout the summer. There is only one tree in the world the boughs of which make a perfect camp bed. No more restful, comfortable slumbering can be had anywhere than on a balsam bed properly made.

Spruce is obstreperous. Hemlock is lean. But the needles of the balsam lie flat and are friendly. The fragrance of a balsam bed surpasses anything in the Isles of Spice. It is healing, restful, and soothing. A pack sheet and a robe over top of the mattress of branches is my only concession to the desire for creature comforts."

Angell bent down to look inside the wiki-up. "I imagine that you hear creatures roaming around at night when you sleep out here."

"There is a very territorial beaver who slaps his tail on the water of Duck Lake and disturbs the tranquility of this place now and then. Other than that, I have never been bothered much by diurnal or nocturnal creatures."

Angell thought this might not be entirely true, given that it was the human creatures that must have bothered the Governor enough to remove himself to this remote island every summer. This thought prompted Angell to turn his back on the Governor and scan the view of the riverbank. He took an informal census of the closest possible human neighbors. He found none. When he turned around, he was slightly startled to see a large, furry "creature" lumbering toward him with only the Governor's legs below to assuage his sudden fear that this was truly an invading animal.

"Perhaps the creatures of the forest don't bother me because I look so fearsome in my buffalo hide coat! With my wiki-up and my buffalo coat, sleeping in the open air is quite comfortable, and I credit some of the sources of my vitality to that practice," the Governor emphasizing the word vitality. "My habits and stamina have not changed much over the years. And where they have changed, I exercise mind over matter."

Then the "buffalo" with the Governor's legs strode down the bluff toward the library and Angell followed this strange creature into the library. Angell caught up with the shape shifter as he was hanging up his robe on a coat rack in a dark corner of the library.

"Tell me where you would like me to sit."

"The windows in your library are quite high. The light is coming in at an angle that makes the location of natural light not quite adequate for my purposes at this time of day." Thinking that he would be permitted just one objection, Angell chose not to add that the smell of the library was less than intoxicating; it had the musky smell of old books, more than a strong whiff of mildew, and the air was a pea soup of dust.

"I will accommodate you by perching on this library ladder to take advantage of the shaft of light you need." The Governor began to mount the ladder that had treads so narrow that perching was all that would be possible, and the Governor's stamina for perching surely could not last long enough for the first sitting.

"That seems like a precarious position," Angell cautioned. He fought the urge to move closer and spot the Governor as a coach does for a gymnast on a high beam.

"Nonsense! I maintain my excellent sense of balance by standing on one leg each morning while I shave. I did not have the opportunity to shave today, but I would like to be clean-shaven for the bust's final rendition. Can you manage that?"

"My artistic license is up-to-date, so I am sure I can manage it," Angell said. "I can even manage to keep the khaki shorts and high-top canvas shoes you are attired in today out of the bust rendition."

"Ha-ha! It was either my usual camp uniform or my buffalo robe, but it is too warm for that."

"Wise to dress comfortably because our first session will take about 2 hours, if you are up to it?"

"When I was the Railroad Commissioner for the State of Michigan, I made it my business to inspect all 12,000 miles of track, and I viewed them from a seat I had made to fit atop the cowcatcher in the front of the train," Osborn said proudly.

Angell thought that everything that came out of the Governor's mouth sounded like a passage from a Horatio Alger adventure story. "That must have required incredible stamina!"

"Then let's proceed. Full steam ahead with your project!"

"*Our* project, Governor," Angell corrected.

Somehow, Angell managed to finally get the last word in conversation with a man who was used to having the last word. While he worked at his sketching, the Governor became engrossed in a volume in his library about the human esophagus. Angell took note of the book and hoped that the topic for dinner conversation that evening would not be drawn from this most recent research. Gladys had a delicate stomach for that kind of dinner talk. After a while, Angell heard the volume in the Governor's hands close decisively, and it would only be a matter of seconds before the Governor disappeared out the door. The Governor had the habit of making the most of his entrances and his exits. It was as if he considered every interaction a performance. This reminded Angell of costumes.

"Just one more thing before you go," Angell requested. "I noticed that you cut quite the figure in that sombrero you were wearing when you bid us 'adios' last night after dinner."

"I have a collection of international hats given to me by the crowned heads and industry leaders in Europe."

"Anyone I've ever heard of?"

"Mussolini presented me with a hat, but Stellanova hopes that the moths will make a meal of it!"

"How about if you wear a hat for your next sitting?"

"Bully! And I will also come with the story behind its acquisition!"

Angell was not sure that he had actually heard the Governor say, "Bully!" Earlier he had thought that there was a similarity between the Governor being perched up on that ladder and the Rough Rider mounted on his horse. Angell had read about Theodore Roosevelt's vitality, which had been described best by the effect it had on those who witnessed his entrance into a room. Apparently, they felt his energy like an "electric current." Perhaps, the Governor had not really said, "Bully!" but Angell had definitely felt the "electric current" in the room and the absence of it when he exited.

The Panama Hat
August 1937

There was no actual routine for the sittings, except the starting time, which Angell requested, and for which the Governor was always punctual. After that, anything could happen, and the sessions could be concluded at any time, which the Governor determined.

"Good morning, Governor!" Angell enthusiastically greeted Osborn the morning of their first session. That day and thereafter the sculptor always made sure he was at the library first and ready to begin. He did not want to run the risk of being on the receiving end of a gruff greeting, or reprimand, from the Governor.

"I remembered that you asked me to bring a hat for our session today, Professor Angell."

"But you don't seem to be carrying a hat?"

"As an artist, you know that sometimes what is *not* present in an image is as important as what *is*," Osborn said.

"True," Angell answered cautiously. Was the Governor really going to lecture him on art?

"One of the world leaders from whom I *most* wanted to acquire a hat was Teddy Roosevelt. All I had to do was ask T.R., and he surely would have satisfied my request for one of his Panama hats, and then I would be holding it right now."

"So, you didn't get a chance to ask him?" Angell tried to steer the Governor toward his seat, but he ignored the sculptor's hand gestures to shape his behavior.

"I had many chances to ask him when I campaigned for him in 1912 to unseat President Taft. I could have asked President Roosevelt, and he either would have said 'yes' or 'no,' yet I didn't risk the possibility of him saying 'no.' The lesson to be learned from my reticence is that you should be prepared to receive a 'yes' or a 'no' and not slink away without having even tried."

"That is sound advice," Angell agreed, thinking that the Governor had concluded his story. "Would you mind seating yourself..."

"During his presidency," Osborn interrupted, "Roosevelt visited the Panama Canal when it was under construction. and there he was photographed wearing a Panama hat. I promised you a story, if not a hat. There is an Ecuadorian saying, 'My hat instead of myself.'"

'My hat instead of myself," repeated Angell resignedly.

"Meaning," the Governor explained, "that it is preferable to give up one's hat rather than one's life!"

"I can't imagine a situation in which that choice would have to be made."

"In western Ecuador, the Guayas River runs through the Guayas province where Ecuadorians hunted alligators for their hides. Their daring method of conquest involved swimming in the river wearing nothing but Panama hats on their heads and armed with long knives clenched between their teeth." From the nearby table Osborn grabbed a woven coiled basket from his travels in Madagascar, dumped its contents, and placed it on his head. He then retrieved a letter-opener from his desk and placed it between his teeth. "When the hunter was faced with the open jaw of the alligator, he would duck under the water. While the alligator devoured the empty hat, the hunter would deal a death blow with the knife to the underbelly of the beast." Osborn then removed the letter-opener from his mouth and buried it in the clay.

Angell, masking his frustration at not being able to get the Governor's posterior in a chair to pose, did his best imitation of a crocodile smile and said, "And I thought those hats were just for keeping the sun off one's scalp." Angell mused that the Governor was a fascinating creature himself and something like the alligator— living on the shores of permanent bodies of water, resting in burrows and a bit snappish. At the moment however, the sculptor wished for a bit less character and creature and more of someone who would just sit in the chair.

The Four "G's"
August 1937

Stellanova did not really mind having other people around, although there on the island it was most productive and harmonious when it was just the quartet of Chase, Gib, Lee, and herself in residence. If a visitor could just sit in companionable silence from time to time, that was the best tacit agreement. However, she did not think that she and Mrs. Angell would come to such an agreeable arrangement anytime soon. Stellanova simply longed to sit and contemplate something beautiful and then work to describe it in verse. Writing prose for Chase's projects was not quite as satisfying to her as writing her own poetry. A poem could make time stand still, and if she did her work skillfully, any number of moments there on the island, and with Chase, could be frozen forever like something pretty captured in a clear glass paperweight.

She felt the need to exercise her observation muscles like Chase did his daily devotions. Her "prayers" took the form of "Breathe in. Breathe Out. Be still. Listen. Look." For instance, if she stared at that birch tree between the porch and the shore, and described it to her satisfaction as a poet, that would be a devotional as reverent as Chase's. How she longed to have the time and skill to observe nature like Mr. Frost, though. Fortunately, her prayer for inspiration this morning was answered. Her eyes focused on a stump sprout around the original decaying birch trunk standing on the riverbank. The white columns of the living birch trees rose like the ribs of a cathedral. They supported a vaulted ceiling rivaling those of the most sacred places designed by man. The reveler stepped inside the circle of birches and leaned against one of the columns and tilted her chin upward, to marvel at a fresco of blue and white and green that was created and recreated every few moments. Now, Stellanova was eager to translate her observations into crystalline verse. "White columns rise like ribs..."

"Oh, there you are!" Gladys exclaimed. Stellanova jumped and lost the pencil out of her hand. It rolled toward the source of the interruption like a failed baton passing in a relay race, reminding her that this visit with Mrs. Angell was going to be a marathon and not a sprint.

"Oh, you startled me. Did you need something?" Stellanova asked.

"I'm actually here as the messenger, Miss Osborn. Carleton wonders if you would be willing to pop into the library for the sitting because he senses that the Governor will be restless. They are having wonderful conversations, but the Governor keeps suggesting that they go for walks. Carleton thinks the Governor needs to have a focal point, and he notices how he dotes on his daughter."

"Does he?" Stellanova asked in a leading way.

Gladys could not tell if Stellanova asked if Carleton noticed or if her father did indeed dote on her? When in doubt, Gladys had a gift for filling in the blanks.

"A sculptor's work can be tedious, I'm afraid, and so he finds it difficult to work."

Stellanova filled in the blank "...with dogs, children, and iron ore hunters?" With her sly smile, Stellanova displayed her sense of humor and acknowledgement of the Governor's challenging personality. "I understand, but your husband doesn't need me," Stellanova informed Mrs. Angell. "He simply needs my advice. Tell your husband that the Governor will focus if Professor Angell introduces any of his three favorite topics."

"And those are?"

"The three Gs; God, God's country, and the Great University of Michigan...oh, and the fourth G, is the Governor himself!"

Gladys felt a subtle shift in their relationship. It felt as if they were two wives who had been discussing their respective husbands. This almost flustered Gladys, but she quickly recovered. "Men *do* like to talk about themselves, that's true enough, and these two certainly have the University of Michigan in common. I'll go suggest that." She turned, relieved that her role as the messenger was over without having to reveal the message from the original plea for help that Carleton issued about "coaxing the old codger to sit still!"

Providence
August 1937

The subject and the sculptor were collaborators in a sense, and they needed to trust one another, but the sculptor could not even trust himself. Angell felt he had to get something off his chest before he could move ahead on the commission; he was just not sure how. The Governor, although often gruff and self-centered to a fault, did seem at moments like someone to whom one could, perhaps, confess a failing, if only to make him feel superior. Angell could be very wrong about this. He was about to take a leap of faith, but creating itself was a process of taking risks without certain results.

"You appear to be a very pious man," Angell said.

"I have very little claim to piety," Osborn admitted. "I am a praying man, though. My motto is, 'Do your best and do not quarrel with Providence.'"

"I *do* quarrel with Providence sometimes," Angell countered. "I can mold anything that I see, but I cannot give a parent with empty arms anything to ease their grief."

Osborn was uncharacteristically nonplussed. "Why would you make such a difficult task *your* responsibility?"

"In 1927, I accepted a commission to do just that," Angell paused to collect himself. "I was commissioned to create a memorial to the thirty-eight children who were massacred when there was an explosion in their school. None of the children was over the age of thirteen. Some families lost several children in the explosion."

"Oh, yes. The Bath, Michigan tragedy," Osborn said with the weight of the words hanging between them. "That was a sad day; it was also a strange case. As I remember, it was the treasurer of the local school board who planted the explosives in the school. Governor Green, one of my successors, dug with his own hands to help with the recovery effort. I was relieved at the time that I was not the Governor with the responsibility to console the inconsolable. I am ashamed to admit that I have not thought about those children in some time, much less prayed for them and their families, in some time. Lindbergh's trans-Atlantic flight happened at the same time and you'll recall how that event buried the news about Bath before the bodies were even buried, and the tragedy was too quickly forgotten."

"I am haunted by that tragedy," Angell confessed. "I have a recurring dream that while I am creating the memorial, I lose the use of my hands." Carleton stared at his upturned palms and splayed fingers.

"How horrible that would be for a sculptor, even in a dream," Osborn sympathized.

Angell continued, "It isn't, exactly, a nightmare scenario. In that dream, I am oddly *relieved* that I cannot complete the commission and finally have a physical excuse for failing the community of Bath, rather than because of my own inadequacies as an artist. Only later, after I had agreed to do the job, did I learn that it was school-age children from around the State who sent in their pennies to pay for the commission." At this point, Angell struggled to continue.

"Tell me about the sculpture that you made," Osborn said.

"It was of a girl, about ten years old, cradling her pet cat."

"I think there was more to it than that. Tell me."

"The cat was small and fragile and..."

"And the little girl was protecting it."

"But none of us could protect the children."

"Then I think that your sculpture was a fitting tribute. I hesitate to share something with you," the Governor began. "I'm going to have to trust that you will not share this with your wife or with anyone else for that matter, but I believe that God may be telling me to share my personal experience as a grieving parent to help you move forward."

"You can trust that I won't repeat what you tell me," Angell promised.

"I cannot absolve anyone of any guilt, let alone my own," Osborn said, "but I may be able to give you permission to relieve yourself of the sense of responsibility to the grieving parents. Parents who have lost a child think they want to remember in clear detail, but they do not. If they truly remembered their dear child's voice or their laughter, it would be all too painful. Sometimes, memories are more of a curse than a blessing." Osborn removed his handkerchief from his back pocket and used it quickly. "What I do so clearly remember is the gentle pressure of their little hands around my index finger. I miss that trust, that simple gesture of faith. I also miss what that trust—that faith—instilled in me. That is what made me a father. All four of my grown children gradually lost that simple trust in their father as the years went by, that is only natural. However, that trust never had the chance to dissipate with my baby boy Chandler, and then later, with my dear little Trudy."

Angell was about to interrupt the Governor with his condolences, but Osborn waved him off.

"You are not the only one who wants to forget and feels guilty about that," Osborn explained. "Grieving parents want to forget too. Your project was never really about the parents. The purpose of your commission, Professor Angell, was to help the community remember. The community did not require a perfect tribute, just a fitting monument for people who did not have a personal connection to the lost souls."

Angell mulled over these words, knowing first-hand the truth of what the Governor was saying. He had hoped with his Bath memorial to give Gladys something also—to console her over the loss of their first-born, a son.

"I don't suppose there could ever be an adequate memorial for lost children," Angell said.

"No. There could never be. Not on a grave marker and certainly not in a newspaper. I was a newspaperman, yet I know that much of what is written on newsprint is soon used to line bird cages or, baser yet, to serve our needs in the outhouse. And then you are lucky if the ordinary citizen reads anything more than the obituaries and the police beat. My obituary, for instance, will likely fill several columns, but those souls who die as children may only get a line, if that. Justice would be if their obituaries filled several columns dedicated to everything that they missed in their short lives on this earth. People who die after a long, full life should merit only a line in the newspaper—the one thing they really wanted to do or see. Again, I am interested less in what people do than to what they aspire. The entry for my life's end should read, 'Former Governor Chase Salmon Osborn only regretted that he never saw the Grand Canyon.'"

"You give me much to think about, Governor, " Angell said while briefly kneading his temple with his fingers.

"You probably will never stop thinking about the tragedy, but I advise you to stop thinking about it in the same way that you have. There is no door out of that room of sorrow and regret." He stood up. "Angell, my good man, it is clearly time for a walk, the only thing to do when one is dispirited. Pray or take a walk, which, for me, is one in the same. Let us go and clear our heads."

Osborn and Angell could only walk single file on the narrow trails. This meant that face-to-face communication was not possible, but long periods of silence were. Periodically, Angell heard Carleton hum strains of a familiar hymn, but he could not quite place it.

Eventually Osborn stopped and wiped his forehead with his handkerchief and turned around as he folded it meticulously to avoid eye contact with Angell. Eye contact is the most essential thing in a politician's toolbox, so it was unusual that Osborn was not making eye contact.

Osborn cleared his throat. "I'm going to impart to you a harsh reality. You have got to move on, man, from your crisis of confidence. Even loving spouses cannot find the right words to console one another over the loss of a child. How could you be expected to do any better?"

"I hear what you're advising," Angell began, "but I asked it of myself not only as an artist but also as a parent."

Osborn didn't seem to notice that Angell had just alluded to his own personal sorrow. "Actually, if anyone *could* do something to ease the pain," Osborn said, "it would be a poet, a musician, an artist, or a sculptor because words utterly fail unless they are in the form of prayers, but even then…" Osborn exhaled in a way that expressed uncharacteristic resignation. "I was relieved not to have been the Governor at the time of that tragedy. I would have known that my words would have utterly failed that community of mourners and that I would just have to leave it to the hands."

The Governor clasped Angell's hands, much as would a Scottish laird would acknowledge a member of his clan. Then he turned to lead the way again, leaving Angell more than a bit stunned at the sudden and unpredictably warm gesture from the Governor. He recovered and followed the Governor, and recalled the last thing he remembered him saying. "The hands?" Angell asked.

"The hands that searched through the rubble that morning. Also, the hands that brought the hot dishes and the hands that held the parents' hands."

Osborn was slowly building to a crescendo. "The sculptor's hands and, of course, the Creator's hands. The only source of any comfort is to be found only in the attempt, not the result. The only source of comfort in times of despair is helping hands, not necessarily healing hands."

For a man who was known for his excellent skills as an orator, this acknowledgement that words occasionally fail was significant. Angell absorbed the message. "I value your perspective."

"I'm glad. If it's all right with you, Professor, I'm drained. I'm headed for a nap in my wiki-up."

"Of course, Governor," Angell said, relieved but drained as well.

Breakfast Before Dawn
August 1937

Angell awoke, surprised that he was done sleeping so early. Indeed, he had had the best night's sleep since he had arrived. As he dressed, he felt more confident about his ability to complete the commission. The only explanation was that the conversation with Osborn the day before had somehow been a balm for his ailing soul. Now he was eager to get to work. However, as it was Sunday, and the Governor would probably be leaving camp for church.

Angell and Gib exchanged morning pleasantries as the professor was entering the kitchen, and Gib was stepping out after having delivered a bundle of logs and received his list of tasks for the day from the Governor. Two pieces of badly blackened toast popped up, coinciding with Angell entering the kitchen, so his arrival did not startle the Governor as much as it might have. Angell was not the least bit surprised that the crusty Governor liked his toast burnt to a cinder. Lee was not responsible for the burned toast, but she was there to open the kitchen window a crack to clear the air of smoke from the toaster as she greeted the professor. She promised him two pieces of her homemade bread that were not reduced to the remnants of a hearth fire. The Governor was crunching away, and either did not hear what she said or would have been amused by it because she could get away with twitting the Governor having been in his employ for so long.

Not sure if the Governor liked to converse at breakfast, Angell ventured, "Good morning, Governor. Since it's Sunday, I am assuming that we won't get started this morning because you're attending church, perhaps on the island or in Sault Ste. Marie?"

"I pray several times a day, but I do not attend church," Osborn admitted. "You wouldn't be the first person to wonder why. Although, I am asked to give a good many guest sermons."

"I didn't intend to ask you to justify why you don't go to church." Angell made a "mea culpa" gesture with his palm to his chest. "I withdraw the question, your honor."

"I don't mind talking about my faith, especially early on a Sunday morning. For me, the journey of my faith has taken a few detours, which have been even more enlightening than the straightaways. Most of those detours I'll keep to myself, but you might be amused by one of them that actually happened *in* a church."

"Oh?" Angell rose to fill his coffee mug again and refilled the Governor's as well. He did not add his usual milk and sugar to avoid an unflattering comparison with how the Governor took his coffee.

"When I was a teenager, I was attending an evening service with my family." Osborn took the napkin holder on the table, emptied the napkins, and made of the empty holder a miniature church pew. "My nemesis at the time, a youth named Rawles, was seated directly in front of me." Osborn placed the pepper mill between the sides of the napkin holder and placed the salt shaker behind the napkin holder to demonstrate his and the other boy's relative positions in the pews. He continued with the story as he animated the salt and pepper stand-ins. "I wasn't in the most reverent frame of mind, and then young Rawles, in a loud whisper, called me a vile name and followed the insult with the threat that he was going to 'lick the stuffin' out of me' after church. I didn't see any reason to wait until after church, so I vaulted over the pew, hit him in the face, and stuffed him in between the seats where I continued to pummel him. You can imagine the uproar in the church. I was arrested the next day for desecrating a church."

Angell could well imagine the scenario since there was salt and pepper all over the surface of the table after the demonstration of the row.

"But I was acquitted of the charge shortly after that. The incident did, however, make me think it was time to move on to another town. God doesn't mind where you take down a bully, so a pew is as good a place as a playground. And the devil's playground is everywhere."

Angell went to the sink to get a dishrag to clean up the aftermath of the skirmish. "Chalk it up to youthful indiscretion, eh, Governor?"

"I didn't leave indiscretions behind in my youth," Osborn chuckled.

"But then who does?" Angell said.

"Agreed! If you refill our coffee cups, I have another story that will be of special interest to you, Angell, as an art professor." Angell complied and then sat down to savor Lee's excellent coffee and the Governor's next story.

"When I was a regent of the University, there was a professor who was accused of delivering a 'Christ-less' lecture. I am ashamed to admit that I voted with the other regents to remove him from the faculty, but then my conscience started to speak to me most urgently in the form of questions."

Angell nodded knowing that rhetorical questions were a staple of the Governor's speeches, whether he was speaking from the podium or from his spot at the head of the table.

"Do you not know that the fearless teacher presents every facet of the intellect in action? Will you strive to give wings to thought and then kill it when it tries to fly? Next time you oppress an intellectual process, will it be the death of a great truth?"

"But your doubts were raised only *after* the professor was fired?" Angell asked, trying to hide his incredulity.

Osborn halted almost imperceptibly before continuing his story. "It was a close call with my conscience," he explained. "Fortunately, I changed my mind before it was too late. And I was able to convince most of the other regents to change their votes. I concluded that the professor in question should continue to shake things up, and I came to have a large respect for his work without yielding an iota of my Presbyterianism."

"So, your denomination is Presbyterian?" Angell asked.

"If one had a passport for religious affiliations, mine would document that my religion of origin was Presbyterian. However, after all my travel and life experiences, gaining stamps on my religious passport, as it were, I have trouble assigning myself to any one denomination. The trouble with Christianity is that man isn't good enough for it yet. Christ was born too soon," Osborn said.

Angell nodded his head slowly. Clearly the Governor held strong opinions, but they were also nuanced. "Others may not appreciate the passport analogy," Angell said, "but I do."

"I actually have a somewhat stronger allegiance, in general, to institutions of higher learning and to newspaper publications than I do to most churches," Osborn went on. "The work of principled academics and honest journalists can shine a light on the truth, too."

"It is said 'Sunlight is the best of disinfectants.'" The break in the cloud cover outside coincided with Angell's statement and the quote and the dust motes were bathed in light.

"That was the aim of all the newspapermen that I have ever known," Osborn remembered. "Every one of them waged a battle for equality and decency every minute, and it was a prideful thing to know them. So, even though I did not formally join the church, I did enlist for the aims of the church."

Angell wondered what it would be like to be the Governor's age and spout adages as easily as some men spit chewing tobacco juice.

"I can find my sense of spiritual equilibrium without sitting in a church pew. For instance, I find it when I sleep on my bed of balsam boughs—more comfortable than a hard church pew—and I can look to the heavens and smell the boughs as fragrant as incense. In truth, I have not rubbed shoulders with my fellow man in a church pew in several decades, but a good number of my exhalations each day have carried prayers for others. I don't know whether prayers reach a Divine ear but it seems a bit presumptuous to think so. Perhaps prayers are only your good wishes for people. I pray for all my friends, those living and those dead. I pray for my children, grown or gone now, in my daily devotions. I also pray for my children's mother. That topic, however, is between me and my God."

By now, after a few days on the island, Angell could well anticipate when the Governor had finished with a topic or a session, much like he were listening to the final chords of a symphony he'd known for years and could anticipate the end of the piece. He might even have been tempted to applaud, but Osborn would typically be out the door before the curtain call.

An Encore Performance
August 1937

Angell was like an anxious student timidly approaching the office door of a stern professor during his office hours. Rubbing his hands served the dual purpose of kneading out the nervousness he felt while warming his cold hands in the dank atmosphere of the library.

"Professor Angell, just how do you want me to pose today?"

The word "pose" left a slight smirk on the Governor's lips. He then struck a pose mimicking George Washington's iconic figure crossing the Delaware.

"It isn't so much how I want you to *pose*, Governor. I am looking for a particular *expression*. Pretend to be thinking about something important."

The Governor visibly bristled. "I don't ever have to *pretend* to be thinking about something important. I am always thinking about something important!"

Angell realized too late that he should have been able to predict that reaction. He scrambled to recover from his faux pas. "Of course. Of course! How about thinking about something that you are *about* to say. I'm looking to convey the dynamism that I see in your expression when you are..."

Osborn interjected, "...saying grace!"

"No, sir. I'm not looking for a spiritual kind of intensity."

"Hmm. I take it you also don't want me to perform my early morning war whoop?"

"Gladys was quite startled this morning when we heard what she described as 'an unearthly howl.' We didn't know exactly to what to attribute that sound. However, we are accustomed to waking up to an alarm clock, which is startling enough."

Angell caught the Governor's eye for a brief moment of shared mirth.

Osborn proclaimed, "No need for an alarm clock here if you get to bed at an early hour!"

"How about I portray you with the expression that might be on your face right before you are about to begin a speech, Governor?" Angell had seen Osborn bring that kind of intensity and focus to many of their interactions, which tended to take the form of lectures. However, in this instance, something about the Governor's expression at present looked like a reminiscence was bubbling to the surface.

"If I posed like I must have looked before my *first* speaking engagement, I would look like a possum in a poke. You could have displayed me in your exhibit museum on campus alongside the other animals, including the skeletons I donated from my travels to Madagascar, a flying and amphibious lemur, and a pygmy hippopotamus! Maybe you have seen them?"

"I have. Fascinating specimens!"

Angell was more fascinated that the Governor may have fallen short even of his own expectations at some point in his life. "I've heard you on the radio, Governor. Most people would think you were a born orator."

"Well, I do thank God for any natural talents I possess, but if the truth were to be known, I have greater pride in those gifts I have worked hard to attain. The first time I was asked to speak in public was at a banquet in Sault Ste. Marie. I don't really remember what the organization was, or the topic of my address, but I vividly remember the paralyzing dread I felt about having to face an audience. Before I was to give my speech, I took my leave out a window. That was shameful enough, but I forgot that I was on the second floor of the building, and I injured my ankle in the surprisingly long fall in the dark. I was on crutches for months afterward!"

"Forgive me, Governor, but did someone tell you 'to break a leg' before that speech?"

"That would be more amusing, Professor Angell, if I did not still walk sometimes with a slight hitch in my giddy-up to this day."

Angell recalled his wife always telling him that his sense of humor was not always well-timed. Today, she would be right.

"The second speech went better, simply because I actually delivered it! I learned something very important when I gave my third public speech. On that occasion, I remember that the group was the National Canoe Association, and they were meeting in Milwaukee. I fought the urge to flee with advanced preparation—memorizing my speech and rehearsing out loud. The speech was well-received, but several hours later, a brawl broke out, unrelated to the content of my speech. Members of the organization started smashing dishes and even destroying chandeliers—a very Wild West scene. I was called upon to speak again as a distraction to break up the mayhem. I decided to deliver the same speech as before—including every word and gesture as earlier in the evening. The same speech was received with even more enthusiasm than before. After that experience, I never feared an audience again!"

Angell almost applauded, but Osborn had only just taken a quick breath.

"But now I am relieved to say that my public speaking engagements are mainly a thing of the past after this last strenuous tour when I became so run down that I contracted pneumonia. My daughter is insistent upon this. I pretended to put up a fuss, but in truth, I am glad to put all that behind me. However, I still have a pen and a typewriter to share my thoughts!"

Angell still did not have a lock on the expression he wanted to capture with his portrait bust, but he was gaining an insight into this learned yet rugged man. The physical attributes were easy to replicate, although he might have to de-emphasize his bear-trap-like jawline to flatter his subject. His other most prominent features were his dark and penetrating eyes, a barometer for his thoughts. Actually, his gaze did not vary much from the intensity of a hawk's when the Governor was about to prey upon a conversationalist with a weaker intellect—to when he was feasting on new information. Angell thought that the University should have sent a photographer or a painter instead of a sculptor to capture this unique bird.

Poetry, Prose, and Pygmalion
August 1938

The eraser end of Stellanova's pencil was resting on her bottom lip, serving as a divining rod transferring her unspoken thoughts to the page. She was sitting at her desk by the window in Big Duck, but she was engaged so deeply in introspection that she almost did not see Gladys walking toward the cabin.

"Knock, knock!" Gladys sang out. Stellanova wondered why people say that when their presence has already registered? She got up to open the screen door because Lee had long drawn the line at being expected to answer to anything other than a kitchen timer and the Governor's war whoops.

"Miss Osborn, I don't expect you to feel obligated to entertain me. I know that you have your ongoing projects to attend to. I can be perfectly happy curled up with a book on the Gander's porch."

"That's very thoughtful of you, Mrs. Angell. As it happens, the Governor and I are writing another book together." Chase was on a real tear about the renewed accusation in the Detroit newspaper that Longfellow had plagiarized his signature work. His initial rebuke to the paper was in the form of a letter to the editor, but it had mushroomed into a weighty manuscript with footnotes, appendices, and references for Stellanova to manage.

"Isn't it amazing that there are so few words in a poem," Gladys said unwittingly venturing into Stellanova's territory. "Yet it takes reams of paper to explain them."

Gladys forgot for a moment that Stellanova was a poet, but Stellanova's deadpan response served to remind her.

"I don't think that's amazing at all, Mrs. Angell. Sometimes I am amazed by how many reams of paper are used for prose."

Gladys continued undaunted. "We've all read books that make us feel that trees shouldn't have been felled to tell the story. But I'm sure that won't be the case with the book you and the Governor are working on."

Gladys had noticed a pattern to her interactions with Stellanova; they seemed all to be like a fencing match—thrust and parry, thrust and parry— at least until she could capture her full attention. The predictability of these interactions inspired a fanciful image to come to Gladys's mind—that of she and Stellanova in a verbal fencing match with giant pencils made her smile ever so subtly. "As it turns out," Gladys finally returned to her initial purpose in seeking out Stellanova. "I didn't bring enough reading material for my stay here. I knew that I would probably have plenty of time to read, but I didn't anticipate the almost total lack of distractions."

"You're bored?" Stellanova asked, but not without an air of censure.

The match was continuing, but Gladys was agile at feinting when faced with a conversational challenge. "No. Well, maybe just a little. My life in Ann Arbor has consumed my time and made me feel like a gerbil on a wheel with weekly and monthly commitments year in and year out. Here, for the first time in quite a while, I'm able to think my own thoughts, and blissfully, I don't have to share them with anyone if I don't care to. Conversations at the faculty women's groups I attend have to be peppered with just the right amount of travel anecdotes, Hill Auditorium concert reviews, and book critiques. And you're always supposed to be brilliant at playing bridge, and I don't even like playing bridge."

Stellanova, too, remembered that atmosphere in Ann Arbor. There were *too* many friends and *too* many pleasant invitations and activities. They jostled each other and jostled her; life was a choppy sea there with continual pleasurable excitement. She loved it, and yet resented the competition for her time and thoughts. "The only bridge you will ever hear about here is the Governor making his case for a bridge over the Straits."

"That's a relief!" Gladys said, also with relief that she now had Stellanova's attention and agreement.

"Mrs. Angell, you were seeking some additional reading material. I have just the title. *Invasion* by Janet Lewis." Stellanova rose from her workspace to find the book in her glass-fronted bookcase.

"*I'm* afraid that military history is not my favorite genre," said Gladys.

"Mine either," replied Stellanova. "This is a novel based on the lives of Jane and Henry Schoolcraft, who were a married couple from two different cultures. They lived right nearby in Sault Ste. Marie."

"That sounds like just the kind of book to keep me company here!" Gladys said appreciatively.

Stellanova resisted the urge to try out the lecture on Gladys that she had recently written about Jane Johnston Schoolcraft's life for a speaking engagement for the Sault Ste. Marie Women's Reading Club luncheon later in the fall. Researching was something she was used to doing, having written for an encyclopedia publisher in New York City years before she became Chase's chief researcher. Stellanova needed to do some preliminary research about Jane Schoolcraft for the book she and Chase were writing, and she could prepare her lecture for the women's group about Jane at the same time.

While Gladys exited with the novel about the Schoolcrafts, Stellanova thought that she should practice her delivery of her speech to see if what she had written sounded pleasant to the ear. Chase was always coaching her to do that so that her writing sounded less like an encyclopedia entry and more like a conversation, something that would engage the solitary reader or a live audience. Sometimes, Stellanova felt like she was the statue Pygmalion molded and then brought to life under the sculptor's hands. Maybe that was why she was so drawn to the story of Jane Johnston Schoolcraft, who had been molded by her father and then married to a man who continued to direct her education and dictate almost all other aspects of her life.

Stellanova realized that if she were honest with herself, she had more in common with Jane Schoolcraft from the previous century than she did with women like Mrs. Angell. That is why spending so much time researching Jane's life did not feel like a solitary experience.

Stellanova paced back and forth, struggling with how much to divulge about Jane's life to an audience. She worried about including the information about Jane's opium addiction, not only because of the stigma, but the source of information about Jane's problem was Henry Schoolcraft's second wife. Mary Howard Schoolcraft would have been privy to her husband's knowledge of his first wife's shortcomings, but she might also have been motivated to put her predecessor in the worst possible light. Stellanova was particularly sensitive to this issue, being the person who had supplanted Chase's affections for his wife. However, she would never stoop to write about Chase's wife Lillian. Should she disclose Jane's personal failings and struggles to a group of women in Sault Ste. Marie, who might also gossip about her and Chase?

So, she was protective about Jane's legacy. After all, Jane, her kindred literary light, was a beacon and a balm for the loneliness she often felt because she could not forge a genuine friendship with another woman when she could never be forthcoming about the most central fact of her life.

Stellanova picked up Jane's book of poetry—the book that she had purposely not given to Mrs. Angell, and leafed through its pages that often bled with the poet's pain—not unlike her own—both of them, in their own time and circumstance—living in the shadow of a man who could not wholly acknowledge her role in his life.

The book fell open to a poem whose first stanza could have been written by Stellanova herself.

The sun had sunk like a glowing ball
As lonely I sat in my Father's hall;
I walk'd to the window, and musing awhile,
The still pensive moments I sought to beguile.

A Heavy Lift
August 1937

Somehow Angell needed to explore his subject's full emotional range. Having a living, breathing subject was welcome, but also problematic—maybe even enigmatic. His access to his subject was extraordinary and Osborn was an open book of sorts talking almost incessantly about himself, yet there had to be more. Angell sensed that the Governor's bravado was masking something on which he could not quite put his finger, but probe he must as another day's work session began.

"I understand that you've been very generous to the University," Angell prompted.

"And I suppose that's why there will be a bust of me. I would prefer that a building be named for me, but I guess that we can't exactly choose monuments to our legacies."

Osborn's jab at the relative merits of architecture versus sculpture registered with the sculptor and his anger was briefly transmitted through his fingertips to the clay. Since the Governor was getting underneath his skin and clay was now underneath his fingernails, he thought it better to move the Governor onto another topic.

"I've also heard it said that you're a self-made man. There's a good story there, I'm sure," Angell urged.

"Ah, everyone likes a rags-to-riches story, don't they?" Osborn rubbed his palms together, almost as if there were a slender stick between his palms, and he was trying to create enough friction to rekindle a memory. "But…" the Governor held up a sizeable knotty index finger to signal a changing wind in his narrative, "do they appreciate a riches-to-rags-to-riches story?" The Governor was clearly warming to this topic and happy to have an audience for his campfire chat. "In any case, I see no shame in telling you that my father lost all the family money when I was a small boy. When my parents and their seven children left our little log cabin in the backwoods of Huntington County, Indiana, we moved into a large three-story house in Lafayette. It seemed like a palace to me and my siblings. Then when I was eight years old, everything changed. All I remember is that I seemed to go to sleep in the big house and to awaken in a little frame shack, with only two rooms and a lean-to. All of a sudden, we were a family translated from luxury to necessity—from affluence to abysmal poverty. Much later, I realized that even though poverty cramps, it can eventually expand the soul."

"I'm prepared to believe you," Angell said, "but what does that mean to you exactly?"

"Generally," Osborn explained, "young children are blissfully unaware of their parents' financial footing. However, when things change, especially for the worse, they readily absorb the values of thriftiness and a healthy work ethic that is necessitated by a reversal of fortune. You could say that I did just that. Iron-ore prospecting, working in and around lumber camps, learning the newspaper business, and eventually buying newspaper outfits all have their origin in this misfortune. All this turned out to be a lucrative combination and fueled the fire in my belly to have an influence on the communities where I lived and worked."

"And that led you to a life in politics."

The Governor continued, "As it turns out, I was always in politics even before I was elected or appointed to any official civic position. I wasn't afraid to speak my mind, no matter what I might set ablaze by doing so."

"I would never have the stomach for politics," Angell said.

Osborn's good-natured laughter burst from his barrel-shaped chamber of a chest. "Of course, you do! Universities are the most political organizations that exist! Jealous colleagues, dysfunctional departments competing for funds..."

Angell signaled surrender and agreement in one gesture. "Blissfully, I have escaped the battlefield of department meetings here at your camp. Still, I suspect the academic arena isn't nearly as rough and tumble as the boxing ring of politics."

Osborn leaned forward like he was about to impart a guarded secret and spoke in a tone that did not match the bellowing sounds of his usual proclamations. "The things that scare most persons in politics are the most attractive to me. I like the strife, the pawing, the goring, the tragedy, and not to mention the comedy that comes from the friction, the impacts, the *slander*, and the abuse of a public contest." Osborn paused briefly as if he needed to swallow something particularly distasteful. Then he continued with his usual appetite for feeding his ego. "I have a good temperament for a row. It's kind of like seeing how much you can actually lift."

Angell contemplated Osborn's mien. If Angell had put his finger on the Governor's pulse at that moment he said "slander," his blood pressure would have risen sharply. Angell could now add fear to the emotional range of his subject. The "heavy lift" was not the fear of a fight. No. The tang of fear on his tongue when he said "slander" was because what this man most feared was the loss of his reputation.

Closet Contents and Discontents
August 1937

Stellanova and Lee had already talked about the menu for the evening meal, a strategy session of sorts as was their daily habit. Because it was going to be a very warm day, Stellanova had urged Lee to take a rest in the afternoon—which, on Stellanova's part was at once sympathetic and strategic—She looked forward to those moments when the kitchen that was not hers, but could momentarily be hers to make something without the scrutiny in the older woman's domain. Lee, a taciturn woman just north of 60 years old, had cooked for the Osborn family ever since the Governor's tenure in the State's capital had ended and had served him through the close of other chapters in his life as well. She had heard and seen much, but mainly she made her presence known by the aromas from what was bubbling on the stove or baking in the oven and by occasionally humming French-Canadian folk songs when her normally taciturn demeanor was put on the back burner.

Stellanova now had the chance to engage in a baking ritual that was as comforting to the maker as it was to the partaker. She prepared the blueberry pie filling, plenty tart just like Chase liked it, and rolled out the crust. Stellanova folded the pie crust on itself two times like folding a dinner napkin and lifted it into an old rose-covered pie dish with a crackled glaze creating a stained-glass effect on the surface. As she unfolded the crust, she mused about how many times that dish had been heated and cooled over the years. That was the kind of sentimental family heirloom that convinced one that a pie never tasted just right unless that particular pie dish was used. She then rolled out more dough to make a latticework top crust, weaving the strips of dough as she contemplated the warp and the weft of her culinary project and the weaving of her life and sacrifices into that of the Governor's life. One of those sacrifices was Chase's lack of enthusiasm for her efforts in the kitchen, which would cool like a pie stored in the pie safe that Gib had made for her. Stellanova predicted that Chase would not do his "whoop" that he reserved for registering pleasure in Lee's cooking, because he would not dare to risk expressing that kind of unbridled enthusiasm in public for *anything* she did for him. That made her think, again, of the lavish praise that he had heaped on George and the hospital staff, but not on her.

However, she would seek appreciation elsewhere—however small. Yesterday, she had asked Gib to pick enough blueberries for two pies—one for dinner and one to send to Gib's aunt. Her pie's latticework top crust had to be perfect because Gib's aunt was an expert weaver of ash baskets. If the blueberry-stained ash basket that they used to collect berries was not on the shelf in the summer kitchen, Gib had remembered. She should resist the urge to check behind Gib because he was always so reliable. Her mind's eye anticipated that in the early evening, Chase would challenge Carleton to crank the ice cream machine to make vanilla ice cream to go with the blueberry pie. Stellanova smiled to herself to think of the blueberry-vanilla-ice-cream-slurry on the plates after dessert.

Stellanova heard a knock at the door, but her hands were gloved in flour. "Come in! I'm in the kitchen!"

Gladys entered, saying, "Just the smell of the blueberry bushes here is intoxicating. I think that my taste buds have been primed for blueberry pie ever since we got here. I hope I didn't eat so many berries while walking along the path that there won't be enough for a pie."

"The bears are more of a threat to the supply than your grazing," Stellanova said.

"That's a sobering thought," said Gladys as her eyebrows went north and were in no hurry to return to their normal position.

"Actually," teased Stellanova, "it is more likely that you'd see a buffalo around these woods."

"You can't be serious!" exclaimed Gladys.

"You may see the Governor lumbering around in his buffalo coat from time to time," Stellanova explained. "Although August sightings are rare given the heat."

Gladys heard a segue to her initial purpose in seeking out Stellanova. "Although, I find that the evenings here do get surprisingly cool. Could we trouble you for an extra blanket for our bed? I'm afraid we are a bit soft from not having camped much in recent years."

"You consider this camping?" Stellanova asked.

Gladys was beginning to find that trying to converse with Miss Osborn was like being blindfolded, spun around, and told to pin the tail on the safe topic for conversation. "No, no. The cabin is so beautiful that it makes us feel close to nature. But we feel a bit chilled having become accustomed to our new central heating system at home."

Because Stellanova had turned away to start another pie crust, she missed Gladys' body language, indicating she was catching a chill—from the frosty conversation.

"There is a fireplace in your cabin that Gib keeps supplied with logs and kindling for starting a fire," Stellanova said, underlined the obvious.

"Although, my husband works with his hands, I have to admit that he is not a very good fire builder. I suppose everyone should know how to do practical things like build a fire or make a pie." She was watching how effortlessly Stellanova could turn out a piecrust. She used the roller like she was ironing a tablecloth on short notice.

Stellanova couldn't suppress a brief smile, "The Governor does lead a rather spartan lifestyle here—often sleeping in the out-of-doors, but there's no reason that his guests have to adopt his habits, that is with one exception; the setting of watches to 'Osborn time.'"

"Yes," Gladys acknowledged, "We've learned to set our watches a couple of hours ahead, so we don't miss any meals. We learned that lesson straight away."

"I am truly sorry," Stellanova apologized, "that you missed your first breakfast here."

"Well, it did make us more keenly aware of the meaning of the word break-fast."

"Glad you have found the humor in it," said Stellanova. "I advise that you don't lose that sense of humor for the remainder of your visit here because you will probably need it."

"I promise," said Gladys, "I won't be a wet blanket about it."

"The blanket!" Stellanova exclaimed. "Follow me upstairs to the hall closet where I keep the extras." Stellanova led the way up the narrow staircase that was behind a door in the kitchen's corner, which Gladys had previously assumed was a pantry door. At the top of the stairs was the hall closet, and Stellanova needed to get a sturdy desk chair from the nearest bedroom to serve as a step ladder. Gladys held it steady so that Stellanova could safely reach the top shelf. She then handed a couple of blankets down to Gladys.

"These are beautiful blankets. Such a distinctive pattern," Gladys remarked sincerely as Stellanova passed several into her hands, all of white wool with green, red, yellow, and indigo stripes.

Stellanova answered with some degree of pride. "They're Hudson Bay blankets. They've got quite a history. Two hundred years' worth, in fact."

"The pattern is familiar to me," Gladys said, "but I don't know anything else about them."

"Their history goes back to when the Hudson Bay Trading Company used to trade these blankets with the Indians for beaver pelts," Stellanova said. "The company also made these blankets into hooded coats called capotes; they were particularly popular among both the Natives and the French-Canadian voyageurs."

"They're heavy. They'll be warm." Gladys said.

"They're heavy because the wool is boiled, and that

creates a dense weave," explained Stellanova. "I have several sizes of these blankets. See these black horizontal stitches along the selvage? They're called points. The points indicate the weight in pounds of each blanket. A full stitch, or point, indicates a pound. A half stitch, a half-pound. The more stitches, the heavier and larger the blanket."

"I'm now glad that Carleton can't build an adequate fire; otherwise we wouldn't have had the chance to sleep under one of these beautiful blankets," said Gladys.

" I think I'll get one down for myself," Stellanova decided.

"Let me step into this bedroom and put these down on the bed, so that I can steady the chair for you again," Gladys offered.

Having turned away, and just as Gladys lay the folded blankets on the nearby bed, Stellanova cried out. Gladys rushed out into the hallway expecting the worst. Instead, she found Stellanova still standing on the chair, but holding a cardboard box, looking crestfallen. "There's evidently a leak in the roof that has soaked this side of the closet. My correspondence is damaged!" Stellanova exclaimed in dismay.

"Miss Osborn, please be careful. Hand me the box and put one hand on my shoulder to get down off that chair." Stellanova stepped down with Gladys's help and eagerly took the box back from her arms.

"I'm afraid to open it to see the damage."

"Maybe it is not as bad as you fear?

Stellanova put the box on the chair and lifted off the top of the once white, but now water-damaged, herbarium box. She dropped its lid on the floor and started peeling back through the years of unbound pages in the box.

"Not everything is ruined," Gladys said eager to assure Stellanova as she looked herself into the box.

"Yes, but the letters with the earliest dates, the most dear to me, are the most damaged."

"Let me help you separate the pages. We can lay them out to dry," Gladys offered.

"No! No, thank you!" Stellanova answered abruptly. "Thank you, but I can do this," Stellanova assured her, not wanting to let on to Gladys how very personal this damaged correspondence was. "I should have stored the letters in the Governor's library!"

Stellanova stood awash in regret over her choice of where she had stored her letters that documented ten years of correspondence between her and Chase. She barely remembered that Gladys was still standing there.

Gladys could see that the damaged letters had a profound effect on Stellanova and knew that since she could not help, she needed to leave Stellanova to her private agony.

"I'll just take this blanket," Gladys said, turning to retreat.

"I'll see you in a few hours at dinner, Mrs. Angell." Stellanova tapped her watch lightly. "Osborn time, remember," she said with as much of a smile as she could muster. The letters documented what had taken place, what was between them that had also happened on "Osborn time" and their present-day arrangement that was also on "Osborn time."

Embers
August 1937

Stellanova had read Chase's letters so often that she could almost believe those exchanges had occurred face-to-face. The frequency of their letters and the fact that they often crossed in the mail also fed the fantasy that they had shared their thoughts and feelings in person.

In the spring of 1922, Stellanova was embarrassed to have written a particularly uninhibited letter to Chase. This was before she had met him and long before she had any realistic claim to his affections. At the time, she dearly wished that she had not had the temerity to send it. For some reason, the delivery of that letter had been delayed by several weeks; this was odd as all later letters she wrote to Chase had reached him in a timely manner. Stellanova suspected that the receipt of that letter was held back *after* it had been delivered. Her return address, written in a feminine hand, on the envelope must have been like the telltale message lipstick leaves on a starched white collar. If she had known then that Miss Hadrich, Chase's secretary, was reading and screening even his most personal correspondence, she would not have written the things she did. Only much later did she come to understand that that letter eventually did reach Chase, but only after one, or even two, other women had read it.

If she had known then, what she knew later, that Chase was a man who was impossible to embarrass, then she would not have agonized over that letter sent in the spring of their May–December situation. Much later, he wrote to her about his recollections of their trysts. Things said in the heat of the moment were erotic, but they made her cringe when she read how Chase had "transcribed" them in letters to her. They were so graphic that they were both romantic *and* repugnant. At the time, she thought she should burn them, but she did not. During the many years they were apart, those letters were the only manifestation of their physical relationship. Perhaps, the water damage had washed away the ink and extinguished the old flames? It was not the loss of the letters that she now feared. It was the loss of *that*.

She needed to set that thought aside, as the memory of another missive between them came to mind. That missive, too, like several other of their letters, had traveled a circuitous route. It was 1922. It was Chase's first invitation to Stellanova that she might visit him that summer on Duck Island. What Stellanova now most remembered was that that invitation was rescinded almost immediately after it had been offered. Even more memorable was how cryptic was his note abruptly taking back the invitation. The reason he gave for the change in plans was "a worse than fatal *influence*." The edited version, supplied by his secretary in a follow-up letter, was stranger still. Miss Hadrich wrote to explain that the Governor had intended to type "a worse than fatal *illness*." Could it have been that a "worse than fatal illness" were the words Chase had chosen to refer to his feelings for her and that the "worse than fatal influence" was how he expressed his wife's jealousy? In any event, the invitation evaporated; probably because the scent of their ardor in their correspondence did *not* evaporate with the days it took for a letter to travel between them.

In her early letters to Chase, what was it exactly that had attracted him to her? Did he hear in that early correspondence a youthful naiveté, a vulnerability that he could exploit, or a chance to cast himself in the role of parent or paramour? How consciously had she communicated that she might be a willing participant in either of these two very different relationships? That question troubled her. *She* fell in love with his impressive biography, and those eyes. What did *he* fall in love with? Certainly not her biography, which, at that time, was a bit thin. Did he simply fall in love with the opportunity to fall in love? Did this make their relationship built on any less solid ground? Should she simply trust in fate and not question or doubt his genuine regard for her from the beginning?

Fifteen years later, she could see these letters as breadcrumbs that had led her on a winding path into an uncertain future where, even on the straightaways, there were so many obstacles. And she could never seem to see around the next bend. Yet, that path led her to this very cabin and this life. She could not honestly say that this life simply happened to her.

Stellanova was more comfortable posing these questions to herself than she was at seeking the answers directly from Chase. They had always been better at communicating on paper, and now that they did not send letters to one another, she could not find a way to broach the topic of dissecting their relationship. However, they did so *ad nauseam* when they were ardent correspondents. Maybe it was the fact that she was as curious about their relationship as those were who gossiped about them? Gossip or not, at some point, she had consciously chosen this concubine-like existence, which became the central conundrum of her life.

Whispering Angells
August 1937

Gladys peered into the mirror that was attached to the old vanity. The reflection from the once silvered surface of the mirror was now worn and cloudy, so she could only intuit her image. The lighting in the room offered no help. It was dim with no overhead ceiling light and only two small bedside lamps. The low light and the antiqued quality of the mirror were working their magic and consorting with Gladys to obfuscate the effect of the decades between her appearance now and when she considered herself to have been in her prime. Since she could barely see her own reflection, her mind's eye had conjured Stellanova's image; the subject of her recent preoccupations.

"It's so curious that Miss Osborn always refers to her father as 'the Governor,' yet she refers to her mother as 'Mrs. Osborn,'" Gladys said as she settled at the vanity's seat and addressed her husband.

Carleton sat on the bed taking off his shoes. The bed was newly topped with the Hudson Bay blanket, and he briefly paused to notice the texture of the weave before taking up the thread of the conversation. "Well, even though he occupied the Governor's office for only a single term, years ago, the title does seem to permeate his persona."

"That may explain the formality between them, something I find a bit strange for a father and daughter," Gladys said. "I don't know, but I sense there is something more. How can I describe it?"

Carleton gazed toward his wife's unclear reflection in the mirror as she brushed her hair. What he saw clearly was her present temperament, which he could always read by the ferocity with which she went about this nightly routine.

"Miss Osborn is attractive, but more so she's beguiling even, and she is obviously a highly educated woman. What is she doing here in this remote compound as the Governor's handmaiden?"

"Dear," Carleton said gently, "we're not here to psychoanalyze the Osborns."

"I know, Carleton, but I also know that *you* can't help analyzing your subjects either."

Carleton rolled his head slowly from shoulder to shoulder, easing the muscular tensions and draining away his preoccupations of the day. Gladys knew that Carleton only did these mini-calisthenics just before bed when his current project felt more like work than creating.

Carleton rose, removed his wristwatch, crossed the room, and placed it on the corner of the vanity. He reluctantly continued the conversation. "I have to admit that Freud might find fodder for his research on the ego by interviewing Osborn, not to mention his narcissism. Nevertheless, I do find myself quite drawn to the Governor. After conversing with him for hours, it seems he has lived the equivalent of three lifetimes."

"I agree, he does seem larger than life," Gladys said. "He is a very compelling person."

Carleton placed his hands upon Gladys's shoulders as he dodged the last tallied brushstroke. He leaned in and made eye contact with Gladys in the clouded mirror and said a bit mischievously, "You seem to be falling under his spell."

Gladys broke eye contact with Carleton in case her eyes would mirror her soul and he could interpret her expression.

"Just teasing, Gladys darling. You are certainly not the first person to have found him, at the very least, intriguing."

Gladys blushed because while she found the Governor to be a bit brutish and so unlike her gentle Carleton, she had to admit, to herself, that she had been captivated by receiving Osborn's penetrating gaze and felt a bit unsettled in his presence. Gladys shivered involuntarily.

Thinking her cold, Carleton responded by warming her arms with his hands. Gladys felt thoughts of the Governor seep out of her pores under her sculptor's skillful hands.

"Let's turn in," Carleton suggested, then teased, "and I'll try to break the spell old Chase has cast on you. Hmm?"

Gladys, with a slightly scolding look, shook her hairbrush playfully at Carleton. "And I'll do whatever I can to assure you that I can put the bristly Governor out of my mind and focus on you...and I'll take whatever shape you mold me."

Diplomacy in a Teacup
August 1937

Gladys usually had a light step on the floorboards, especially when she was a guest in someone's home. However, she didn't want to seem like a stealthy eavesdropper, so she cleared her throat as she entered the kitchen in the Gander, where Miss Osborn and Lee were having their morning meeting about the day's menu.

"Good morning, ladies. Miss Osborn, I have some letters to mail to my children. I believe you said the mail goes out a couple of times a week?"

"And you're in luck, Mrs. Angell, since this is Thursday. The mail goes out on Mondays and Thursdays."

"Washday and baking day," Lee said, "so I'll take my leave of you to put some loaves in the oven at Big Duck."

"That sounds heavenly. I can look forward to the delicious aroma of baking bread every week." By then Lee was out the door, leaving Gladys alone with Stellanova. "So, I can mail my letters to my children today, and that will give me the weekend to write to my mother."

"I write to..." Stellanova stopped herself short, adjusting what she had intended to say. She then resumed. "I, too, *wrote* to my mother often." Stellanova thought to herself that even in these small details she was practically dictating her autobiography to her guest.

"By the way, were you able to save any letters from the damaged box?" Gladys asked. "I hope you didn't lose any of the letters from your mother."

"Thank you for asking. Fortunately, I had stored my mother's in a different spot. The letters that were in the box under the leak were letters I received in the 1920's from," again she stopped, and then quickly added "...a friend." Stellanova, again, seemed helpless not to provide Gladys with unnecessary personal details. "I laid some of them out to dry on the bed in the guest room. I fear some of them may be irrevocably lost, though. I think I will be able to decipher even the most damaged ones because I remember the general content of them."

Stellanova realized that she might have broken the seal on her public façade. Thank goodness that Chase's handwriting was atrocious, even back then, for anyone not familiar with his hand, it would be almost impossible to decipher. Stellanova did not exactly know why she felt compelled to share something of herself with Gladys when she already felt over-exposed. Even the small details of how she had dealt with the letters seemed much more than was required, much more in retrospect than she really cared to divulge. In truth, her paper trousseau of love letters was as fragile as the essential secret of her life.

Shaking herself out of her ruminations, she decided that one way to keep a lid on her life, perhaps, was to busy herself with a mundane task like making a pot of tea.

"Mrs. Angell, I haven't exactly been a proper hostess. "May I offer you some tea? I'll brew us a pot. Stellanova motioned for Gladys to make herself comfortable on the settee on the porch as she herself stepped away to set the kettle on the stove. As she walked into the kitchen, Stellanova contemplated that she had almost referred to the settee as a "Chesterfield," a common name in Canada for a couch. But, fortunately, she had caught herself when she realized that to have done so would have revealed her origins and, more troubling still, would have exposed her true parentage. The teakettle's whistle and whine prompted Stellanova to focus on her hostess tasks. She soon brought out a teapot and a small plate of shortbread that Lee had provided. The slight rattle of the empty porcelain cups shivering on the saucers before the hot tea quelled their fragile nerves was a welcome sound to both the women who dreaded the likely return to their stilted conversation and needed a ritual with familiar rules of etiquette.

"I hope you like Rose tea," Stellanova said. "I mean Rose brand tea. It's orange pekoe, actually."

"That sounds lovely." Gladys was relieved that this would be much less formal than the Faculty Women's teas on campus.

The steam from the teapot brought forth a memory in Stellanova as if an unbidden genie had accidentally summoned it out of a magic lamp's spout. Stellanova was reminded of sharing tea with another coed where they lived in Helen Newberry Hall on a cold and dreary November day in Ann Arbor. That was a pleasant memory of a time she actually enjoyed the company as much as the tea. Soon, however, the sound of the spoon in Gladys's hand stirring and gently hitting the sides of her teacup, brought Stellanova back to the moment and the challenge of conversation immediately at hand.

"Red Rose tea used to come with fortune-telling cups for the reading of tea leaves." Stellanova looked over her cup mischievously at Gladys as she took a tentative sip of the hot tea.

"Don't tell me you read tea leaves?" Gladys almost sputtered.

"No," Stellanova reassured. "The Governor would frown upon that, being a man of God—the ultimate reader of tea leaves, you might say."

Gladys's laughter pleased Stellanova. Making Chase laugh, more often than not, had to do with him identifying something in her that was naïve or lacking, and therefore the source of humor.

"I hope that one day I have occasion to use that observation and pass it off as my own," Gladys said.

"I would be flattered," Stellanova answered.

While Stellanova had been seated on the edge of the settee, she now settled back into the cushions as she felt her edginess seeping away as she sipped. "I should tell you that from the outset I was less than enthusiastic about the bust commission, but that doesn't mean that I can't be more civil to you," Stellanova admitted.

Gladys looked like her thoughts had been divined by a mind reader, if not a tea leaf reader, but chose to take another sip of tea instead of respond while Stellanova continued.

"I was skeptical," Stellanova ventured further, "about many aspects of the commission, from your husband's skill to…"

Gladys was quick to come to her husband's defense. "My husband is a true artist." The empty teacup in Gladys's hand was also shaking and chattering away to help her defend her husband. "His work is well regarded in the University community and…"

Stellanova leaned forward and interrupted. "My candor was not meant to insult your husband's ability to carry out the commission. It's just that I'm not ready to face the Governor's mortality. The creation of the bust seems to mummify him prematurely. He's still a vital man, and he has so much more to contribute; indeed, he has almost as many adventures ahead of him as behind. The bust will essentially put a bookend on these later years of his life."

Gladys was surprised by the words pouring out of Stellanova's mouth, the most extended utterance yet. "I don't doubt anything you say. I have had a rather steady diet of Chase Osborn in anticipation of our visit here, and Carleton continues to fill me in about their discussions after their sessions."

"I am sorry that you find the details of the Governor's life so trying on your patience," Stellanova bristled.

Gladys made a face like she had burned her tongue, but it was the impact of Stellanova's sometimes acid tone. "Oh, no. On the contrary," she rushed to explain. "The more I learn about your father's life, the more I truly want to know about him." Like adding milk to hot tea, Gladys had quickly cooled the conversation to an acceptable temperature.

"I would also like to learn more about the strong woman behind the great man."

"You flatter me again," Stellanova said.

"Yes, you, but I also meant Mrs. Osborn," Gladys explained. "Your mother."

"Lillian?" Stellanova asked, realizing immediately that the conversation had once again turned in a direction that she did not want it to go.

"Yes, your mother," Gladys reiterated.

Stellanova poured more tea for Gladys, signaling a new cup of tea and a new topic.

"I cannot enlighten you about Mrs. Osborn, at least, not in the way that you may assume I can."

Had Gladys been reading a novel with this exchange between characters, she would have reread the last page because she had lost the thread of it. In this case, however, she needed to move the dialogue ahead. "Your china tea set is exquisite," Gladys said from her fallback position of dispensing compliments.

"You seem surprised to find signs of civilization here," Stellanova observed. "In fact, you would encounter fine china and the accompanying manners and customs to go with them—even a hundred years ago—at tea parties given by..."

"Jane Johnston Schoolcraft!" Gladys answered like a schoolgirl too eager to answer to raise her hand. "I am enjoying the book about her that you loaned to me."

"Someday I would like to write a scholarly treatment of Mrs. Schoolcraft's poetry, but that will have to wait. The book that the Governor and I are writing now about *Hiawatha* is consuming all my attention, I'm afraid."

"Not Longfellow's *Hiawatha*?" Gladys asked.

"The very same, although I like to think that the stories are less by Longfellow than by or at least belonging properly to Jane Johnston Schoolcraft's ancestors."

Gladys touched her temple as if to pinpoint a place in the roadmap of her memory where she had fixed the coordinates of a long-ago school day recitation. And there she found it, right where she had stored it years ago. "By the shores of Gitchee Gumee, By the shining Big-Sea-Water, Stood the wigwam of..."

Stellanova chimed in, "Nokomis Daughter of the Moon, Nokomis. Dark behind it rose the forest, Rose the black and gloomy pine trees, Rose the firs with cones upon them," Both women recited in unison, with mirrored smiles. "Bright before it beat the water. Beat the clear and sunny water. Beat the shining Big-Sea-Water!"

They shared a laugh, which subsided into sips of tea. "I have been so steeped in stories about the Schoolcrafts' scholarship and marriage," Stellanova explained, "that I have not been spending much time with the living recently. That might explain my awkwardness in making small talk."

Gladys nodded in understanding. "Small talk is an art form that I have had to master for my survival as a spouse in the arena of academics. Along with the spoons, knives can come out at faculty dinner parties, and especially at faculty women's teas."

Stellanova nodded and smiled in appreciation of the social climate in Ann Arbor. "Would you like some more tea?"

"No, thank you, but I will take another piece of shortbread." She reached for the plate Stellanova held out.

"What a pretty pattern on the shortbread."

"It's a thistle," Stellanova answered.

Gladys thought that the bristly thistle was a perfect family crest for the Osborns, even as she was beginning to think much more kindly of Stellanova. "Now that my teacup is empty, I am tempted to look at the bottom to see the company's name. I'm interested in china generally as an art form. Royal Doulton?" Gladys asked.

"That's right, but I don't know the name of the pattern," Stellanova replied. "I know that it must be very old as Mrs. Osborn brought it to the marriage as a family heirloom."

"Your mother would be pleased that her daughter continues to use her tea set after her passing," Gladys noted.

"More tea, Mrs. Angell?" Stellanova said. "Oh, I already asked you that."

"Let me help you take the dishes back to the kitchen," Gladys offered.

"Thank you, Mrs. Angell. Then I'll head across the way to Big Duck to collate my correspondence. It should be dry by now." Stellanova was eager to assess the damage to her personal archives and the damage to her heart when she reread the anguished letters from a very difficult decade.

A Difficult Decade
August 1937

From the second-story bedroom window of Big Duck, Stellanova watched Gladys walk from Angell's vehicle around to the river side porch of the Gander. Since her visitor was toting a bag that was bulging with some sort of knitting project, Stellanova calculated that Gladys would likely be occupied and out of the way for some time. She saw this as her chance, in private, to gather her pages of correspondence that had been drying. But checking on the pages was only a small part of what was on her mind. What truly beckoned her attention was an anxious desire to begin stitching together the patchwork fragments of correspondence into a whole, a narrative, convincing if only to her, that might provide justification for her difficult choices in the not-too-distant past.

A decade ago, Chase had suggested, indeed nagged more than once, that Stellanova write a novel about her life. At the time she thought he probably meant for her to write solely about the parts of her life that did not include him as he could not possibly have known that the rest of her life's story would include him. He told her that she should keep a diary to document her experiences when teaching in the Ozarks, something that would also serve as a kind of therapeutic exercise to clear what he referred to as "her muddled mind." There was nothing muddled about her mind. Her mind was clear, and she knew what she had wanted from the very beginning. Him.

As it turned out, she did not need to keep a diary. Everything that mattered most to her, she wrote in her letters to him. He kept all of her letters, except the early ones. He returned all the others, not in a fit of pique after a lover's quarrel, of which they had many, but to serve as material for the novel or diary he had urged her to write. For her part Stellanova kept every scrap of correspondence from him. The letters told their story with the rawness and audacity that a reader would never believe were it to be written in a novel—the one she might write, not the one that he had envisioned. Were their relationship to be reconstructed merely from her diary, it would only represent one side of the story. In the letters, it was all there, both sides, and the whole had been in that box whose contents were now an uncertain, fragile record of two lives that had once come together in words she still wondered if they ever should have been written, let alone stored away for herself or perhaps even, scandalously, for posterity.

The Blouse

August 1937

Stellanova turned her attention to see what else was stored in the closet that might also have been damaged by the leak. Parting and peering between the many hanging garments was like trying to open heavy stage curtains. Among these Stellanova discovered an old suit coat of Chase's hung over the same hanger as a monogrammed blouse. Stellanova sniffed the collar. The blouse had taken on a scent that Stellanova could not identify. Perhaps, it was the faint fragrance of a perfume Chase had given Lillian? Finding Lillian's blouse under Chase's coat made Stellanova feel as if she had interrupted two lovers in an intimate embrace. It didn't help that the blouse was embroidered "LOJ." She wondered if this was his way of concealing that he had kept this blouse for sentimentality's sake. Or had Lillian pointedly left it behind as a final salvo to Chase? Or was it a pointed message to Stellanova that she would never deserve the "O" at the center of any monogrammed clothing as had been the right of Chase's proper spouse?

She hurriedly took Chase's coat off the shared hanger. She was not sure what possessed her to try on the blouse. When she buttoned it up, she noticed that the top button was missing, so she used a cameo pin from her jewelry box to close the gap. Now committed to this ill-conceived costume, she went downstairs to work on correspondence, but that was not her objective. Her real intent was to deliver her message to Chase and get a rise out of him when he came in mid-day to check for his mail and saw her wearing the blouse with the unspoken and pointed message delivered in just three letters.

Stellanova had not anticipated that it would be Gladys who was the first to see her wearing the blouse. "Excuse me, Miss Osborn," the older woman announced herself as she rapped on the door, "Somehow, I brushed up against some poison ivy, even though I kept chanting, 'leaflets three, let it be.' Do you have anything for this, ugh, itching!"

"Oh, dear. Have you ever had a reaction like this before?" Stellanova asked, motioning for Gladys to enter as she turned around toward the bathroom and it's medicine cabinet. She returned, shaking the brown-tinted bottle to mix the lotion that had separated, but the cap was loose and some of the pink liquid splattered on the blouse. Even in her dismay caused by the spill, Stellanova caught Gladys's gaze lingering on the monogram; she seemed to be trying to make sense of the initials, almost as though she was moving the letters around like a jumble puzzle. Stellanova turned her back on Gladys to avoid her staring at the monogram and got a hand towel from the bathroom to blot the lotion on the blouse. When she looked in the bathroom mirror, she could see Gladys approaching. Her hand moved to her chest, and she felt the smooth abalone shell surface of her cameo pin. This gave her a way to deflect Gladys's evident curiosity about the monogram. Stellanova turned around and returned to the living room.

Gladys inclined her head ever so slightly to examine the monogram yet again, but this time more closely, but Stellanova pointedly interrupted her train of thought as she handed her the lotion. "You must admire cameos," Stellanova said.

Gladys met Stellanova's gaze. "Sorry for staring, but that is a...very unusual cameo."

"My college friend Yuki gave this to me. She sent it from Japan."

"It's lovely! Gladys said. "What is it made of?"

"Abalone shell." Stellanova unpinned the cameo so that Gladys could hold it.

"It is much more colorful than any of the cameos I've ever seen," Gladys remarked.

Stellanova gently guided Gladys by the elbow closer to the window to show the cameo's iridescent surface. "The woman's profile is also different," Stellanova said. "Notice that the nose is very pointy, almost a caricature."

"Sometimes cameos were profiles of actual people, weren't they? Royalty, I think," Gladys added.

"Yuki told me that you could see in this cameo how Japanese artists often generalized Western European features. So, it's rather a curiosity, too, in that regard," Stellanova said.

"Do you still keep in touch with your friend in Japan?" Gladys asked.

"I do. Our lives have diverged since college, though. She has children, and I do not. Oh, that reminds me, you received some mail. From one of your children, perhaps?" Stellanova retrieved an envelope from an ash basket on a table near the door.

Gladys exchanged the cameo she held in her hand for the letter. Stellanova was painfully aware that the real treasure was the letter.

"It's from my youngest, Jenette," Gladys said.

"I don't want you to delay your reading of your daughter's letter, so I'll leave you to it. I'm feeling a bit off, actually. I think I'll lie down upstairs and read some of my old correspondence while you read your recent one."

"Thank you, Miss Osborn. I hope that a little lie-down will make you feel better. And thank you for the calamine lotion."

After Stellanova had climbed the stairs, that slight bit of exertion had caused what felt like a small dam breaking and then she noticed the blood—a rivulet of disappointment. She knew in that instant that her brief hope that she would finally have Chase's child had quietly burst like a fragile soap bubble. Perhaps, she had never been pregnant. And maybe she simply could not be, now or later, as she was entering a phase of her life when she would be experiencing unpredictable cycles. That meant that not only Chase but now her body, too, would be giving her an emphatic "No" to the most pressing question she had ever asked of him *or* of God. She had prayed to God and pleaded with Chase to allow her to be a mother, instead of just a mistress.

Stellanova resented that Chase had denied her the one thing she wanted from him more than anything else from him. He had wasted years of her life engaging in fruitless foreplay, and even that was mainly on paper. He touted his generosity in giving away land and money to friends and universities. The planting of his legacy was his actual motive, yet he would not let his seed take root within her to create the most lasting legacy she could imagine and give him—a young child, many years younger than those he had had with Lillian, one who would live well beyond those other, now grown children. She did not get to be with Chase during his best years. Now, it turns out, he did not get her best years either— when she could have borne him a child.

She had to change everything below the waist; she took off the blouse as well, setting aside her thoughts moments ago of toying with Chase by surprising him with its monogram of another now on her. Stellanova consoled herself by thinking that a monogram stitched on a blouse was nothing compared to the many times Chase had written in ink, in his own hand, "Dear Stella."

Lost Angels
August 1937

Later in the afternoon, Stellanova descended the stairs to find Gladys sitting in the chair by the window in the living room, taking advantage of the natural light for her reading.

"I hope your daughter's letter put your mind at ease that's she's doing fine alone at home," Stellanova inquired as she picked up a stack of Chase's mail by the door.

"Yes, it did," Gladys said, using her daughter's letter as a bookmark. "If I could only hear from my other children, but they're young men, so it isn't likely that they'll write to their mother, unless they need money, of course."

Stellanova was jealous of Gladys; she at least had children to worry about. "How many sons do you have?" Stellanova forced herself to ask as she sat down on the end of the couch nearest the window and began to sort through Chase's correspondence.

"Three," Gladys answered with a slight hesitation. She actually lived in dread of this question. No matter how many times someone asked her, she was never really prepared to respond without betraying her mother's heart.

"Are they scattered to the winds?" Stellanova asked.

"Douglas and Donald are in college."

"And your third son?"

"We *had* a third son, our first child, but I don't often talk about him because it makes people very uncomfortable."

Gladys offered this and hoped that their conversation would soon move to another topic, for when people tried to offer her comfort, it generally fell short, and then she blamed them for their insensitivity. It was a vicious cycle. She found it best simply not to set that sad cycle in motion. At least that was what Carleton advised.

"Yet it seems you've opened the door, perhaps, for me to ask?" Stellanova placed the mail down on the end table. "I fear it would be insensitive of me at this point not to ask about your first child, no?" Stellanova ventured while she moved to sit on the edge of the chair opposite Gladys by the window.

The questions did not bother Gladys as much as the "answers" some well-meaning, but misguided, people offered. It was "God's will" or "God needed another angel."

"Our dear baby boy David. He had just turned one year old when he contracted polio and his little body succumbed to it. We thought that the doctors at the University could work, well, miracles, but it turned out that they were nearly as helpless as we were."

"My heart was so broken that I was just not in the right frame of mind to be a loving mother to my second son. I gave birth to him not quite three weeks after little David died. I don't know when I stopped wishing that he were David. What kind of a mother would wish such a thing? Douglas deserved to be loved as himself from his first day, but I..."

Stellanova reached out and gently put her hand on Gladys's knee as she sought to make eye contact with her. "I am sure that you did the very best you could. Your baby could never have known you were grieving for another. Most assuredly, he, Douglas, felt safe and protected, and fully loved in your arms. He could feel your heart beat when you held him close. He couldn't have known that your heart was broken."

"That is a comforting thought. Thank you," Gladys said quietly.

"I cannot imagine the pain that you have been through and still feel." Stellanova expressed as she settled back into the chair and shook her head. "I will never be a mother, so I can't pretend to know," Stellanova admitted.

"I hope that you will be a mother one day, if that's what you want."

"It was what I did want, but now I am resigned that it will never be."

"I am sorry that you may miss out on being a mother. You're such a devoted daughter and very protective of your father's legacy."

"Yes, I am that, at least," Stellanova sighed.

Gladys straightened to take a full breath. "It's important for me to tell you about an extremely difficult project that my husband undertook a few years ago," she said tentatively.

"More difficult than dealing with the Osborns of Sugar Island?" Stellanova asked.

"If my husband's commissions were all of living subjects, like Governor Osborn, it would be so much easier for him."

"Easier?"

"Yes. He became quite...haunted by a commission he accepted just a few years ago. We both did, actually."

"Haunted?"

Gladys needed to pause to ask Stellanova for a glass of water. Stellanova quickly obliged, and after Gladys accepted the glass gratefully and took a couple of sips, she was ready to continue.

"Carleton was tasked with commemorating the dead. This isn't unusual for a sculptor, of course, but the subjects had been recently murdered."

"Oh, my goodness. You mean the work of art was about the murdered individuals? It was to represent them?"

"Yes, that was the challenge. Of course, Carleton didn't know any of the subjects, but he truly grieved for them. In fact, he had nightmares about them, those little souls."

"*Little* souls?" Stellanova hesitantly asked.

There was the slightest trill in Gladys's voice. "Yes, little children, I should say. Carleton was commissioned to produce a sculpture for the town of Bath, Michigan, after the..."

Stellanova gasped. "Oh, yes, the elementary school bombing? That was a *horrific* tragedy! I remember the newspaper coverage. How many years ago now was that?"

"It was in '27. I'm glad you remember it. Thirty-eight precious children left for school one morning in May and never returned home to their parents," Gladys said.

"All those devastated families," Stellanova whispered.

"Carleton ran the tragedy over and over again in his mind as he struggled with how he or any artist for that matter, could give the town something that would provide even the smallest measure of comfort. Frankly, his was a real crisis of confidence in whether he had the ability, really the insight, to do their little souls justice," Gladys sighed.

"Nothing would ever be good enough, though," acknowledged Stellanova.

"Carleton tortured himself over the commission, and eventually, he came to think *he* wasn't good enough either. His style of sculpting changed after that commission. It became very stylized and less realistic. I have never dared to ask him about that. I'm not an artist, after all. Still, I didn't think it was an artistic choice as much as...it was a way to avoid falling short of representing his subjects faithfully."

"The sketches he's made of the Governor are certainly realistic," Stellanova said.

"You're right. And I was so relieved to see him sketching the Governor's likeness in that manner. You know for years, even after that commission, Carleton continued to make sketches trying to create a better tribute to the lost children of Bath. The work was long done; he just seemed to need to do this for his own peace of mind, though I don't think he has ever really gotten there."

"It was an impossible task," Stellanova consoled. "On some level, as a poet, I understand that what you create can never do your subject justice. I can only begin to imagine the weight of that artistic task."

Gladys released a shuddering sigh. "I have never told *anyone* about Carleton's personal, I mean professional, difficulties before. Please keep this all in confidence, even from the Governor."

"Of course, Mrs. Angell," Stellanova promised. "If we are keeping confidences, we are more than strangers at this point."

"Please call me Gladys."

"As you know, the Governor calls me Stellanova, but my given name is just Stella. That's what my friends call me. Sometimes, Stellanova sounds like just too many syllables between..."

"Friends," Gladys interjected as she reached out to place her hand on Stellanova's shoulder.

Stellanova rose and said, "We need some fresh air. Will you help me fold some sheets from off the line?"

"Why, of course."

As they walked toward the clothesline, side-by-side, it felt as if the stiff breeze swept away some of the sorrows they had just shared. The sound of sheets snapping in the breeze simply held them, blissfully and less painfully, in the here and now. As Gladys helped Stellanova fold the sheets, the scene was evocative of times and tasks immemorial. It was like two women performing a choreographed Renaissance dance. Nothing about it required any words, but Stellanova thought to herself resignedly that more sheets needed to be washed when they had visitors, but also because when visitors were present she and Chase did not share a bed.

The Bust Gets a Makeover
September 1937

The Governor's library had turned out to be a sufficiently adequate studio for Angell although there was just enough room to set up his modeling stand or step back to critique his work. However, when the Governor was present for a sitting, the room felt almost cramped; accommodating not just the physical Osborn, but the legend, too, and that voice. The makeshift studio had its advantages; the eclectic collection of books and Osborn's travel paraphernalia provided a welcome distraction when Angell needed a break, and the library was warm when it was chilly and cool when it was a little too warm. However, the climate for conversations was solely up to the Governor's disposition.

Angell no longer needed the Governor to sit still because the sketching phase of the project was done and the sculpting phase had begun. So the Governor was free to move about his library as his topics for conversation roamed and ricocheted off the walls. Meanwhile, Angell listened and commented as he worked the clay, periodically standing back to evaluate the progress on the bust.

"Stellanova is worried that you'll have me looking like one of your museum exhibits—a piece of taxidermy. Maybe she's right. In any event, let's give her a bit of a shock, shall we? I could don my buffalo robe, and you could sketch me looking like a bagged trophy mounted on the wall." Enjoying his own sense of humor, as he regularly did, Osborn led with that tremendous chin and stretched his neck to imitate the posture of a taxidermic prize. "She is not overly fond of that coat. When I wear it, the sight practically raises the fur on the back of her neck."

"I wouldn't want to deprive you of such fun, but personally I wouldn't dare tease your daughter or test her hospitality, on which we still depend yet for a couple more weeks," Angell said.

"You have spent hour upon hour listening to me, Professor Angell. In truth, I am starting to bore myself!" Osborn laughed, again finding his own amusement. "Seriously, I would like to learn from you; I consider everyone I meet, whether he is with or without a degree, to be a professor from whom I can learn. My experience has been mainly in the scientific fields, and so I lack some in my knowledge of the arts. Tell me something about portrait busts," Osborn said as he sat down behind his desk and eased back into his banker's swivel chair. "Do enlighten me!"

"I'm happy to oblige you." Angell took a damp studio cloth and wiped the clay patina from his hands. "Realistic portraiture, especially in busts, has a long historical tradition beginning with the Roman Republic; a sizable number of portrait busts of notable citizens and politicians survives from that period. With the exception of the occasional medieval reliquary, of this or that saint's head, that portrait tradition lay essentially dormant for much of the middle ages until it came back into favor in fifteenth-century Florence, in the Renaissance, that is."

"In fact, I think I have a volume about Bernini on that shelf up there," Osborn said as he pointed to an upper shelf. He got up and walked across the room to mount the library ladder. He took the book off one of the higher shelves and held it out to Angell to take it from him before he descended the few steps. Angell again quickly wiped his hands, this time on his trousers before taking the book.

Angell put the book on the desk and started turning the pages carefully. "One of the reasons I spent so many sessions sketching you before putting clay on the armature is because the greatest sculptors of the Renaissance and, later during the Baroque and the age of Bernini, did the same thing. Bernini, in particular, made sketches that were as realistic in his day as photographs are in ours." He pointed to one of the plates in the book, the bust of a certain Monsignor Pozzo. "Here is an example of how Bernini was able to translate his life-like observations of the moment into the permanency of the marble without losing anything of the speaking likeness of the man."

"Excellent lecture, Professor Angell! I don't know much about sculpture, but I do appreciate it. Art is a link that connects us with men and things of the past—Egyptians, Greeks, and Mayas and their cultures." Chase laced his fingers for emphasis. "We are brothers and heirs linked across time."

"Well said," Angell agreed.

"I once saw a bronze 'Lupa di Roma' in Bucharest and was quite taken by it," Osborn added.

"You don't say. I actually know that piece. It's from the founding legend of ancient Rome."

"Yes. The mythical twins, Romulus and Remus, suckling on the teats of the she-wolf. That one I saw in Bucharest, I had a copy of it cast in bronze in Naples; they worked from my own photograph. I presented the sculpture to the City of Sault Ste. Marie. You can see it if you go to the grounds of City Hall," Osborn said.

"What made you select that particular piece for the city? Does Sault Ste. Marie have some kind of connection, however distant, with Rome?" Angell inquired as he swiveled the pedestal on which the bust rested so that he could face the Governor straight on.

"No, no connection, at least in the traditional sense. Rather, I gave the piece because this Upper Peninsula is still wild and sparsely inhabited by humans, and since most of the people who live up here have a good bit to do with that wilderness, they truly understand the precarious and interdependent relationship between animals and mankind," Osborn said.

Angell sat on the stool next to the pedestal, and with his elbows on his thighs, he rested his chin on his clasped hands as he fixed his gaze on the Governor. While it had not taken long for Osborn to bring the conversation back to himself, and an opportunity to interject a reference to his travels and his generosity, Angell started to think how he could use this moment as inspiration for the bust. "If only I could communicate something of what you just said in how I depict you, Governor, you know, about the natural affinity of man and nature. That is, I'd like the bust to communicate that somehow in fixed bronze something of your instinctive and dynamic vitality."

"No need to flatter me, Professor Angell," Osborn said, standing up. "I have had my fill of sycophants in my years in politics. I vowed to be a one-term Governor to avoid those types." Chase put one leg on the edge of his desk. Angell noted this informal pose as he imagined that the Governor had perfected ways of signaling that he was a man both of the people and craftily capable of manipulating them, even Angell himself in that very moment. The Governor had this way in their sessions of suddenly taking control and being, well, the sculptor of his own bust.

"Stellanova has been focused on the finished product of the bust," Osborn said while casting his hand in the direction of himself in wet clay, "but I am more interested in the process. Continue, Professor Angell."

Once again, Angell was not entirely sure where the Governor was leading, so he decided simply to provide the dry details of his craft. "I created an armature for the bust. And then I applied about 50 pounds of this grey-green Roma plastiline modeling clay onto it," Angell explained while he worked with a hoop tool to shape and smooth the different planes of the torso.

"I trust you need to work quickly before the material dries?" Osborn asked.

"Not necessarily; since plastiline is an oil and wax-based clay, it never completely dries or hardens before the bust is cast in bronze. This explains why we can have multiple sessions and I can return to work on the same material, one day after the next as we've been doing."

"So, you can alter the image if need be?"

Angel began to think that he could now see where the Governor was going, and he feared that his subject might ever so craftily be attempting to switch roles. "Is there a problem with the bust, Governor?" Angell's voice betrayed his anxiety.

Osborn left his perch on the desk, walked over to the bust, and pointed an accusatory finger at his image. "Do you not notice the resemblance of my bust to the father of our country?"

Angell's shoulders slumped as he gazed at his work. "I see what you mean about George Washington."

"As much as I admire Washington," Osborn said with some levity, "I hold in higher regard Alexander Hamilton and his contributions. But that's another matter. To your work, I don't know whether to be flattered or frustrated that I've spent so many hours posing when it seems you could have merely put a dollar bill on your easel for inspiration! I think that the University is significantly overpaying you for your work," Osborn said laughing at his humor.

Angell's face started to harden into a cringe as he realized that the bust did indeed bear more of a resemblance to George Washington than to that of the Governor. "You are justified in being frustrated, Governor."

"I'll settle for being flattered, rather than being frustrated. If you could just make me look less like the planter of Mt. Vernon and more like 'The Laird of Duck Island,' that would better serve the spirit of the commission, don't you think?" Osborn said.

Angell imagined that Osborn was likely storing this moment away to entertain future dinner guests long after the commission was done and he and Gladys left the island.

Since he would be taking the clay study home with him to Ann Arbor he would be leaving behind on Duck Island nothing but this story for the Governor to tell, and tell he certainly would.

"Back to the drawing board," Angell said dejectedly.

"Small matter," Osborn consoled. "I have started over many times in my life. Show me a self-made man, and I will show you a man who has re-made himself time and time again, so it makes sense to me that my bust would need to be made over, too," Osborn said as he clapped Angell on the back.

"That's generous of you, Governor. It won't take me too long to make the necessary changes," Angell said.

"You won't have much time before the University committee arrives to see the progress on the bust, and I'm off to Boston for a week!" Osborn said as he took his leave but left the words ringing in Angell's ears as he stared at the bust that now mocked him.

Old Baggage
September 1937

Stellanova was relieved to be rummaging through another closet—one that would not hold any unwelcome, saddening surprises. She was looking through Chase's collection of neckties to select a few he might like for his upcoming speaking engagements in Boston. With her back to the bedroom door, she was startled less by Chase's appearance than the oddness, the formality, of his clearing his throat as he entered as if she were a trespasser in the bedroom that they usually shared.

"I know that you'll be busy in Boston, but I hope you'll take a few moments to write a note to me on hotel stationery like you always used to do," Stellanova asked, glossing over his disgruntled entrance. "I remember especially liking the hotel stationery that boasted 'Absolutely Fireproof!' It gave me comfort."

"And wasn't the *Titanic* advertised as, 'Absolutely unsinkable!'" Chase teased.

"In any event, I shouldn't have to subscribe to the *Boston Post* to get the news about your comings and goings."

Stellanova draped two ties over each of her shoulders to model several possibilities for Chase. He selected the paisley pattern and the one with the single fleur de lis. "I won't be gone so very long, my star. I'll be returning before a letter could be delivered to the light station." Suddenly playful, Chase draped one of the unchosen ties around Stellanova's neck and started to tie a loose Windsor knot necklace. A smile played on his lips as he worked.

"That's not the point, Chase darling. I miss the way we used to communicate. I miss our letters. We haven't written letters to one another for over seven years...ever since the adoption."

"Why haven't you mentioned this for the last seven years? Why now?" Chase asked.

"I've been reading through our correspondence recently. You used to be so ardent. I miss that."

Chase moved his hands from threading the tie to resting them on Stellanova's shoulders. "So, you're getting nostalgic on me."

"Yes, I guess, but not so much so that I would want to revisit those difficult times." Stellanova at once spoke and seemed to retreat into her own thoughts. "I'd just like to return, in a manner, to the best part of that time in our lives." She reached out and put her palm over Chase's heart.

Chase bowed his head, putting his hand over hers. "I don't miss *any* of that part of our lives when we were apart."

"I do miss the exchange of letters, though."

"We exchange information with one another every day in person, Stellanova."

"But it's the sharing of ideas and news about things beyond the everyday, beyond even our academic projects. As in those years, when you are away from me, I want to know, 'How was your speech received? How many people were in the audience? And...how does it feel to be away from here, away from me?" She looked up at him as she removed his loosely knotted handiwork from around her neck.

"If I tell you all that in a letter, then what will we talk about when I return?"

Stellanova moved to the bed to drape the tied loop over the post of the headboard and opened Chase's suitcase to put in a third tie—one that she had given him during the years that their emotional ties were often quite strained. "We will still have our guests when you return, Chase, prying eyes and pricked ears, I continue to fear. A letter from you would allow me to carve out some time that we could share—just the two of us." She got Chase's travel alarm clock from the drawer in the bedside table.

When she handed the clock to him, Chase accepted it, took her other hand in his, and leaned in to whisper in her ear. "Cheer up, my dear Stellanova. You won't be lonely." Chase straightened up and struck a profile pose. "You can always converse with my bust!"

"That is not even remotely amusing! What is more, you would *not* want to hear what I would tell your stand-in!" Stellanova flashed the sly smile that Chase first saw in her University of Michigan graduation photograph she had sent to him years ago.

"Oh, no?!" asked Chase, a bit mischievously, and then the intensity of his gaze ratcheted up just a notch.

Responding, Stellanova took off her glasses to increase the intensity of her own gaze and said, "Talking to your bust, let alone a dialogue between it and me wouldn't put either one of us in the best light, Chase."

Chase held up a finger to quote one of his favorite adages, "Bringing light to a subject is rarely, if ever, a bad thing."

"That works if what you are discussing is a grocery list or the day's chores. It would be quite another matter if the light you so praise was to provide illumination, so to speak, for someone reading the letters we once wrote to one another," Stellanova warned. She fogged up her glasses with her warm breath as she looked seductively at Chase and then wiped them clear with the handkerchief she took from his luggage.

"Oh?"

Stellanova moved directly in front of him and placed a finger on his chest for emphasis. "You may not remember all the things that you wrote, but *I* remember my letters and certainly remember all of yours!"

Chase took his handkerchief from her and moved to the open suitcase. "That, my dear, is because you are excavating and examining our relationship as it was during a time before everything was settled." Chase snapped the suitcase shut as if to say, 'Case closed.' "That is not an emotional journey that *I* am interested in retaking."

Stellanova lightly wrapped her knuckles on the suitcase. "Well, that's the trip I am going on while *you* are gone to Boston. It is one way to keep you close to me." Then, playfully tugging on his lapels, smiling into his face, "If wishes were aero-planes, I would be with you wherever you go."

Stellanova initially felt reassured by their intimate conversation, however much they did not meet in agreement, but then, on further reflection, there was something contradictory and disturbing in what Chase had said about bringing light to a subject that cast a shadow on her mood. A subject if ever there was one, their whole life together was lived in the shadows. Yes, Chase was a man who lived by maxims, but not in every case. Had he been willing to take her hand in marriage and walk with her from the shadow of uncertainty, and shame, into the light of open love, their relationship would be so much more satisfying.

Sometimes, Chase seemed so cool and distant that Stellanova wondered if it was far from an act, a protective posture; perhaps he actually believed the lie he hid behind to be with her. The likelihood of that was considerable as his life had not really changed much, but hers had, and the discrepancy between his reality and hers made for a complicated plot that she at least found exhausting to play out and rehearse for others day in and day out. It was like she was in a one-woman play, a romantic tragedy of sorts, but the drama was not measured in minutes or hours, but weeks and years. She alone was carrying the burden of the ruse, especially when Chase was traveling and she alone, among so many guests, had to keep the story, that fiction moving forward. Thank goodness the Angells would be going off-island for a few days.

The Braver of the Two
September 1937

Stellanova sometimes did her writing at the kitchen table in Big Duck between breakfast and lunch. This worked well as Lee was very quiet in her own work at the counter, and her steady activity of cutting, chopping, or stirring this or that pot on the stove helped Stellanova to stay focused on her writing and also gave her an excuse to take a break periodically to talk with Lee. Today, however, she interrupted her work and Lee's to make what she thought was a simple request.

"What do you think about a special dessert tonight for Professor Angell? I'd like to acknowledge all the efforts he's made on the commission. It's nearly their last dinner and soon after they leave, we'll have three more guests from Ann Arbor. I assume the Governor mentioned that we'll have a forestry professor by the name of Ramsdell and his grown daughter, and the 'pièce de resistance,' a Dr. Clover who is a woman and apparently quite an adventurous botany professor."

"Yes, I'm aware of those three. But for this evening, what did you have in mind for the menu, I mean for the dessert?" Lee asked as she wiped her hands on an embroidered tea towel (probably a wedding gift for the woman who wore the embroidered monogram) hanging from the oven door handle.

"An angel food cake."

"Angel food? I haven't made one of those for years and there are many reasons for that," Lee said, reaching for a well-worn cookbook stored on a shelf just above the kitchen window. While obviously considering the request while she paged through the book, Lee nonetheless voiced a litany of pitfalls that carrying out Stellanova's suggestion presented with *her* commission for a cake. "With that cake the batter easily goes out of balance. Too much sugar and it falls. If the flour is damp, you get a sticky crust. If the oven is too hot, the crust is hard. If the egg whites are under beaten, it's dry. If the eggs are overbeaten, the texture is coarse."

"Oh, is *that* all?" Stellanova asked mischievously.

"You jest, but angel food is devilishly hard to make!"

Both women burst into laughter. "How about this? Angel food it is, but I'll make a back-up dessert—a blueberry cobbler."

"Sounds like a good plan, but you know that I hate to fail in front of an audience, especially when the Governor is in camp."

Years ago Stellanova would never have dared to spring a last-minute menu request on Lee. Rather, she deferred to Lee because the older woman had lived with the Governor much longer than she had. Initially, she was very apprehensive because she assumed that Lee's loyalty to Lillian would make their relationship strained. Stellanova felt that she did not have the opportunity to ease into her relationship with Lee by coming as a visitor first. Instead, she came as a legally newly minted family member in the summer of 1931. Yet, over the years they had come to an unspoken understanding of their respective roles at the Osborn camp. They had bonded one memorable morning when they each rolled their eyes simultaneously in the other's direction. That morning Chase had expressed his satisfaction with Lee's cooking by throwing back his head, and letting loose with one of his startling wolf howls. It was then that they realized that both of them kept the Governor together, body and soul, and they both needed to have a sense of humor about it.

The reverberations of that outlandish howl and their shared astonished amusement over it were behind today's conversation and concord about the eventual angel food cake. Later, with the cake safely shepherded from mixing bowl to oven to counter, Stellanova set the table with Lillian's china. The elegant dishes had a warm white glaze with gold leaf edges. The formal place settings seemed at odds with the Osborn camp's rustic setting—a far cry from the life Lillian must have imagined when they were first married, lived in the Governor's mansion in Lansing, or resided in their beautiful home in Sault Ste. Marie. Lillian could not have predicted that living on Duck Island was the next logical step in their social life. There were a few missing pieces of the china, noticeable when they had larger gatherings at camp. Stellanova's imagination was such that something beyond the mundane always entered as a possible explanation for why something was or was not there. She wondered under what circumstances those pieces were lost—perhaps shattered in an argument? She had inventoried everything at camp like an archivist trying to piece together Lillian and Chase's married life from the chards Lillian left behind.

Chase offered nothing to Stellanova about his marriage to Lillian, either out of loyalty to his true spouse or his aversion to acknowledging any failures or shortcomings on his part. The only information Stellanova had to go on was in Chase's autobiography. There Lillian was described in glowing terms. Even though the autobiography had been published a couple of years before she started writing to Chase, Stellanova could not resist being jealous of how Lillian was portrayed, and not just as a loving spouse. There in the pages and for posterity, she came across in ways in which the younger woman could never compete. "There never has been a time in the African jungle or any other place demanding courage," Chase had written, "when my wife has not been the braver of the two."

How could Stellanova be equal to that kind of praise? And not for the first time, there setting out her predecessor's china, she worried whether she would make, maybe even was making the same missteps as Lillian had, living as she was with the same man. Could not this man to whom she had tethered her fate decide again that a bond with a woman was fraying? Most vexing of all was the thought that maybe Lillian had done nothing at all to alter things between them, except perhaps graying, as she herself had begun to do.

That evening at the dinner table, as if summoned by Stellanova's preoccupation, the specter of Lillian was raised aloud, but in an unexpected manner. She heard Chase mistakenly refer to Lee as Lillian when regaling the Angells about his adventures in Madagascar. Chase never mentioned Lillian's name. Stellanova was stung by the mention if even by mistake, after all these years. Chase continued to regale the Angell's about his adventures in Madagascar, oblivious to his gaff. It felt as if Chase had practically raised a toast to her predecessor, her rival really, whom she had never confronted in person, yet faced every day in some way or another.

Stellanova was so rattled by Lillian's name being spoken that she needed to find an escape to conceal her emotional reaction. She arose quickly to take some dishes, any dishes, as an excuse to repair to the sanctuary of the kitchen and, perhaps, the council of Lee. Stellanova was barely aware that she had cleared some of the dishes a bit prematurely.

She had not wanted to attract any attention to herself, if at all possible, but that plan shattered as soon as she swung the door to the kitchen open with her hip. It was then that the cream pitcher, which she held in her trembling hand, seemed to have leapt off the matching saucer and on to the kitchen floor breaking into jagged pieces awash in a puddle of cream. With her hand to her mouth to stifle her horrified gasp, Stellanova stared in shock at the carnage of china on the floor.

Lee moved quickly to Stellanova's side and put her arm around her shoulders knowing instinctively that first she needed to help in some way with what was broken within the younger woman, rather than what was broken on the floor.

"Stellanova, it's alright. Really, it is. Accidents happen."

"I'm not sure it was an accident, Lee," Stellanova said tentatively.

"Of course, it was, dear. Don't torture yourself. And let me tell you, this isn't the first time I have helped to clean up broken pieces of this very same set. It is a good thing that it was originally a 14-piece set."

"I had not realized before that there were that many pieces missing."

"Missing in action, you might say," Lee explained raising her eyebrows.

"Missing in action?"

"I'll explain later after we serve dessert. Here. Grab a dish rag to sop up the cream and I'll pick up the chards and dispose of them discretely."

"Thank you, Lee. Truly," Stellanova said feeling now that she could rejoin her guests and put up a brave front, or at least, a composed one.

After dessert was served—the requested cake and not the substitute cobbler— Stellanova and Lee found themselves again in the kitchen, washing and drying Lillian's dishes. As Lee had alluded to earlier, she opened up about that "missing in action" comment and the dynamics of the former Osborn household. She told Stellanova that while Lillian had relished her role as the Governor's wife at the capital, she was equally happy to return to their life in Sault Ste. Marie. However, Lillian did not embrace living on Duck Island or sharing in her husband's amusement at the quaint notion that he had been born in a log cabin and had returned to living in one. Also, because Chase was then accepting many speaking requests, he was often gone, which left Lillian behind in surroundings that were far from anywhere and far from her choosing.

From Lee's perspective, the Osborn's relationship was already fractured when Stellanova and Chase started to correspond. Lee confirmed something else that Stellanova had only suspected. According to Lee, Chase's secretary, Mary Hadrich, who was loyal to Lillian, had tipped Mrs. Osborn off as to the frequency of the letters from Stellanova. Lee also told Stellanova that that telegram from Chase, canceling her first invitation to Duck Island, had been sent after quite a row with Lillian and had resulted in reducing the inventory of china plates—a casualty of the set-to. An infuriated Lillian had demanded to know why a young woman had been invited to visit Duck Island, particularly one who did not have the pedigree, social or academic, or any other professional reason for being entertained by the Governor. That row had to have been the reason, the "worse than fatal illness," that Chase hinted at in that telegram in explanation of why the visit had to be cancelled. This reminded Stellanova of Chase's characterization of Lillian as courageous and brave in his autobiography. Lillian was courageous enough to stand up to him and, ultimately, brave enough to leave him. Stellanova had been brave enough to come to Duck Island under extraordinary circumstances and stay. Sometimes, though, she wondered if she would be courageous and brave enough to wait him out until she got what she wanted.

Father Figure
September 1937

Angell had the Governor's permission to work in his library between sessions. He liked to keep the door open, for the extra light and cooling breeze but also to see the occasional boat traffic on the St. Mary's River. On this particular day, he was deep in thought when the light source was suddenly diminished by the appearance of Osborn's broad form. Without greeting Angell, Osborn entered, proceeded to his desk, and produced a sheaf of papers that he placed on the desk and then began to riffle through his desk, evidently looking for something of great import to him.

"Ah! Here it is!" Osborn held up a necktie pin; Angell leaned toward what the Governor held, discovering that the pin was decorated with the State of Michigan seal. "I am sorry, Professor Angell, that I have to leave the island during your stay. I accepted the speaking engagement in Boston before I knew about the timing of your visit. Perhaps, while I'm gone, you might like the break from your work to see the surrounding area?"

Angell kneaded clay in his hands as he answered. "I might like to see more of Sugar Island, perhaps get over to Mackinac Island."

"I haven't been to Mackinac Island in years. Not since I stayed at The Grand Hotel when I was Governor."

"Gladys has always wanted to see The Grand Hotel. I think I'll surprise her with a dinner there," Angell said.

"Good idea. It's aptly named The Grand. You would undoubtedly have an enjoyable visit, but I have never returned because the service was, well, grand."

"And that was a problem?" Angell asked.

"As Governor, I attracted too much attention from the management, the staff, and especially the guests who recognized me. It was all well-intentioned, but under those public circumstances the hotel is not the kind of a place where one can truly rest. I think it would be better to have a private Governor's residence on Mackinac Island for keeping a lower profile while on vacation."

Angell took an appraising look at the Governor before he pinched off a bit of clay and applied it to the bust's neck. "I also have a professional interest in seeing Mackinac Island. Somewhere on the island, there's a bronze statue of Father Marquette by the Florentine sculptor Gaetano Trentanove," Angell mentioned.

"The name Trentanove sounds familiar to me, but I cannot think why that would be."

"Perhaps, because he had a studio in Wisconsin?" Angell said, prolonging the conversation to give himself more time to make comparisons between the subject before him and the bust.

"That could be it. As worthy a subject as Father Marquette is, he is an odd choice for an Italian sculptor, don't you think?"

"Not necessarily. Sculptors tend to go where the commissions lead them," Angell said with a wry smile playing on his lips.

"Did this Italian sculptor visit Mackinac Island? I don't remember reading about his visit in the Soo paper," Osborn said.

"Apparently, the sculpture on the island is a copy of a marble original, installed in Statuary Hall in Washington. I've only seen a photograph of the marble, so I would like to see the bronze copy," Angell said.

"I remember now why the sculptor's name sounds familiar. There was some hubbub of a church vs. state nature about the placement of that marble sculpture in the nation's Capitol. Threats to the statue. An armed guard. I hope the placement of my bust on campus will not prove to be so controversial!" Osborn said. They shared a chuckle.

"Actually, the installation of the bronze of Marquette on Mackinac Island caused its own set of challenges too," Angell said.

"That's a shame, especially since Father Marquette is a much-revered figure in this area."

"The problem was monetary, not philosophical," Angell said. "Apparently the funding for the statue was slow in coming, though it finally came through. Ironically, the man who was the greatest champion of the statue's installation would never see it in place because he died in 1908. The funding source was a bequest he made in his will, and the statue was erected the next year."

"You must be talking about Peter White," Osborn said. "After White died, I took his place on the U of M Board of Regents. Big shoes to fill. There really should be a bust of him at the University."

"Funny you should mention that. Trentanove did make a marble portrait bust of Peter White, in a tuxedo, no less."

"Did he? And yet I get the common treatment of an open work shirt," Osborn chortled as he pointed to the bust.

Angell extended his arm with his thumb up in the pose an artist often assumes when he is gauging the scale of his subject. With one eye closed, he said, "You seem to be more of a 'come as you are' sort, at least here on Duck Island."

"Yes, I suppose you're right," as Osborn pretended to straighten an imaginary tie and said, "I have more formal attire packed in my bag for Boston, I assure you. By the way, you better pack a coat and necktie for dining at The Grand Hotel. They will not seat you without proper attire. If you didn't pack a coat and necktie, you could borrow something from my closet," Osborn offered.

"Thank you, Governor, but Gladys packs my bag and plans for all contingencies. Plenty of short-sleeve shirts, for instance, to avoid my habit of ruining cuffs when I sketch with graphite."

"My daughter proofreads my speeches for my trips, but she doesn't pack my bags, other than selecting my neckties."

"Well, she is your daughter, after all, and not your spouse."

Osborn ignored or did not hear what may have been the exploratory undertow in Angell's comment. "I like to pack my own grip, so nothing extra is included," Osborn explained. Then he seemed to inventory the pages of his speech and, holding them upright, tapped the pages on the desk like three exclamation marks. "I need to be light on my feet in case I decide to exit through a window again before delivering my speech!" Osborn forced a laugh. "And now I must practice my speech, as I regularly do here in the library. Forgive me, but the acoustics are greatly improved when no one else is about."

"Ah. Very good, I'll leave you to your practice," Angell said as he quickly cleaned his sculpting tool with a rag. "Have a good trip, Governor," he said making his exit, but he did not take but a few steps beyond the door that he had purposely left ajar. He wanted to listen to the man who had a reputation for delivering stemwinders on a wide range of topics. Osborn did not disappoint. Within just a few minutes, Angell knew that the orator's reputation was well-deserved. He felt rather like the son who suddenly realizes that his old man is wise after all. Indeed he was "The Sage of the Soo."

Just Below the Surface
September 1937

Carleton and Gladys had wended their way over a couple
of footbridges to reach Sweet Gale Lake, the north shore of
which bordered Duck Island between the Osborn Camp on
Duck and the Gander on Sugar Island—serving as the laird's
moat. As promised, they found the Governor's yellow canoe
beached on the shore, nearly hidden by reeds. The dense
shore vegetation encroached on the open water of the marsh,
and the reflection of the leafy branches doubled the effect of
swallowing the open water.

Carleton stabilized the canoe until Gladys got situated
in the bow. He then pushed the canoe into the water as he
deftly slid into place in the stern and they got underway.
Gladys immediately wished that she had had the foresight to
bring a towel to cushion the wicker canoe seat because she
could feel the cane seat making a waffle pattern on the flesh
of her backside. Soon, however, there would be other sources
of discomfort.

It was entirely predictable that there would be
a "stowaway" or two— a homesteading spider and the
exoskeleton of something that still had the unnerving ability
to cling like a ghastly broach. Then a hitchhiker in the form of
a dragonfly landed on Gladys's head. Carleton was amused
that it looked like a decorative, almost Art Nouveau, hair clip
come to life. Gladys, however, was relieved that the dragonfly
quickly abandoned her head as a vantage point and next
selected the canoe's bow where she could observe from a
less irksome distance, the beauty of the stained-glass wings

and iridescent body. Then to her delight, another dragonfly alighted, only to start making a meal out of "her" dragonfly. She could not stomach watching nature take its course, so she used her paddle to escort the "pair" off the premises and into the water.

Gladys needed to replace the visual image of the cannibalistic dragon hunter drama, and Carleton came to the rescue by pointing out a male red-winged blackbird that captured her attention with its distinctive "conk-la-ree" call and epaulet-fluffing as if in readiness for uniform inspection.

The marsh was humming away in many keys at once. The cacophony of nature's sounds might normally have stilled conversation and cleared the mind, but not for Carleton, not today.

"Carleton, you have a gift to see through to the very bones of a person."

"I do not know if I would put it that way, but I like the 'you have a gift' part."

"Don't be modest. You're an artist, and you are very analytical about your work."

"Darling, I'd be a full professor by now if you were on the promotion committee."

"Yes, you would!"

"Why do you mention 'my gift'? Are you worried this project is intimidating me? That the Governor is getting under my skin?" Carleton questioned as he slapped at a mosquito that inserted its proboscis, like a hypodermic needle, into the back of his neck.

"No, but something about the Osborns has gotten underneath *my* skin," she said as she flicked a small beetle off her arm, and looked into the water only to notice a large submerged tree limb. "Watch out!"

Carleton paddled backward to avoid the hazard. Once clear, he asked, "What do you mean?"

"You know how sometimes I can sense things beforehand?"

"Before you have evidence?"

"Okay, you've got me there, but you need to accept that the kind of evidence I occasionally provide is real, if more intuitive. Today, I saw a look that passed between the Governor and Stellanova, that made the hairs on my forearms nearly stand on end." Gladys could sense from the halt in the rhythm of his paddling that Carleton was about to refute her ability to sense what was just below the surface of interactions. "Now Carleton, hear me out, please."

"All right, but quietly. Sound travels clearly and a long distance across the water. We are still within sight of the cabins."

She turned in her seat to attempt eye contact. "Don't the Osborns seem *less* like relatives and *more* like, I don't know, a married pair?"

"Why? Just because they collaborate on books?" Carleton at once answered and challenged.

"I think you know what I mean. I think they may do something *else* between the covers—and I don't mean *book* covers!" Gladys whispered insistently.

"I think you should have brought more reading material with you for this long stay on Sugar Island." Carleton playfully flicked water droplets from his fingers in Gladys's direction to cool the sizzle of gossip. She quickly turned to face forward again and dipped her oar. Carleton mused that canoeing should be a solitary activity.

"Please don't discount my observations. Your observations help you to understand your work. Mine help *me* to help *us* navigate our social life on campus and maybe here at the Osborn camp, too."

Carleton rested his paddle on his lap and spoke with a resolute tone. "And your observations can be a bit intrusive, darling, especially since we are their guests. I agree they are an unusual pair, but they are not a couple. A widower might *naturally* come to rely on his daughter."

"Rely on, yes. Dote on even. But there is a different dynamic between the two of them," Gladys insisted, then dropping her voice, "Carleton, I'm telling you. There is an undercurrent between those two."

Carleton had not expected to talk about much of any consequence when he suggested he and Gladys go canoeing. Canoeing usually gave him the illusion of having the ability to stay above the fray—gliding soundlessly over submerged rocks and logs. He enjoyed the secret thrill when the bow of the canoe parted the reeds near the shoreline, like opening a curtain to reveal the backstage activity of the animal actors being themselves until they made their exit—a family of ducks quickly taking off into the water or sunning turtles slipping off a log. Catching these animals unawares was a much more pleasant diversion, than contemplating the disrupting nature of the Osborn's relationship—peering like a voyeur between the curtains of the Osborn's domestic life.

The Guest Book
September 1937

Of all the volumes in the Governor's library, perhaps no one was more precious to him than his guest book. It was his record, indeed his reassurance that he was and continued to be a sought after someone. And he wanted his guests to know this. So, when he produced the guest book for a visitor to sign, he would always remove the ribbon attached to the binding that marked the page of the last entry so his so his guest would need to page through the entire parade of luminaries.

Osborn rarely invited people to be his guests on Duck Island because most guests contacted him and asked to visit. Yet, every once and a while, he would extend a special invitation like the one he sent to Dr. Clover, a professor of botany at the University of Michigan. Initially, Stellanova assumed that Dr. Clover was a man but soon found out to the contrary. When Stellanova first heard her full name, Elzada Clover, she pictured her as an eccentric old priestess of plants with a gray topknot, dirty fingernails, and a sagging bosom. How wrong she was. Though unmarried, that much was true, Dr. Clover turned out to be an adventurous woman about Stellanova's age and the only thing that sagged was Stellanova's self-confidence in Dr. Clover's presence.

Dr. Elzada Clover was the first woman to travel the entire six-hundred-mile length of the Colorado River as it runs through the Grand Canyon. During the forty-three-day trip, Dr. Clover cataloged the plant life found at the bottom of the canyon. She was just barely home in Ann Arbor when Chase practically summoned her to visit him and give him a firsthand account of her adventures.

After Dr. Clover arrived and got settled in, Stellanova sought out her own audience, surprising herself at finding the professor already at work in the makeshift lab she made of the Osborn's Rittenhouse picnic table on the sleeping side of the Gander. She was taking plants from her dented and dimpled metal vasculum and carefully placing them between the sheets of her plant press—a guest book of sorts for botanists.

"Hello, Stellanova! What a beautiful name," Clover remarked, adding "I guess you know it literally means 'the star lover and his star.'"

"I thought it meant only 'new star,'" Stellanova said noticing that the professor made eye contact with plants and people with equal curiosity.

"It's unusual to have a name that describes a relationship, rather than simply an attribute. That makes it an even lovelier name. Much like plant names."

Stellanova found her smile most disarming. "Thank you, Dr. Clover."

"Please call me, 'Elzada.' Forgive me, it may seem an awkward way of greeting someone, that is, beginning by analyzing a name, but I'm afraid that it's an occupational hazard. I think about Latin roots constantly since I work daily with the Latin names of plants.

Stellanova's closest friends from college still addressed her in their letters as "Stella." She often thought that she should have left that as her legal name, keeping

Chase's pet name for her private and reserved for intimate moments between the two of them. Not so much concealed as treasured. However, she had legally changed her given name the day that they had formalized their relationship, or rather their arrangement in adopting her as Stellanova Osborn. Stellanova contemplated that it might have been better if the water from the leak in the closet had erased the evidence that she was once so naïve and pliable in Chase's hands, molded into a shape for which no other man was a possible fit. But it had been a two-way street. Unconventionally achieved though it was, they shared a last name, Chase, Lillian, and she.

Suddenly realizing that she was not holding up her side of the conversation, Stellanova made a much-too-obvious observation. "Your last name is so fitting for a botanist."

"I've sometimes wondered if I was destined for my profession," Elzada said.

"It's a good thing that you're not married, Dr. Clover," Stellanova blurted.

Dr. Clover looked at Stellanova with the pleated brow of incredulity. "Excuse me?"

Stellanova's hand moved reflexively to her mouth. "I'm sorry. I've said a very clumsy thing. I only meant that it would be a shame to change your last name, so appropriate for a botanist, to adopt something less fitting in the last name of a spouse, like Miller or Smith." Stellanova wished that her tongue would curl up like a fiddlehead fern.

"I wholeheartedly agree," Dr. Clover said as she smiled good-naturedly and turned her attention back to her plants.

This time she moved from her press to a small, portable microscope that she had set up on the table.

Stellanova watched for a moment and then offered, "Someday I would like to try my hand at looking into a microscope for inspiration. But with my limited scientific vocabulary, I would utterly fail in describing what I saw."

Dr. Clover stopped looking into the microscope, pausing to clean its lenses with a bit of special paper from a small pack that she had placed beside the microscope, together with a pair of forceps and a box of glass slides.

"You shouldn't trivialize your gift as a poet. A botanist tells only a fraction of the story about the natural world, the part that is as flat and dry as the plants mounted between these herbarium sheets."

Dr. Clover then cleaned her glasses with the same care and attention she had given her microscope. She seemed constantly to focus and refocus from the tiniest detail of the plant to the larger picture of life itself. "The botanical illustrator and the poet give a plant a more accessible description for most people than a professor ever does with her lofty Latin descriptions."

"I suppose the scientist and the poet both describe a plant with the same economy and selectivity of words about what they observe," Stellanova said.

"I'd have to agree. I would like to read your work, and especially if any of your poems are about plants I might collect here on Sugar Island. Wouldn't it be nice if botanists could affix poems to the scientific descriptions on their herbarium sheets?"

"If you did that, I am afraid that you would be labeled as an eccentric, Dr. Clover."

"Again, please call me Elzada, if you're comfortable. That label, not Elzada, but 'eccentric,' has already been practically pasted on my forehead. Yes, I'm an eccentric, pants-wearing, unmarried female academic."

"I'd rather be known as an eccentric than an old maid," spurted Stellanova. She did not quite know why she felt comfortable with Dr. Clover so soon after making her acquaintance. Perhaps, because she had been swimming against the current of truth for so many years the presence of this unconventional woman, presented her with the license she never had before to be more frank, more uninhibited, even with herself.

"Stellanova, I have a feeling that you are *not* an old maid," the professor said as she looked over the rim of her glasses.

"You are equally observant of both plants and people," Stellanova said with some trepidation in intimating that Dr. Clover was "on to something."

Not exactly wanting to go where Dr. Clover seemed to be headed, Stellanova deflected. "I have been observing you, too, and I've noticed that you look up from the Governor's graces at the dinner table before he is done."

"Guilty!" admitted Dr. Clover.

"You're not a particularly religious person then?" Stellanova ventured.

"Maybe not in the conventional sense, but as a scientist I do have questions that challenge some beliefs and some that confirm a certain brand of faith. How can one look into a microscope or see the Grand Canyon and not believe in God?" Elzada looked again at her plants collected in the canyon and seemed to revel briefly in finding them in such a beautiful habitat. "In any case, I'm sorry that I have been less than reverent at the dinner table, though. I guess thanking the Lord for all the dead organisms on the table is not as inspiring as giving thanks for seeing flora and fauna in their natural habitats. I think that I will take a little field trip around Duck Island to work up an appetite and, perhaps, a bit more conventional piety."

"And I need to see Lee about dinner," Stellanova signaled her own need to move on. "Please don't be late for dinner, Elzada," Stellanova called. "What I mean is, I know the Governor's appetite for the account of your trip will be ravenous."

The Guest of Honor
September 1937

"I thought you might be here," Stellanova said, addressing the Governor as she entered the snug one-room cabin Chase called Little Duck. He had built the cabin for himself as his domicile in exile, or at least estrangement, from his wife, Lillian. Stellanova often had worries that this cabin might one day serve the same purpose again. These worries were amplified when the presence of guests necessitated that she and Chase sleep apart.

In this moment Stellanova sought out Chase to talk about something of no real import, except that it was an excuse to maintain a tie to him while talking about household matters. "We have never had place cards for dinner, but with the collection of guests being so eclectic this week, I feel we need to give this some thought," Stellanova said as she leaned against the opened door, never feeling entirely welcome in his lair.

"First come, first served, I always say," Chase pronounced as he put his book and reading glasses aside.

"Well, that takes care of where *you* will sit, but I think I know whom you would like to sit next to."

"Dr. Clover. She will add intellectual flavor to my dinner. Remind me, who else is arriving today?"

Stellanova gave him an incredulous look.

"Don't look at me that way. I am *not* entering my dotage. Not yet, and you well know it. I've simply been preoccupied with my upcoming speaking engagements in Boston. I've gotten ahead of myself and the calendar. Now, my starry guide, tell me again, who will be seated at our table tonight?"

"Professor Ramsdell from the University's Forestry Department, and his daughter, although I've forgotten her name just now."

"Ah! Of course. The rough and ready Ramsdell! He will one day be the custodian of our property here once we have a sit-down with George to hammer out the details with the University."

Stellanova involuntarily flinched when Chase mentioned George and "hammering out the details." She felt she had a legitimate reason to fear that George would conspire to wield the biggest hammer and drum her out of their enclave on Duck Island after Chase was gone. There might be little she could do about that, but she would endeavor to make a positive impression on Professor Ramsdell. She would start by not being as invisible as she often was in the presence of guests. "Where should I seat Professor Ramsdell and his daughter? Mrs. Angell has a daughter about her age, so I could seat her at the end of the table next to Gladys. And I'll put Professor Angell directly opposite you at the other end of the table."

"But that's usually *your* spot," Chase said.

"True, but that spot is conventionally reserved for the lady of the house, and that isn't my role, is it?"

"Stellanova, let's not revisit this topic. Not just now."

"Maybe I should take cues from the young Miss

Ramsdell for how I should act the part of a grown daughter in the presence of her father. Forgive me if I'm a little rusty in that role."

"You are not rusty, my smooth skinned beauty." Stellanova's position in the natural light by the door highlighted the clean planes of her face that made her as handsome as she was beautiful. "You *are*, however, a bit testy."

Stellanova crossed her arms in silent acknowledgement and agreement with Chase's assessment. "Planning dinner may take my mind off my grievances, at least for a little while. So, we have seven for dinner. I don't think an odd number is ever ideal."

"It will be fine, my dear. Numbers tonight won't matter in the slightest. You and Lee will doubtless prepare a menu that would garner the seal of approval from the Chamber of Commerce, and Dr. Clover will regale us with tales of her adventures on the Colorado River."

"You're probably right, we'll be fine. I'll be off to talk to Lee about dinner."

"Leave the door open. That way, I can watch you as you walk away."

"I'll feel your eyes on me," Stellanova smiled.

"That's the idea," Chase said in a tone that was playfully seductive.

Stellanova made her way across the compound, never turning around to see if Chase was indeed watching her, though she suspected he was, yet there was always that fear of discovering that he might have returned, indifferently, to reading, before she disappeared around the corner of the Gander.

Stellanova's meeting with Lee was a brief one. Although Stellanova made a show of planning a different menu for camp guests, Lee knew that any menu at this time of year would not vary much because the bounty of the land and water in Michigan in August was sweet corn and whitefish, and for dessert, what else on Sugar Island, but maple syrup drizzled over homemade vanilla ice cream? Lee also knew that as much as she endeavored to serve the main course hot, it often cooled significantly while the Governor said one of his infamously long graces.

A few hours later, the dinner guests were gathered around the large rustic varnished pine table inside the Gander and seated according to Stellanova's conversational choreography.

"I'm very pleased to introduce Professor Ramsdell to you, Professor Angell," Osborn said. "Have your paths ever crossed on campus by chance?"

"No, Governor, we haven't met before," said Angell. "I'm pleased to meet you, Professor Ramsdell. This is my wife, Gladys."

"I am happy at last to make your acquaintance." Professor Ramsdell rose to his full height of well over 6-feet. He looked more like a lumberjack than an academic with a heavy black mustache that almost had its own rhythm of speech apart from the words coming out of the man's mouth. He had a cowlick of thick black hair that he had to keep smoothing back off his forehead, which he did before he extended his long arm across the table to shake Angell's hand. He turned to Mrs. Angell. "Please call me Forrest. And *this* is my daughter Helen," he said, beaming as he might if this gathering were doubling as the lovely blonde's coming out party.

The Governor broke in to say, "Professor Ramsdell is here to discuss how my property will be managed in the future. I shall be happy to deed my Duck Island Preserve of three-thousand acres to the University with no restrictions, except a life tenancy on Duck Island. My library of some seven-thousand books will go with the gift as well. Since Professor Ramsdell is an expert in forest land management, I am confident that my gift will be preserved and valued as forest land going forward."

"Isn't it amazing that Father's first name is Forrest?" Helen interjected. Stellanova was instantly envious of the young girl's confidence in her role as a daughter to jump right into the conversation. Unfortunately, she did not have a ready comment, and whatever space there might have been for that was immediately taken over by the girl's father.

"I don't know how amazing it is, dear, but it does create a bit of confusion sometimes," Professor Ramsdell acknowledged.

"Having the last name of Angell, with two 'Ls' no less, can be rather confusing, too," Angell said.

"Well, now that we have established who we are, we can be seated for grace in front of the correct place cards," the Governor directed.

All heads were bowed in anticipation of the Governor's grace, except Helen's. She used her blond waves as a curtain to surreptitiously maintain eye contact with the whitefish on the platter in the center of the table served with its head on.

Osborn intoned, "Father and Mother of the Earth..."

Stellanova was hesitant to alter the well-established schedule for eating on "Osborn Time." Still, she had noticed that the guest of honor was missing. "Excuse me, Governor, but we're missing one of our dinner guests."

Osborn had noticed that Dr. Clover's seat was empty, but the Sovereign of Sugar Island did not renegotiate with his subjects to suit their routines. Barely looking up, he said flatly, "I don't pause to take roll, Stellanova."

"I'm concerned about Dr. Clover's whereabouts, Governor," Stellanova persisted.

The tension between them was palpable to the guests, and they joined Helen in staring at the fish. Angell, however, stole a look at the Governor and, noticing his stony rigidity, mused to himself that he might have chosen granite for the medium for the bust.

"Perhaps, she's gotten lost. I know she was taking a walk before dinner, and she did know when dinner was," Stellanova said.

The door opened, and all heads turned, expecting to see Dr. Clover, but it was Gib bringing in some firewood.

"Dr. Clover is certainly no stranger to navigating woodlands. You're painting her as a shrinking violet when she is more like a resilient woody plant," Osborn said. The comment elicited nervous laughter because the diners, for their part, clearly were in need of some levity.

At the risk of this interchange sounding like a "Please, help me in the kitchen" conference between spouses, Stellanova pressed on. "Humor me, and please send Gib out to find Dr. Clover." Stellanova remembered Gib had told her that Dr. Clover had struck up a pleasant conversation with him about her time supervising an Indian mission school in Texas.

"Very well, my dear daughter," Osborn reluctantly capitulated. "If Dr. Clover does not turn up in the next quarter-hour, I will send Gib out to find her. Gib, please help Dr. Clover navigate the trails if need be. Take my first aid kit, just to be prepared."

"Yes, sir, Governor," replied Gib.

"And whether Dr. Clover needs any first aid or not, she will certainly find your knowledge of medicinal plants of great interest," Osborn said.

"A young woman should not be traipsing off alone into the woods," said Professor Ramsdell.

"Forgive me, but hasn't Dr. Clover proven her mettle just a month ago by boating down the Colorado River?" Gladys countered.

At that moment light footfalls were heard coming up the central stairs at the back of the Gander. Stellanova pictured Elzada treading the boards like an actress and hitting her mark on cue as the audience first saw her silhouette behind the scrim of the screen door of the dining room to deliver her first line of the evening's entertainment. "The woods prove no more a challenge to me than to a man, Professor Ramsdell. Just because the only other woman to attempt to boat down the Colorado drowned does not mean that women have any more reason to fear that adventure than any man."

"Dr. Clover! You have returned and no worse for wear!" Stellanova exclaimed.

The Governor motioned for the professor to take the seat immediately to his right. Elzada sat down as she made her apologies for her late arrival. Clearing his throat with unassailable authority, Osborn once again intoned, "Father and Mother Earth, Almighty one, Lord of all, commander-in-chief of the universe. Help us to be a Christian people in truth as well as in name fitted to be thy instrument for good in the world. And help each one of us to do our part to make it so. Amen."

"Gib. Thank you for being on hand to be our search party," said Stellanova, not exactly wanting to give up her earlier sense that something could have been wrong.

"Of course, Miss Osborn," Gib said as he moved toward the door. "Is there anything else you need?"

"Would you like me to ask Lee to wrap up some dinner for you to take home?" Stellanova asked.

"No, thank you. My aunt is expecting me for dinner tonight, and I better arrive with a good appetite."

"Goodnight, then, Gib. We'll see you tomorrow," the Governor said.

With a hunger for information as intense as his guests' appetite for dinner, Chase got right down to his "main course" of discussion as he began to fill each guest's plate himself. "Now then, Dr. Clover, please tell us about your recent expedition, though I admit I'm jealous of your adventure."

"I'm happy to do that. And I'm looking forward to this dinner," Dr. Clover said, leading the quest for food. "I must say I've been on a rather subsistence diet of Post Grape-Nuts for weeks! They were stored as great big marbles, so we had to hammer them into smaller pieces to eat. However, the centers were almost always wet and moldy. I suspect I will have a lifelong aversion to that cereal!" she said, eyeing the food as the Governor added an ear of corn to a laden plate.

"Better to stick with Kellogg's corn flakes," Osborn advised. "Dr. Kellogg happens to be a friend of mine. Did you know that C.W. Post, inventor of your Grape-Nuts, was at one point a patient at Dr. Kellogg's sanitarium? It was there that he got the idea to start a rival cereal company in Battle Creek. I consider Kellogg to have the better cereal though."

"I also don't want to drink Postum ever again!" continued Dr. Clover.

"Not to worry. After dinner, we'll retire for real coffee," Stellanova promised. "But now, let's give our guest of honor a chance to eat, and then we'll be able to hear about the rushing waters of the Colorado without being distracted by the rumbling of our empty stomachs." Stellanova picked up her fork as though conducting the official opening downbeat for dinner.

Ever the newspaperman, Chase found it difficult not to interview Dr. Clover during dinner, but he did not show as much restraint in showing how enamored he was with her. Chase had led the life of three men, so perhaps, Stellanova thought, he might seek a third companion? She wondered what ruse would he come up with the next time? Stellanova felt off-balance in Dr. Clover's presence and even though Clover was nearly her same age, she thought that their guest just seemed to be aging at a different pace or in a different way. Dr. Clover was the embodiment of vigor. Her complexion alone—still flushed from her climactic experience of riding the Colorado River's rapids— lit up the lowlight of the cabin. Stellanova felt more like a fading plant in Chase's eyes, drying up and pressed into a fixed pose in the professor's plant press.

She realized that if she were honest with herself, she was as attracted to Dr. Clover as Chase was. Not since college, when she had published "The Whimsies" literary magazine with her fellow co-eds, had she felt a real kinship with other women. That kind of connection was one of the casualties of her all-consuming relationship with Chase.

Lost in thoughts borne of her insecurities, Stellanova, unfortunately, missed most of the casual conversation during dinner. She was nonetheless awakened from her regretful reverie when she heard Helen exclaim, "You see, Father, unmarried women *do* have the best adventures!" This comment felt like a slap to Stellanova's cheek. Helen had managed at once to go to the very heart of Stellanova's anxiety over her limited life and to make everyone in the room—male, female, married, and unmarried, feel uncomfortable. That young woman could no more divert her stream of "thoughts" than water could be stopped from spilling over Tahquamenon Falls.

Stellanova realized that she alone, at the moment, had the power to steer the conversation around these rapids as she hastily looked about the table to make sure the diners were done this time. "It's time for coffee, and it's a lovely evening for sitting outside on the porch. Helen, will you help me with the trays, please?"

Dessert and an Appetite for Adventure
September 1937

The diners resettled on the porch. As they surveyed the porch furniture, they tried to decide which chair might be the Governor's. They stalled by admiring the view until the Governor strode to a wicker chair with an upholstered back and a seat that fit him like a well-worn baseball glove. The Governor motioned for Dr. Clover to sit beside him, leaving the remainder of the guests to their own impromptu game of musical chairs. They would soon join the Governor and Dr. Clover who were already taking note of the changing coordinates of the glowing fireflies.

"Thank you, Stellanova, your suggestion that we retire here to the porch provides me, and perhaps also our fine scientist, with the opportunity to illuminate our guests as to the source of the firefly's light," Osborn beamed. "From what I understand, Thomas Edison, like so many others, was curious about the source of the firefly's light. He admitted that he could not produce light as economically as the firefly, but he hoped that man would discover the secret and profit from it. I actually discovered the source, but I haven't profited from it, nor has anyone else for that matter."

"You've discovered the source of the firefly's light?" Dr. Clover asked, at once curious and incredulous.

"The Governor's discovery was published in *The Saturday Evening Post*," Stellanova interjected. "You can see a copy in the Governor's library tomorrow, if you're interested."

"I am. Many botanists, including myself, are very interested in entomology. Knowing the insects that visit the plants I study is an important part of my work," Dr. Clover explained.

"I really shouldn't claim that I *discovered the* source of the firefly's light. I merely made a *correlation* that proved to be conclusive. It may be true of almost every discovery made. One man discovers one thing, one another, and finally, somebody discovers the missing link, the key. Then the facts are correlated, and the conclusion is satisfactory. My idea is at least new, and I think it is indisputable. Those to whom I have submitted it are as firm in their conviction as I myself am."

"I actually thought that the firefly's light was still a mystery," Gladys said, setting her coffee to the side.

"The poet in me almost wishes it were so," Stellanova added.

Osborn laced his fingers, weaving them into nearly a prayerful pose. "For my part, scientific inquiry and discovery deepen the mystery of the Divine. Don't you agree, Dr. Clover?"

"That might be the best summation of my experience on the Colorado River," Clover offered, really hoping to change the subject off the one of the Governor's choosing that was clearly beyond scientific credibility.

Osborn, not realizing he had been diverted, began his cross-examination. "Did you keep a detailed journal as Meriwether Lewis did on his expedition?"

"Yes, and I'm glad that I did. Not all the specimens I collected survived the trip, so my journals are going to prove indispensable when writing up my research."

"Do you mind, professor, if I sketch you while you're talking to us?" Angell asked.

"I can't imagine that I would be a very interesting subject, but that's fine with me. We had a photographer on the trip who took informal portraits of us, but a botanical illustrator would have been more useful. Do you sketch plants as well, Professor Angell?"

"Animals, mostly, and people, of course the Governor most recently, as you know. I also make plaster models for the exhibits in the museum, of everything from living animals to extinct ones. In a way I try to give them a second life," Angell said.

"I know what you mean. On the expedition, I explored the cave of an extinct ground sloth," Clover said.

"Really? Did you find skeletal remains?" Angell asked.

"No, but I examined the sloth's petrified dung to discover the plants it had consumed. Cactus spines were embedded in the excrement, which provided information about the animal's diet and the dispersal of plants in its habitat."

"Eww! It must have smelled horrible!" exclaimed Helen, wrinkling her nose.

"No, petrified remains have no smell other than the smell, say, of dirt," Dr. Clover responded.

Dr. Ramsdell's face betrayed annoyance that his daughter had once again brought the level of the discussion down. "Returning, if you will, to your mention of the diet of the ancient sloth, I am curious about the variety of cacti that you may have observed in the canyon. How many plant zones did you identify?"

"Five, actually, if you can imagine it!" Clover beamed.

"I hope to do more than imagine it. I'd like to see it for myself one day," Ramsdell said.

"I have never seen the Grand Canyon either," Osborn interjected predictably, "but I *have* traveled to exotic places the world over; most recently to Madagascar where I saw something that you, Dr. Clover, have perhaps never seen, the Madagascar Cactus. The flowers are so fragrant that I wished that I could have bottled the aroma!"

"You're right, I haven't seen that plant," admitted Clover, "but I can tell you that it is often mistaken for a cactus. It's actually a member of the dogbane family. The Latin name is *Pachypodium lameria*. However, I'm glad to hear a first-hand account of the fragrance of the flowers."

"In Latin it literally means 'thick foot,'" explained Ramsdell.

"Yes. That's why the plants are sometimes known by the common name 'Elephant Feet,'" Clover added.

"I like to hear the common names, instead of that scientific mumbo-jumbo," complained Helen.

"Helen, please be respectful of Dr. Clover's expertise," Ramsdell said.

"That's quite alright, Helen. You'll like the common names I gave the four cacti that I discovered in the Grand Canyon; Claret Cup, Hedgehog Cactus, Beavertail Prickly Pear, and Fishhook Cactus."

"I like Claret Cup!"

"That's fine, Helen," her father then continued in an undertone, "Don't persist with that topic, Helen. The Governor's camp is a dry one, not to mention that you are *still* underage."

"I assume you named the Fishhook Cactus because of its appearance and its function, too?" Osborn asked.

"You're correct, Governor. Their hooked spines are indeed strong enough to have been used as actual fishing hooks by native peoples."

Osborn interjected, "This evening truly has the atmosphere of a Chautauqua assembly."

"She-talk-what?" asked Helen.

"It is something like an academic camp for adults," Osborn explained. "The first such camp was held at Chautauqua, New York. President Roosevelt, TR, that is, called the Chautauqua 'the most American thing in America.'"

"Not unlike the University's Biological Station summer session on Douglas Lake," Dr. Clover added with some measure of pride in her institution.

"Yes, that's a fine academic enclave in a beautiful setting," Osborn remarked. "Bay View on Lake Michigan is another fine example of a gathering of intellects, in the case of Bay View, we're talking about lecturers and musicians for the community's edification."

"Circuit Chautauquas have sprung up all around the country," Stellanova said.

"It sounds kind of like a circus without the high wire act," Helen giggled.

Dr. Clover looked at Stellanova, and her eyes mimicked the face of someone who might be about to walk a tightrope. Stellanova felt pleased that she had been singled out by the professor for a private moment of mutual understanding and levity.

"Academia, dear, *is* a high wire act," Professor Ramsdell said, looking pleased that his daughter had given him an opening for a clever rejoinder. He offered her his subtly seedy tweed sport coat, complete with leather elbow patches to make her more comfortable in the night air and gave her an affectionate squeeze on her shoulders as he draped the coat about her.

Chase had a similar jacket for shooting. With equal amounts of disappointment and resignation, Stellanova noted that even though she and the Governor were posing as father and daughter, Chase could never, *would* never, risk any such affectionate public gesture as Ramsdell had just extended to his actual daughter.

"Your talk should continue without further interruptions," Osborn said.

"I fear you're all assuming that I can tell my story in an entertaining way. I do play the harmonica and I played it on the expedition, but I'm not ready to go on the road with my act yet," Dr. Clover laughed. "This will be good practice for me, though, as I've accepted several speaking engagements on campus this fall."

"I often find that the person who is supposed to introduce me to an audience does a poor job. I, however, will give you a proper introduction here and now." The Governor stood and retrieved his reading glasses and an index card out of his chest pocket. Dr Clover tried to conceal her unease that Osborn had prepared a formal introduction to what she thought was going to be little more than a casual conversation about her trip. Nevertheless, Osborn announced, "Professor Elzada Clover received her Master's of Science degree in 1932 and her Ph.D. in 1935 from the University of Michigan. She is an instructor in botany and an assistant curator of the University's botanical gardens. She has just returned from a botanical expedition of great scientific import. Please welcome tonight's speaker, the first botanist to survey the flora of the Colorado River, Dr. Elzada Clover!"

Chase had stung Stellanova by how he hovered over Dr. Clover like she was a rare and beautiful plant that he wanted to examine more closely. Dr. Clover was indeed a distinguished scientist and she had accomplished much, even before her latest adventure. But did he have to be so obviously taken with her? When Stellanova heard the welcoming applause of the assembled guests, she was awakened from her bitter internal monologue and realized that she was as eager as everyone else to hear the professor speak about her adventures.

"Thank you, Governor," Dr. Clover nodded to her host and to her audience as she launched into an abbreviated version of her experience. "There were six of us on the trip. Three of us were scientists—another botanist and my graduate assistant Lois Trotter. However, I felt guilty asking any other woman to share the physical and mental punishment which would be ours. I also asked a young zoology graduate student, whom I selected mainly for his ability to row. The river guide and a surveyor rounded out our crew. We said our 'goodbyes' when we left campus, and to be honest we were not confident of our return. We actually engaged in a bit of dark humor about our prospects for survival, which helped us to cope with the fear."

"We traveled in three sixteen-foot boats, each one weighing about six hundred pounds—from Green River, Utah, north of the Colorado River, to Cataract Canyon, and then through the Grand Canyon. We were not always traveling on the water, however. Sometimes we had to pull the boats overland. And dry land presented us with its own challenges. One time, we had to get the boats up a sixty-foot cliff at a 45-degree angle. Other times, landslides of boulders threatened to harm us. Logs and tree trunks could shoot out of the roiling water like projectiles hurtling 20-30 miles per hour. I would prefer to die doing something exciting, but it was a sobering moment when we reached the Cataract Canyon, known as the 'graveyard of the Colorado River.' At this point, one was cut off from any hope of getting out in case of accident, illness, or fright. It was the point of no return. We could hear the noise of the first series of rapids. 'Ominous' is the wrong word, but we were all pretty serious. The sound of the tremendous waves made the crew mute with awe, fear, and the impossibility of being heard above the roar." She shook her head at the thought of unspoken memories. "It is a great river with a hundred personalities, but it is not kind. The days were 'as hot as Hades,' and the nights were 'colder than hell.'"

Helen audibly drew in air like a Hoover vacuum in reaction to Dr. Clover's use of the "H" word. Stellanova wondered if Helen had never heard a woman swear before or thought it was her place, in front of her father, to be appropriately shocked. It was too bad that the screens of the porch were keeping out the mosquitos because Stellanova dearly would have loved to have Helen choke on a bug for interrupting the professor's story.

"There were so many near disasters," Dr. Clover continued. "One of the three boats (with half of our food) became unmoored, but was later recovered. I will always remember the sound of the water and the birds and, also, the phrase from 'The Rime of the Ancient Mariner' that kept going through my head during the expedition, 'Water, water everywhere, not a drop to drink.' Clean drinking water was a scarcity. We would leave water out overnight to allow the clay silt to settle. However, out of necessity, we sometimes drank water right out of the river from our helmets, which coated our mouths and throats with clay and gave us stomachaches."

"I feel thirsty just listening to your story!" Helen exclaimed.

"Then please, listen, dear, and sip your coffee," Professor Ramsdell firmly advised.

"That's quite all right," Dr. Clover reassured the young

woman. "This is also a good time for me to have some coffee before I continue." She then raised her coffee cup in a long-distance toast in Helen's direction. Stellanova stood and began to offer another round of coffee.

"I don't mean to focus on the dangers and the hardships," Dr. Clover continued. "The scenery more than made up for the lack of conveniences and sanitation. I will never forget singing 'Moonlight on the Colorado' while floating under a gorgeous moon. That particular night was so beautiful that I couldn't sleep. The rigors of the trip even became routine." She held her cup out to receive more coffee and murmured her thanks to Stellanova before continuing.

"Toward the end of the trip, it was just part of a day's work to make a flying leap for shore, to climb steep cliffs after plants, and to get photographs. The trip ended at Lake Mead after forty-three days, and I brought home more than plants and journals." She seemed to be reviewing an internal film reel. "My life has been full of adventure, but this seemed like the ace of them all."

The expression on Dr. Clover's face was rather beatific at that moment. Stellanova wondered if she were the only person on the porch who remembered seeing much that same expression on her face that she had seen in photographs of a triumphant Amelia Earhart? Poor Miss Earhart, probably lost forever. The famous aviator had disappeared just two months before, but Stellanova thought it was possible that her spirit lived on in this extraordinary woman in their midst.

"You must have been so relieved to have returned home safely," Gladys said.

"I feel very fortunate, but I must admit that I already miss the daily feeling of uncertainty and expectation. People who have not fought with such elements cannot realize how petty and trivial are the things two-thirds of us worry about in civilization. In a way, what a shame to have to get back. Present company and surroundings excluded, of course."

The Governor picked up the thread of Dr. Clover's story and put a button on the evening's thought-provoking discussion by making his exit as he announced, "Evening prayer affords one the opportunity to focus on the less petty and trivial concerns of our days." The suggestion was the dry camp director's idea of a "night cap." As a result, the evening ended all too abruptly for the rest of Dr. Clover's rapt audience.

A Bitter Aftertaste
September 1937

Gladys and Stellanova were sitting in the shade of the small pergola-like shelter, what the Governor referred to as the Go-Down. Built by a local Chippewa, it was a 10-by-12-foot structure with no walls and a thatched roof. Its location on the St. Mary's with a view of the Canadian banks on the opposite shore made up for the structure's lack of aesthetic. From this vantage point, the women could see and almost hear the Governor at a distance, engaging in hand-picking produce from a local farmer's rowboat. The farmer's young son and daughter were sitting on the dock sharing with Gib their own brand of current events.

Stellanova and Gladys overheard the men discussing the prediction in the Farmer's Almanac's for the first frost and how purple turnips can tolerate a frost. "Anything can serve as food for thought for the Governor," Stellanova said almost to herself. "And he also has eclectic tastes in food from all his travels around the world."

"The Governor has very eclectic tastes in reading too, it seems. I even noticed books by one of my favorite authors in his library, Gene Stratton Porter."

"Yes, I love her work, too. The Governor has fond memories of his Indiana boyhood, actually very near where Stratton-Porter lived," Stellanova said.

"Think of all the books she might have written had she not been killed so young," Gladys sighed.

"An automobile accident, wasn't it?

"Yes. She had moved out to Hollywood, and she was in the back seat of her chauffeur-driven automobile when it ran into a streetcar. She was thrown from the vehicle and killed instantly, I guess," Gladys said.

"I believe that she lives on through her stories and poems, though," said Stellanova.

"I would agree with you about that. Have you read *Girl of the Limberlost?* Gladys asked, hopefully.

"Yes. I found it moving—the story of a daughter's devotion...and what it cost her." Stellanova bit her bottom lip in a futile attempt to catch the words that had just tumbled out.

Gladys seemed not to notice the subtext of Stellanova's comment or her reaction as she took a turn down an easier conversational path. "I find the ending is so satisfying and memorable, especially since the characters end up on Mackinac Island. I've always wanted to visit there and step into the pages of one of my favorite books from childhood. Do you think I could borrow the Governor's copy for our trip to the Island?" Gladys asked.

"I didn't know that you had plans to go there. But of course, yes, you can." Stellanova might have felt a muted sense of coming abandonment, somewhere between the leave-taking of a family member and the feeling one gets when a pet leaves your lap to choose someone else's.

"We didn't originally plan to leave Sugar Island before work on the commission was completed, but since Carleton will have this break when the Governor is in Boston, we are on a lark to Mackinac Island for a few days. I want to sit on the porch of The Grand Hotel and read *Girl of the Limberlost*," Gladys said.

"That's a pricey porch, if you plan on staying there."

"Yes. The price will come dear, but then Carleton calls me his dearest, so..."

"You can wear him down!" Stellanova said.

Both women laughed conspiratorially, admitting to a ploy that they had both used. Shortly afterward, Stellanova experienced the bitter aftertaste of the comment on her tongue. Her life was peppered with doubts about whether she and Chase were together because Chase could not imagine a life without her...or whether she had eventually just succeeded in wearing down his resolve to stay apart?

Woven Baskets and Family Ties
September 1937

Before his departure for Boston, the Governor had informed Professor Angell that soon after his return, Dean Cooley and Professor Hopkins were coming to see the progress on the bust. The uncertainties of that coming visit, that inspection really, made it difficult for Carlton to completely relax while he and Gladys were on Mackinac Island. They did, however, manage to enjoy an elegant evening at The Grand Hotel, beginning with drinking cocktails on the porch as they appreciated the spectacular view and gentle breeze off Lake Huron. Then they enjoyed the spectacular indoor view of the hotel's expansive dining room adorned with several dozen elegantly attired guests whose conversations provided a pleasant counterpoint to the light classics being performed on the grand piano. Every aspect of the evening was a novel experience including the presentation of the fresh whitefish from Lake Michigan, which had been prepared and served on a small cedar plank.

When they returned to Duck Island, Gladys soft-pedaled her and Carlton's recounting of their luxury excursion, because as guests at the Osborn camp, they appreciated that on the scale of Duck Island, the Gander was The Grand. Still Gladys satisfied her urge to share her reflections on the trip by writing picture postcards she had purchased of the hotel's porch, the view of the Straits from Fort Mackinac, and the horse-drawn carriages on Main Street.

Carleton discovered upon his return to camp that even though the Governor was off-island, he was still setting the daily agenda. The Governor had asked Gib to take over some of the obligations of hosting their guests by giving them a taste of what Sugar Island had to offer: catching northern pike, hiking old Indian trails, and picking blueberries from which Lee would make a delicious blueberry cobbler—a little less tart than Chase liked it since he would be out of camp. On his own, Gib added a visit to his Auntie Kateri's camp on Sugar Island, a couple of miles from the Osborn property.

There were three people on the roster for the excursion; Carleton, Gladys, and Dr. Clover. There were three people not on the roster. Stellanova stayed back to do more research on Jane Schoolcraft. Professor Ramsdell begged off so that he could catch up on correspondence, walk the property that the University would be acquiring, and meet with George. Helen did not go on the foray because she had packed only dress shoes.

Those with proper footwear headed out with sack lunches made by Lee to follow Gib for the two miles through the woods at a pace that was a stroll for Gib and Dr. Clover, but a bit brisk for Carleton and Gladys. At Gib's pace, it was not long until their vista opened up from an oak bluff at the southern tip of the Island. There the two arms of the St. Mary's River met just a few nautical breaststrokes short of Lake Huron. Those traveling overland came upon a simple two-room dwelling wrapped in pebbly tar paper with a metal chimney extending from a sidewall like an arm, halting strangers from coming closer. In front of the modest home, there was a fire-pit rimmed with puddingstones, which looked like petrified clumps of fruitcake batter. At the head of a semi-circle of black ash stumps sat Gib's Aunt Kateri, sitting in a weathered Adirondack chair surrounded by her ash basket-making materials. Her dark and slightly wavy chin-length hair was crowned with a men's black felt hat, and she wore black work boots making her bright yellow dress seem oddly fussy with its three-quarter length sleeves trimmed at the cuffs with a border of red, white, and green ribbon. A wide chevron across the bust of the dress outlined in the same pattern of ribbons but with the added adornment of a row of metal cones the size of pinky fingers made out of snuff tobacco tins. The shimmery pattern was repeated on the skirt and the hem of the dress. Gladys thought that Kateri's attire was reminiscent of a flapper, albeit with a more modest hemline and heavier footwear. The metallic fringe caught the sun's attention and Gladys's, too. As Gladys walked toward Kateri sitting in the clearing of low-bush blueberries, she was so mesmerized by Kateri's appearance that she forgot to be vigilant about avoiding the poison ivy until Dr. Clover broke the spell by chiming "Leaves of three. Let them be," while pointing at the ground immediately ahead of Gladys's path.

As they came into her house's clearing, Kateri called to her nephew, "Gib, why haven't you been around to bring me more ash strips?"

Gib raised his voice to reply, "The Governor keeps me very busy, Auntie!"

"Gib, show me your hands! Where are the calluses?" Kateri asked accusingly as the party drew near.

Gib ignored her command. "Today, I am a guide, Auntie. While *I* talk, *you* can demonstrate."

"Your hands have gotten soft, but your tongue is rough," Kateri scolded.

Gib crouched to be eye-to-eye with his aunt. "I'm sorry, Auntie Kateri. These are the Governor's guests. This is Professor and Mrs. Angell and Dr. Clover. Will you please show them your baskets?" Gib asked.

Carleton took a step forward. "We're very pleased to meet you. You live in a very beautiful place," Carleton said.

"The view of the St. Mary's River from here is spectacular. What an idyllic place to live," Gladys added.

"Try visiting in winter," Kateri countered.

"Yes," Gladys said, fanning herself. "Sometimes I don't know what is worse, extreme cold or extreme heat."

"Come in January, and you'll have your answer," said Kateri. "Gib, go ahead and talk about harvesting the strips." Speaking in Ojibwe, she said, "Miidash nongo gaawiin kanendiziin waazhichigeyin." *Now, you won't forget how to do it.*

Gib had hoped that the presence of visitors would temper his aunt's penchant for speaking her mind. His best tack was to continue their exchange in Ojibwe. "Kiikendaan geyaabi nakaazyaanh ninjiin nokiiyaanh, Nizigos." *Auntie, you know that I still work with my hands.* "Wegnesh dash nawe deweganan gaazhitooyaanh giinakaazyaanh kakjiish weyaan." *What about the drums I make from woodchuck hides?* "Kiinoondaw niibnanching dewegeyaanh." *You've heard me play them many times.*

Aunt Kateri countered, "Gaawiin maampii gda'aasii wiidewegeyin piichi biboong, nimaajaayin minising, baawiijiiwaad Gechinagozod." *You're not here to play the drums during the winter when you go off the island with your Governor.*

"Geyaabi ndobaanagam minwaa ndodewege enjinkweshtaadwaad Gechinagozojik." *I still practice by singing and playing for the Governor at their gatherings.*

"Miidash nongo maaba gdogimaa?" *So, he's your Chief now?*

To the others there was no mistaking that Gib and his aunt were arguing, even if they were not doing so in English. Carleton reached to take a long thin curl of wood from the ground. "Why is it that you use black ash?"

Gib was visibly relieved. "Black ash wood is the most flexible."

Dr. Clover was keenly interested. "You harvest the strips in the spring, then?"

"Yes. When the buds are just coming out. The sap is running, and there's a spongy layer between the growth rings that is easy to separate when you pound on the bark."

Elzada also picked up a strip of wood and produced a hand lens that hung from around her neck on a leather cord. Holding the lens near her eye and focusing, "The black ash tree doesn't have fibers connecting the growth rings to each other," she explained for the Angells' benefit. "That's a unique characteristic among all other tree species in North America," passing the hand lens to the Angells so they, too, could see the growth rings more closely.

"I make a wedge with an axe at the end of a section of pounded wood to peel the growth ring off to make strips and then split again to make very thin strips," Gib explained.

"I could demonstrate the process, but it would take more time than I think we have today."

"You're always in too much of a hurry when you come around." Kateri shook her head from side-to-side in resignation. Finally coming to the end of her grievances, she turned her attention to the guests. "We've woven ash baskets for thousands of years. Fishing creels, berry baskets, and cradle baskets."

"What plants do you use to dye the strips? Lichens, by any chance?" Dr. Clover asked.

"Lichens make beautiful colors, but you have to collect too many of them to boil. It's easier to use flowers, fruit, mushrooms, or roots even."

"Some of the strips on your other baskets have interesting designs," Carleton noted, thinking that the designs reminded him of hieroglyphics.

"These are my sweetgrass baskets," Kateri said pointing to the baskets laid out on the ground on a tarp next to her chair. "I decorate some with porcupine quills, others with birch bark bitings."

"Bitings?" Gladys asked, noticing that Kateri's teeth were worn down.

"Yes, I use my teeth."

Gib would later elaborate on the ash basket-making process on their walk back to camp. He explained that the women used their teeth to smooth the willow or bulrush strips, so the best basket weavers had worn their teeth down to the gums. Most in the party were shocked, but Carleton remarked that it was not uncommon that any artist might suffer a disfigurement for their craft. He imparted that apparently Michelangelo had smashed and disfigured fingers.

Kateri folded a piece of birch bark in half and put it in her mouth, exposing the smooth cinnamon-colored side to her jaw's vise. She took it out to unfold it. "I bite traditional designs into the strips. If I like how it looks, then I weave it into my basket."

"It's unusual to see bitings woven into baskets nowadays because not many people know how to do it anymore," Gib said, "but Auntie Kateri does. I remember my favorite was one that she did of a bald eagle in flight."

"Her bark is worse than her bite," Carleton whispered playfully into Gladys's ear.

Gladys mouthed the words. "You're awful!"

"Excuse me, Professor Angell," Gib said. "Even though dinner is going to be later with the Governor away from camp, we should start back."

"Before you go," Kateri said, "I want to give you some berry baskets. Gib, go through the house and get them from the summer kitchen."

When Dr. Clover received her basket, she took a moment to inhale its sweet aroma. "What a lovely souvenir of our visit."

"Carleton and I will treasure ours, but it is so lovely that it will be hard to use it."

"They're meant to be used," said Gib. "They may even be useful today with the blueberries ripening. We may be able to pick some on the trail back to camp," Gib said, urging their departure.

"But do *not* pick the first berry you see," Kateri shouted as she gave the ash strip in her hand a shake at the departing party. They looked back with puzzled expressions as Kateri added, "because then you will never take the last one."

"We'll make it an honorable harvest, Auntie."

"See that you do," Kateri said as the metal cones on her dress winked in the sun, perhaps masking a parting wink she had given her nephew.

The party took its leave of Gib's aunt and headed back to the Osborn camp. As they returned along the same root-ribbed trail, they discovered a new obstacle in the form of a newly-downed maple tree across their path. To go around the limb, they had to leave the trail for less even ground and suddenly there was a shriek as Gladys fell.

"Gladys!" Carleton cried, hastening to her side. "Are you hurt?"

"I don't know. I may have sprained my ankle," Gladys said as she rolled over and sat up. "I just didn't see that hole there."

Carleton helped Gladys hobble over to sit on the downed tree trunk and knelt beside her to take off her shoe— a familiar storybook tableau. "Let me see your ankle, darling. I need something to wrap it because we still have a little way to go to get back to camp."

Dr. Clover quickly untied her headband. "Here. Use my bandanna."

"I'm sorry," Gib said. "I should have warned you about the Indian pits."

"Gladys, I think that you've stumbled upon quite a find!" Dr. Clover said.

"Forgive me if I am less than enthusiastic about this so-called 'find,'" Gladys winced.

"I didn't notice these cache pits until just now. I thought they were tree tip-ups, but they are all too regular in size," Dr. Clover said.

There were circular depressions of a uniform size dimpling the forest floor on the bluff near the water's edge. The small shallow craters were all around them.

"What was stored in the cache pits?" Carleton asked.

"Food mainly. Stored by groups of Indians who would settle here year after year," Gib explained.

"I would expect that you would find evidence of dried fruits and some nuts?" Dr. Clover asked, all eagerness.

"Dried fish and corn, too," Gib added. "Some pits were even dug for sap vats. How is your ankle feeling now, Mrs. Angell?"

"The throbbing is a little slower now, thank you, Gib, but I'm afraid I'll need a few more minutes to rest before I can get going again."

"Gib, what else can you tell us? It might distract Gladys from the pain," Carleton suggested.

"Yes, sir. Not all pits were used for food storage."

"Don't tell me that I am sitting at the edge of an ancient grave!" Gladys said.

Gib had a musical laugh that they had not heard in the Governor's presence or his aunt's.

"No, ma'am, but the pits were sometimes used as ovens or to boil down maple sap into syrup. Some of the pits were used to store maple-sugaring tools like sap taps. Others were probably used as wild rice jigs."

"Rice jigs?" Dr. Clover asked.

"Don't look at me," Gladys said. "I'm in no shape to dance one!"

"Not like a jig you dance," Gib said. "Jig is an old word for a container. The pits were sometimes used for hulling wild rice."

"How exactly was that accomplished?" Carleton asked.

"The pit was lined with an animal hide, and rice was poured on the hide. Then someone would stand in the pit on top of the rice and move their heels from side to side in a twisting motion until the hulls fell off," Gib said as he demonstrated the motion.

"Kind of like stomping on grapes to make wine," Carleton said.

Gladys held out her hand, and Carleton moved in close to support her. "I could really use a drink to dull the pain," Gladys whispered to her husband.

Carleton put his arm around Gladys to help keep her weight off her injured ankle. "I did buy a special bottle of amber liquid on Mackinac Island," Carleton responded. And then, rallying enough to demonstrate a sense of humor, Gladys added, "You better be talking about something stronger than maple syrup!"

"That's my girl," Carleton said as he patted his wife's hand that was holding on to his shoulder.

"Do you think that you can make it back to camp, Mrs. Angell? It's only little farther," Gib said.

"Yes. I think I should be able to make it if we go a little slower. I am sorry to be such a bother."

"It's no bother. I just hope that you can get your foot up as soon as possible. Miss Osborn will be concerned about our late arrival, though, so I may hurry ahead," Gib said, but instead of taking Gib's cue, Gladys engaged him in more conversation to take her mind off the pain and satisfy her curiosity at the same time.

"How long have you worked for the Osborn family? Did you work for *Mrs.* Osborn, too?" asked Gladys.

"Lee has worked for the Osborn family much longer than I have," Gib said as he turned to lead the party forward.

"Nice try, darling," Carleton said when they were just far enough behind the group to have a private comment stay private.

"What do you mean?" Gladys said innocently.

"Just because you stumbled into unearthing the Indian cache pits doesn't mean that you can do an archeological dig into the relationship between the Osborn family members," Carleton cautioned.

"I am not digging. I am merely scratching the surface."

"Well, please try to resist the urge to scratch unless the itch is caused by a mosquito."

Searching, But Not Lost
September 1937

Stellanova had initially intended to work on her research while Gib took the Angell's and Dr. Clover on a hike to his aunt's camp, but she decided that it would be more rejuvenating to work on her poetry. However, when they departed and a solitude of sorts could be hers, unfortunately, Stellanova's mind was cluttered with the feelings exhumed from rereading the letters she had dug out of the closet. Yes, the letters traced a history of her tenuous hold on Chase's affections, but that had been largely resolved by their arrangement. Then, why did she feel like she was not standing on more solid ground now? Going forward into an uncertain future, she realized that she was much more preoccupied with his intentions, rather than his affections. To be sure, she had followed a convoluted path in her life to pursue her education, her career and her heart. The center and the destination for her, for many of those years, had been Chase, even before she met him in person—ever since she had read his early responses to her letters. But that was all history now. It was the present and the future that had no clear course she could see, let alone follow.

As it turned out, what she needed was not an opportunity to sit with her research or her poetry, but to rise and walk outside to commune physically with her surroundings. At least in this way she could feel like she was literally on more solid ground, while her thoughts flitted like butterflies looking for a host plant. So, ultimately, she found herself drawn to the labyrinth that Gib had helped her build by gathering fieldstones to map out the ancient design she showed him. Stellanova had mused more than once that the irony and, in fact, the mystery of walking a labyrinth was that the spiritual pilgrim often experienced a moment of clarity by following its seemingly meandering way toward the center. Such was her hope and her need—for an epiphany.

Stellanova paused in the middle of the meadow in the hip-high grass, barely inside the radius of the ring of the dinner bell but far enough that she would not feel obligated to answer any call or sense of duty from the main house or the Gander. Here, the path she was traveling was hidden from others and obscured even from herself. Entering the opening of the labyrinth, she was both alone and not alone because she found herself playing out dialogues in her mind's voice between herself and Chase. Conversations that had actually occurred and also those that she was rehearsing for an opportune moment between the two of them. Today, as she reached the center of the labyrinth, she was rewarded once again with some small insight. She was prompted by some unseen source of counsel to acknowledge that the serenity she sought did not mean that her life or her relationships needed to be predictable or static or even conventional. Here in the meadow, Stellanova noticed and felt that everything was moving, changing, growing. Could she then not do the same?

Her introspective mood was interrupted and almost mocked by the locusts making haphazard arcs across her path. It was a bit unnerving, but she could see the humor in her modest attempt at a spiritual quest being interrupted by a plague of grasshoppers. What would be next? Frogs and gnats or some other pest? In fact, Stellanova became aware that her spiritual sphere had just been breached by none other than Helen.

"Miss Osborn! Did you lose something?"

Stellanova saw the slim figure of Helen apprehensively picking her way into the meadow wearing a floral dress that Stellanova thought might attract the grasshoppers.

Had she lost something? Only her patience, thought Stellanova. She could understand why Chase barked when his daily devotions were interrupted. When Helen was closer, Stellanova offered an answer, albeit an obtuse one, in W.H. Auden's words, "I'm only lost until I see I'm lost because I want to be."

"Excuse me?" asked Helen, as she tucked the loose strands of her stylish blond bob behind her ears, exposing more of her heart-shaped face and guileless expression.

"No, I haven't lost anything. I am walking this path as a spiritual exercise," Stellanova said. She was not sure if she felt irritated with Helen specifically or if she was having another one of those days when she had the irritable sensation that she wanted to shed her own prickly skin.

"That doesn't look like much exercise," Helen said.

Stellanova inhaled patience and exhaled in reply. "Not physical exercise. It's a metaphor, a saying for life's journey."

"Oh, how lovely. It's a maze!" Helen blurted out, not even stopping to wonder about what she had just been told.

"It's a labyrinth."

"Aren't they the same thing?" asked Helen as she shielded her pale blue eyes from the noon sun and squinted at the labyrinth.

"No, they are quite different. A maze is more like a game, designed to confuse, but a labyrinth provides the path taker with a sure route to the center. There aren't any wrong turns, so you can never really be lost."

"I think I understand. I'm sorry for distracting you," Helen apologized. Stellanova was grateful that Helen, at least, had understood the most important message; that she was seeking solitude.

"Thank you for wanting to help me, Helen," Stellanova said with some sincerity. "You're welcome to walk the labyrinth any time, but I have to warn you about the grasshoppers. They don't observe the traffic pattern."

"If I could walk the labyrinth without the grasshoppers, I would probably enjoy it," Helen said without much conviction. "I'll see if I can help Lee with something for lunch," Helen said with much greater conviction.

Stellanova was relieved to be free to attempt to reclaim her contemplative state of mind while retracing her steps from the center of the labyrinth out. However, this opportunity proved to be a fleeting one and her concentration was again broken by the distant glint off of Professor Ramsdell's binoculars. Stellanova thought that Professor Ramsdell might be embarrassed that she had noticed she had been the subject, momentarily, of his observation of nature. Stellanova observed that the professor was as overly prepared for the outdoors in attire and footwear as his daughter was under prepared. He was sporting jodhpors and the kind of lace-up cavalry boots similar to the ones that the "Dough Boys" had worn in the war, to survey the property. Stellanova thought that Chase would be amused by the professor's costume because he tromped all over the property in shorts and high-top canvas shoes.

Professor Ramsdell was definitely on a mission. He had remarked at dinner the other evening that he wanted to become familiar with the property before meeting with George Osborn, who was expected to arrive the next day. Stellanova was anxious about their meeting, but not because of anything that George might show the professor about the property. As Chase's longtime confidant, George was aware of Stellanova and Chase's relationship, almost from the beginning. Chase even let George read some of their personal correspondence. It made her feel uncomfortable at the time, but at least it made George aware of their true feelings for one another. George was initially tolerant of his father's infatuation with a student closer to his own age. He humored his father, probably thinking that the relationship would burn itself out in due time. However, when the relationship became permanent, George had not embraced the idea that he now had *four* siblings, according to the law, instead of the original three. Stellanova experienced such a keen sense of dread in anticipation of his visit that it seemed like she was having a premonition that George would steal up behind her, put his hands on her shoulders, and whisper in her ear that, in the end, she would have no legitimate claim on his father's estate. Stellanova shuddered as if to shake off the mere thought of George's hands on her shoulders.

"Miss Osborn!" Gib called. Gib, having had a part in constructing the labyrinth, he alone seemed to understand the significance of her spiritual quest and would never interrupt her unless he had an important mission of his own.

With some degree of trepidation, Stellanova turned to see Gib running, but at an easy pace, toward her. She stepped through the border plants outlining the labyrinth's path so as to reach the edge more quickly. Gib stopped before he would have broached the outer rim of the labyrinth, and from there he held out a telegram to Stellanova.

"It's from Colonel Osborn. I thought that it might be urgent." It was never lost on Gib that the Osborn men liked to keep their titles.

"Thank you, Gib. It may be important since the Colonel, the Governor's son rather, is due to arrive tomorrow. I'll make sure that he sees it."

"I'll be heading to the shore to do some work the Governor asked me to do on the *Water Bug* before the Colonel's arrival."

"That's fine, but I don't know whether he'll sleep in a hammock on the porch of the Gander or on the houseboat. It will depend on the weather, of course, so thank you for getting the houseboat in ship-shape all the same."

"Of course, Miss Osborn," Gib said as he took off toward the shore where the *Zheshebe Minis* ("Duck Island" in Ojibwe) was also moored. Gib took great pride in the sleek cruiser and was trusted to be at the wheel whenever the boat was underway to collect the mail or to take the Osborn's visitors on tours around the island.

Stellanova took only a few moments to contemplate whether or not to open the telegram herself. Since there had never been any hesitance on Chase's part to share Stellanova's letters with George over the years, she felt very little hesitancy about reading his telegram before delivering it to Chase. Also, he was not in camp to receive the telegram. All the same, that did not mean that she did not hold her breath as she read the short missive—dreading the message, fearing as she always did, perhaps irrationally, that it might have something to do with her. As it turned out, George was merely communicating that he would not be arriving the next day since he was detained indefinitely due to a recurring back spasm. Frankly, she was glad. She bore no ill will toward George, but she was relieved that his visit would be delayed. It had increasingly proved to be a strain to pretend, in the presence of guests, that she liked him. George had poisoned the well with his suspicion of her motives where Chase was concerned. Her reservoir of goodwill had dried up long ago where George was concerned.

The three of them, Chase, George, and Stellanova were locked in a drama. When the time came when just two of them were left together onstage, she was afraid that George would be successful in writing her out of the script and forcing her to make an exit. She had been auditioning for Chase almost all of her adult life. Chase for his part had finally cast her in a role, but she was determined to play two more roles in his life. She was resolved to be the playwright and the director, and she hoped that George, at some point, would be relegated to being a benign presence in the audience. Unfortunately, the lesson of the labyrinth, born on the wind that moved the surrounding grasses, was temporarily lost in the burr of the stage whisper that she imagined was in George's voice.

Facing the Future
September 1937

Angell had gone outside to where his automobile was parked behind the Gander. He had no intention of driving it because there really wasn't anywhere for him to go. He admired the stylish Buick that still looked as new as the day he bought the coupe two years earlier. Its hood stretched out in front as if to nose ahead of all other automobiles on the road. The wheel wells gracefully broke over the tires like waves that could not possibly impede the car's progress.

Angell's preoccupation was interrupted by a pine cone projectile that landed on the hood of his car from the canopy that the Governor considered a suitable carport for Angell's automobile. Osborn insisted this was the only place to park. When Angell leaned over the hood to remove the pine cone. It was then that he noticed something more insidious than even a barrage of pine cones; the quiet drip by drip assault of pine sap threatening to mar the formerly pristine finish. He knew he should have asked the Governor if he could have parked the car out in the open and not under the trees. The car was a mess. Angell's fury would fuel the elbow grease necessary to clean the car. From the dingy look of the Governor's automobile, a homely flivver, it was clear that it received washing only when nature took its turn. Angell would not wait for nature to take its course. He had already done that. He would, instead, go in search of bucket and sponge.

Later on, as Angell scrubbed away at the sap splats, the progress on the chore put him in a better frame of mind to continue to contemplate his pleasure in owning such a fine machine. He couldn't help but admire the hood ornament. Having teased Gladys more than once about her penchant for flashy broaches, he could not possibly tell her that, initially, he may have been attracted to this particular auto because of the ornament, a small figurine, a sculpture really, designed by Casimer Cislo, an acquaintance of Angell. The sleek design and lines of the whole automobile seemed to begin and return to that figurine, that objet d'art of a tiny goddess. Nearly nude as she leaned forward with the wind in her face as if flying heroically into the distant space ahead. With the goddess hood ornament, the car looked as if it were in motion, even when parked, even with a cooled engine. He had the faith in his diminutive muse that the ancient seafarer had in the mermaid-like figurehead on the bow of his ship. He was lost in these thoughts and the exertion required to rub out the spots as he muttered, "Out, damned spot!" In a few moments, Angell would have reason to worry that his muttering had been overheard by the Governor.

"Good morning, Professor!"

"Oh. Hello, Governor! You surprised me a bit, although I did know that you were back from Boston. Your car's here, and I saw that the flag had been run up the flagpole again." It was the practice at the Osborn camp to fly the State of Michigan flag whenever the Governor was in residence. And a week ago Angell had seen Gib take down the flag after the Governor's departure. In fact, he did so even before the dust had fully settled as Osborn's car moved out of view down the two-track on the way to the main road.

"Yes, it's a ritual we observe at my Possum Poke camp as well. In any event, I want to show you the particular State flag that I have in my library."

"I'd like that. And I'd like to show you the progress on the bust."

As Angell followed the Governor to the library, he felt something between apprehensive and optimistic about what the Governor's reaction might be to the nearly finished bust. He had been inspired by the expression on the statue of Father Marquette. He had found that the missionary's resolve was rendered by the sculptor to be wholly immutable, and he wanted the expression for the Governor's bust to be equally so. If he had also gotten the Governor's jawline correct, he would have cleared a significant hurdle. As long as the Governor did not still think his bust looked the father of our Country, Angell felt ready to finish.

The Governor entered and went straight to the corner where a hat rack and a small flagpole stood. He held up one corner of the flag and said, "This is the flag that flew over the Michigan State House on the day of my inauguration."

Angell leaned in closer to read the State motto, "'Si Quaeris Peninsulam Amoenam, Circumspice. If you seek a pleasant peninsula, look about you.' I couldn't agree more. Living here in this peaceful place, I can see how that motto might often come to mind."

"It's almost too easy to forget about the turmoil of the outside world when we live here. At this point in my life, I want to commit my efforts to a wider definition of peace. Iron ore from this Upper Peninsula has been shipped through the Soo locks to the steel mills to feed the war machine before, and it will be again, now that another global conflict is brewing over in Europe."

"Yes," Angell answered soberly. Here in this tranquil place, he had almost been able to forget that the war machine might swallow his own sons' futures. He turned from the flag and walked to his workstation. "I imagine that you'll make your views known in the local Sault Ste. Marie and Detroit papers?"

"I'm thinking on a larger scale than opinion writing. It's still a great source of disappointment that the United States never ratified the League of Nations, never got behind Wilson on that. Now it's likely we'll need an organization that has even more clout than Wilson promised for that, God willing, if we can't avoid another war." Osborn rapped his large knuckled hand on his desk to punctuate the word "clout." "To my way of thinking, such an organization ought to be established right here at the Soo," Osborn proposed as he tapped his index finger three times on, "right here at the Soo," on the desk to emphasize his proposed location on an invisible map.

Angell disguised his skepticism about Osborn's wild idea by looking as if he were critiquing the bust. He then put his sculpting tool between his teeth using his thumbs to make some small indentations in the planes below the Governor's cheekbones. "Will this issue take you out on another speaking tour?"

"I hope not. As I suggested, I'd rather people come here to see first-hand why this is the perfect meeting place for an organization focused on maintaining world peace. If Sugar Island were the official meeting place, I wouldn't need to travel, *and* I would only need to change my shirt and wear long pants to attend the meetings!"

Angell laughed, and the tool was dropped from his mouth and fell to the floor.

"I am quite serious about Sugar Island, actually." Osborn bent down to pick up the errant tool and handed it to Angell. "This island is the perfect backdrop for peace negotiations."

By now, Angell knew that Osborn did not mind a foil in conversational banter. "With the challenges involved in traveling to Sugar Island, it doesn't seem like a very practical idea, Governor, that is, for most people. I mean, you'd have to have dignitaries from all over the world making their way to this out-of-the-way place."

"Practicality is the enemy of the possible," Osborn quickly countered. "Yes, I'll grant you, the current conditions are not conducive to travel, but I've personally lobbied President Roosevelt on the idea of building a bridge over the Straits through several letters and in person as his guest at the President's Winter White House at Warm Springs. And as a result of that meeting, I'm confident I've won his support for a bridge over the Straits of Mackinac."

Just then the Governor's expression, as a determined visionary, was precisely what he was hoping to capture in the bust, that Marquette element he observed. If he could capture that essence and remove what troubled him most about the bust—showing the man looking a bit vacant or, worse yet, senile.

"That's promising, Governor," Angell offered as he contemplated the fine line that existed between what was considered visionary and what was considered, well, a bit kooky."

"I notice that you've got my chin right this time," Osborn said. "I don't know if I was born with that chin or if defiance itself sculpted it as my most prominent feature."

Angell contemplated the question by glancing back from his subject to his sculpture. Nature, maybe, but surely it was also his art; one way or the other, on both the bust and the man, it was a good face.

Parting Gift
September 1937

Gladys found Stellanova working with a small pitchfork in the garden plot next to Big Duck. Stellanova was covering tomato plants with straw. She hummed as she worked and did not notice Gladys's approach, that is until she turned around to follow the flight of a bald eagle.

"Gladys, shouldn't you be staying off your ankle?"

"The swelling has gone down, and it feels much better. Just a little stiff and sore."

"Let's sit on the steps for a bit," Stellanova offered.

"Thank you, Stellanova. I brought a hostess gift for you," handing her a very slim package.

"That's not necessary, Gladys. I've become rather accustomed to the steady stream of the Governor's visitors over the years, and I never expect anything in return."

"But how many of those visitors stayed for six weeks?"

"Your extended stay was necessary for the project."

"Well, *my* presence wasn't necessary," Gladys said.

"A woman is often her husband's muse."

"A muse. I don't know about that, but I do enjoy seeing his projects take shape, and we do occasionally talk about them over dinner or on our evening strolls."

It occurred to Stellanova that Gladys' deflection of her role as a muse was actually, in its simplicity, a confirmation of it. Stellanova had been coming steadily to the realization that her romanticized notion of what it meant to be a muse, or even a wife, was antiquated and narrow. For years, she had tried to convince Chase to make her his wife, but when she finally received his resounding rejection of that, she had been willing to settle for simply being his amanuensis, nothing more than a stenographer really. Then, as the years went by after his decision to formalize their all-too-private love, she had failed to notice that she actually meant much more to Chase than she may have in any of the other roles she had begged to play in his life. After all, much like Gladys and Carleton, she and Chase talked, almost incessantly, in fact, about their joint writing projects as he read over her shoulder at the typewriter, and discussed their shared literary passions during dinners, and afterword during the long, quiet evenings spent on the porch. It was she who kept him engaged in his writing, kept him company, and kept him, well, young. She was his muse, was she not? This slow dawning epiphany would be the real parting gift for Stellanova.

As if Gladys had been privy to Stellanova's thoughts, she said, "I wasn't sure what sort of gift I should bring because I didn't know your tastes before we arrived," Gladys said.

Stellavova, seizing on the words, "your tastes" looked around her and realized that even after seven years, her tastes still were not evident anywhere here unless she could count a stack of books of hers here and there and the footprint of the labryinth.

"I was so relieved when I saw that you had a phonograph," Gladys continued.

"We didn't play much of anything while you were here, and I'm afraid that the Governor's tastes run to listening to nature's music over recorded music," Stellanova apologized. "He talks more *about* the phonograph than he *uses* it. Mostly, it's here as a prop for him to remind people that Michiganders can claim Thomas Edison as a native son."

"But I've heard you put some music on to play, from time to time. I loved listening to the music of Irving Berlin and the Gershwins that you put on the phonograph sometimes. It was a welcome break from the operatic and symphonic music, as glorious as that is, that we typically hear back on campus at Hill Auditorium. I took a chance and brought you a recording of Enrico Caruso's recital that he gave at Hill Auditorium several years ago," Gladys said, pointing to the still unwrapped gift in Stellanova's hands.

Stellanova opened the package and held the gift, an album, at arm's length, in both hands, like welcoming the return of a loved one. "Oh, Gladys! This reminds me of one of my most treasured memories from my student days in Ann Arbor."

"Might you have attended this performance?" Gladys asked, referring to the recording.

Stellanova lovingly brushed the record jacket with her hand. "No," she said regretfully. "At the time, I didn't think I should spend the money to buy a ticket. The day before the concert, which happened to be an unseasonably warm day for March, I walked past Hill Auditorium and walked up the steps to the piazza to read the concert flier on the kiosk. Stellanova made a slow sweep of her hand to make a marquee in the air. "It read. 'Caruso—Himself. The World's Greatest Artist Will Appear in Concert!'"

"The doors to the auditorium were open, so even though I had earlier made my decision, I stepped into the lobby and went directly to the ticket booth, only to find a sign on the window that read 'Sold Out!' I could have kicked myself for having been so miserly. But all was not despair," Stellanova added, smiling as she put her hand on Gladys's arm to signal a pleasant turn of events. "At that moment, I heard a piano. Then Caruso himself began to sing! I couldn't believe my ears! Since the doors were open, I sat there on the steps along with a few other impromptu concertgoers who had also happened by this unadvertised practice of the master. And I remember being flabbergasted at seeing people walking past the auditorium on the sidewalk, obviously hearing, or perhaps not, this glorious music, as if they had someplace more important to be than listening to Enrico Caruso." She smiled wide. "Oh, Gladys, this is actually quite wonderful. I will treasure your gift forever!"

"And I will treasure *your* gift, Stellanova."

"My gift?" Stellanova had a moment of unease, thinking that Gladys assumed she had a gift for her, too.

"Yes, a gift—the story of you and the Caruso practice. You have given me a remarkable story for when I need something to share when next I'm at one of those interminable faculty women's teas, or even during an intermission at Hill Auditorium when I'm forced to stand with others in the long line for the ladies' room."

Stellanova smiled and nodded turning the record cover over to read the selections on the recording and the liner notes.

"It's the very story that led up to your experience on the steps of the auditorium." Gladys noted with satisfaction in the surprising appropriateness of the gift.

Stellanova was so moved by Gladys's gesture that, unprompted, she began to read aloud from the back of the album.

> "'To book the famous Italian tenor Enrico Caruso to perform in the small mid-western town of Ann Arbor was a long shot. Skeptics thought that the local Ann Arbor audience would lack the sophistication to appreciate Caruso's performance; in fact, few had any faith that the University Musical Society (UMS) would be able to persuade Enrico Caruso to perform or pay his high fee of over $13,850. Charles Sink, the first Director of UMS, traveled to New York City to meet with Enrico Caruso, and they struck up a friendship—and a deal. Caruso agreed to come to sing in Ann Arbor! At that point, nothing could stop Caruso from coming to Ann Arbor, except the Spanish flu. The concert, originally scheduled for October of 1918, was postponed until March 3rd of 1919. Contrary to all expectations, the Ann Arbor audience loved Caruso, and the famous tenor loved the Ann Arbor audience. What was more, the exceptional acoustics of Hill Auditorium and the linked reputations of the hall and the University Musical Society were effectively raised. The fortunate result was the University Musical Society began to attract many more high-profile musicians.'"

"Gladys, let's listen to this together. I want to share it with you before you have to leave."

"That would be a delight. Let's also have an 'intermission' so that we can have tea and talk some more," Gladys suggested.

"Agreed!" Stellavova said.

Hidden Charm
September 1937

Stellanova's thoughts were stalled for some reason. No matter what she did or didn't do or think, she could not seem to make progress on either her research or on her current poem. Vexed at every turn, and anticipating continued frustration, she thought that she might as well turn her attention to household tasks; changing the sheets on her bed was as good a place as any to start. As she gathered up the old and smoothed and tucked in the new, she remembered that her reading glasses had slipped off her head the night before, dropped behind the headboard, and remained there as she had been too tired to retrieve them. So, as much as she could, she shifted the heavy bed frame away from the wall only to hear something else hit the floor, something that didn't quite sound like her glasses. Extending her arm between the wall and the headboard, she felt about and soon recovered a hand-sized hoop. She had almost forgotten that she had tacked the hoop on the backside of the headboard, out of Chase's sight. She sighed. It had held special significance for her—at least over an extended time when the possibility was nightly there of its power and of its discovery.

So, it wasn't exactly that her thoughts were stalled; no, they were there, just not on research or poetry but on a subject that she couldn't escape but felt powerless to control. Holding this hoop, she wondered if when the Angells were gone from the island would Chase resume his amorous visits? But as she pushed the bed back into its normal position, she exerted equal effort in pushing away this unresolvable thought, this question for which she was fairly certain of its answer. As had long been her habit, she actively moved in thought to another subject, far from the one that really interested her. This time it was to when she had just arrived on Sugar Island, about seven years before, and she and Lee had gone to the farmer's market. They stopped at Mrs. Kateri Church's stall to buy a couple of jars of maple syrup. Lee liked Mrs. Church's syrup because it did not have the watery consistency or the smoky flavor of some others. Mostly, Lee was aware of how important maple syrup was to the Governor who prized and carefully portioned it, even with himself, taking care not to pour it too liberally, especially when he was down in Georgia each winter where there was no possibility of securing more.

Stellanova remembered Lee commenting on the Governor's guardianship over the syrup; but on this day, as she sat on the bed, hoop in hand, it was another memory of that earlier day that held her attention. She remembered that they had to wait for a few minutes to purchase their syrup because Mrs. Church would not be distracted from finishing her handiwork. She was working on a small round willow frame with a woven string spiderweb pattern radiating out from the center. She made quick work of attaching a long deerskin ribbon to the edge of the frame and tying on a few beads. Stellanova thought it might be some sort of rudimentary sieve, but the webbing was too wide to strain or catch anything. Observing the young woman's puzzlement, Mrs. Church explained she was making a spiderweb charm that would hang on a baby's cradle. She continued, noting further that Ojibwe mothers and grandmothers made these to snare and prohibit any harm that might hover about a small child. Stellanova remarked that such was a lovely tradition and that it had to give mothers some much-needed peace of mind. To her surprise, Mrs. Church handed the charm to her, refusing the money that Stellanova hastened to offer.

It was a gift. What was more, it was a gift that was a prediction, a hope. That gift had surprised Stellanova then as more recently, just days earlier, she had been surprised in another way by Gladys's gift of the Caruso album. Rising from the bed, taking a few steps across the room, she sat down at her desk and without any preparation, and certainly without any forethought, she began to wrap a small present for Gladys.

The Committee Convenes and Critiques
September 1937

Stellanova did not mind visitors to Duck Island as long as she and Chase had time to themselves in between visitors where they could fall back into their comfortable routines and be less vigilant about posing as father and daughter. That just was not possible in August and September of 1937. The Angell's stay was challenging enough before it was compounded by the arrivals of Dr. Ramsdell and his daughter Helen, and Dr. Clover. Then, without a break, that whole group was to be joined by more newcomers from the University: Dean Cooley of the Math Department and Professor Hopkins, Director of the Summer Session. Stellanova could not help but feel overwhelmed and a little crowded, though she did find herself a bit interested in meeting Hopkins. After all, he was the man responsible for Carleton's summer posting to Sugar Island and the eventual immortalization of Chase in bronze.

When the day finally arrived, Stellanova recalled that she had met Cooley before when he visited their Georgia camp. She recognized the tall-dark-and-handsome Cooley in casual camp attire, but her attention was drawn to Hopkins because he looked a bit like a migratory bird from down south. She was amused by his summer plumage of all-too-new plaid shorts and short-sleeved shirt making him look like he had been blown off course by a northerly gale and a bit ill at ease on his foray into the Osborn camp. Hopkins was also sporting brown and white saddle shoes. This Dapper Dan looked like he was in search of a putting green. Chase had often expressed to Stellanova that he did not believe that one should judge a book by its cover, but he did have a theory that a man could be judged by his footwear. Stellanova could easily predict that Chase was certain to deem Hopkins, when he saw his choice of golf club footwear, to be a man who was "highly recreational" and far from a serious companion for a rigorous hike or a worthwhile conversation. Unfair? Yes. But then, she suspected that she was often unfairly judged by their visitors. Stellanova often found that once she was introduced as "Miss Osborn, my daughter," that quickly relegated her to being as invisible as someone in a bird blind. However, it did allow her to hear and observe much in their presence without any expectation that she might contribute.

So, as she prepared to deliver Dean Cooley and Professor Hopkins to Chase's library, she knew full well she would be noticed about as much as the flagpole propped up in the corner of the library.

"I've heard that the Governor's library is quite impressive," Hopkins said.

"I've never known an autodidact quite like Osborn," Cooley said.

"He has a degree from Purdue, doesn't he?" Hopkins asked.

"And a good many honorary degrees as well," Hopkins added.

"But I've found that the breadth of his knowledge can be explained less by his academic history than his extensive travels and reading," Cooley added.

Stellanova was pleased that these emissaries from the University had a good impression and a good assessment of Chase, but as she stood back and allowed them to knock on the door, this was little comfort as her mind was focused on the coming reception by the Governor. Even though they were expected, and Chase looked forward to their visit, she still feared they just might run afoul of the Governor, particularly in this moment as they announced their presence at his library door. They did.

"You are interrupting my morning devotions!" the Governor growled as he answered the door to find the two academics hovering at the entrance. Since the pair were backlit from the glare off the water, Osborn initially noticed only their relative stature—Hopkins being a head shorter than Cooley— of the two silhouettes. The Governor was no more capable of disguising his pique at the unrecognizable figures at the door as he would be if he immediately recognized the men as his guests.

"Excuse me, sir, maybe we should return at a more convenient time?" Hopkins suggested.

"No need. The break in my concentration cannot be mended. Come in, come in," Osborn acquiesced, evidently still miffed.

"These shelves must be groaning with the weight of all these books," Cooley remarked as he moved into the light highlighting his resemblance, in Stellanova's mind, to an older but well-preserved Tyrone Power. She sympathized with Cooley's attempt to play a valiant role in this drama to move the moment beyond their awkward arrival. Hanging back, as she regularly did, Stellanova at once recognized the professor's attempt and also understood its initial futility.

Then, as she had observed on more occasions than she could count, Stellanova watched Chase pivot, gradually, to being the consummate host as he usually did. She smiled slightly, thinking that the Governor's quiver had been emptied with his initial salvo from inside his fortress.

"They'll hold. After all, these bookcases are made out of winter-cut northern white cedar," Osborn said.

"Locally made then on the island?" Cooley asked.

"No. They're Rittenhouse, made in Cheboygan," Osborn said.

"Sheboygan, Wisconsin?" Hopkins asked, giving the shelves a closer inspection through his round tortoiseshell glasses.

"Cheboygan, Michigan with a 'C,' an old logging town southeast of Mackinaw City where you took the car ferry. The Rittenhouse Furniture Company started out, years ago, making railroad ties. After the area was logged over and the railroads went into decline, the company changed over to making heavy, sturdy furniture and other pieces for cottages, like my shelves and this lectern here."

"Interesting that you have a lectern here in your library," Cooley said.

"Of course. I accept many speaking engagements, and I practice right here in my library," Osborn said.

"If these walls could talk," Hopkins mused.

"They would say, 'Talk less and read more!'" Osborn said, making Cooley and Hopkins laugh nervously.

"Stellanova, did you bring our guests here straight away? Have they met Professor Angell?"

"Not yet, Governor, but Professor Angell intended to meet with your guests just outside the library."

"Well, shall we step outside then? Let's have an unveiling of Professor Angell's bust! It is a true measure of his artistic skills," Osborn announced as he approached the door, "*and* a real tribute to my patience in posing for it," as he strode out the door without holding the door or looking to see if his guests were following.

The group followed, as it was obvious that they should. As promised and anticipated, Angell was waiting outside with the bust on his sculpting platform and a camera on a tripod. Angell knew his role in this scene and, initially, let the bust and the Governor speak for him.

Osborn looked the bust over with a quizzical expression, a bit feigning that this might be the first time he had inspected the sculptor's work. Far from it. "Well! I declare I feel that looks like me! But what a rugged customer he is!" Cooley and Hopkins again laughed, a bit less nervously this time, but evidently unaware that this moment was pure theater.

"Oh, Dean Cooley and Professor Hopkins, I'm glad to see you," Angell said as he continued to busy himself with the camera, inadvertently breaking with his supporting actor's role in the Governor's present scene.

"Professor Angell, you've accomplished far more than just capturing the Governor's likeness," Hopkins said.

"Thank you, Professor Hopkins."

"I would agree he has," Osborn chimed in. "Put that bust in bronze and send me the bill! In fact, even though this is destined for Ann Arbor, I would like a copy for my library."

Stellanova was watching the scene from the doorway of the library as Chase rather awkwardly posed with the bust, although she was pleased with the likeness, she hoped in vain that Chase's request would not be granted. This bust was all too realistic, and would one day, all too soon, be a painful reminder for Stellanova.

Cooley looked at Hopkins and said, "I don't see why not?"

"Thank you," Osborn responded. "It will remind me of the many pleasant hours I've spent conversing with Professor Angell," said Osborn.

"Excuse me, gentlemen, but lunch is ready for you in the Go-Down," Stellanova said.

"I'll be just a few minutes behind you," Angell interjected, "I don't want to miss this light for a few photographs of the Governor with the plaster." Angell stepped behind the camera and continued his adjustments to its lens. "Oh, Stellanova," that reminds me. You mentioned earlier that you would like some photographs of me working on the bust. This is good light for that. Maybe you could stay behind, just for a minute or two, and we'll make those images, too?"

"Certainly Professor," Stellanova answered, "Governor, may I ask that you lead our guests to lunch?"

Angell finished adjusting the camera, made a few photographs himself of the bust, and then asked Stellanova to look through the lens. "Here, I think it's ready for you."

Stellanova was no stranger to a camera and even without saying so communicated to Angell that she knew her way around the instrument. Confident that she had matters in hand, Angell stepped over to the bust and pretended to put on various finishing touches.

"That's good, that will do nicely I think," Stellanova said after making three or four exposures. "Let's make our way and join them for lunch. After lunch I'll ask Gib to lend you a hand in moving your work back into the library."

"Actually, I need to prepare the bust for travel down to campus. I'll need to miss lunch because I need to apply a couple of inches of plaster of Paris to the bust, wrap it in burlap, and pack it into the crate that I have in the backseat of my car. I will take Gib's help then to load it into the crate."

"I'll leave you to it then," Stellanova said handing the camera back to Angell before she left to meet the others at the shore.

Later on, Stellanova pressed Lee to relay what she had overheard Hopkins and Cooley discuss before she had joined them for lunch. Stellanova had often marveled at Lee's ability for near, even exact recall, something she saw almost daily as Lee worked from recipes in her head as she prepared their meals. Even when Lee needed to look at a recipe, she seemed to do so only once and then she had it all, step by step, committed easily to memory. The same was true of her recounting of the professors' conversation. "Well, it began like this," she said without any uncertainty or hesitation,

> "The Governor certainly seems pleased with his likeness," Cooley said.

> "But should he be?" Hopkins questioned.

> "What do you mean? Didn't you just praise Professor Angell's work?" Cooley returned.

> "Yes, but I don't think that the bust is altogether flattering," said Hopkins

> "The profile seems fine," Cooley said.

> "I agree. In profile, you can see the resolve of the rugged Renaissance man, so to speak, but head-on?" said Hopkins.

> "Angell has captured the Governor's eccentricity, but I acknowledge that that could also be interpreted as senility," Cooley said.

> "That's what concerns me," said Hopkins. "At least the job's done, and we have something that satisfies the spirit of the commission. Also, as old as he is, the Governor could peg out at any time."

When Lee had relayed this last comment, it made Stellanova gasp as if by doing so she could breathe for the specter of the "soon-to-be-expired" Chase that Professor Hopkins had conjured with his insensitive and dismissive prediction of Chase's mortality. Had Stellanova been apprised of this conversation before lunch, her serving of hospitality would have been severely rationed where Hopkins and Cooley were concerned.

While Stellanova and Angell had been finishing up at the library, the Governor's party was watching Gib, the de facto host for these fresh air repasts, as he made the preparations for toasting lunch sandwiches, balancing them expertly on a forked green stick over a semi-circle of rocks that he had laid for cooking over an open fire just outside the Go-Down.

In anticipation of lunch, the Governor intoned almost a grace, albeit secular in nature. "The hills on the Canadian shore are the oldest things in the world if geological chronology means anything. They are more the backbone of the North American continent than are the Rockies." Then Osborn launched into a more traditional grace expounding on that theme and surprising his guests that such an oration would precede a humble picnic.

After a most satisfying lunch, Cooley said, "I've visited you in Georgia, but you seem to be even more at home on Duck Island, Governor, than at your winter camp."

"You have something there. Stellanova knows that if I happen to die during the winter or spring at Possum Poke, she is to bury me here on Duck Island. Although she doesn't like me to say this, her promise to honor my wishes actually makes it's easier for me to leave Sugar Island each fall because I am certain that I will return—one way or another!" Osborn joked, which made Stellanova visibly cringe that he could speak so lightly of what she so greatly dreaded.

Cooley changed the subject. "I've often heard of the beauty of this area of Michigan and particularly the Straits of Mackinack."

"That pronunciation grates on the ears of a local, doesn't it, Gib?" Pulling Gib into the conversation as the true local in the small party. Gib's lips stretched ever so slightly in amusement, but he quickly looked down to conceal his reaction from the professors.

"The pronunciation of 'Mackinac,'" Osborn continued, "is only an approximation of the sound of the Ojibwe word for a 'crack in the land,' that we commonly refer to as The Straits."

"I appreciate your frustration," Cooley said. "As you know, Governor, I own a 'PEE-can' grove near your camp in Georgia, and locals are forever correcting visitors who insist on saying 'puh-CAHN.'"

"Potato. Po-tah-to. Let's call the whole thing off," Hopkins sang awkwardly in his unpredictable tenor.

Osborn stared at Hopkins uncomprehendingly. Stellanova knew that if Chase was speechless, he was genuinely flummoxed by Hopkins' strange rejoinder. Stellanova felt a little sorry for Hopkins as he had no idea that Chase would not have been current with popular culture and certainly not familiar with one of the newest Gershwin brothers' tunes. Stellanova observed that sometimes there was a strait, a wide divide, actually, between the Governor, a man born when Lincoln was president, and his visitors, yet they continued to seek him out. As did she.

The Last Supper
September 1937

Stellanova was relieved that the season for visitors was almost over, although she would miss Dr. Clover and the Angells. She had long been aware that most guests to the island were there for their own ends, wanting something from the Governor that might advance their lives. The visit of Dr. Clover and the Angells was different. Dr. Clover had come at the behest of the Governor. Professor Angell was there to carve out a small niche in history for the Governor, and Gladys, however too present at times, had helped Stellanova understand something of her own unconventional past and still unsettled present. So she wanted their final evening to be memorable, and it proved to be just that. Stellanova and Lee planned the menu of venison stew, but the side dish of confrontation was served up by the Governor.

Osborn's dinner table etiquette was rife with routines that his guests could only learn through their unwitting infractions. The mix of formalities and informalities made it even more difficult for guests to navigate. The guests were expected to be punctual (on Osborn time) and they could also expect to be the audience for the Governor's blessing, really an opening address before the intellectual nourishment that was on the Governor's menu for conversation on any given evening. The meals were served family-style with the serving bowls brought directly to the table. Professor Hopkins assumed that this meant that the guests would pass the bowls around the table. He thought that by not serving himself first, and initiating the passing of the serving dishes to the right, that he had cleared the first hurdle of the obstacle course that would be dinner.

"This venison looks delicious," Hopkins remarked as he passed the platter to Gladys. "Some people find venison gamey, but if seasoned just right, it can pass as a fine grade of beef."

"Speaking of passing, I always serve my guests myself!" barked Osborn.

The dishes were cooling in the chilly atmosphere and were quickly passed to the steaming Governor. Instead of the usual course of lively conversation, there was little more than the banter between the forks and knives, so the guests busied themselves by cleaning their plates in just a few minutes. Once the sound of the flat wear died down, that was Osborn's cue to play the cowbell by his empty plate, which summoned Lee to clear the dishes and bring in dessert, an apple pandowdy. However, Professor Hopkins' plate still had some food left on it when he handed it to Lee.

"Eat that potato!" Osborn ordered.

Professor Hopkins looked startled, as though not sure whether the Governor was specifically addressing him.

Osborn gestured with the dessert serving spoon. "Do you hear me? Eat that potato!"

"I do not *care* for more potato," Professor Hopkins answered firmly.

Osborn and Hopkins were in a stalemate and the others, the Ramsdells, Dr. Clover, Dean Cooley, and the

Angells were frozen in an awkward tableau of diners caught in the crossfire. Since Osborn had already crossed the line between host and the sternest of father figures, the next step was not much of a leap for him. "Then, you get no dessert!" Osborn bellowed.

"Then I'll *forego* the dessert," Hopkins said decisively, yet feeling off-balance as he tried to reconcile the man he came to meet, who was the worthy subject of the bust commission, with the irascible man at the head of the table.

After a tense, raised eyebrow exchange between Stellanova and Chase, he backed down, and Professor Hopkins got his apple pandowdy. Stellanova breathed a barely noticeable sigh of relief. She did not only worry that visitors to the island might discover the true nature of her relationship with Chase, but might also discover that it was even more difficult to reconcile the difference between the myth and the man—especially recently.

As everyone had buried their forks and their gazes in their desserts, Dean Cooley threw out a conversational life ring. "I feel like the guest of honor has been left out. The group was a bit taken aback as it was not clear who exactly was the guest of honor, even though this was the Angell's last meal. That Osborn had made nothing special of that fact, all were left wondering whether even he might be unaware that this was their "Last Supper," so to speak. "I mean, the the Governor's doppelgänger!" This was followed by a stifling silence that threatened to suffocate Cooley's effort. "I mean the bust!" Cooley said.

"Ah!" Osborn responded. "I think I would be a bit uncomfortable sitting down to eat with my doppelgänger, as you call it. Seeing one's double was once thought to be a harbinger of bad luck."

"True. In ancient Egyptian mythology," Angell said, "the 'ka,' or 'spirit double' was credited as having the same memories and feelings as its counterpart. It was even thought to perform actions in advance of the person it resembled."

Stellanova thought, "As if I didn't already have enough feelings of misgivings about that bust."

"The Finns," Osborn added, "many of whom call the Upper Peninsula home, call a similar spirit 'a first comer.' This discussion has been amusing, but we need to give Professor Angell more credit than for merely copying my image. This is what impresses me most, Angell. You managed to work into the clay something more. I suppose I am more or less like the Northland, which has rugged terrain and rough facets like your treatment of the bust. Yes, I am well pleased with Angell's work!"

"Let's all raise our glasses to Carleton!" Ramsdell chimed in.

"To Carleton!" they all exclaimed.

Everyone would leave the next morning, except Professor Ramsdell. Helen would travel back to Ann Arbor with the Angells so that her father could meet with the Governor and George to work out the final details of bequeathing the property to the University.

Of course, Stellanova considered the gift of land to be the best possible monument to Chase, yet she had reservations about granting the land to the University. George had always been the advisor on whom Chase relied the most, but Stellanova had her own advice for Chase, and she would endeavor to make her case before George arrived. She would warn Chase that he should not forget the cautionary tale of King Lear, who gave away everything, only to live on in years finding himself unwelcome in his own kingdom. Yes, King Lear came to mind, but only part of that drama. She herself could never be cast by anyone, in the role of Cordelia, Lear's daughter, whom the King had drowned for refusing to flatter him. God knows she had never spared in efforts to flatter Chase. No one had ever been more genuinely impressed with his biography than she. Still, she worried about *George* finding a way to disown her.

The meetings between Chase and Ramsdell, after the departure of the other guests, took their predictable course with discussions about Ramsdells' forays into the three thousand acres and the twelve miles of shoreline that would make up the preserve. What was also predictable was Stellanova's unease about arrangements for the future of her haven where she had felt closest to Chase, where she so hoped she would continue to live after he passed on.

A Widow Returns
April 1949

The barge bearing Chase's body was expected from the Soo. The casket was too heavy for the footbridges at the usual landing edge of the island, so it had to be brought down shore closer to the Osborn property where there was no bridge to traverse on the way to the burial site. Stellanova lamented that it all was a bit too much like moving heavy freight, not a person, not her Chase. Surely a Governor's burial should merit more ceremony, yet his sole mourners for the burial would be herself and Gib.

"Mrs. Osborn, I brought you a chair to wait for the barge," said Gib, easily addressing her formally, as he always did, but with the title she had only acquired recently.

"Thank you, Gib," Stellanova replied as she continued to look down river. Do bring one for yourself, we might be waiting a while as the water is quite choppy today."

As Gib walked away toward the Gander, Stellanova's mind wandered back to Chase's final days, earlier that month, at their Georgia camp. If it were not for the nurse's bedside notes, it would be quite a blur. There would be, however, three events that would always be in sharp focus. The annulment. The marriage. The last breath. All of this could never make sense or satisfy any sense of propriety among others, but it made sense to her. At long last it made her whole, or so she thought.

Lillian's own last breath had come fourteen months before Chase's. She died more or less alone, at least without

Chase by her side. News that she had passed arrived some days later by letter from George, who added that his mother had wished to be buried in a cemetery in Sault Ste. Marie. She had read the letter to Chase after she and Gib had transferred him to his wheelchair one morning to sit by the window at Possum Poke. Chase took in the news with a nod of his head and some sort of audible acknowledgement that was difficult for Stellanova to interpret. He did not make eye contact with her, instead, he stared out the window, and after a point bowed his head. Stellanova did not know, and she would never know, whether this was in prayer, regret, or even shame.

When Lillian died, all of her arguments that she had laid out for marriage in her pleading letters and in her recurrent discussions with Chase might have seemed moot. But now the real waiting began. For months after Lillian's death, she wondered when Chase would accept and acknowledge that he was a widower and finally free to marry her? Now, sitting with Gib, awaiting the barge, Stellanova remembered how it was that she was waiting for her husband's body and not her father's. Armed with George's letter, she had finally possessed the single most persuasive argument in her hands. Yet, fourteen more months had passed with no change in her status until "the eleventh hour." When Chase began to fail in April, her anxiety over the past, the present, and, more importantly, the future merged and guided her hand through the annulment of the adoption and the signing of a marriage certificate.

Posterity would never know of their most intimate conversations in recent months that finally brought them together as husband and wife. What existed was something altogether different, the bedside log that had been filled out by the nurse in Georgia who was there in their home for Chase's final days. The log was now in Stellanova's possession, as she needed it to be. Factually, it described Chase's deteriorating condition between April 5 and April 11 of 1949. But that was not why she had been eager to take hold of the log and keep it from the eyes of others. There was a timeline on those pages that Stellanova worried might raise questions someday.

> **On April 5:** Chocolate milk, egg. Later, milk, grape juice, oatmeal, egg yolk, yawns, slight hiccups. Dislodged considerable mucus. He called. When I asked what he wanted, he said, "Mostly you." Awake. Slightly feverish. Up in chair, pedicure, back to bed; slept quietly. Grand mal. Began like a petit mal. Mouth noises and tremors. He met death in the form of three violent consecutive convulsions that racked him for an hour. Streptomycin and penicillin administered every 3 hours.

> **On April 6 & 7:** His position was changed every half hour. Pulse weakened and irregular in the morning. He seemed stronger late evening. Seven coughs and yawns. Smiled twice. Difficulty swallowing. Position changed every half hour. Streptomycin and penicillin administered every 3 hours.

> **On April 8:** He battled down a stubborn high fever with four ice baths, excepting imminent convulsions. Nasal oxygen begun. In two hours, he regained normal temperature and clear consciousness. Removed mucus from throat with an aspirator. Two yawns, one cough. Position changed three times. He opened his eyes and smiled at the night nurse. Penicillin was administered at 9 p.m.

> **On April 9:** He married. Heart failure brought five hemorrhages, and all hope was gone.

> **On April 10:** Since he refused to die, we tried to bring him back again. One chance in a thousand became two chances in a thousand. Then the other side of his heart failed.

On April 11: *Pulse becoming weaker. No response to wife's voice. Dr. Crumbley here. Rev. W.C. Smith here. An hour after the weakening of his breathing became apparent, he was gone peacefully. Time of death 5:25 p.m.*

Were George, or anyone else for that matter, to read this, he would surely find reason to contest Stellanova's status as Chase's wife and heir. She was resolved to keep the existence of the log, and her possession of it, a well-guarded secret.

"Do you need a lap robe from the cabin?" Gib asked as he set his chair next to hers.

"Yes, it's a bit cold out here. That's so thoughtful of you. Would you bring one of the smaller Hudson Bay blankets?"

"Absolutely," Gib replied, even as he was into a running pace back in the direction from which he had just come. Ever a man of the woods, and of outdoor chores and pursuits, Gib was still fit and he never went off anywhere, except at a run. Against the cold she crossed her arms and closed herself in tighter to her wool sweater. She then dropped her hands down to her lap and rubbed her hands together. Normally, like anyone else, she would do this almost absent-mindedly, without even looking at her hands, but not this time. She couldn't help but see where there was not a ring, where there was no conventional symbol that she was actually the Governor's wife, now widow.

She stroked the arms of the hoop-backed chair and reflected on what sort of eulogy would be fitting for this homely funeral attended by only two mourners and perhaps a few barge hands. After all those years and all those meetings with notable people and important visitors to the island, this role fell solely on her. She had never discussed this possibility with Chase, but she had once asked Chase if he was worried about dying. His answer was far from atypical, questioning her in his oft-rhetorical way. "Do I mind dying? Of course not. The people who are fond of me will be sad, and that's all that bothers me. I love life, but I am so curious to see what goes on afterward that sometimes, honestly, I can hardly wait." This sentiment had stung her then and did so anew. He also had said that he thought death was "the most fascinating subject in the world; nobody knows anything about it, and most people are too fearful and superstitious to permit themselves to be interested." Stellanova reflected on the fact that she was in that latter camp, less for her own life than what her life would be like without Chase. Her fear had started a decade earlier with the bust commission.

Gib returned with the blanket, and with the same attention he used to take in preparing Chase's wiki-up, he now used to settle the blanket carefully over her. Stellanova noticed that even close up Gib looked almost the same age as when she first met him eighteen years earlier. Gib then sat down next to Stellanova and settled in to wait. Chase had chosen both of them to see him through his later years. Stellanova thought ruefully, "Lord help the employee whom Chase could not trust." Chase had dispatched with a few of them over the years. Chase never expressed directly his expectation, but he clearly appreciated strong, capable, and uncomplaining people. Gib never complained, as he did not, yet again, the previous day when he had had to dig the Governor's grave himself in the gnawingly damp chill.

The chilly vigil reminded Stellanova of the many times that she had sat up, similarly wrapped in a blanket, waiting for Chase to return to the island from one of his speaking tours. That was far from the half of it. Stellanova had been waiting for Chase most of her adult life. She wondered if the waiting had aged her prematurely? The stiff wind caused her steely gray hair to be lifted off her face exposing the extra lines that were etched on her forehead by worry during Chase's touch and go final year. Against the cold, she rubbed her forearms as if she were making up for lost embraces.

The barge was still not in view, but as Stellanova's eyes glanced across the restless water, she began what was, in effect, an impromptu eulogy. "The Governor was a good 'getter' and a great giver. There was a furniture worker's strike when he was Governor. Thousands of workers were off the job, striking for better wages and hours. The strike lasted for months. The plight of all the workers and their families weighed heavily on the Governor, and he worked to convince the legislature to pass the first worker's compensation bill in the country. He also helped workers in the Soo by pressing the government to reduce their shifts from twelve hours down to eight hours, and to pay them through the winter."

Gib nodded. "He always treated me well, too. That's why I stayed with him all these years."

"I can't think of a pallbearer more worthy than you, Gib. You were almost like a son to him."

Gib's voice dropped in pitch. "And he a father to me. If it's all right with you, I would like to do something we do at our funerals."

"Of course."

"It is our tradition to place tobacco on the grave or pour whiskey on the ground for the afterlife."

"But the Governor didn't smoke, well not much anyway, and he certainly didn't drink."

"Don't I know it!" Gib said. "I thought about that and brought something else for his grave," Gib said as he reached into the breast pocket of his coat and pulled out a small flask of thick amber liquid.

"Maple syrup!" Stellanova exclaimed. "How fitting!" And then they both laughed.

"That will be lovely. To the sweet hereafter!" Stellanova said, continuing to smile as she had not in days.

At that point, the barge appeared around the point, and although they had been waiting for it for some time, the sight of it still caught Stellanova off guard. In Chase's later years, she remembered seeing him sit right here on the bluff to watch for the arrival of his visitors. Those were much more pleasant vigils than this one.

She rose out of the chair slowly. The dread of the grim task ahead made the blood in her system seem thick as sap that was boiled down too much. "Gib, while you help the crew bring the casket on shore, I'm going to collect some fresh balsam boughs for the Governor's final resting place, like you used to collect for his wiki-up."

Stellanova was not sure Gib heard her as he had begun to step away, his attention was obviously consumed with helping the men hoist the Governor's casket out of the barge. Counting Gib, there were five of them, and they still struggled under the weight to make their way up the steep bluff. The men initially headed for the library, thinking it was a mausoleum, but Gib indicated the winding way through the woods that led to the largest boulder on the property. As they came closer, the mound of fresh dirt beside the rectangular hole became evident as their destination.

Stellanova met Gib and the ersatz pallbearers at the end of the trail to the gravesite. Gib saw that she had lined the bottom of the grave with the balsam boughs; whether he had heard her moments earlier, he was evidently pleased. Stellanova held one branch in her hand close to her nose to take in whatever healing properties she understood that Gib's people believed balsam to possess. Also, the strong fragrance would have an even more important function presently as it masked the smell of the damp earth and the emotional chill it gave her. She then unfolded a paper to read aloud the poem she had written.

Wilderness Grave

Inept the rake,

the scythe, the spade!

For the plot where we are laid,

with bright blossom and green blade

He who made wild beauty be

will give us for the common sake

care in perpetuity.

"May I try saying one of his graces—as I remember it?" Gib asked.

"Please."

Gib did not bow his head but lifted his chin to gaze up at the canopy of hardwoods that would stand vigil over the Governor night and day. He held his palms up, palms that had worked hard for years for the Governor and therefore showed no signs of blisters from digging the Governor's grave.

"Father and Mother of the Earth, we thank you for sunlight and all it yields. We thank you for the renewal of life and courage. We pray for all men to be in harmony with your purpose, and we ask for patience, understanding, and justice."

Stellanova was pleased that Gib remembered one of Chase's blessings as accurately as he did. Then, what came next, surprised, and moved Stellanova more than she could have anticipated. Gib added, "We pray for Governor Osborn's eternal life and his continued guidance in our daily work. Amen."

Widow's Weeds
April 1949

The day after the burial, Stellanova, for some inscrutable reason, felt compelled to put on Chase's buffalo coat. The coat had lost all traces of Chase's scent and the smell of balsam boughs and had acquired a slightly unpleasant musty fug. The weight of the coat, however, gave her the comforting sensation of being anchored in place long enough for her thoughts and feelings to puddle around her feet and seep into the ground absorbing some of her grief. However, wearing those "widow's weeds" was not altogether comforting. Stellanova remembered that when Chase put on that coat, it was a signal that he would be sleeping in his wiki-up and not in her bed. She would never know whether Chase wore the coat to connect with something primal in himself or in an effort not to cave in to the domesticity that Stellanova craved.

The hide coat was lined with an old blue and white wool plaid topcoat of Chase's. It was not one that Stellanova had ever seen him wear. Since Stellanova had always done Chase's mending, she wondered if this was Lillian's work. The image of Lillian's wifely attentiveness to the lining of Chase's prized coat was an unwelcome vision, especially at this difficult time. Stellanova did not want to think of that. She did not want to think of Lillian. So, she looked straight ahead and felt again the weight of the coat upon her shoulders. The long sleeves formed a muff-like embrace as she clasped her forearms in front of her. The wool lining of the coat felt abrasive against her skin and made her feel agitated on a deeper level, too. She could have taken the coat off, but she wanted to stay in touch with that odd sensation so she could hold on to the thread in her thoughts—a memory unspooling from her childhood of a disturbing fairytale.

There was a king who promised his dying queen that he would not marry again unless he found as beautiful a woman as she to marry. He did not have to look far, for that woman was his very own daughter. The king's daughter devised a way to delay the wedding by asking for three gowns to be made before the dreaded incestuous union would take place. The first dress was to be as "golden as the sun." The second as "silver as the moon." The third as "dazzling as the stars." The daughter also wanted a cloak fashioned from the feathers and fur of every bird and animal in her father's kingdom. When all her conditions were satisfied, she had no choice but to flee, and she took her trousseau with her. Unfortunately, her escape was brief, and she was captured and returned to the castle where she lived out the rest of her days as a disenfranchised heir consigned to the life of a kitchen maid without even possession of her given name.

What had nudged that strange fairytale off her mental bookshelf was wearing the coat. She felt as if the psychological tome that was her unconscious life had hit the floor and awakened her conscious mind. With sudden clarity, she saw herself not just a little in the king's unhappy daughter. Stellanova realized that it had been she herself who had delayed the wedding by accepting Chase's terms; in being so accepting of those terms it was as though she was as much an author or, at the very least, a complicit co-conspirator, playing out their ruse.

Stellanova should have negotiated much earlier for a legitimate, unfalsified place by his side. Her position as his legal wife had been so very brief that the public, fooled for so long by a story, a tale actually, would not be easily convinced that the marriage had even taken place. She had never found comfort in the fiction of her life as a ward. Now it frightened her that for the rest of her life she might never find peace and acceptance even as his true widow. She became cold, even as the coat remained about her increasingly lonely self.

The Turn of a Key
April 1949

Stellanova considered searching the pockets of Chase's coat for a few moments before she actually did it. It might feel like sticking her hand down a snake hole. She could be bitten by what she found, but she was more likely to find a pocket knife or a bit of iron ore. When she reached in, what she did find was only a bit of lint and tin of Altoid mints with the manufacturer's claim of "Curiously Strong Mints." Stellanova was amused because Chase himself was "curiously strong." As she moved to place the tin on the bureau, its contents rattled, but not with the sound she might have expected. Inside she found no mints. Instead, there was a small key and a book of matches from a Detroit hotel. Chase had traveled so much, especially across the State, that there was nothing odd about a matchbook from a Detroit hotel. What made much less sense was that key, especially since she didn't know Chase ever to have locked anything away.

She felt like Alice in Wonderland holding the key to a door that might make her feel smaller, might even upend her world. Somehow, she knew that she was not meant to find this key. She came to this conclusion almost instantly knowing that Chase must have banked on the fact that she had always had a visceral dislike of the coat and would never search the pockets. Keeping the key in the pocket of this coat was as good as putting it in a strong box, hidden well beyond view or detection.

Stellanova could think of nothing in Big Duck or Little Duck with a lock on it, and personal items were not kept in the Gander. The only possibility was that the key had to be for a drawer or a cabinet in Chase's library. She turned the key over in her palm. Thinking. She was not sure if she wanted to know what might be locked away. She sensed that she needed to get what was in front of her behind her as quickly as possible, almost as if the White Rabbit was badgering her that she was already late for a very important date. She took one tentative step, and then her resolve quickened her steps toward whatever secret the library-crypt held... for her.

It did not take Stellanova long to discover that the key opened the lower, left-hand drawer of Chase's private desk. Having swelled with the humidity, the drawer squeaked gratingly. The sound startled her as if Chase had found her reaching deep into his past. Stellanova pondered whether it was possible to trespass in the past, or was she simply doing the dogged work of a historian? She could hear Chase intone the familiar words from the Lord's Prayer, "And forgive those who trespass against us."

The unlocked drawer revealed a well-worn leather-bound Bible with an embossed image of the Holy Family on its cover. She ran her hand over the cover and thought wistfully that it was almost like rubbing her hand over the surface of Chase's leathery and deeply veined hands when he was hospitalized that last time. She had seen Chase read his Bible in Big Duck every evening shortly before bed. It had never occurred to her that he might have more than one. This Bible was much larger. It fit into the drawer as closely as a coffin into a cement burial vault. She carefully wedged her fingers between the spine and the drawer's side to excavate it from its tiny tomb. The weight of the pages and the thickness of the spine made it difficult to lift it out of the drawer.

At that moment, with the Bible in her hands, an odd memory resurfaced, like a thorn working its way out of the skin. Several years ago, she had developed a cyst on her left wrist as a result of all the typing she had been doing on their *Hiawatha* manuscript. The cyst had become a source of considerable discomfort such that she stopped typing one day to apply a green tea compress and Chase asked her what was wrong. When she held out her hand for him to see, he immediately said, "This looks like a job for a Bible." She was not nearly as apt to pray as Chase was and said, "I will not pray for something as trivial as a bump on my wrist. I will save my chits for more troublesome problems." Then Chase explained, "It's the kind of large cyst, or 'Bible cyst,' that they used to eliminate with a whack of a Bible, hence the name." Stellanova replied that she might be willing to try that treatment if the compresses failed to relieve the dull ache. He never mentioned at the time that the remedy, in the form of the heaviest book in his library, was so close at hand in his locked desk drawer. Curious that he would not have produced the weighty tome then if only to see her eyes bug out at the prospect of submitting her wrist to the Good Book's guillotine. But then, maybe, at that point, the Bible was not there?

One way or the other it was here now. She opened the book, randomly, perhaps, hoping for some timely wisdom, but that turned out to be a futile effort. She then turned to the birth records page for the Osborn family.

Chase Salmon Osborn (born 1860)

Lillian Gertrude Jones (born 1863)

Married May 7, 1881

    Children

        Ethel Louise Osborn (born 1882)

        George Augustus Osborn (born 1884)

        Chase Salmon Osborn, Jr. (born 1888)

        Emily Fisher Osborn (born 1889)

        Oren Chandler Osborn (born 1891–died 1892)

        Miriam Gertrude Osborn (born 1900–died 1902)

The first several entries brought no surprises, but there were entries there that were a revelation to Stellanova. She knew that Chase and Lillian had had four children. She had no knowledge of the others. She took a seat in Chase's chair, putting the heavy book on her lap (because her wrist sometimes still ached) and sat there trying to absorb the weight of this new information. Maybe this was why Chase would not, or perhaps could not, think of having a child with her.

Then she went looking for something else she needed to confirm. She turned the page, but nowhere could she see her name entered. Her birth and name, not even her adoption date, had ever been entered. Were George ever to see this, this alone would be all the evidence he would need to deny her what was hers. But that wasn't anything near to what really troubled her about this. She was not in the Osborn record, not in the family Bible, not where names were sacred among other sacred names. All she knew was that she was never supposed to see this.

Stellanova rose to put the Bible back in the drawer. In the moment she could think of nothing else to do with it. She then noticed what she thought was a piece of yellowed paper lining the bottom of the drawer. It was instead an old over-sized envelope that had been placed facedown at the bottom of the drawer. She placed the Bible on the desk and used a letter opener from the middle desk drawer to gently raise the brittle edge of the envelope in case there was something of value in it. The metal clasp on the envelope was rusted and broke as she bent the prongs. She pulled out a sheet of paper and tilted it toward the light. The heading did not immediately make sense to her, expecting some sort of legal document like a deed or perhaps documentation for the gift of the property to the University. She had to read the title of the document aloud to convince herself of what she was seeing.

Decree of Separation.
Signed by
Chase S. Osborn and Lillian J. Osborn
August 22, 1923

Chase and Lillian had been legally separated. He had never told her this, only that they had grown physically and emotionally apart. But it had been legal. Had this been locked away for two and a half decades? Stellanova was now even more incensed that he had not taken the next legal and logical step and divorced Lillian years ago. The secret had been locked away in that drawer for two and a half decades!

It was evidence of his public shame in getting a separation decree and his private shame of the dissolution of his family— his first family. His *only* family of record in the Osborn Bible.

Chase had made it clear that he would never divorce his wife. Chase's pronouncement consigned Stellanova to being his daughter in the understanding of many and his perpetual mistress in the knowing eyes of only a few. He used the law to alter his family's configuration by adopting her, but he would not avail himself of the legal system to be free to marry her. That would have made a fundamental difference in their lives, *especially* in her life.

Stellanova had romanticized the notion that she and Chase were family once the adoption had been finalized in 1931. Chase called her his "true North." It was one of the most romantic things he had ever said to her. She thought that it also meant that he would always come back to her. Now his actions were coming back to her—to threaten to erase the significance of her place in his life. Now she knew that he never even entered her name in the family Bible. This revelation unmoored her. She had thought that nothing could be more distressing than being separated from Chase, but finding this cut her adrift in a sea of much deeper sorrow.

At that moment her eyes went to the other side of the library where they fell on the copy of the bust that Angell had had cast personally for Chase. Remembering that summer of its creation, that summer with the Angells, when for weeks on end the mockery of her relationship was in constant threat of being revealed, the bust was no longer a portrait of Chase; it was a mockery in bronze that their relationship had always been of fragile clay, a constructed sham and, what was worse, her very existence was denied in this sacred of all family documents, paces away, over there on Chase's desk. Moments earlier her initial thought was to return the Bible to the locked drawer and throw that key into the depths of Lake Superior and never open that drawer again. She decided instead to rid herself of Chase's bust.

The Veil Lifted
July 1958

For years, Stellanova's resolve to dispose of the replica of the bust was firm, but a hefty bronze bust resists its own passage from one place to another and one's custody to another. It is not like a collection of letters that can be stored or thrown away or donated to an archive. A bust has a stubborn staying presence. Stellanova learned this after making numerous inquiries about an off-island destination for the bust. Initially, she had thought that a bust of a former Governor of the state would have been graciously accepted for display in a government building in Lansing or in a library in the Soo. However, these seemingly promising pathways eventually led to dead end after dead end. Even though the gift of the bust came with no price tag and none of the proverbial strings attached to significant gifts, time and taste had passed by Chase Osborn's reputation, even though his reputation had been fiercely guarded.

Stellanova had resigned herself to the idea that she might have to keep the bust after all, but relegate it to a dark corner of Chase's library, covered against all possibility of being seen by her. And then Stellanova received a postcard from Elzada Clover that was postmarked "Pellston, Michigan," a small village about twenty-five miles south of Mackinaw City. Elzada explained that she was teaching a course on Boreal Flora at the Biological Station on Douglas Lake. She wrote that she had brought her signed copy of Stellanova's "Balsam Boughs" book with her to camp and had enjoyed re-reading the poems inspired by the habitats that both she and Stellanova loved to study in their own manner.

Stellanova had sent Elzada early drafts of some of the poems for her critique. They had developed a friendly correspondence over the past decade and this gave Stellanova the courage to write to Elzada seeking her assistance in finding a new home for the bust. Not too many days later, Elzada's welcome response and resolution arrived in the post. Stellanova was delighted to read that Elzada had approached the director of the Biological Station, Dr. Alfred Stockard, who was aware of both the reputation of the Governor and the artistic skills of Professor Angell, and decided that the bust would grace the library (that Stockard had designed) at the Biological Station. With the exchange of another couple of letters, the two women came to an agreement for a date yet that summer while Elzada was still to be at the Biological Station and could receive both her and, so to speak, her late husband.

Stellanova decided that the delayed exodus of the bust actually had been fortuitous. Now she could take "Chase" over the Mackinac Bridge for which he had so passionately advocated, but had not lived to see it completed. On the appointed day for travel, driving across the Straits of Mackinac from the Upper to the Lower Peninsula seemed like crossing a border. Stellanova was glad there was nothing more than a tollbooth on the St. Ignace side of the bridge and not a customs agent ready to question her about what or *whom* she was bringing across the bridge.

Stellanova would be traveling less than two hundred miles round trip, but the trip represented a much longer journey for her. She was not traveling alone exactly. Chase's bust was in the back seat inside an old pillowcase she had shrouded it in a decade ago, and concealed by his buffalo coat.

As she drove across the bridge, she thought of what Chase probably would have told her, namely to trust in the sound engineering of the colossal structure. Unfortunately, his voice was merely of her creation, and her real anxieties were right there in the car with her in the more pressing form of her discomfort in negotiating the strange road that was the bridge, its guard rails so low that she only wanted to drive on the inside lane. This was small comfort as that lane had the unnerving effect that its surface of grates, in lieu of pavement, made a roaring sound under the wheels. By a force other than her own, the car tracked one groove to the next, jerking the steering wheel right and left under her white-knuckled grasp. And if that were not enough, it was foggy.

The shroud of fog that morning may have been a blessing, though—obscuring the bridge's height and the water's depth. She began to talk aloud to steel her courage. "Chase, you would be distraught about the billboards—not just the size, but the so-called Upper Peninsula attractions they advertise—fudge, pasties, and more fudge—obviously targeting a certain ilk of tourists. The visitors we wanted to attract to the area were none other than delegates to the United Nations. Your bridge would have made that dream come to fruition."

While gripping the steering wheel, she was forced to acknowledge that she could no more escape the chasm between the peninsulas than she could escape the chasm between her past with Chase and the present and future without him. She had been Chase Osborn's ward for eighteen years, his wife for only two days, and his widow for more than a decade now. Stellanova realized with a burgeoning sense of clarity that her lingering grief had created a scrim, like the fog she drove through, muting the many shades of color in the water below and the forested land ahead onshore. Her general outlook, since she had lost Chase almost ten years ago, had been obscured by melancholy as if she were actually wearing a widow's veil, but she was taking an important step today as she put each mile behind her.

Dr. Clover's instructions were good. Before long Stellanova was turning into a forested road that was marked as the entrance to the University of Michigan Biological Station. The road led slightly downhill toward the shore revealing a seemingly self-sufficient rustic summer resort. Many of the small cabins looked like metal-sided ice shanties that had been stored on shore to double as domiciles for the summer. There were a few larger two-room tar paper shotgun shacks and a log cabin or two indicating that there was a social hierarchy in this backwoods enclave. Continuing to follow Dr. Clover's directions, she came to what appeared to be the center of the camp with structures that served as lab classrooms, a dining hall, a lecture hall, and the newest building easily recognized, by its form and function, as the library and the pre-arranged place to meet up with Dr. Clover.

Stellanova stopped the car in front of the library under a large red oak tree. She climbed the few steps to the front door, eased open the screen door, and stepped gingerly across the tile floor along the central aisle of bookshelves and past several long library tables to the back of the library where a young woman sat at a reference desk. Before Stellanova could inquire about Dr. Clover's whereabouts, Elzada appeared behind the screen of the back door. Stellanova found herself being as relieved to see her as she had been a decade earlier when Elzada had finally arrived for dinner after a walk about Duck Island.

"Good morning, Stellanova. It is so good to see you again after all these years," Elzada said in a stage whisper in deference to the scholarly space.

"Likewise," Stellanova whispered, limiting her response to avoid any annoyed glances from the students whose heads were bent in study or somnolence.

I hope you didn't have too much trouble finding the Station," Elzada inquired while motioning for Stellanova to follow her out the back door of the library to stand along a fieldstone retaining wall frothy with green vegetation.

"Your directions were perfect," Stellanova assured her.

"And you arrived in time for lunch. Will you be my guest? That will also give us the opportunity to catch up with one another."

"That's very thoughtful of you as I eat a good many meals by myself. I would really enjoy sharing a meal and conversation. I would also like to thank Dr. Stockard for agreeing to give the Governor's bust a niche here."

"We'll undoubtedly see the director at lunch. I've asked a couple of men from our work crew to remove the bust from your car while we are at lunch and place it on a table at the back of the library near the window. I imagine that you would you like to check on it before you leave this afternoon?"

"No," Stellanova hesitated a moment. "I don't think so. I've said goodbye to the Governor so many times over the years, for one reason or another. I think I'll forego saying goodbye this time. Besides, I prefer to delude myself sometimes by pretending that he is simply away on a speaking engagement."

"And what better place than here?" Elzada kindly supported Stellanova in her obfuscation.

"Indeed," Stellanova said, relieved that, once again, Elzada had demonstrated that she understood her.

An hour later, Stellanova was headed north again. Her load going over the bridge was lightened by more than just the weight of the bust. As she neared the opposite shore, she was moved to open the window and let the breeze over the Straits lift her spirits and, in effect, lift the veil, a bit, on her lingering grief.

Epilogue
Burnished Bronze
October 1980

The young woman, a University of Michigan sophomore, had yet to choose a major and, in fact, had not really chosen her college either. Anne was the daughter of a botany professor at Michigan, so she hadn't really gone very far for college. During freshman year, she was disappointed that she had not decided to apply to a college further afield. Living at home made her feel as if she were repeating her senior year of high school minus marching band practices and prom date drama. Sophomore year, however, Anne was more or less happily resigned to being a commuter student. After all, while living at home she had avoided the distractions of dorm life, the freshman fifteen, and contracting mono. She had also enrolled in her favorite class to date—an art history survey course taught by Professor Hoover. He looked too "hip" to fit the stereotype of a history professor. He had a mop of salt and pepper hair—like an aging Beatle. His relaxed posture at the podium, silhouetted against the big screen in the darkened auditorium, made it look like he was in the middle of a cigarette break in a film noir rather than a professor lecturing to 300 students about the artistic luminaries of the past.

It was October and they were nearly halfway through the material of the course that would take them from the distant Italy of Cimabue and Giotto to the nearer America of Jackson Pollock and Andy Warhol. This midway point had them in the Baroque, Professor Hoover's specialty, and today he was showing the students the image of Bernini's portrait bust of the Roman Cardinal Scipione Borghese. Professor Hoover was in his element describing why this work looked so real. He told the students how Bernini had followed the Cardinal around his palace for several days, sketching him at breakfast, drawing him as he held meetings, and capturing him in animated conversations.

Sometimes, it was difficult for Anne to choose between taking copious notes and just listening to Professor Hoover's scholarly observations such as, "Mostly what Bernini carved in stone was the vivacity of the man, his appetites for all things worldly, mostly food, and all this literally bursting forth in the incriminating detail of a strained button on his robes. This represents the very 'speaking likeness of the man.'"

That was Wednesday's class. The Friday lecture class was, for whatever reason, cancelled and instead, students were to meet either Thursday or Friday in their smaller discussion sections. Anne was in a Friday one. It was a beautiful afternoon on the eve of the much anticipated and emotionally charged Michigan-Ohio State game *and* it was a home game. So, it didn't surprise her that only seven of the fifteen students showed up for the discussion. Anne never skipped class. That could be attributed to the commuter's conundrum—Where else would one go, but to class? As she entered the small classroom, there stood Professor Hoover in conversation with the graduate assistant who led the section. Anne watched the two men talk for a few minutes and she noticed that the younger man had adopted some of Hoover's mannerisms over the course of the term. Apparently, once or twice a semester, Professor Hoover, would take over and lead a discussion section. She knew this was going to be interesting, and she felt a bit smug that she was among the few conscientious students who had shown up for class on a beautiful fall afternoon.

"Professor Hoover will be teaching our section today," said the pseudo-Hoover grad assistant. "Let me quickly hand back the quizzes. You did pretty well on these. We can talk about them next week."

"We're heading over to the Union," announced Hoover.

The class was hardly out of the building when Hoover lit up. He was definitely a chain smoker, and this was probably why, when he took over a discussion section, he would often hold that section outdoors. As the group approached the Union, Professor Hoover took one last drag on his cigarette before discarding its butt to the side of the entrance. Already with a momentum set in motion from the art history building, the students kept moving assuming that they were heading into the building. But then the professor stopped, and so did they, now facing him directly as he turned around while simultaneously pointing to the ground, to the very place where they were standing.

"President John F. Kennedy once stood on these steps. He stood here at two in the morning on October 14, 1960. The historical marker commemorating this event is right here. And it was on this very spot, Kennedy announced his idea to create the Peace Corps. Despite the very late, or very early hour, Kennedy was cheered by a large and enthusiastic crowd as much for the hope and promise he represented as for the fact that he referred to Harvard (his alma mater) as the "Michigan of the East." Hoover's students indicated by their light laughter that they also appreciated the nod from an ivy league alum.

"The image on this plaque on the wall here, captures Kennedy's youth and vision," Professor Hoover continued as he gestured to Kennedy's portrait in relief mounted on the brick wall. "The profile is not unlike what one typically sees on a coin. I must say that it's more than a little disappointing to watch so many students pass by this site, oblivious to the significance of this marker. It is not too far a stretch to say that this is hallowed ground. The choice of the profile portrait, the typical manner of presenting a statesman, is not insignificant. Kennedy's concept for the Peace Corps initiative was itself a prescient act of statesmanship. Not many on the campus know that the announcement about the Peace Corps occurred here and many fewer know anything of this sculpture. My point is that the biography of the man, in this instance, has almost totally overshadowed the work of art. We study art history as an insistency that images matter; that images speak truths. Hold those thoughts and let's head inside to the lobby where there's another sculpture that has suffered much the same fate as this image of Kennedy."

Anne was struck by the fact that Professor Hoover's lecture style was no less formal or eloquent just because they were gathering in an informal way. She and the other students followed the staccato beat of Hoover's sleek Italian leather Chelsea boots into the building, up a flight of stone steps, and into the Union's main lobby. There the beat stopped as he paused before a bronze bust of a man. The bust was positioned at eye level on a pedestal that stood against the wooden paneling of the room. For a moment, Hoover waited for a small parade of publicly exuberant sorority wannabees to pass by. This also, evidently, allowed him time to catch his breath.

"Like the Kennedy image outside, you've probably walked right past this bust many times, he began. "I did much the same, when I was a student here. I never took notice of it."

Anne acknowledged to herself that she had never taken notice of this sculpture either. Yet, she had a nagging feeling that she actually *had* seen this sculpture before, but not in this setting. Could this be the same sculpture, or some version of it, that she had seen many times, many summers past, and many miles north of where she was standing now?

"This bust was a University commission, a work that came about in the formal manner that many works of art, particularly the portraits we have been studying in class. Think, for example, of Bernini's Sciplione Borghese, the work we were discussing in class the other day. Like that masterpiece, this is no less a 'speaking likeness of a man.' In this case, Chase Osborn, a former Governor of the State of Michigan and a Regent of the University."

As he always did in class, Professor Hoover began to draw the group deeper into the work with his close description of its overall form, its details, and the surprising "presence" of it. Yet, Anne was distracted because of her recognition of the bust. However, she tried to stay focused by taking notes as Hoover provided more context for the work.

"Let's consider the realism of this work. This is clearly Governor Osborn right here before us. In this attentiveness to the man, the sculptor was obviously working in a long-standing tradition of realistic portrait sculpture that goes all the way back to ancient Rome. Upper-class citizens, especially political figures, routinely had their portraits carved in marble, and they were surprisingly life-like. That tradition survived, to a degree, into the medieval period in things like reliquary busts that gave every impression that you were looking at this or that martyred saint. The tradition is then picked up in the Renaissance, specifically in Florence, and then it thrives again in the Roman Baroque as we've recently seen with Bernini's work."

Anne furiously turned the page in her notebook and the ruffling sound momentarily interrupted Hoover or maybe he was giving her time to record his every word. He shifted his weight and put his hand lightly on Osborn's pate.

"The history of art is filled with real people essentially presented in all their reality, be it in marble or, in this case, bronze. And beyond physiognomy, that is the sitter's face, an attentiveness to the reality of the here and now continues in the treatment of what the man is wearing. Note the clothing. It's a casual work shirt and, what is more, it is open, unbuttoned at the neck, revealing his upper chest. This Governor Osborn as the man he was, not delivering some speech, certainly not in a pose suitable for an image on a coin."

"That seems like an odd informality for a subject of his age and stature as a former governor," one student commented.

"Unusual yes, if again we insist on putting portrait busts, their sitters, and their artists on remote pedestals, so to speak. In some respects," Hoover said, pointing to the pedestal underneath the work, "this whole tradition of pedestals does a disservice to the very works that are literally upheld by these platforms. I think what's at work here is more.

The artist's determination to make an intentional statement about the man's down-to-earth quality, his make-up as a real man. The presence of this work shirt surely contributes to the 'take me as I am' attitude that seems to be projected by our subject," Hoover surmised.

Anne decided to sacrifice her note-taking and ask a question. "Professor Hoover, I get the idea of a 'speaking likeness,' in the case of Bernini, and I follow you on this 'take-me-as-I-am' treatment of this person, but I'm confused. In our class we've been studying specific artists as great artists. What confuses me is whether a commission like this actually inspires artistic creativity? Where is there room for the great artist to create?"

"Excellent point. Go on," Hoover urged.

"I guess what I'm trying to say is this. Is this about the subject, this man, or is it also about its artist? The subject is this governor, Osgood or Osmond."

"Osborn, to be precise," Hoover interjected with a smile.

"I just don't 'see' the artist in this work. This portrait business just seems like, you know, a business arrangement instead of an artist creating what is important to communicate as art."

"Well said, and spoken like a true art history major, which I presume are are! Someday there'll be a place in History of Art 102 for you!" Professor Hoover quipped as he was now back with the reins of the class in his hands. "True, yes, but the pressure caused by hunger and deadlines, as any students with a paper due can attest, can spur creativity." This brought forth a laugh from a few of the students.

"I hear what you're saying, but I still think that certain commissions could be very limiting artistically," a male student parroted Anne—probably because he trying to impress her more than he was trying to impress Hoover.

"You are right, in most cases," returned the professor. "Let's take the opposite. Doesn't an open-ended assignment sometimes give you so much freedom that you end up spinning your wheels, so to speak, not knowing where to turn? The absence of structure, or parameters, can also stymie creativity." Hoover stepped back a bit and folded his arms as he looked appreciatively at the bust. "Carlton Angell obviously knew that he had to represent the man. However, what he had to search for, what I think makes up the intangible presence of this work, is what was below the surface or contours of the man's face. When we look at this face, at the intensity of evident introspection, I think we can only conclude that its sculptor had to have invested something of the same kind of time and energy that Bernini did when he followed Scipione Borghese around his palace, observing him when he least felt himself observed. Does that answer your question?"

Anne nodded affirmatively as she continued to take dictation on his observations.

"I don't think that Carlton Angell could have made this work as it stands before us, raw and real, without investing something of his own artistic commitment," Hoover said as he rested his case just in time for his next nicotine hit. "If you need a chance to grab a coffee in the Union or at Drake's, we can break for a few minutes before our next destination on campus. Let's reconvene on the Diag in about ten minutes to continue our tour of campus monuments. Next stop—the pumas in front of the Natural History Museum."

"I've heard that the pumas only roar when a girl passes by who is still..." said the same student who had tried to get Anne's attention. She took note of his comment and would steer clear of him at her next discussion section.

"I'll have to cut you off right there," Hoover interjected. "To regroup, Carleton Angell, the same artist who accepted this commission, created the pumas. Judging from the look on the face of the bust, I conjecture that the wild and exotic pumas did not present as ferocious a challenge to the sculptor as did his subject Governor Chase S. Osborn, but then we'll never know."

As Anne's classmates and Professor Hoover would never know, and she could not have imagined at the time, she would one day unearth the story behind this intriguing tribute, as mysteries are only worthwhile as an inspiration to act.

"A Fine Romance"

Correspondence between
Chase S. Osborn
and
Stellanova Osborn (née Stella Lee Brunt)
(1921-1931)

"You Do Something to Me"

My Dear Miss Brunt,

Your letter of May 6 reached me on my way home from the West. I do not know what it means because I have seen no impertinent letter from you. I have asked my very exacting secretary whether you have written to me anything that could possibly have been interpreted as in any way disrespectful or unkind or crude or improper, and she says you have not. If you wrote that way, it did not reach me, and if you wrote that way, I am quite sure it would have reached me, so I am very certain you did not.

I am compelled to feel extremely decent these days. I am to deliver the Commencement address at Northwestern June 10 and get another degree. That does not mean a great deal to me, and it may transpire that the address will mean nothing to the audience either.

I have just read your "In a Ford." It is song, and consequently poetry, and perhaps plus. If you write a book or anything else that is purchasable, I will buy it.

With kind wishes, I am,

Yours Sincerely,

Chase S. Osborn

Dear Miss Brunt,

Your letter of May 29 really gives me a great many pleasant vibrations.

It is odd that the letter you refer to should not have been received. If I had gotten it and had reacted as you suggest, I should feel ashamed of myself for life.

If Mr. Frost blue-penciled "The Robert Frost of the Whimsies Evenings," I don't think as much of him as I did.

Just one thing as to riches. There is only one test of wealth—that is, if one is able to serve without expecting compensation in the form of money, appreciation, or so-called gratefulness.

Yours Cordially,

Chase S. Osborn

Dear Miss Brunt,

Your letter shall be a dear one, and you are a sweet girl to write me so richly. However, anyone with youth and wit and imagination can have a busted heart is quite bewildering to me. Now do not go to the Ozarks to stay too long at a time any more than you would elect to slumber in a rose garden. But go and see and drink and feel. Please do not go to the Ozarks without seeing the Lake Superior country. The geo-antithesis of Arkansas.

Someday, I hope to see you, and as I am a grandfather of eleven grandchildren, is it not all right for me to ask you to come to my Duck Island camp in the St. Mary's River? It is just a camp, but the roof does not leak much, and we eat a little three times a day. Perhaps Mrs. Osborn would be there, and like as not, she wouldn't. But if you are so rigidly conventional, you may bring a chaperone, and there will be room and a welcome for both. There have been quite a many honeymoons at the camp and several planted, but in the latter case, you need more than a chaperone, whatever is a chaperone.

Twice now, you have written to me in so kind a style that I feel I know you and desire to advance it beyond theory. Good old summer times will cure that heart disease you think you have. The record of the thing will be preserved only, and you shall not care.

Yours Respectfully,

Chase S. Osborn

Dear Miss Brunt,

Indeed, Duck Island will be open August 20, and if anything, it will be the very best time for me to have you and Miss Osawa, and I think you will like the North Country.

There is no requirement of dress whatever. In fact, the thing I wish you to have in mind, in justice to me, is that it is a backwoods log camp. There will be a place to sleep and food that will sustain you, and if you find it very, very disagreeable, you may be assured that it is still worse in the Ozarks. I shall expect you both August 20.

Let me know exactly when you are to arrive so that I can meet you and convey you to Duck Island. My secretary, Miss Mary Frances Hadrich, 601 Adams Building, who takes care of every detail when I am absent, will be glad to assist you in any arrangement that will add to your comfort. Mrs. Osborn will be camping near at hand, and I hope you will see a great deal of her.

Yours Cordially,

Chase S. Osborn

Dear Miss Brunt,

A tragedy in my family in the form of a threatened fatal or worse than fatal influence compels me to cancel all invitations to my camp for this season. This is painful to me in your case and Miss Osawa's, and I even fear and hope you also will be disappointed. It is an unforeseen turn of the Fates. Another year I hope to run my camp as usual and have my friends about me. And I shall not be satisfied until you have come.

All of your letters and your anticipations terminating for the time in disappointment would make me hate Heaven if anything could. I am just taking my bitter drafts and shall have to ask you to swallow yours for the time being.

Please do not misunderstand me in the proposition that if you and Miss Osawa will undertake a trip and vacation anywhere as my guests, I will most happily meet all expenses. I suggest you go on your Mississippi trip, and with all my powers of insistence, I hope you will send me the bills because you know you are my guests now. This proposal seems neither rude nor impossible. Please do this.

Most Sincerely Yours,

Chase S. Osborn

My Dear Miss Brunt,

Please read "illness" instead of "influence" in Governor Osborn's letter to you from Duck Island, August 3. I did not catch the typographical error until the letter had been mailed. It was sent up from camp.

Since then, Governor Osborn has been in town for a few hours and has written you in reply to your letter of July 26. He is keenly disappointed and deeply distressed by the necessity for canceling for this season the invitation to Duck Island. In fact, I do not know when anything has troubled him more. He will not be content until another season has permitted a visit from you and Miss Osawa, and we shall all simply look upon it as postponed.

Yours Very Sincerely,

M.F. Hadrich

Secretary

My Dear Miss Brunt,

I love your letter and the questions you ask. And I wish you could know my pain at not having you and Miss Osawa here at this time, but you are surely going to come some time.

I wish that you were coming in middys and knickers. That would be just the thing. And when you do come sometime, those are the uniforms. You could not wear ruder clothing than would fit this rugged land. The only thing one who knows the country expects to do up here is to keep his body clean, and everybody does that now. Clothes do not count. I meant to have you stay at least a month or longer, but the destinies have determined otherwise now. Very evidently, from what you say of your walk at dawn, you will fit this country perfectly.

Yours Cordially,

Chase S. Osborn

"Always"

Dear Chase,

 Are you sure the picture on the shelf in your cabin had nothing to do with your surrender? Dear, I had no thought of boldness. I just loved you and belonged to you and stood there thinking it to you as I had thought it over and over again since the first day I saw you. I began belonging to you then, Chase—almost from the first minute. All these years, I have belonged to you, keeping myself back, as I thought, keeping myself all fragrant and molten and lovingly tender for the time when marriage would let me "make delivery." The picture on your shelf was taken for you. The woman in it belongs utterly to you! Her heart and mind and spirit think the same thoughts now as then; her body has an even dearer message for you. My breasts have not been cured of their longing, Chase.

 It was a unique joy to try to take care of the woman's end of things, to set tables, and serve, and sit at the end opposite you, and have you boss me when I didn't do exactly right. I've never been outstandingly domestic, but I could be, for you. But I can darn beautifully, and sew on buttons. And I'd love all your clothes, from your rubber heels to your Stetson's crown—I'd love them all into wholeness and cleanness, and as for you inside them! You'd have to boss me off! I want to come and play and work with you for you. (Sleep with you, too!!!!) And it's more than for my own sake, dearest. It is not wise to live alone as one grows older. Companionship would do more for you than you can know—loving companionship. I was born

to spend my days in the making of your happiness.
You say "impossible," but my heart keeps saying
still, "The day will come." The courses of our lives
have turned toward each other slowly—no?

Stella

Dear Chase,

I am unable to be ashamed or sorry for our dear time of utter understanding and acceptance. I will not have it called a slipping or an error, even a flagrant error. It was sweet and proper—fitting—perfect—all-beautiful—and I shall be proud and joyous and at peace because of it forever! It was not marriage? I am not so sure. It had deep meaning for us both. It was the outgrowth of the years of our affection, the next step in our constant growing closer to each other. Dear, there was too much of a drawing to each other to let us live our lives apart. Lines that are not absolutely parallel cannot be kept from convergence if drawn out long enough. Passion brings lives together at sharp angles, quickly to merge and quickly to separate. Love keeps lives apart so that they run along together, side by side, like a true pair, both before and after union. Union is dear and right.

What matters if you are not my "husband." You are the nearest to a husband I have ever had. I have given my vow to God to hold you so, unto and through death. No, you are not my husband; you are much more than merely that to me. After all, "husband" is only a term authorized by law, cancellable by law or death. The term is applicable to a man married to a woman while both were drunk or wild with a rank passion; applicable to a man married by a woman who marries for need of food—and—home—and luxury—providing powers, has found it sensible to trade her body; applicable to one who marries a girl three days before he flies to Europe, and is at once divorced; applicable to men whose wives have murdered them.

I do not grieve inconsolably because I cannot call you by a name that means so little in this year of the world. Who knows exactly in these days just what the word is worth? The laws themselves have robbed it of its meaning. It is part of an orderly arrangement whereby society tries to keep track of its property rights and to keep prostitution limited. It is orderly and right. And yet—we love each other so truly and tenderly—so dearly and abidingly. God meant love to be so. It is the closing of the circle, the last arc that makes the full sweep of perfection. No one was hurt. So long as it hurts no one, so long as we ourselves are not hurt. Whatever you are to me, whatever I am to you, there is a union that is more than legal marriage, and with me, the ceremony shall be binding till I die.

Only dear, we must avoid all double-dealings. Neither of us can be happy, as you say, entangled among tricks and disguises. Let us continue to be friends as we have been for all these years; we have not changed. Write to me as you have through all these years—a little oftener than for the first four of them, about as we have written this last happy year. And I will write to you as always, not too often. Perhaps a dozen times a year?

Stella

Dear Stella,

So, you heard I am hard to live with.
Anybody whom I wish can live with me
forever if they are two things: First, they
must be honest. You are. Next, they must
not fight me. You would have too much
sense than that.

You tempt me by saying maybe you
could not abide me long? Maybe not?
Some do. No one ever leaves me who
works with or for me. I have people for
a quarter of a century to decades. I have
always employed labor and have never
had a strike or a moment's trouble. My
men stay with me forever.

Miss Hadrich was my intiMATE
secretary for 35 years—stayed much too
long. Cooks and men have been with me
for a quarter of a century. So, you might
find me just.

I know I am "strong" going. Also,
I have never lost a friend who did not
come back, and seldom they go away
at all. How about my standing in the
Sault? I have lived there almost a half-
century and my standing is all one could
ask anywhere. In fact, they honor me
far beyond my desserts, as YOU also do.
I have never deserted a friend. In the
case of Mrs. Jones Osborn, she left me
repeatedly, but I NEVER left her.

As to my pursuit of women, you are
as attractive a girl as ever I knew (most
so) and see how I fought you off. It was
for your own good as I saw it. Now I
have surrendered. We can lie together in

289

bed—undressed—so near and warm and
vital and sweet and passionate and all
purest holy body for you ARE MY WIFE
from God.

Lovingly Forever Your Friend,

Chase

Dear Chase,

We have been growing in love for each other for enough years to understand, to know, to believe that we shall dearly love each other until we shall both die. Love binds us now, knits us; we two are truly one, heart and body, mind, and spirit. We have each other, in unflagging and imperishable love—forever.

Always one of the pillows on my bed has been your pillow, but now I know exactly which one is yours; and you are there each night and morning as before, only with a dear difference. No longer a foolish dream for which you scold me—but a dear memory and a glowing hope. My breast dreams that it is a pillow for your beloved head. I will make up to you in tenderness all that the years behind or the years ahead may rob you of. Dearest, dearest!

One must have love, or life goes grey. George should be happy that you have me—he should be glad. George is your son. He has to do what you tell him. He could be your ambassador. I know we'd like each other. Perhaps George thinks I'm a siren. He said something in his letter about not being a radical—does he think I am one? Please tell him if he comes to see you, or when you see him that I like him very much and would like very much to know him. Tell him I'm a very dangerous person so far as you are concerned, and that, if he has any filial affection, for your sake, he should do some spying on the attacking army!

My life begins and ends in you. I am not Stella any more, Chase—only the Stella-part of you.

We should not have to live apart.

Stella

"Love is Here to Stay"

Dear Chase,

Spring makes me feel very young. Does it you? I came across a prescription against old age the other day. It was Roger Bacon's! He suggested listening to good music, listening to stimulating conversation, wearing your best clothes, and talking with pretty girls. Evidently, his recipe was intended for you, not me. About the fourth ingredient, I'm afraid I'm hardly either pretty or a girl anymore, and you can't talk to me; but I am young enough to have blood that sings for you like all the birds in the spring, and we can talk with the sign-language of our pens, so perhaps we can help each other to cheat the years a little.

You must not think me too near perfect, Chase. I might come to live with you someday and have to dispel your illusion painfully. There are many things about me that may try your patience, even in letters—lapses in attention and memory; displays of ignorance; streaks of stupidity; and some of them are past curing. It is good to feel so sure of forgiving and being forgiven, and so perfect that we shall both be trying not to need forgiveness. If we don't be careful, Chase, we'll be making each other over into a new being, after all —a cross between a diplomat and angel! Between the two of us, we're going to create a great deal of happiness for ourselves and for every life we touch. I know that I care more for everyone because of you.

My life has always had two currents—to you!—and to writing.

Stella

* I was wearing the blue dress I wore when we met to exchange our vows—wearing it for the first time since. Always I thought of you, loving you, trying to be worthy. I shall love my blue dress always.

Dear Stella,

I do not marry for a day. You are my God-given wife forever. There is all that is right and happy in our relation now. You are my bride and ought to be in my arms this moment. I am so sorry I was not stronger when we were wed by Jehovah. Darling, you came so fully and so completely. As you were in my arms, I was nearer bliss than ever before. It was the perfection of rhapsodic love. I have surrendered to you completely, and you shall have to protect me. For now, I am the weak one as the man always is when he gives in. If it were possible, I would marry you and espouse you. But that is impossible and maybe for the best. No act could add to our perfect love or the divinity and the sublimity of it.

Please come to me when it is safe for you to do so and when you would ENJOY doing so. There are not so many years left. I fought against the selfishness of it for a long time. NOW I am yours, and you are mine. Passion is the smallest part of it all, but we do like the love word better than before. I salute you and fondle you and kiss you from your brow to your toes with a special sweetness for your lips and a long caress of your sacred holy of holies. My loved one. My bride.

Come closer and closer and closer and melt into my being.

Chase

"It Had to Be You"

Dear Stella,

One thing you never have taken into consideration, and that is that several other women claim to love me as much as you do. Of course, they do not, and most of them are trying to get what LITTLE I have. Mamwolves are always sex-hunting. They know and read certain marks that are sure signs and act accordingly. They get to be experts in determining if a woman has had "experience." Even I think I can tell, and I have never pursued a woman in my life.

Biggest thought I have ever had about you is that I KNOW you are honest and not designing and selfish. I cannot start a harem even of honest women who would be my wives or "mistresses." Of course, you would never have been my mistress, but you said you would be exactly that and in those words. That did not fool me at all, and it led the way to the "Lansing experiment." As to mistresses, the entire scheme is a damned fraud on women, and any woman ought to know it. You tried it. Men use women as vehicles of passion and then drop them when a new model comes out. The woman being the custodian of all the jewels, will be the only loser. But, sure as the devil, if we were together up to the time I could not, I fear you would not prevent me from seducing you if you could now call it that. Otherwise, I would try my best to have you come to Duck Island instead of Manitoulin. And if you came, it would be "all off," so we MUST NOT??? I'm trying to be decent and square, and so are you.

Faithfully Your Friend,

Chase

Dear Chase,

When you wrote as you did, it troubled me. I had called out to you in a crisis—weakly, foolishly, and yet with some vague hope that it might make you shake yourself free. It was not a call for you to come any way. May not one in torture cry out his suffering? But you wrote that was the "siren way" and that there was no chance that you could break loose. For a while, it seemed as though your answer was an offer only to take advantage of my situation.

All this, weighs on my mind. You know the scales that the world keeps for weighing men and the special standards that men require of their own sex. I know that by the measure of the average man, and of men as a group, I am fair game; that few men would think one whit the less of you for any advantage you might take of my attachment—and few women. If you had been weak that way, you would have made a dozen surrenders in these long barren years, to a dozen of all these women who have been attracted to you. You have a way with women, Chase, whether you mean to or not; you appeal to them, draw them; it is in your letters and in your cards.

I haven't any right to expect you to treat me as if I were an untouched girl—and yet, somehow, that is what I want from you, what I am trying to deserve. I am trying to be my finest and best, Chase, but I do not want to be so painfully virtuous for the mere pride of being so.

Stella

Dear Stella,

You who are so able and sensitive, and in some things sensible, must know that I cannot, Dear Stella, and no one can answer such a remarkable "book letter" as you for the autumnal equinox. It might be approached personally in conversation and discussion but not in such a letter as I feel I must write. Then there are the subtlest interpretations to be made. Perhaps you can get an idea of my attitude when I tell you that it even does not irk me to have you state for the nth time that you might have married sundry persons if it had not been for your love for me as if I am responsible for that. Maybe it may be or have been an invention and an intervention of Providence to keep you from mooring to a rotten dock. Better love purposely and purposelessly as you do than to love where it would breed trouble and better to love an idea or an ideal or me than not to love at all. But how futile in the ordinary way your love for me.

Usually, love means home and marriage and children and car and food and a lot of ordinary and extra things. Your love for me can mean none of these things. If it keeps you from scattering all right. You ask if I care if you love me; if I wish you to? That is beyond me. I have not asked you to. For your sake, as I saw it, I have treated you brutally. I have refused to see you or have you near me. All this could have been different and sweet if we could have been SAFE friends. Always you think and write of its bearing upon you and do not seem to realize me and my situation. There are so many in Heaven whom I have loved; my mother; and others that I shall under God do nothing to you or anyone that shall have them look down in shame and pain. Then I have had public honors I ought to try to be worthy of. And many have named babies for me, and that is a sacred responsibility. All these things are beside you. As to you, I think too much of you to abuse you, and if you came too near me too often, I MIGHT do that. I do not wish and cannot afford to have a mistress. You are too excellent in my esteem to think of as one. And yet, that is what you potentially suggest all the time.

Best thing in your letter is you say you are well in body and mind—your torso shows attractively in one of the Kodaks. Thanks.

Your Friend Indeed,

Chase

Dear Chase,

Dear Love, the secret way in life is harder than the open. Life, at its simplest, is hard enough and gives rise to overmuch misunderstanding. Lover, our way together cannot be easy—There are great troubles on every side—we must go very carefully—Perhaps, dearest, a woman is a bit like a horse or a dog in having instincts which seem nervous and fussy but are to be trusted when the way leads through the dark. My fear is part of our protection—if we are to proceed in secrecy. I long for the open, the happy unafraid! I do not know—now—what is best. Aren't we a family, too? You say that it is impossible for me ever to be your wife. And I say it is impossible for me ever to be your mistress.

Guess there's nothing left except for me to be your sweetheart!—all the days of my life: all my life's love and respect and devotion, my one sweetheart.

Faithfully, but as always.

Stella

p.s. Someday, will you tell me, in your beloved, plain Anglo-Saxon, the stark meaning of the Latin word "impossible?"

Dear Stella,

YOU pursued me like a hunted animal for seven years. I thought I was hooked, but it is impossible legally because my marriage is the only marriage that is recognized or defined. You at once reacted against the entire situation. You "divorced" me as fully as you "married" me to use your terms.

I think I am beginning to understand you. A sex urge comes to you, and you spill over, and you offered—more than once—to be my mistress. I would not accept or allow it. And I will not do so NOW. You say you did not suggest such a thing, but then you remembered and repeated the offer.

Again, and ever I am,

Chase

"When I Lost You"

Dear Stella,

You say you love me. You don't, and yet you do. You love yourself as you should, and yourself is so wonderful and so complex that you do not know your own self. If you were near to me, you would not find me wonderful nor yet ideal only as you kept your eyes closed as to me and open as to the strange population of your own BEING.

Spring brings to you a special surge of sex and life passion, and then you think of its or their realization, and you think of the purest and safest avenues. Those are distant and worn smooth by time, and the rut can be followed and do danger or the minimum of risk taken. Please try to understand this. You even say you do not know how anybody can love anyone less able than they are. That is a personal vanity. And how can you measure so-called ability? College boys down here starve, and men who cannot sing their own names have Rolls-Royce cars. Not that having is a measure of ability. Beazel says success is happiness, and there he stops. I say it is, too, and that the only way one can be happy is to build a fire of joy in another heart and warm at it as girls inflate their skirts over a warm air furnace and men back up to a blaze or a base-burner.

You speak of going to the convocation at Michigan State College and telling the girls you love me, etc. I have no objection to either. There is but happiness in the way we love even if it is long-distance platonic and only such because it is long distance. For as you say at times, "you are an answering woman." I am still able to be an "answering man." Not for long, but now. And if you go to the convocation, I shall probably fall down and disappoint you, which might be a good thing to do. I am ever expecting anyhow to fall down; to fail, but up to now, I have muddled thru or gotten thru somehow.

Your Pateraurelius,

Chase

Dearest Chase,

This morning I am up and dressed and allowed to walk to the sun porch and back. A man in the sun porch who looked a bit like you, so far as the crown of his head was concerned, and the rest of his face was buried behind a newspaper, so I fancied something happy for a minute, although I knew it couldn't be.

Chase, dear, I'm thinking you must either be in California or withdrawn into yourself in terrible distress. You can't be silent toward me, while I'm not well, just to break me of my caring for you. You can't. I know you too well now. I shall be glad to have your letter when it comes.

Really, Chase dear, I could see you often now. Once every spring, once every fall, as you go north or south, spending a happy week-end with you, a happy week-end together as in Lansing, only there need never again be another time like that Friday night. Our times together could be all Sunday mornings, all quiet happiness. All the storm of longing passed once and for all. Let me at least come to know you as the closest of friends—trust me, command me.

Stella

Dear Stella,

I am NOT to answer your astounding
and endless letters, DEAR STELLA, they
are art and heart, and all that, but to
persist in them, only nourishes the
insanity of impossibility. If you will allow
me, I shall be your loving friend. But
the way you go and do makes it and you
dangerous. We NEVER shall live together.
If it were a sane possibility, I would not
write thus. You with goiter and one lung
and rabid sex hunger and me with one
foot in the grave and other on the edge
and rheumatism and approaching sex
death—the whole idea is preposterous to
the point of insanity. If you cannot see
this as I do, you are unworthy of yourself
and the friends who have honored you
and the beautiful world you have made
for yourself, as you graphically describe.

I shall do my best to be worthy of you by
saving you.

Chase

Dear Chase,

I try to answer your letter and tear up what I write. It is all so complicated. Only one thing is always clear.

If we are the finest friends, we are in need of no disguise? We have a subtle, delicate way to steer to keep out of duplicity and keep in ways that are quiet and unadvertised because they are our own. I think I see the way for us, clear and fine and right and pure, and all that the way of two should be. Let us go on as we have gone, in open friendship under the open sky. Our friendship is known and respected. All of my friends know of our friendship that it is fine and fearless, unwaveringly deep and loyal.

If we have come to be to each other more than friends, that is between you and me. I know its beauty and its rightness, things being as they are. Let our letters go on as before, often enough, but never too often, to Miss Stella Lee Brunt from her good friend ex-Governor Osborn. Let us be proud of them. Let us go on as always, having nothing to hide. For the rest, for the nearness and dearness that belongs to you and to me alone—it is of the things the world has no need to share.

Stella

Dear Stella,

The fact is that if our friendship cannot be placed upon a PROPER basis and KEPT there, it ought to end so far as correspondence is concerned. It appears from your confusion and feelings to be a crazy affair anyhow. Perhaps again, it is PROVIDENCE working in a mysterious and helpful manner.

I have the kindest possible feeling for you, but evidently, I do not feel as you do. My plans at the time appeared entirely all right to me, but you wrecked them. I expect NOT to be here at Christmas. It is all a disillusionment????

Hope to get to Duck Island. Due at state convention about two weeks after the primary whether I win or lose. Things as you know look good. Your letter is nice but thoughtlessly long. Glad you got the A.

Faithfully and Affectionately Your Friend,

Chase

Dear Stella,

One would think I was the trapper when I even as late as Christmas, warned you not to come. It would be far better if you would just forget I am on earth. I mean, BETTER FOR YOU. When I am gone, you can take "Possum Poke" and your mother and do what shall make you happy. It is to be a pleasing thing to me also BOTH BEFORE AND AFTER! Now please do not have another fit when you read this. I simply do not know what you want. And are not satisfied when you "get it." THERE CAN NEVER BE A DIVORCE. I made that directly and honestly clear. And there ought NOT TO BE any other arrangement. When you are sex normal, you have sense. When you are sex hungry, you have NO SENSE. You have stirred up the whole situation.

I was happy and getting along, and you "burgled" me. I shall love you as long as I live if you do not drive me mad with your tempest of inconsistent words. I shall have to restore the old status.

Please do not change your mind for I would not have you here, as secretary, or any capacity would only make endless trouble!!

Please DO NOT come to Detroit Feb. 25 or 26 when I am there. Much better for you!

Chase

"How about Me?"

My Dearest Friend,

I'm not going to write about nothing in particular—just to talk to you. Since your eyesight—and the evenness of your disposition mean more to me than my time; and since, too, it is bad enough to have the obstacle of hundreds of miles of distance to hinder our conversation without having unreadable writing to add to the difficulty; —I am going to type out the rest of the pencil scrawling for you. I hope you haven't given up in discouragement before you got to this point.

One of the original Whimsies—is in town this year, working for her master's degree in philosophy. That is Doris Gracey. We eat together at a students' boarding house (thirteen meals for six dollars!); and I get modern, medieval, and ancient philosophy with every other mouthful. My course is just beginning with Heraclitus, Thomas Aquinas, and Francis Bacon; and a good deal of Wenley. It is rather fun. Doris is a real Phi Beta Kappa who mentions the society at least once a week, wears her pin frequently, and is as sure of her opinions, their uniqueness and their exclusive claim to being the best, as I have been at several stages in my career. Interesting girl! Her mother died when she was three; her father when she was sixteen, leaving her a house and a housekeeper in Marietta, Ohio, a farm nearby, and some stocks with coupons on them to be clipped occasionally. She still has all these, plus a college education, an Airedale called Peter, also two trips to Europe. Having never had an ungratified wish in her life, so far as I can determine, and being perpetually in the state of being thrilled by everything, she thinks she believes in the essential tragedy of human life. Funny girl! Although her father was a Democrat, she became a Republican at the age of two or three because someone gave her a McKinley flag to wave and taught her to say "Yay, McKinley!" Today she told me that she gave up Christianity at the age of seven because her grandmother told her that her pet chickens couldn't go to Heaven with her. She preferred to go with her chickens rather than with her grandma! She will not hear anything good about the English because there happens to have been some Irish blood in one of her remote forebears and she adores everything Irish. Doris is the most interesting combination of foolish prejudice and excellent brain that I have ever known. Another of her deficits: she is twenty-eight years old and hasn't, I'm sure, ever thought twice about any man. She LOVES ideas. It is so much happier to be able to love both! Doris seems only half a human being to me, somehow. But I do like her! We're going to join the Cosmopolitan Club together and attend the concert series with each other.

All this activity is in prospect. Saturday night the Cowdens had half a dozen of the nicest possible, and most interesting young women over to dinner. I was there; but felt somehow "out of it." All but one of us were ex-Whimsies. I begin to feel older and not so sure of things as the very young and very brilliant and very sure-of-themselves. I _care_ too much about too many things; I'm sentimental perhaps, too sentimental to think clearly. My judgments get all gummed up somehow.

Writing that essay took me clear out of the world for a week or two. It's gone now. I'm glad. But my thrill with it has gone, too, since I've thought it over. I actually thought it was splendid, for a while, the best I had ever done! I am rather tired tonight. Been over-doing. Need to be bossed into not working hard. You know I haven't had a spare

minute since I came to Ann Arbor. Worked foolishly
hard on the essay—but don't know how else to
work! Had to start out in life that way to get
anywhere; now can't stop. Can't teach an old dog
new tricks! This afternoon I stayed home from the
office and tried to sleep. I will make up the time tomorrow. My work is fascinating at the office.

I still like Woody's ideas, Chase. I like them
thoroughly. They have made me actually think
of going into political science. You know that
our machinery of government is in pretty bad
shape, that it does need repair—some of it, even
scrapping. That's what would be fascinating in the
study of political science: to discover the essential
purposes of institutions, wherein they are falling
short, what would put them back into alignment.
That would be fine hard work, fun! Really, I got a
tremendous lot out of those books of his. Have
you read them? (his Literary and Political Papers
and Addresses). Would you like to have my copies
to look over? Sometimes I've marked "CSO" along
the margin! What he says so often, to me, points
straight at you. Of course, I may be prejudiced.

There was one whole day while I was in the
trance of trying to express my thoughts on his
thoughts, that I didn't even think of you, except
when it was time to look for letters. Funny, how I
look for what I don't expect! This summer has got
me into a bad habit that I am even more sensible
than now, perhaps you will think it permissible
to write a little oftener, perhaps once a month
instead of once every three. Letters are such good
company. Some above others. Mrs. Shy writes: "My
own dear Girl;" Florence Fuller, in Lansing, says
"Darling Stella; violet-like Nona, in Washington
begins "Dearest Stella;" and Roger Thomas, getting
his Ph.D. at Harvard sends two cards to remind
me that he would like a letter. I like them all, very

much, and am very happy to find a word from them tucked in between the bannister rails at the foot of the stairs. But there is always another letter I look for besides. If there wasn't a paper with possible news of you, I don't know what I'd do.

Your note came this afternoon. I found it, between the railings, as I went out to supper. How can I ever give you back some of the happiness you give me! It is almost more than I can bear. All the hard things in my life are more than paid for by that one note from you.

Now we must get these dogs straight. Red Jim is one of the puppies, then. And Nick is one of them, too? I dreamed of those dogs, last night! At least there were puppies in one dream. They began as five baby chicks that I was carrying to Mrs. Shy's; and ended as puppies, finally dwindling down to one, as things will do in dreams; and Mrs. Shy wasn't pleased even to have that one brought home!

The other day, I came upon a book called, well, something about genealogies of the "first families of America." I looked for you, and there you were! Even if I were a radical and hated first families on principle, I should like them very much better, having found you listed among them! There should be all possibilities of you going on down into the coming generations. And Chasie is the only one in the third generation who carries your name on, isn't he? You should have had at least a half a dozen grandsons bearing your name.

And now I suppose I've been preaching a small sermon to something I think a part of Chase Osborn that isn't him at all! You know, though, Chase, there isn't even an implied criticism in that sermon. Something has happened to me this year. I'm completely unable to find a thing that needs even improvement in you! Isn't that a desperate situation to have fallen into? And I had such a good collection of human failings for you before! You'll have to do something, talk a lot and reveal yourself, shock my eyes open again. This will never do at all! Of course, you've one BIG fault: You're so hard to really get to know! You're so hard to get to really understand! One knows you are fine and big the first word you speak, but it takes so long to really get to realize the whole big news and fineness of you. Of course, that is the BIG fault with even such things as great truths: easy to recognize, needing a lifetime to appreciate. Now, isn't that a nice compliment? Something bigger than a compliment. I mean it to be.

There was one thing you said once about George being finer than you, that I've wanted to argue about ever since. I DON'T BELIEVE IT! You know what is in your own mind. but you don't know what is in his! I doubt if he tells you everything, any more than you told him what was in yours! George may have a higher polish of a certain kind, the polish of his fine alma mater and his DEKS, and, I am sure, an innate fineness of his own; but there is a fineness in you that cannot be surpassed, Chase. I back you against all comers!

People can misunderstand self-effacement for self-sufficiency, think you don't want affection rather than the truth that you won't see yourself deserving of it. I thought you so once!—for a while; or at least wondered if you weren't so. And everybody isn't a stubborn "cuss" like me, to hang on till the bitter truth is out—or discovered not to be. You know you must allow people to think that you're at least a tiny bit dependent on them—even if you aren't at all!—just to make their affection seem a useful thing.

You are always to keep anything I write, if you want to, even when what I write exposes me at my worst. I wish you had kept all the letters I ever wrote you, though I know how crazy and wild and silly some of them were. You are nice not to have kept them. And yet, I wish you had. Someone would have found them someday and learned a little of how fine a man you are. I had rather you were known to be what you are than that I should be given credit for being what I am not.

You are nice to insist on paying me for what work I do for you. I am glad that you believe I want to do it only for love of you; glad that you have common sense beyond mine. I see now what you see plainly; that you could not accept my labor at all unless you paid for it. I am willing. You shall pay me whatever is the current pay for anything I do. And now, please let me work with you often, whenever you can manage it?

My pictures are coming from Hamilton this week. I can hardly wait till they come. There are only two of them I really like—one a little boy, sunning on the top of a hill against a blue sky; and the other a little etching of a chapel in Paris. There's one, too big, with grand brown-gold sails, fishing boats on the coast of France; a Japanese print, interesting but not attractive; and an etching by an artist I met in New York. When I get them up, and get the cover for my trunk which Mrs. Bliss is going to help me make, I'll have a hyper-thrill. I do like my house! And imagine making over a trunk—which has given one the blues to have to live in it every bit of one's life, making it over, with a bit of padding on top, and a frill around three sides, to bring a little joy! I think life should be only that, shouldn't it, my dear one!—not wishing for something that is not and believing one could be happy if that something only could be, but just to take the raw material as it comes, and out of that, just that, make as much as possible of beauty and happiness. I love my little house; I don't believe anyone could be happier than I am.

About Christmas, for instance. I'd like to buy you a bow tie, for one thing: a black bow tie, warranted to stay in place for 729 days in a row. Do you suppose I could buy you a tie? It's heaps more respectable a gift than a towel! Or sleeve-holders, or garters, and such. I don't want to send you books and books and books—and mostly books you don't exactly want. Of course, the tie might be that, too! Or I might try a picture that you don't exactly want, for a change? Lots more to say to you—in December! It is very hard not ever to see you, hard not to be able to write to you often and not to hear from you often. But I don't know any sacrifice that you wouldn't be worth! Yes, sir—- and I'm going on thirty-four years old.

One of two things, or both, I would like from you for Christmas, besides the answer to my next letter. That you think of once, on Christmas morning, and wish I could go walking across the fields with you; and that you rake up some kind of a job to do that I can help you with! Please? Please!

Once upon a time there was a French girl who lived at Newberry, who didn't like lots of American dishes. She was invited once to spend a week with some American friends. They had pumpkin pie for dessert the first night; she could hardly bear to eat it; but, just to be polite, when they asked if she liked pumpkin pie, she said she liked it very much, that this was unusually nice. The next night her hostess brought on a beautiful cake, which made Marinette's mouth water; but also, alas, another pumpkin pie, saying, "You liked the pie so much last night, that I baked another one tonight on purpose for you!" Marinette said she'd never be polite again.

SO, when I ask you as I ask you now, "Do you really LIKE a long letter like this?" "Are you POSITIVE that it doesn't bore you to tears? I could talk to you forever, I'm afraid. Wish you were here to defend yourself! Even to return the onslaught!

Did you have a big storm last night, Thursday? Is there anything bigger than a whale? If there is, I guess this letter's one.

Bless you, my dear—God give you many years, and work worthy of your powers to crowd them with—and a little that I may help you. I don't really believe in God, and yet I pray to him for all fine things to come to you.

It's nine-thirty, dear Chase. If wishes were aero-planes, I'd be in Arizona tonight!

Your faithful friend,

Stella

p.s. You'll be in Battle Creek this week. If I knew where you were to be staying, I'd be tempted to write you a little note to meet you on your arrival. Oh, just for fun! Perhaps it's just as well. After all, I've promised only to write you only according to schedule. But I might address an envelope to you with nothing in it but anything you wanted to imagine there? I hope your delegation was successful in its aim; and I hope you have not come home unduly tired. Tell me when you expect to break up camp. And where, and on what dates, you expect to speak. I promise not to turn up anywhere unexpectedly; that would not be either kind or fair; but I would like to know what corner of the world you're holding down while you're on your way south.

p.p.s. Tell me about Little Duck: it is built of logs, of course. Filled in with what? Fireplace? How many rooms? Not more than two I hope. Do you keep it in "literary disarray?" Draw me a picture like stage directions, please. Windows look out upon...? What do you do on rainy days? What do you do of an evening?

Wildest Stella,

You make everything harder than
it is. I know what I am hungry for
and what you are. And I know it is
IMPOSSIBLE. George is here. I showed
him your letter. Maybe he shall tell
you his reaction if you do not get away
before he goes to Ann Arbor, which may
never be. But he said he would like to
call on you. And when he saw your last
snap, he said you are better looking all
the time. If you write George much, his
wife shall appear!

I have seven chicks and twelve grand
ones and a thousand godchicks and no
end of dogs. Even the dogs know that
you <u>cannot</u> come and stroke my fevered
brow. All that tenderness shall have to
come in hell where I think I'm going to
have a ringside seat.

As to my heart, you hurt it more
than anyone else for when I get to a
point of thinking we can be SAFETY
first friends. You load all kind of tear
bombs and gas and smoke screens and
heavy shrapnel. And you come at me
with submarines and dirigible blimps and
one-o-planes and two-o-planes and horse
and feet. And all this when I had actually
planned how you might come safely to
this rude place in the wilderness where
the loon shrieks at night and the wild,
fierce gulls threaten me ala Prometheus.
Also, there are herrings running like
miniature sharks. But all these could not
hold your foolishness down when it is in
high run. BUT Dear Stella Star, do read
your letters after you write? They sound

goofy. And do allow me to be Your Real
Friend—

Esbjerne (Osborn)

    P.S. George has seen all your letters.
He is interested in our friendship, as he
knows my sense of it. My heart acts up,
but that is a sign also of life. When it
does not, I shall indeed be finished. And
it does not worry me a bit. If I had you,
it would not, and I would not last two
weeks. So that's another good reason.

YOUR FRIEND,

Chase

Dear Chase,

I do so want to see you. Must it always be IMPOSSIBLE? It seems unnecessarily hard, unnecessarily precautious like the practice of the early church fathers who forbade the marriage of third cousins in order to be sure that second cousins should not. We are not children. I would die rather than hurt your honor or your self-respect. George understands. Do not say "impossible." Some safe and proper way can be made, George knowing. Sometime when he is with you could you not let me come? I wish it could be for a month, so that I could see you every day, as you go through the ordinary small affairs of living and meet the ordinary challenges of the day, so that every shred of dream and illusion might fall away from my affection for you, that I might see clearly for once you by yourself and fasten my affection unquestionably there. But it would do my life good to see you only an hour, Chase; only five minutes. If you still think you cannot, one of these days I shall be writing George and asking him to help me. It is hard for me to bear, this never seeing you, when you are not as strong as you have been. I cannot stand it always.

When, reporting to my Hamilton doctor this summer, I told him that I had not ceased to care for you, he shook his head and said that I was rather the kind of woman who should marry a man younger than herself. He was right, of course; but, unfortunately, only a part of me is that kind of woman; and the other and finer and strong side inclines in the contrary direction. The doctor shook his head, too, at Yuki's scheme to get me to forget you; he said that was the worst possible plan—the way to cure me was to let me see you often, when actuality would scare the dream away.

You see, it is really doctor's orders that I see you. To disprove his statement is an added reason for my wanting to come. He thought that you were canny not to let me. Perhaps it is only the logical thing, Chase, to put my conviction to the crucial test. I will fight hard to grow well and strong in body and mind, for your sake. I have tremendous ideals for the person I would have caring for tremendous you! And I have tremendous ideals for you—activity that will weigh substantially at least till you are eighty. So, don't you, please, take any chances with your heart or your constitution in that icy water, will you? Please be good and set me a good example! I love you very much. Dear Chase! I have never known the day I liked you less than on any day before.

God keep you well—goodnight.

Stella

"They Can't Take that Away from Me"

Dear Stella,

Do you think it easy for me to take the position I have in reply and response to your arguments and dictum? Your statements are irrefutable in a sense. I shall never cease TO LOVE YOU. And there shall be a growth of that love. There must be no deceptions, no dual personalities, nothing to hide, and nothing to explain. The ancient Chinese adage is right in morals and policy: IF YOU DO NOT, YOU CANNOT BE CAUGHT. I feel a nobility and a lofty sense of being right that compensates for the loss of the baser, but sweet things.

My prayer is to love you and help you and not to harm you. Please to discharge your sex mania and be motivated ALL THE TIME by your nobler self in which you are as the evening and morning skies in purity.

Lovingly Yours,

Chase

Dearest,

I have hated every kind of deception; but henceforth I know that your life and mine as they may touch each other is the affair of no one but ourselves. We must somehow see each other oftener now—-oftener than three years! Perhaps if some day we may spend all our days together it will be better that we have not left too much till then. Don't care if you don't care. I do! I want you to go through life with me for many years. Wish you might companion me into my sixties. I want to add and add to your life, never to subtract from it. This way perhaps, anyway at the beginning, I can let us have each other without fear. If we were together all the time, I'm afraid I'd be afraid about it all the time.

Stella

Dear Stella,

OUR prayers are answered. I have asked God to show me how to help you and not to harm you. There is LYRIC LOVE, and there is LETHAL LOVE. The former is of God and HIS harmonies. The latter is of the devil, all hellish and destructive. You have played with that, and you are still doing so. It shall kill you. It would murder me. I do not count. YOU DO. To my mind, love helps and cares and comforts and is not just an orgasm of passion. I do not wish to go back on a single thing that is right and good. In a little time, if I lived, you would curse me, and when you had killed me a bit sooner than might be, you would hate my memory for permitting it. We can be the most noble and loyal friends.

Always Your Friend,

Chase

Dear Chase,

Passion is a wind blowing where the heart is a desert, it is a burning gust that passes, leaving only a desert as before. But our hearts are in flower for each other—-trees in blossom—that have been blossoming for each other year after year. Passion sweeping through us as a gust of fragrance.

I wanted you badly to be with me in my bed. You were! My arms and all my body said sweet things to you; my heart was happy; and our minds and spirits spoke together. I have heard it said that the intercourse of body is an ugly thing. How false that is! It is only partial knowledge that could say so. To me, the hours in which our bodies lay in loving closeness, are the highest beauty I have ever known. No dream has ever imagined such beauty. Those who say that body love is low—how wrong they are—how better they know—how much they have missed.

Stella

Stella,

I AM TOO OLD FOR YOU. I am tied
to the mast and no thundering forts to
pass and no mines to run. I am as well
as I deserve to be for 69 (near). I shoot
as well as ever. My heart seems to be
"coming back." At least I have been more
careful than usual. And as to means I
have scant to do me for the few years
there are.

You have such priceless values. It is
a crime for you to throw them away in
a cemetery. I have learned to love you,
but it is an unselfish love in every way.
There can be no harm in lightening your
heart with a general love. I think love
abideth in you as the essence of a flower
and blooms in seasons. One moment you
ask me not to write. At the same sensible
instant, you say we must need each
other, not oftener than once a year. But
you expect me to carry all the load of
discipline and restraint. All right; I love
you enough to do it.

I had come to devour your letters.
Now you must only write once a
year. Our love is above and beside the
nourishment of the written word. I
return to the belief that has been host
within me all these years that you
love some self-created ideograph or
monograph or an indeterminate and
immeasurable thing. To permit you to
hunger for anything you call ME is an
idle and unwise and improper weakness
on my part. It is really the God thing.
Just now, you give it my name. Once you
gave it another. Again, you shall name it

someone, something else. This is only an attempt at evaluated analysis.

I greatly desire your happiness but can contribute little to it. I insist on our relation and love being impersonal. It is the only way it can endure and be of any value to either. I AM OLD. MY HEART IS WORN AND WEARY. I love you more than ever, and if it could be, I would be your husband. I am your friend. I am a thousand times more your friend in this refusal than would be by connecting.

Undoubtedly there never has been such a woman as you are. Please direct your genius and your power in worthwhile directions. What I am writing is in obedience to what I interpret as real love—best expressed in the moment when sense and not passion ruled, away with the consuming fire. Come the crystals of purity.

Faithfully Your Friend,

Chase

Dear Chase,

Today, because it was hot and because I am thinned down so that I do not need them, I left off every semblance of a corset, except the brassiere on my "teddies," and so went out to dinner. The wind blows clear through one's flesh and it is good. My body was so quietly proud, dear—because it is yours. My breasts were talking to you dearly. They seemed like live and thinking things, like perhaps, knowing so well what body they are born to snuggle to. Dear, isn't it strange that always it is my breasts that do the calling—until you come—and then all of me is one great cry, for all of you. The softness of your flesh haunts me, dearest. You were so dearly soft to my touch —so sweetly soft. (I thought you might be old—you ought to be!) After I was away from you I discovered one morning how soft a sumac is when it is young—the green stems and the under-side of the leaves—soft as the softest surface in the world. So now I think of two new things—the velvet of the Manitoulin sumac and the dear velvet of you! You are so dear!

I lay down a little while ago to rest, for I have need to. But I could think only of you. I had you lying there with me—you are beside me always. Wonder if we are always to be together in this Siamese-twin fashion, now. How shall I ever get anything done, dearest, if I have no privacy? There's only one thing I aspire to now in this world and that is to love you marvelously. I know I will try to be sensible and wise.

Perhaps it is only this Swiss muslin dress that makes me want you here to hold me closely. It tasted the first kiss we gave each other, in the hall outside my door. It let my breast and your loved hand first meet. It helped betray us to each other—as we were all desire to be betrayed. I am afraid it would do the same today, if you were here.

328

Heat or no; tired out or no. My heart and lips and breasts and body would speak sweetly to you—if you were here.

Stella

Dear Stella,

You gave me a fine choice of letters today. One was all fragrance, and the other was as sassy as one could wish. I liked it best. You have dander. Good! From the way you kick back, I conclude that I was more right than I knew. And it is a new idea of you I exposed. I am host to the vanity that I know you better than you know yourself. And now, as to hating me, go ahead; it is a fine business and will not interfere with my friendship for you in the slightest. All my life, I have been hated and have the best of the bargain because I almost never (I think never) hate. It is a weakness that I do not hate and have not, I suppose.

Flowers everywhere now; in my heart; in the yard; in the fields and woods—everywhere.

Please hate me.

Chase

Dear Chase,

You must not mind my praying as though I were your loving wife. It means nothing except to me—no claim, no expectation, only an expression of my vowed fidelity, only an expression of my happiness and peace. I have given up the thought of wanting to be Stella Brunt Osborn, Chase. No—I shall always want to be or to have been. But I have given up the hope—except that perhaps someday should sickness come...

Stella

Dear Stella,

I am no less your friend than ever,
Dear Stella, and I wish —pray God would
show me how to help you. We must not
correspond. This is imperative. There
was a dangerous, fatal trend and no
temperance in it. Providence intervened
at Lansing.

I showed your letters to my devoted
son George, who has both sense and
sympathy. He agreed in the wisdom of a
major operation—cut all out and off at
once.

I hope deeply, Christmas will not be a
mockery to you.

Chase

Dear Chase,

The germ of the "fatal trend" lay in the things you said to me during the eight times you were with me in New York. If there was no hope of that "one perfect year," why did you say that you had nothing much to offer me? Why did you take pains to assure me of the comparative youthfulness of your "generative organs?" It was then you should have considered my feelings, not now. You have caused me terrible troublings since then— troublings that have been responsible in part for my two illnesses. MY FAITH IN YOU HAS DIED! That death separates us, but only I must suffer.

Goodbye.

Stella Lee Brunt

Dear George Osborn: Since your father has shown you my letters (some of my letters) and asked your advice about his encumbrances, I send this copy of my last letter to him for your information. He has given me the greatest trouble in all my unhappy life. He does not realize. Please do not judge me harshly nor him.

Sincerely,

Stella Brunt

"I've Got You Under My Skin"

Chase Dear,

The big envelope was to have been just a bit of fun between us—a trick-package wrapper within wrapper. I thought you might be led, by all the envelopes within envelopes to expect something very terrible inside, something unforgivably indiscreet. And I guess, after all, there is enough of the indiscreet in it to prevent your being altogether disappointed!

Maybe it's just as well I didn't re-write the note. For if I had, I was going to be wearing the bewitching soft and silky wrap that Yuki sent me to Missouri—to wear when I stole out by moonlight, to play havoc with some man's heart! I have so often wanted you to see me in it, and to enmesh you in its softness, that my visit to you on the porch at "Possum Poke" might have meant more music to us than the frogs and whippoorwills and crickets and all the singing things of the night could make. We should not spoil the beauty of the night, nor the beauty in our hearts; but perhaps, moved by my love for you and radiance it gives me, you might let us pretend for once that we are sweethearts.

You know that the stars are really suns. So, I thought that perhaps because of all the things you have kept from, all your life, because you have denied yourself what most men would have taken, God has given you my love for a special sun to bask in during the last decades of your life. Stars are suns a long way off. But they can give a warm and tender glow; they are a beauty and a comforting assurance. You don't really need a star. You are a sun—yourself and to me. But perhaps even suns like faithful company? I'm really more like a satellite of yours—anyway, our orbits are going to be always parallel, even if they never cross! And if ever the time comes, or the proper accident occurs, I'll cease to be sun or satellite and be just a meteor flashing through space to join and be a part of you!

You tell me that I have my own place in your heart, which is deep happiness for me, Chase. It is the glow of that deep happiness I want to give to you today and always.

Stella

Dear Stella,

You wrote some time ago that you wanted me to fuck you. And I wish to every night and a lot of days. I could sound your sweetest depths right now if there were safety and sense and honor in it. I wish to lie on your snowy teaties ala Solomon and fuck you to the walls of Heaven. Then when we had done and spent ourselves, we would wish the fool-killer had gotten us before. I'd love you for a bride if it were possible.

Lovingly Yours,

Chase

Dear Chase,

A widow once told me things about the difference in the way men talked to a woman who had once been married and the way they talked to women who were not supposed to know things, or who had husbands to protect them. And it does stand to reason that what a man says to women will be based on what is common knowledge between them. I am Miss Brunt. I have never been talked to as women are talked to who have known men. No one else but you have ever been able to think of me from that point of view. Your words came as a shock, and my heart sank. But now, I understand. We cannot help, we who talk as frankly to each other, speaking our whole thought out of our whole, common experience.

You will say, I suppose, that I, on my side, said some shocking things to you. I know. But, Chase dear, it is queer how names can bother a woman. The way I said it, somehow didn't seem so bad! Or at least not so open to question as lacking respect. And you wrote that it wasn't bad at all, but a straight invitation. It makes me smile at women and life. We both meant the same thing and with equally primitive intensity, and yet your way of speaking bothered me.

Professor Strauss said, one day, that women rarely sanctioned the indecent, but were often very much more immoral than men. Shakespeare was often indecent, he said, but never immoral; women writers were often flagrantly the latter, rarely the former. Perhaps that explains my feelings about some of the things you said. But I would have you know, Chase, that so long as you maintain in me the assurance of your respect, no word of yours can even be anything but dear to me.

And I should like you to know, too, as this incident is closing, that just as I never knew love until I knew you, so I never knew what passion was until your words burned themselves into my consciousness.

Stella

Dear Stella,

WHAT YOU NEED and WHAT I'D LIKE is a great and good fuck once in a while. And the time is coming when I cannot "fucktion." Now, however, when you write about your sweet and soft teaties, my old phallus prick gets as big as a tree, and I could make you sing. Once my prick was so big, I could have made you cry out in screams of purest pain of joy. When we fucked we had both worn ourselves with longing until neither was at the best. Your love juice did not flow as free— as it could, and my prick was small as compared even with normal. I wish to kiss your honey box right now and then have you kiss my prick and then thrust it into you to the hilt and jerk and jam ferociously until we both lose ourselves in the finest fuck and COME TOGETHER and then drop listlessly into each other's arms and I get another "hard on" and then at it we would go like a pair of loving fuckers forever. If you plan to come at the Easter vacation, you can come as a writer or a newspaper person or as for some magazine. Then if I am in the condition I am NOW, YOU SHALL BE FUCKED PLENTY!!!!!

Is the word "fuck" repulsive to you or repellant? Tell me. It is not to me. I love it!

Chase

Dear Chase,

It is dangerous, perhaps it is wrong, but my famished heart is feasting on the passion you have given me across a thousand miles. How can I tell you to cease telling me what I have been wanting you to tell me all these years?

But you passed over all the ordinary conversation in my letter, neglected almost every ordinary question, to answer my "suggestion." And even when I asked something in the harmless direction of investments, you twisted a phrase back toward our danger zone and answered only that.

I do not want you to stop saying mad and terrible things to me. Your words are as stark and strong—and as sublime—as the nudes of Michelangelo. I yield to you in glory. All that you are I want. All that I am, I give. I am your mistress in glory.

When one loves, and has confessed, and has been allowed to hover near the loved one, it seems that the body forgets its proper place sometimes—it is a child of spirit that takes all the wisdom and patience of its elders to subdue. Children who have been allowed to play normally, to be normally active, to work off their energy, are easier to manage. Repressed children are likely to break out at times, to make too much noise. My body is a repressed child, Chase. So is yours.

You are a funny boy! You tell me not to let my body talk to yours, but you do not say you are displeased. You only say, "I love your coming closer; only you must stay away." And I must answer, as always, I have answered you, I love you, and I love you, and I love you! And I will come always closer till I come entirely to you in an honest union, or to the last point, this side of stealthy liaison.

There is distance between us. That I will help you keep. But I will not be the one to stop this nearness we have come to in our thoughts and letters. This business of us both wanting to stop, but neither wanting to forego answering reminds me of a law in force in a western state to the effect that at a certain stretch of single track, trains coming toward it from both directions should, at their respective ends, come to a full stop. Neither should proceed until the other should have cleared the single track by a hundred years! Or yards?

Stella

Dear Stella,

DARLING, the sweet, tender, hottest,
juiciest FUCK you sent or BROUGHT was
so exquisitely real. My PHALLUS was
like a peeled pine tree a hundred feet
long. Your honey box was warm and then
hot and flowed mild and honey. I did not
kiss your lips. I sucked them. And then
with mouth to teat, I fucked you, and you
rolled in unison and pressed me until I
thrust you thru and thru. Then we CAME
TOGETHER and then subsided into each
other's arms. I buried myself in your
breasts. My belly was fast to yours. Then
I kissed you from head to foot lingering
at the honey port. Then you did the
same thing to me. Then we fucked again
and repeated. Then we fucked again. In
all, we had four perfectest fucks. And I
wished my phallus might stay IN YOU
forever, making us inseparably ONE.
Solomon never had such a feast nor
such a glory of a FUCK. Language is as
inadequate as it is to build a fire of or
perfume a honey port. You said PLEASE
FUCK ME AGAIN. And I did. And I WILL.
When? Please come some time. Time is of
the essence!

Wish you could be at Duck Island
when I am there??? Then you would
indeed be ravished if I have remaining
strength.

Chase

Dear Chase,

It is going to be very hard for me as it is, my sweetheart. I have played the game with all my cards face up upon the table for the last ten years, in the utterest kind of frankness and openness; to pick them up now, all at once, is impossible—and terribly distasteful. The one thing in my life—-my later life—that I have had to comfort and encourage me has been my absolute honesty with all men.

You make me worry, loved one, remembering last night in the car. Hunger is a terrible thing, and you have starved so long. And I, who love you, love your every touch—love you wildly and tenderly—must put away your hands from touching me. And so, you are gone away again uncaressed, uncomforted—to hunger still, as you never did before, poor, hungry you being driven north again.

Dear, it is a bad thing to be hungry for so many years, then to surrender, and then be given only a crumb. My heart is aching for you. It is not right. It is not fair. It is not good for you. By rights, we two should spend our days together—playing and working and loving side by side. The ravenousness would go away soon. I cannot stand it to have you so needing and denied. Something will have to be done. Chase, perhaps you will have to break free for both our sakes.

Dearest, often enough, I could believe that we were guilty of bad judgment in giving to our hungry bodies the dear taste of each other. The need of you, the being always away from you, has all my mind these days, and I am good for nothing else.

You are my life, it matters not so much how I shall spend it for you so that I give you all that is just and true, give you all, that is the thing. But you must not be so upset by the need of me! I shall break my heart if I so spoil your life. There is so much for you to do.

Our love must not be like a wine that weakens—but cool, clear water from a deep living well. Chase, dear, you wander crying, thirsty, in the desert; while I wait, wasting, longing to have you.

My happiness is yours dear, understanding, steadfast affection is going to drown the other half of my lifelong hunger. Passion does not last—it is the vanishing fraction of a constant relationship. All but that I have of you—the best and the dearest. I ask nothing more. Having known both kinds of love.

Stella

Dear Stella,

I MISS YOU. If it were not for the AFFLATUS, I could almost wish you had never come??? It is like Tantalus letting one down for a sup, then rudely yanking the cup away. But I wish to feel the loss. And I am accustomed to suffering, and the adjustments demanded. All of it shall give me the burning refinement I need. It is the way of GOD??

You make me wild with your suggestions, and I try to think as well as act right. I just wish I were between your ivory thighs and penetrating you to the depth of bliss and exploring wildly your holy of holies. It is not enough to kiss your honey box in my dreams. Now please do not mention sex or else keep far, far away or I'll bite your neck and lie on your breasts and give you all I have, but it is unfair to tantalize me.

You can dream as I shall, but you MUST NOT come, and I must not allow you to do so. It is the biggest job I ever had, for we could have the sweetest fucking in the earth. You must not be a WHORE, and you would be if we do things wrong in meditation. If we are catapulted into each other, and I mean INTO, that is another thing. Now let us be a real hero and heroine in this struggle. And if we love each other, we must help each other!!!! In fact, I love you more than mere sex. Divine as sex is!!!

Faithfully and Affectionately,

Chase

"Where's the Mate for Me?"

Dear Stella,

I like every word of your letter in which you accuse me of being a reef. I must write to you now and then as a real daughter and always honestly. Now, as to drifting, you are; and your illustration of the ship and the reef is not good. A ship cannot "jump" a reef, and a shore is even worse than a reef. I have been neither so far as being alluring and showing false lights. I really have helped you get your reckoning to a degree. I want you to lean on Stellanova Brunt and sit on her and stand with her and have confidence in her and courage with her. One can die of lack of courage as quickly as from T.B., and when there is both, it is time to take another tack. You ask if you should adopt a child in order to make a home—no! You can make a home in your own heart and then in a house with a lot of girls until you can snare a boy. Quit trapping for old men. You are bright and pretty and sweet and attractive and would make the dearest wife for some kiddoo. But forget the sex and the baby part. And they will come along in their own time, and if they do not, you can do something else.

Just as you say, the fact you resent what I charge against you is some evidence of its truth.

Faithfully Yours,

Chase

Dear Chase,

Chase, I am afraid that, if we let love draw us as she wills, I shall bear you a baby; for no woman-soil since ever procreation began has so completely, so perfectly, received the seed of man. It is not sensible, it is wild, mad—-and perhaps I shall wake rudely from the madness some tomorrow—but I desire intensely that you shall give me a baby—more than one baby! I would have your babies as often as I could, as long as you could give them to me. And they should be so much like you, dear one, since I have a woman's share of many of your greatest qualities. To project you through your children into the future would be the greatest work I could do; I would give up everything for that, I would center all my interest and all my love on your children.

I long to give the gift of life to my children as the trees desire pollen to have fruit. But, dear, if ever I do bear your children, I shall be to you like the orange tree that even while bearing fruit does not cease blossoming. I am all love for you, down to my deepest roots. But I alone have completely engrafted upon you, beside you, BENEATH you, BENEATH you, most exquisitely adored!

I know that there are those who think it "indecent" for a man past sixty-five to have children; but, dearest, those who are best able to produce better children should not come under any such rule. You have so much with which to endow the future, Chase. Four children of your own flesh and blood are not enough. Half of your good, your great qualities, may have failed to go into the making of so few. Am I wrong in believing I am better soil for your seed? I have some of your vision, your strength, your mind, and honesty, And I would spend all my earnestness and ambition and ability in helping them to be what you would wish them.

We shall defend our babies, who cried so hard to be born! Our babies, who have cried to be born—remain only cries and dreams.

Stella

"I Can't Give You Anything but Love"

Beloved,

Your letter makes it hard for me.
I shall have nothing to WILL to heirs
except a good name. We cannot be
married in the ordinary sense of the
term. There is NO property reason at all
why we might not marry. But there are
many OTHER reasons. You ought to be
able to see them even more clearly than
I do.

If my family and the world knew
the holiness of our hearts, there might
be not so much to misunderstand. They
do not and cannot. Then I have been
honored and trusted, and my name and
my reputation do NOT belong to me or to
you alone. They are the property of those
who have trusted me and have believed
in my sense and judgment. It would
look to the public as if I am insane and
that you are mercenary. It is not enough
for us to know to the contrary. I shall
pray for a time when we can live and
work together in close communion. This
is a simple, clean, trusting, conventional
region. I do not belong to myself alone.
There are many other reasons, not easily
phrased. It does not worry me if persons
slander me unless it is true.

Try to be satisfied with what I am
now giving you, which is more than I
have ever given before.

Affectionately Your Friend,

Chase

Dearest Chase,

Your invitation came yesterday afternoon. I knew the answer as I read it; yet it set me trembling. Last night I sat here until after twelve trying to write the answer, and when I gave up could not get to sleep. I knew the answer. And I knew that you no more would let me come, even if I would, than you would let me see your room at Lansing. I knew though the permission to see you (which I have begged for three years) had seemed to come at last, it meant nothing, that more than ever before it was shut out by the word that is yours. IMPOSSIBLE. I know it is only a new way of trying me—that you wouldn't let me, if I would!

You speak of promises that you have given to the living, and to the dead, that you must keep. There are other promises that you have given—-the tacit agreement between you and your friends and all your people that you are what you seem to be. If I should come and that which seems inevitable now should happen, you would be playing false to all these three. There is laxity in the relations of men and women today; perhaps the changes that go in a direction in the future will be considered sensible and right. But you and I do not belong to this experimenting generation. We are too sure in our hearts of a few of the fine, old-fashioned things? How could you believe in keeping one kind of promise and not the other! It is not so bad to break a legal promise that can legally be dissolved as it is to break the moral responsibility to be honest which nothing can remove. I had rather see you dragged Kresge-like through the ditches of newspaper notoriety, talked about unpleasantly for no fault of your own—rather see you live alone and lonely, without even a dog for company—rather see you live alone and hungry—searching out wistfully across a thousand miles toward my hunger that keeps crying to you—I'd rather any of this should be than that, because of me, you should have actions that needed to be hidden, that brought any fear of discovery to make shadows in your heart.

Chase, dear, my heart is hungry for the closer tie that would then come to knit us—not the tie of marriage, (which is denied) but just the greater closeness the claim that I would have on you, the actual belonging, the excuse to cling!

I had rather see myself a harlot, or a pervert, or a suicide, or a mental wreck from struggling, than have it said about you truthfully, as I have heard it said—and hated for the moment a world so empty of understanding, and so cruel!—that you were "no better than you ought to be," with further incriminating statements—and no longer be able to defend you with the full depths of my convictions as I have done!

How could I keep my reverence for you, knowing that you pretended to be one thing, being another? How could you trust me if you knew me capable now of living a lie? I should not truly love you, Chase, if I could wittingly make you less worthy of respect. The idea of anything illicit does not go with the name Osborn!

Why do you torture me with the long-wanted invitation, now that we know that I may never come to visit? This is my punishment for creeping too close to you with my words! Yet I can't be sorry—for my words—or for yours—that I must try not to remember! I will remember them—but I will not come.

You will be at Duck Island, and I shall be in Manitoulin that you gave me, just as we were last summer. Yet not the same. I cannot love by stealth, under the shadow of deceit and fear; love is too high and beautiful a thing.

I haven't seen you for three whole years, and sometimes your letters wring my heart with your recurrent telling that you wish that I didn't care for you; sometimes, I think that my affection means less to you than your affection for your dogs Red Jim or Bono Bynx.

Stella

But I am yours utterly, dear Chase, and unto death.

Stella

Dear Stella,

I agree that it is FOOLISH and DESTRUCTIVE to think of doing ANYTHING in a sneaky way. I shall NEVER marry at all. If I were young, I would consider marriage or any arrangement that would be just to you and make you happy. If fate throws us together is one thing. If we deliberately run into the thing just for a few fucks, it would be wicked and even cheap. This is not an easy decision, for I would like to fuck you to pieces and crush you and have you and all that, but there are things bigger and better and happier and safer and sounder than the orgasms of a moment. I have a clean heart and clear head as I type this and ALSO a big prick.

There can be greater loftier holier, more enduring love in being right than in doing what both of us well know is _wrong_; a sin; a sorrow; a shame; even a crime???

Affectionately Enough (quite enough)

Chase

Dear Chase,

You were not like other men. You were iron-strong—-you would wall me out. Your uncomplicated life story and your avoidance of more unpleasant publicity meant more to you than me, or the regularity of my life; I should have liked you less for thinking so; but I began rather to like myself less for putting my own self above you, my life story above your life history and your public career. You were the more important of us two, by far, you knew your own mind and your future plans, and you were strong-willed as steel. It had taken five years of my life to make my love seem desirable; —iron man!

I am not altogether foolish, nor altogether weak. I know that she is wise who withholds her favors until she has been deeded, by law, the right to a man's name for her children and the right of maintenance for herself and them; that the way to make a man marry her is to arouse his desire and then deny it—all very subtly—until he promises. I know that women who give themselves generously, rashly, get sorrow for their pains. I know that the wise virgin, when her man bids for her favor, should "play her cards" evenly. But I am neither worldly-wise nor very much of a philosopher. Mostly I am woman. I wanted of you above all a tender human attachment, not an intellectual relationship. I sat beside you at the breakfast table and felt a gap of necessary coldness rise between us. "The matter that is now closed." I had lost you!

Stella

Dear Stella,

I am not divorced and not likely
to be. I have four children and twelve
grandchildren and hundreds of children
named for me. I have been trusted and
honored. If so easily I could brush these
things aside, I could as easily wave you
off someday if things were crosswise. But
if I am honorable in these things, there
is a likelihood that I will be an honorable
friend to you.

Good friendship is surely better than
bad love; I know full well that you think
you love me. But it is not that at all. You
are hunger. It is a spiritual desire around
which gathers other things; a little sex, a
little wish to be cared for; a little heading
for a port. I know what it is, but it is not
easy to tell you. Again, I tell you that you
must find God; The Great All. He can cure
everything. I know it.

Faithfully and Affectionately Your Friend,

Chase

Dear Stella,

I propose to be your loving and kind and helpful friend if you shall and will but help me to be. You near shoved us into the maelstrom of hell, and I near let you do it. The slide down was so sweet. Please have your goiter removed and then you can be my "mother" and take care of both of us as mothers always do.

With Loving Friendship,

Chase

"Let's Face the Music and Dance"

Dear Chase,

I came to the Sault with no thought at all of an immediate change in our relationship. I would be your sweetheart until death or your wife; the intermediate kinship was impossible. I knew the weary and fearful road of one who has something to be hidden, had left it all behind eleven years ago and knew the joy of being 101% honest and unafraid. I knew the beauty of the theory of absolute honesty; that all human relationships are based on the assumption of trustworthiness. Therefore, honesty must be followed always. And I believed, in this day, with divorce no longer a stigma. There could be absolutely no occasion for an irregular union. You said marriage was impossible; I declared quasi-marriage impossible also.

I have thought a great deal since early June of the idea of divorce and you. The papers are full of news of them—but always of grants to half-wits or harum-scarums and moving picture people. And yet nice people are also separated from their mistakes and their misfortune: a number of people on the faculty here have legally canceled their marriages, and have even married again. And I do believe in divorce—since the bonds so often are so far from heaven-made. It is the publicity I dislike for you. It could not be avoided, could it? And if afterward, the woman whom you happened to win and want were younger —no one would understand. There might be more unpleasant publicity. And yet, Chase dearest, if that were the only thing in the way. If a woman's consent to be quietly divorced were all that were necessary to give you all that you have a right to, I should beg you to do it.

Stella

Dear Stella,

You speak of divorce, which we dismissed. I confess I feel you are driving me into a cul-de-sac —a POKE. YOU may not or may be conscious of it. If you had not talked indiscreetly no one would be on the "watch" even as they are NOW???? Much the best not to discuss me with anyone. I never do you. It seems too sacred.

We can be anything we can be if you just can get it into your head that I am not a free man. I am morally, but not in the law. I AM MARRIED legally NOW. We can NEVER marry. No other way. There are ten thousand reasons.

Then I have so many whom I love to live up to. My code has been that nothing is wrong that does not injure; does not hurt someone or THE ONE. We have been tested in the fire, and if we clinched lovingly at times, it would be right if we thought it so. Anyhow there shall not be much time to think of such things as I am beyond the age limit now.

You ask me to write to your mother when you have deceived her all your life. It looks a bit like a trap. Now you are big enough to interpret this without tears. Personally, I think it is your penchant for the decent and the safe. You shift positions so rapidly it is not only confusing but also highly irresponsible. You unsettle me terribly. IT IS NOT LOVE. I am glad you came to "Possum Poke" if the issue is a finished one so far as leading to an impossible impasse.

I am in the late evening of life. The shadows are falling softly, but certainly. They are rose-hued and sweet. I wish to keep them that way.

Please only write once a year or all business. I'll do the same.

Chase

"I Want to Be Married"

FREEDOM AND PUBLIC AVOWAL
FOR AND AGAINST MARRIAGE

by Stella

<u>FOR:</u>

- TOGETHER ALWAYS

    (instead of a few short, difficult times
    a year)

- No fear

- No repression

- COMPANIONSHIP now, when needed most

- A LIFE ALMOST PERFECTLY HAPPY.

- CARE, for always.

<u>AGAINST: PUBLICITY, BUT...</u>

- Soon over

- It has not hurt hundreds of many in
  political and professional life

- Not much news involved since it would be
  only a step confirming separation of which
  everyone knows

- It could have no effect on your public
  standing—the separation and the rogue
  talk having done its worst long ago

- It would be less hard on your family and
  friends than the slow-leaking out of
  an irregular connection (which I feel is
  practically inevitable)

AGAINST: DECEMBER-AUGUST UNPLEASANTNESS, BUT...

- I am _not_ young—nearly middle-aged

- You are no longer wealthy
  (And I would sign papers waiving all
  dower rights. I want only you!)

- I have no money, no family, but I am a star
  graduate of a star university

- You have recognized literary and
  intellectual leanings, with outstanding
  achievement.

- Everybody knows that a man needs
  someone to take care of him as he grows
  older.

- Everybody expects a man to have a
  woman—if he hasn't one legally, they
  accuse him of having one or many sub
  rosa.

- We know that we are ideally mated—spirit
  and mind and body and disposition— every
  way—joyously.

- We know that we are mated for life—
  that we are to be a shining example of a
  steadfast, happy marriage come what may
  (even when I bring up a topic verboten!)

- Why should we care for anything said if we
  know the happy truth?
  —Our friends all would soon know it, too.

It is not so bad to have it said that a woman
married an older man for his money than it is to
have it said that she lived with him extra-legally for
a competence, which is one risk we are running now.

It is not so bad to have it said, of a man, that he married a younger woman for sex reasons, as well as for company and care as it is to have it said that he lived with the younger woman for sex reasons, at intervals and to have it said also that he would endanger her reputation without marrying her, which risks we are now running for you.

Either way, there is trouble of a kind. But the one way there is certainty, safeness, and the maximum of happiness. Beloved, even outside of dictionary things, your Starry may be right—You are so grand, so dear—it is for your happiness I struggle as well as for my own—for what seems to me so plainly the wisest and best.

Scold me if you will, but I cannot change the thought, dear. And all my heart and mind are full of love for you. Think it through with me, darling—weigh it point by point. For Starry, and for Bruin, who love and need each other.

We have only each other—I could cry, having you riding away alone with your need of me and your longing for me as great as mine for you—and me left somewhere far behind longing and needing too—Life is nothing without you!

Stella

"My Heart Belongs to Daddy"

Brilliant Starry Guide,

YOU arranged to come at Christmas. I shall leave it all to you as you know best. No need to rush things with your mother. She might not exactly understand. When it comes time to go to Duck Island, have her come with you??? Why not?

But the thing that worried and pained was the fact of your vacillation and irresponsible temperament. How am I to know you shall not relent in a few weeks or so? This is the third time you have almost completely destroyed my FAITH in you. Please distinguish between "faith" and "love." Now that I love you, it shall never be driven out. But you have caused me anew to doubt and to be shaken as to certainty that you know what you are doing. I hesitate to take any step or make any argument to persuade you. I must allow you to follow the bent of your desire. My love is as unselfish as a human can feel.

I saw Col. Perry. He is to send you a paper to sign. Please do this and mail at once as time is an essence if we are to get into the April term of court.

Adoption proceedings are often complicated, but in this case, there appears nothing complex. That you are more than 21 simplifies things. You need consent from only yourself. If I had a wife, she would have to consent. Having none that is out of the way. That you are a Canadian seems to offer no impediment.

Your mother cannot realize a lot of things. She does not know me. She does not know that I had nothing to do with initiating the "going" of Jones-Osborn. She does not know that Jones-Osborn NEVER was my wife in the way of making me want for her or miss her or anything of the delicate things of heart and sentiment obtained in a perfect wedding???

I let my "boy" go because he had become the intimate in this camp "household." I did not wish him or anyone as an INTRUDER upon OUR dear privacy?

For the sake of argument, let us give heed to your mother's doubts (unfounded as they are). As my daughter, you would not be displaced sentimentally or legally by any possible situation that arises. Your mother does not know that the children are all married and have places of their own and have practically deserted me and I them. This was before you came on the scene. You cannot be blamed for anything providing your love is lasting and sane, and you are certain of what you are doing and wish to do.

Of all the things I do not wish, one is to keep you on the defensive and explaining. There is nothing to defend or explain. Explanations are nearer than first cousins to excuses. If you need any defending at any time, I claim the right and the duty to do that. Things that need explanation usually cannot be explained, and those needing none explain themselves like "gun powder."

You are my precious First Mate.
Actually, you are the FIRST MATE ever I
have had. I wish to be your guide; your
friend; your daddy; your crutch; your
ALL it is in my power to be. But you
must be CREW. Can be no mutinies; no
half-hearted allegiance. NOW you have
enlisted under new colors and have
your rights in some hurtful directions
curtailed for your own good. No more
shall you be cheap. You are to hold
yourself above all.

My only prayer is to HELP you and
never to HURT you, for I LOVE YOU.

Bruin

Dear Stella,

Your mother's letter does not affect me. I had not proposed to adopt her! Nor shall I consider the adoption of you unless you are certain and steadfast and enthusiastic for it. At worst, you would be a legal daughter. At best, you would have so much more.

Your allusions to Bliss are nauseating. Whatever can you have done that gives that Bliss beast a right to question you or be so contemptuously familiar? My word, how cheap you have been. It tries my love, and my love is equal to this and every test. It is divine and transcends all sex and selfishness; shall at once have Col. Perry hold the matter of adoption in abeyance. This vacillation makes me cheap, too. I had thought it all out.

No matter what the vulgar and cheap Bliss and others say, it cannot be more than they have said already. Our only concern is to do right by each other and to be right and to have a clear conscience before God. Mine is.

I repeat that if you are of uncertain mind, just quiet and let time tell the story more plainly. My love shall not change. If it stands the attacks of your irresponsible wobbling, it can stand anything. But I confess I am sick at heart as well as in mind and stomach. You pursue me seven years and then throw the whole thing over and down in a moment's fit of some

strange aberration??? You are not to be
depended upon?????

Chase

p.s. It makes me sick when you wobble-
waffle-wobble.

Dear Chase,

Mother does not understand you or your name as the Cowdens do. She may not ever quite understand. But she will not oppose and in no time at all will be seeing our way. We can make her happy in many little ways. We must make allowances for her, sweetheart—even I come to understand you and your place in the world only gradually. You will find out at once what will be necessary to make me of your own family? About my name, for several reasons, I should like to be Stella Brunt Osborn ("Sally" and "Starry" for love); but if you take me for your child, I shall be yours to name. If George and Mother raise no great objection, and if it can be done in a short time, perhaps we may affirm the bond between us then? We need not tell any more than seems necessary just go along in our own way and let it be known, as it will be.

It is a tremendous thing that we are doing, dear. It is for all our lives—all that we have been and are, for all the years that are left to us. We have aired all our needs and all our doubts, and the one doubt that mattered has been thrown out as groundless. It is no quick, shallow assent now, no argument of the heart with the head silent. Darling, I am all one, undivided,

After all, the fear of harming you was needless, such a load fell from me. All the load of the years fell away, and I felt free—free to come to you at last, joy of my life! Won't ever call you father though—only dear and dearest and maybe a few other names.

Dream of me, dear, these last few nights before we have the right to claim each other. In two more weeks, I come. How grand a time of meeting it shall be—different from all before—

Beloved, life turns us a new page henceforth—
one page for both of us. All the deep, fine, joyous
things we shall write on it together.

I am your girl until I die—and beyond death—

Sally Starry

Stella Brunt Osborn

"Something Peculiar"

Date: March 31, 1931

Miss Stella Lee Brunt
P.O. Box 107
Ann Arbor, Mich.

Dear Miss Brunt,

At the instance and request of Hon. Chase S. Osborn, we are enclosing herein to you an original petition filed by the Governor here in our Superior Court, for the purpose of adopting you as his daughter, which you will understand by reading.

It is necessary that you acknowledge service on this petition, and we have written out the acknowledgement of service on it, which you will sign opposite the pencil cross, and when you have done so, please return it to us at your earliest convenience.

Yours very truly,

PERRY & TIPTON
Attorneys at Law
Sylvester, Georgia

April 1, 1931

Miss Stella Lee Brunt
P.O. Box 107
Ann Arbor, Mich.

Dear Miss Brunt,

In mailing you the original petition of Governor Osborn filed in our superior court asking that you be adopted as his daughter, we failed to enclose a copy of the same, and we are herein enclosing a copy, which you can retain for your files.

Yours very truly,

Perry & Tipton
Attorneys at Law
Sylvester, Georgia

Stellanova Osborn, 1922

Photograph taken on the occasion of the graduation of Osborn
(then Stella Lee Brunt) from the University of Michigan.

She graduated Summa Cum Laude
and was inducted into Phi Beta Kappa.

Harkness Photography, Hamilton, Ontario

Credit: Stellanova Osborn Papers

Bentley Historical Library, University of Michigan

Chase S. Osborn, circa 1898

Photographer unknown

Credit: Chase S. Osborn Papers

Bentley Historical Library, University of Michigan

Chase S. Osborn, 1910

Photographer unknown

Credit: Michiganensian, p.8

Chase S. Osborn at his desk in his
executive office, Michigan State Capitol.

photographer unknown

Credit: Wikipedia

Chase S. Osborn, 1906

photographer unknown

Credit: State Archives of Michigan

A DAUGHTER AT 37.—Because Chase S. Osborn, 72, philanthropist, lecturer, writer and former Governor of Michigan, found his literary work too arduous for his advanced years, he adopted Miss Stella Lee Brunt, 37, his secretary, at Sylvester, Ga. Now she can give him constant attention.

Stellanova Osborn, 1931

photographer unknown

Credit: New York Daily News (by Associated Press)

"Stellanova Osborn and Chase S. Osborn, September 8, 1935,

at the home of Dr. E.C. Elliott, President of Purdue University,

Lafayette, Indiana

J.C. Allen & Son, photography, Lafayette, Indiana

Credit: Chase S. Osborn Papers

Bentley Historical Library

University of Michigan

Chase S. Osborn and Stellanova Osborn, 1938

Credit: Chase S. Osborn Papers

Bentley Historical Library

University of Michigan

Carleton W. Angell and Chase S. Osborn with clay model, 1937

Stellanova Osborn, photographer

Credit: Chase S. Osborn Papers

Bentley Historical Library

University of Michigan

Carleton W. Angell, Chase S. Osborn, clay model, 1937

Stellanova Osborn, photographer

Credit: Chase S. Osborn Papers

Bentley Historical Library

University of Michigan

Carleton W. Angell, Chase S. Osborn, bronze bust, 1938

University of Michigan

Credit: author of *Ward, Wife, Widow*

Carleton W. Angell, Chase S. Osborn, bronze bust, 1938

University of Michigan

Credit: author of *Ward, Wife, Widow*

Discussion Questions

for

Ward, Wife, Widow

What do you think motivated Stellanova Osborn to donate her personal correspondence to the University of Michigan archives?

Do you think that letters of a personal nature, even when donated and archived for public access, should be used to inform the author of a novel or biography?

President Jimmy Carter's personal letters to Rosalyn Carter were published by Jonathan Alter. President Ronald Reagan's letters to Nancy Reagan were published by Nancy Reagan herself. Martha Washington and Eliza Hamilton, however, destroyed their personal letters. Do you think that such documents should remain private?

There is no clear timeline for the exit of Mrs. Lillian Jones Osborn and the entrance of Stella Lee Brunt as Chase Salmon Osborn's lover. Do you believe that Stella Brunt bears some responsibility for the dissolution of Chase's first marriage?

Should we judge Governor Osborn's decisions or morays by his time or our time? Are his actions so quixotic that it doesn't matter from which perspective he is judged?

Should the author have made the characters more sympathetic, that is, more appealing to the reader, or less so?

What accounts for Stellanova's change in personality from the letters of the 1920's to the perspective she has in the late 1930s?

If you were an offspring from the first marriage, could you have accepted Stellanova's role as an adopted daughter or a second wife at the eleventh hour?

Compare the relationship of President Franklin D. Roosevelt and his secretary to that of Governor Osborn and his secretary. How are they similar and how are they different?

There is far more scrutiny now about which public figures are deemed worthy of a statue in their likeness. Would Osborn meet today's standard for being honored?

What do you think about the deathbed annulment and marriage of Chase Osborn and Stellanova Osborn? Chase Osborn had many months to change the status of their arrangement after the death of his wife, but he did not do so. If Stellanova did not have his consent, was she, as his common law wife, entitled to his estate? Did the affirmation she sought justify what she may have done to secure her role as his wife of a few hours and his widow of many decades?

The State of Michigan makes more than a cameo appearance in the novel. Did this enhance your interest or detract from it? Could your home state or adopted home state play as important a role for you in a book you might author?

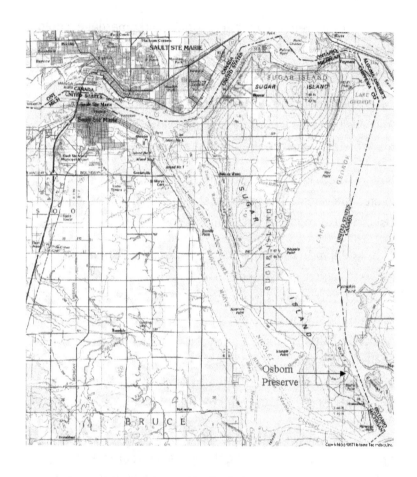

Topographical map of Sugar Island and surrounding region
https://sites.google.com/a/umich.edu/bug-camp—bvk/
home/properties-maps

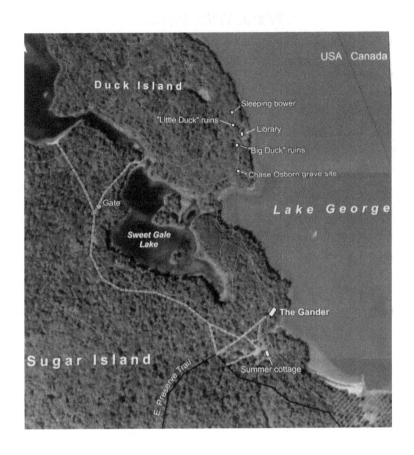

Google Maps aerial view of the site of the Osborn Camp
https://sites.google.com/a/umich.edu/bug-camp—bvk/
home/properties-map

Endnotes

for

Ward, Wife, Widow

Dedication

Inscription in Frost's hand in his own copy of *You Come Too*, the poet's book of verse for children. The inscribed volume is in the Bentley Historical Library on the campus of the University of Michigan. Frost presented this copy to Stellanova Osborn in April of 1962. For the inscription, see Warner, Robert M., "Frost-Bite & Frost-Bark: Robert Frost at Michigan," Ann Arbor, Michigan: Bentley Historical Library, University of Michigan, 1999.

"Always" Lyrics
https://www.lyrics.com/lyric/16113884/Irving+Berlin/Always

All Alone

For this undated letter, from Stellanova Osborn (née Stella Lee Brunt) to her mother, see Stellanova Osborn Papers, Bentley Historical Library, University of Michigan, Ann Arbor, Michigan, 1918-1949.

On a Whim

This letter was not written by Stellanova Osborn, although much of its content here is a composite from other sources. Nevertheless, such a letter likely did exist, and, as with others of the earliest letters from Stellanova to Chase Osborn, it was probably not saved by the recipient.

"...a not-at-all-trim man of medium stature in a not-too-well-pressed grey suit, with fair and not-too-tidy hair." James Tobin, "Robert Frost in Ann Arbor," *Michigan Today,* June 9, 2010. https://michigantoday.umich.edu/2010/06/09/a7771/

"...he speaks lightly enough, with a whimsical, skipping surface over his comments, there is a lasting tang of significance in the stuff of them. The conversation of Frost sparkles, more elusively, and is at its best in the pauses—when it is in his eyes, between words." (written by a fellow member of the Whimsies, and not actually attributed to Stellanova. Osborn).

"Would it surprise you to know that he is also an excellent gossip?" See Warner, 1999, p.19.

"He could be both humorous and ruthless. It was a harrowing experience for me when Frost kept scolding me over the same old faults—not making my meaning clear and using old phrases. My nerves were all on edge, to begin with, and that about unsettled me. I didn't sleep all night." (from letters from Stellanova Osborn to her mother) See Warner, 1999, p.17.

"...not to even twirl his thumbs if he does not so desire." See Tobin, 2010.

For the story about the events surrounding the home game (Yost) vs. Hill Auditorium (Frost), see Warner, 1999, p.23.

Toll

This letter was not written by Stellanova, although much of its content is a composite of material from the correspondence between her and Chase Osborn in the Bentley Historical Library at the University of Michigan, 1918-1949.

For the poem "Toll," see Stellanova Osborn, *Summer Songs on the St. Marys,* North Star Communications, Sault Ste. Marie, Michigan, 1982.

The Proposal

This letter is not the actual letter from the University of Michigan to Chase Osborn, but such a letter did exist and the content of the letter is supported in several sources listed in the bibliography.

"...the state deficit was eliminated; a workmen's compensation bill was sanctioned; and a presidential primary law was authorized. "Chase Salmon Osborn." *National Governors Association*, https://www.nga.org/governor/chase-salmon-osborn/.

The Patient

For the Letter to the Editor, printed here in full, see Chase Osborn, "Gov (sic) Osborn tells how it feels to be seriously ill; lauds Sault hospital. Experiences in delirium of pneumonia described by former governor, now recuperating at his camp," Evening News Sault Ste. Marie Sault Ste. Marie, August 5, 1938, The Library of Congress, https://www.loc.gov/item/rbpe.0840270b/.

The Arrival of Angells

For this journal entry, see Carleton Angell, "The Laird of Sugar Island Chase S. Osborn," *The Quarterly Review of the University Alumnus,* December 10, 1938, pp.19-21.

"So, you think you're a sculptor, Professor. Angell?" See Angell, 1938, p.22.

"I do the best I know." See Angell, p.22.

"I admire your honesty. Well, some men are sculptors in stone and bronze, while others are sculptors of men!" See Angell, 1938, p.22.

"Our span of life is ticked off by springs of iron ore in clock and watch." See Chase S. Osborn, *The Iron Hunter,* Detroit, Michigan: Wayne State University Press, 2002, p.144.

"Let those who produce it hold up their heads with dignity." See Chase S. Osborn, 2002, p.145.

For Osborn's intake of liquids, see Stellanova Osborn, *Eighty and On: The Unending Adventurings of Chase S. Osborn,* Sault Ste. Marie, Michigan: Sault News Printing, 1941.

...[he] growled, 'Osborn, do you know how near a fool you are?' I replied, 'Two feet.' It was not an original retort, I am certain, but the psychology of it was that its very boldness gave me a greater confidence in myself." See Chase S. Osborn, 2002, p. 64.

God's Country

"No one has finished seeing the earth with satisfaction until he has circled Lake Superior both by land and water." See Chase S. Osborn and Stellanova Osborn, *Schoolcraft, Longfellow, Hiawatha*, Lancaster, Pennsylvania: The Jacques Cattell Press, 1942, p.42.

"The winds that blow from the Northwest, even today, are never breathed by man until they get to where the Indians lived and where the whites now have taken their place."

See Osborn and Osborn, 1942, p.41.

"The air is the clearest and most vitalizing on earth, for it is as invigorating as that of the Alps without the danger and discomfort attendant on high altitudes." See Osborn and Osborn, 1942, p.49.

"...could walk off his feet up to the knees!" See Milton Mac Kaye, "A Rugged American," *Redbook*, Janunary-1940, pp. 46.

"There is only one tree in the world the boughs of which make a perfect camp bed. No more restful, comfortable slumbering can be had anywhere than on a balsam bed properly made. Spruce is obstreperous. Hemlock is lean. But the needles of the balsam lie flat and are friendly. The fragrance of a balsam bed surpasses anything in the Isles of Spice. It is healing, restful, and soothing." See Chase S. Osborn and Stellanova Osborn, *Northwoods Sketches*, Lansing, Michigan: Historical Society of Michigan,1949, pp. 57-58.

The Panama Hat

Tom Miller, *The Panama Hat Trail*, Tucson, Arizona: The University of Arizona Press, 2017.

Providence

"Do your best and do not quarrel with Providence." See Chase S. Osborn, 2002, p.281.

Breakfast Before Dawn

For the source of this story, see Chase S. Osborn, 2002, p. 65.

"...in a loud whisper, called me a vile name and followed the insult with the threat that he was going to 'lick the stuffin' out of me' after church." See Chase S. Osborn, 2002, p.65.

"Do you not know that the fearless teacher presents every facet of the intellect in action? Will you strive to give wings to thought and then kill it when it tries to fly? Next time you oppress an intellectual process, it may be the death of a great truth." See Chase S. Osborn, 2002, p. 236.

"...shake things up, and I came to have a large respect for his work without yielding an iota of my Presbyterianism." See Chase S. Osborn, 2002, p. 236.

"The only trouble with Christianity is that man isn't good enough for it yet. Christ was born too soon." See Mac Kaye, January 1940, p.61.

"Every one of them waged a battle for equality and decency every minute, and it was a prideful thing to know them." See Chase S. Osborn, 2002, p. 94.

"I did not formally join the church, I did enlist for the aims of the church." See Chase S. Osborn, 2002, p. 89.

"I don't know whether prayers reach a Divine ear or not. It seems to be a little presumptuous to think so. Perhaps prayers are only your good wishes for people. I pray for all my friends, living or dead." Mac Kaye, January 1940, pp. 46–49, 60.

An Encore Performance

For the source of the story about Osborn's early speaking engagements, see Chase

S. Osborn, 1941, pp.61-62.

Poetry, Prose, and Pygmalion

"There were *too* many friends and *too* many pleasant invitations and activities. They jostled each other and jostled her; life was a choppy sea there with continual pleasurable excitement." See Stellanova Osborn Papers, 1918-1949.

For excerpt from the poem "Pensive Hours," see Jane Johnston Schoolcraft and Robert Dale Parker, The Sound the Stars Make Rushing through the Sky: The Writings of Jane Johnston Schoolcraft, Philadelphia, Pennsylvania: University of Pennsylvania Press, 2008, p.109.

A Heavy Lift

"All of a sudden, we were a family translated from luxury to necessity—from affluence to abysmal poverty." See Chase S. Osborn, 2002, p.50.

"Poverty...cramps...and...expand(s) the soul." See Chase S. Osborn, 2002, p.50.

"The things that scare most persons in politics are the most attractive to me. I like the strife, the pawing, the goring, the tragedy, and the comedy that comes from the friction, the impacts, the slander, and the abuse of a public contest. I have a good temperament for a row. It's kind of like seeing how much you can lift." See Robert Warner, "Chase Salmon Osborn 1860-1949," *Michigan Historical Collections*, Bulletin no.10, January 1960, p.26

Diplomacy in a Tea Cup

"By the shores of Gitchee Gumee, By the shining Big-Sea-Water, Stood the wigwam of..." See Chase Osborn and Stellanova Osborn, 1942, p.41.

"Nokomis Daughter of the Moon, Nokomis. Dark behind it rose the forest, Rose the black and gloomy pine trees, Rose the firs with cones upon them." See Chase S. Osborn and Stellanova Osborn, 1942, p.41.

"Bright before it beat the water. Beat the clear and sunny water. Beat the shining Big-Sea-Water!" See Chase S. Osborn and Stellanova Osborn, 1942, p.41.

The Braver of the Two

"There never has been a time in the African jungle or any other place demanding courage, when my wife has not been the braver of the two." See Chase S. Osborn, 2002, p.88

Dinner Guests

"I shall be happy to deed my Duck Island Preserve of three-thousand acres to the University with no restrictions except a life tenancy on Duck Island. My library of some seven-thousand books will go with the gift as well." See Norman H. Hill, "Osborn Gift Enriches University: Valuable Land and Large Library Are Presented and Accepted by Board of Regents," *The Michigan Alumnus*, vol. 36, no. 3, 1929. file:///Users/mary scholtens/Downloads/osborngift%20(1).htm

"Just because the only other woman to attempt to boat down the Colorado drowned does not mean that women have any more reason to fear that adventure than any man." See Kim Clarke, "River Rat." *University of Michigan Heritage Project*, heritage.umich.edu/stories/river-rat/.

"[Grape-Nuts]...were stored as great big marbles, so we had to hammer them into smaller pieces to eat. However, the centers were almost always wet and moldy." Elizabeth Wason, "Down the Great River: Diary of a Cactus Hunter." U-M LSA U-M College of LSA." *U*, May 20, 2014. lsa.umich.edu/lsa/news-events/all-news/search-news/down-the-great-river.html.

Dessert and an Appetite for Adventure

"Thomas Edison, like so many others, was curious about the source of the firefly's light and admitted that he could not produce light as economically as the firefly, but he hoped that man would discover the secret and profit from it. I discovered the source, but I haven't profited from it, nor has anyone else for that matter." See Emerson Hough,

"Out-Of-Doors: The Firefly's Light." *The Saturday Evening Post*, vol. 188, no. 41, April 8, 1916, p. 36.

"I made a *correlation* that proved to be conclusive. It may be true of almost every discovery made. One man discovers one thing, one another, and finally, somebody discovers the missing link, the key. Then the facts are correlated, and the conclusion is satisfactory. My idea is at least new, and I think it is indisputable. Those to whom I have submitted it are as firm in their conviction as I myself am." See Hough, 1916, p. 36.

The following quotations from the section on Elzada Clover's Colorado River trip are taken from Clover's journals as reported by Wason. See Wason.

"Cactus spines were embedded in the excrement, which provided information about the animal's diet and the dispersal of plants in its habitat," See Wason.

"I felt guilty asking any other woman to share the physical and mental punishment which would be ours." See Wason.

"...prefer to die doing something exciting." See Wason.

"...cut off from any hope of getting out in case of accident, illness, or fright." See Wason.

"We could hear the noise of the first series of rapids. Ominous is the wrong word, but we were all pretty serious. The sound of the tremendous waves made the crew mute with awe, fear, and the impossibility of being heard above the roar." See Wason.

"It is a great river with a hundred personalities, but it is not kind." See Wason.

"The days were 'as hot as Hades,' and the nights were 'colder than hell.'" See Wason.

"We would leave water out overnight to allow the clay silt to settle. However, out of necessity, we sometimes drank water right out of the river from our helmets, which coated our mouths and throats with clay and gave us stomachaches." See Wason.

"...night was so beautiful that I couldn't sleep." See Wason.

"It was just part of a day's work to make a flying leap for shore, to climb steep cliffs after plants, and to get photographs." The quotation is attributed to Elzada Clover in this novel, but it is actually a quotation from Lois Jotter. Sevigny, Melissa L. "The Wild Ones." *The Atavist Magazine*, November 1, 2019, magazine.atavist.com/the-wild-ones-grand-canyon-colo rado-river-first-women.

"My life has been full of adventure, but this seemed like the ace of them all." This statement from Elzada Clover's journal is a caption used in the video associated with the Wason article online at minute 1:47). See Wason.

"...feeling of uncertainty and expectation," See Wason.

"People who have not fought with such elements cannot realize how petty and trivial are the things two-thirds of us do in civilization. What a shame to have to get back." See Wason.

Woven Baskets and Family Ties

For information about the black ash basket weaving craft, see Lester Graham, "Artisans of Michigan: Anishinaabe Black Ash Baskets." *Michigan Radio*, National Public Radio, September 1, 2017. www.michiganradio.org/post/artisans-michigan-anishinaabe-black-ash-baskets.

"Never take the first, because then you will never take the last." See Robin Wall Kimmerer, "Braiding Sweetgrass," Minneapolis, Minnesota: Milkweed Editions, 2013.

Parting Gift

For information about the Caruso performance, see Sophia Kruz, *A Space for Music, A Seat for Everyone: 100 Years of UMS Performances in Hill Auditorium*. MLive Media Group & Detroit Public Television, 2013.

The Committee Convenes and Critiques

"You are interrupting my morning devotions!" See Louis A. Hopkins, "The Governor's Bust: Dealings with the Unpredictable Genius of Duck Island," *Quarterly Review of the Michigan Alumnus*, vol. 62, Spring 1956, pp. 237.

"Excuse me, sir, shall we walk along the path [back to The Gander] and return at a more convenient time?" See Hopkins, pp. 237.

"Well! I declare I feel that looks like me! But what a rugged customer he is!" See Angell, p.26

"Put that bust in bronze and send me the bill!" See Hopkins, p. 240.

The Last Supper

"I serve my guests myself!" See Hopkins, p. 238.

"Eat that potato!" See Hopkins, pp. 238.

"Do you hear me? Eat that potato!" See Hopkins, pp. 238.

"I do not *care* for more potato," See Hopkins, p. 238.

"Then, you get no dessert!" See Hopkins, p. 238.

"I'll forego the dessert." See Hopkins, pp. 238.

"I suppose I am more or less like the Northland, which has rugged terrain and rough facets." See Warner, 1960, p.29.

A Widow Returns

For Chase Osborn's nurse's log, see Stellanova Osborn Papers, 1918-1949.

"Do I mind dying? Of course not. The people who are fond of me will be sad, and that's all that bothers me. I love life, but I am so curious to see what goes on afterward that sometimes, honestly, I can hardly wait." See Mac Kaye, p.61.

"...[He] was a good 'getter' and a great giver." See epithet on marker as seen on the following video: *Possum Poke – The Winter Plantation of Michigan Governor Chase S. Osborn-Poulan, Georgia*, 12 June 2009, www.youtube.com/watch?v=uGojXkH-Voc. (@min 1:56)

For the poem entitled "Wilderness Grave," see Stellanova Osborn, *Iron and Arbutus*, Northwoods Press, Michigan 1962.

Widow's Weeds

For the fairytale "Allerleirauh," see *Wikipedia*, Wikimedia Foundation, December 29, 2020. en.wikipedia.org/wiki/Allerleirauh.

The Turn of a Key

For biographical information used, see http://friendsofallencounty.org/20050034/getperson.php?personID=I06272&tree=MICHGOV

Epilogue

For information about John F. Kennedy's visit to the University of Michigan, see "A Special Milestones Edition, Commemorating the Peace Corps Announcement," *AnnArbor.com,* October 11, 2010.

www.annarbor.com/news/this-week-in-ann-arbor-history-a-special-milestones-edition/.

The source of the information about candidate John F. Kennedy's speech at the University of Michigan Union is a video of John F. Kennedy's address on the occasion of announcing the founding of the Peace Corps on October 14, 1960. https://www.peacecorps.gov/about/history/founding-moment/#video-modal-0

A Fine Romance

For the source of the letters quoted, see Stellanova Osborn Papers, 1918-1949.

Bibliography

"22 Things You May Not Have Known about the 1927 Bath School Massacre," *MLive*, May 18, 2017. mlive.com/news/2017/05/10_things_you_probably_didnt_k.html.

"Allerleirauh." *Wikipedia*, Wikimedia Foundation, December 29, 2020. htpps://en.wikipedia.org/wiki/Allerleirauh.

Angell, Carleton, "The Laird of Sugar Island Chase S. Osborn," *The Quarterly Review of the University Alumnus,* December 10, 1938, pp. 19-27. loc.gov/resource/rbpe.0840270d/?sp=5&st=text.

"Bath School Disaster." *Wikipedia*, Wikimedia Foundation, February 26, 2021. en.wikipedia.org/wiki/Bath_School_disaster.

Brisson, Steven C, "A Nobel Figure: The Story of The Marquette Statues," *Mackinac State Historic Parks*, vol. 3, no. 4, 2000.

"Bust of Ex-Governor Osborn is Completed," Bessemer Herald, Bessemer, Michigan, February 25, 1938, page 12, column 2.

"Carleton Angell, Long-Time 'U' Artist, Dies at Age 75," *Ann Arbor District Library*, Ann Arbor News, June 2, 1962.

aadl.org/aa_news_19620602-carleton_angell_long_time_U_artist_dies_at_age_75.

"Carleton Watson Angell (1887-1962)." *Find A Grave.* findagrave.com/memorial/23432394/carleton-watson-angell.

"Celebrating Women's History Month: Elzada Clover, Pioneering Michigan Botanist and Colorado River Whitewater Rafter," *Matthaei Botanical Gardens and Nichols Arboretum*. mbgna.umich.edu/celebrating-womens-history-month-elzada-clover-pioneering-michigan-botanist-and-colorado-river-whitewater-rafter/.

"Chase Salmon Osborn," *National Governors Association*. nga.org/governor/chase-salmon-osborn/.

Clarke, Kim, "River Rat," *University of Michigan Heritage Project*. heritage.umich.edu/stories/river-rat/

Derieux, James, "Sage of the Soo." *Collier's*, March 28, 1931, p. 28.

Dickson, James, "A Special Milestones Edition, Commemorating the Peace Corps Announcement," *AnnArbor.com*, October 11, 2010.

annarbor.com/news/this-week-in-ann-arbor-history-a-special-milestones-edition/.

Frank, Mary Jo, "U Receives Materials from Robert Frost Family Archives," *The University Record*, University of Michigan, December 14, 1998. ur.umich.edu/9899/Dec14_98/6.htm.

"Gene Stratton-Porter," *Wikipedia*, Wikimedia Foundation. en.wikipedia.org/wiki/Gene_Stratton-Porter.

"Governor Chase Salmon Osborn (1860 – 1949)," *River of History Museum: Sault Ste. Marie, Michigan*. riverofhistory.org/index.php/articles/governor-chase-salmon-osborn-1860-1949/.

Graham, Lester. "Artisans of Michigan: Anishinaabe Black Ash Baskets," *Michigan Radio*, National Public Radio, September 1, 2017. https://www.michiganradio.org/post/artisans-michigan-anishinaabe-black-ash-baskets.

Hill, Norman H. "Osborn Gift Enriches University: Valuable Land and Large Library are Presented and Accepted by Board of Regents," *The Michigan Alumnus*, vol. 36, no. 3, October 10, 1929.

Hopkins, Louis A., "The Governor's Bust: Dealings with the Unpredictable Genius of Duck Island," *Quarterly Review of the Michigan Alumnus*, vol. 62, Spring 1956, pp. 237–241.

Hough, Emerson, "Out-Of-Doors: The Firefly's Light," *The Saturday Evening Post,* vol. 188, no. 41, April 8, 1916, p. 36.

Howard, Saralee R., "Famous Michiganians," *Great Lakes Informant,* series 1, no, 2, Michigan Department of State, Michigan History Division.

friendsofallencounty.org/20050034/getperson.php?personID=I06272&tree=MICHGOV. (Information about the birth and death dates for the Osborn family)

"Hudson's Bay Point Blanket," *Wikipedia*, Wikimedia Foundation, December 18, 2020, en.wikipedia.org/wiki/Hudson%27s_Bay_point_blanket.

John F. Kennedy's Address to the University of Michigan Campus on the Occasion of Announcing the Founding of the Peace Corps, October 14, 1960.

peacecorps.gov/about/history/founding-moment/#video-modal-0.

Kimmerer, Robin Wall, *Braiding Sweetgrass*, Milkweed Editions, Minneapolis, Minnesota, 2013.

Kruz, Sophia, *A Space for Music, A Seat for Everyone: 100 Years of UMS Performances in Hill Auditorium*, Detroit, Michigan: MLive Media Group & Detroit Public Television, 2013.

Lewis, Janet, *The Invasion*, East Lansing: Michigan State University Press, 2000.

MacKaye, Milton. "A Rugged American," *Redbook*, January 1940, pp. 46–49, 60.

Maynard, Charles. "Spring Pools and Clock Towers: Robert Frost, Michigan's Poet-in-Residence: Literary Traveler," *Literary Traveler*, April 13, 2012, literarytraveler.com/articles/robert_frost_annarbor/.

McClinchey, Florence E., *Joe Pete*, Sault Sainte, Marie, Michigan: Zhibi Press, 2018.

McDiarmid, Hugh. "Stellanova Osborn, Married Ex-Governor after Adoption," *Detroit Free Press*, March 20,1988, p. 8a.

Miller, Tom, *The Panama Hat Trail*, Tucson, Arizona: The University of Arizona Press, 2017.

Mires, Charlene, "Sault Ste. Marie as the Capital of the World? Stellanova Osborn and the Pursuit of the United Nations." *Michigan Historical Review*, vol. 35, no. 1, 2009, pp. 61–82. jstor.org/stable/25652151.

Osborn, Chase "Gov (sic) Osborn tells how it feels to be seriously ill; lauds Sault hospital. Experiences in delirium of pneumonia described by former governor, now recuperating at his camp," *Evening News Sault Ste. Marie* Sault Ste. Marie. August 5, 1938. The Library of Congress, loc.gov/item/ rbpe.0840270b/.

Osborn, Chase S., *The Iron Hunter*, Detroit, Michigan: Wayne State University Press, 2002.

Osborn, Chase S., and Stellanova Osborn, *Northwoods Sketches*, Lansing, Michigan: Historical Society of Michigan, 1949.

Osborn, Chase S., and Stellanova Osborn, *Schoolcraft, Longfellow, Hiawatha*, Lancaster, Pennsylvania: The Jacques Cattell Press,1942.

Osborn, Stellanova, "A Conference on Michigan Politics at the Little White House, Warm Springs, Georgia." *The Georgia Historical Quarterly*, vol. 29, no. 4, December 1945, pp. 217–221. jstor.org/stable/40576993.

Osborn, Stellanova. *Eighty and On: The Unending Adventurings of Chase S. Osborn*, Sault Ste. Marie, Michigan: Sault News Printing, 1941.

Osborn, Stellanova, *Summer Songs on the St. Marys*, Sault Ste. Marie, Michigan: North Star Communications, 1982.

Osborn, Stellanova, *Iron and Arbutus,* Sault Ste. Marie, Michigan: Northwoods Press, 1962.

Parker, Robert Dale, *The Sound the Stars Make Rushing Through the Sky: The Writings of Jane Johnston Schoolcraft*, Philadelphia, Pennsylvania: University of Pennsylvania Press, 2007.

Peck, Lauren, "The Origin of the Jingle Dress." *Minnesota Good Age*, MN History, March 27, 2019. minnesotagoodage.com/voices/mn-history/2019/03/the-origin-of-the-jingle-dress/.

Petosky, Paul, "Town of Payment: Sugar Island Township, Chippewa County, Michigan," *Michigan Postal History*, Chippewa County Michigan Genealogy & History. genealogytrails.com/mich/chippewa/citypayment.html.

Possum Poke – The Winter Plantation of Michigan Governor Chase S. Osborn – Poulan, Georgia, June 12, 2009. youtube.com/watch?v=uGojXkH-Voc.

"Properties & Maps – Bug Camp – Bvk's Home Page." *Google Sites.*

sites.google.com/a/umich.edu/bug-camp—bvk/home/properties-maps.

Schaleben, Arville, "'Fabulous'—That's Chase Osborn," *Milwaukee Journal*, Wisconsin Historical Society, June 8, 1928. https://www.wisconsinhistory.org/Records?terms=Chase+Osborn.

Scholtens, Mary Crum and Kevin Williams, eds. *Grapevine Point to Pine Point: The UMBS Centennial Memoir Project*, Lulu.com, 2008.

Sevigny, Melissa L., "The Wild Ones," *The Atavist Magazine*, November 1, 2019. magazine.atavist.com/the-wild-ones-grand-canyon-colorado-river-first-women.

Shackman, Grace, "The Pumas," *Ann Arbor District Library*, Ann Arbor Observer, May 2007. aadl.org/aaobserver/18544.

Shaul, Richard D., "To a Different Drum," *Michigan History,* September/October 2004, pp. 26-33.

Shaw, Wilfred B. ed., "Chase S. Osborn Preserve." *University of Michigan an Encyclopedic Survey,* Ann Arbor, Michigan: The University of Michigan Press, 1958.

quod.lib.umich.edu/u/umsurvey/ AAS3302.0004.001/1:2.8.4.38?rgn=div4;view=fulltext.

Stellanova Osborn Papers, Ann Arbor, Michigan: Bentley Historical Library, University of Michigan, 1918-1929.

Stratton-Porter, Gene. *A Girl of the Limberlost,* New York, New York: Grosset and Dunlap, 1973.

"Stella Lee Brunt Osborn (Mrs. Chase Salmon Osborn)." *Michigan Through the Centuries,* Lewis Historical Publishing Company, 1955.

Steere, William Campbell, "The Bryophytes of the Chase S. Osborn Preserve of the University of Michigan, Sugar Island, Chippewa County, Michigan," *American Midland Naturalist,* vol. 15, no. 6, 1934, p. 761. doi:10.2307/2419895.

Tobin, James, "Robert Frost in Ann Arbor," *Michigan Today,* University of Michigan, 22 November 2019. michigantoday. umich.edu/2010/06/09/a7771/.

Warner, Robert M., "Chase Salmon Osborn 1860-1949." Ann Arbor, Michigan: *Michigan Historical Collections,* Bulletin no.10, The University of Michigan, January 1960.

Warner, Robert M., "Frost-Bite & Frost-Bark: Robert Frost at Michigan," Ann Arbor, Michigan: Bentley Historical Library, University of Michigan, 1999.

Warner, Robert M., "Introduction," to Chase S. Osborn, *The Iron Hunter,* Detroit, Michigan: Wayne State University Press, 2002.

Wason, Elizabeth. "Down the Great River: U-M LSA U-M College of LSA," May 20, 2014. lsa.umich.edu/lsa/news-events/all-news/search-news/down-the-great-river.html.

Tunes Referenced

Berlin, Irving; and R.S. Berlin, "All Alone" (1924)

Berlin, Irving, "Always" (1925)

Berlin, Irving, "How about Me?" (1928)

Berlin, Irving, "Let's Face the Music and Dance" (1936)

Berlin, Irving, "When I Lost You" (1912)

Gershwin, George and Ira Gershwin, "Love is Here to Stay" (1938)

Gershwin, George and Ira Gershwin, "They Can't Take that Away from Me" (1937)

Gershwin, Ira and Lou Paley, "Something Peculiar" (1927)

Jones, Isham and Gus Kahn, "It Had to Be You" (1924)

Kern, Jerome and Dorothy Fields "A Fine Romance" (1936)

Kern, Jerome and Oscar Hammerstein, "Where's the Mate for Me?" (1927)

McHugh, Jimmy and Dorothy Fields, "I Can't Give You Anything but Love" (1928)

Porter, Cole, "I've Got You under My Skin" (1936)

Porter, Cole, "I Want to Be Married" (1912)

Porter, Cole, "My Heart Belongs to Daddy" (1930)

Porter, Cole, "You Do Something to Me" (1929)

Acknowledgements

I am grateful to archivists Diana Bachman, Madeleine Bradford, Caitlin Moriarty and Karen Wight at the University of Michigan Bentley Historical Library.

I extend my thanks to Amy White, Director of the University of Michigan Student Union, who "introduced" me to the bust of Chase S. Osborn stored in the bowels of the building.

I am appreciative of Cheryl Brown, ash-basket weaver, for enlightening me about the process of making baskets, Donna Searles, for introducing me to members of the Little Traverse Bay Band, Netawn Kiogima, for translating Gib and his Aunt Kateri's exchange into Ojibwe.

I want to thank friends Barbara Billings, Thom Gerrish. Claudia Jolls, Rex Lowe, Knute Nadelhoffer, Mark Paddock, Marty Samson, Keith Taylor, and Bob Vande Kopple for sharing their interest and perspectives with me on the lives of Stellanova and Chase Osborn.

I wish to acknowledge Nick Osborn Pratt, great-grandson of Chase Osborn, for providing me with proof in the form of a PDF of a legal document that confirmed that I was on the right track with my assumptions about the true nature of the relationship between Stellanova and Chase Osborn.

I am indebted to the Norcross family, Julie, Matt, and Jessalyn, owners of McLean and Eakin Booksellers in Petoskey, Michigan for hosting so many authors over the years who inspired me to dream about one day writing my own novel.

Thank you to Schuler Books of Grand Rapids, Michigan, especially Pierre Camy and Vivian Kammel, for their professionalism in creating an edition of which I could be proud to hold and to share with my readership.

I am profoundly grateful to have selected just the right people to shepherd this novel into the final stages. I could never have found my way through the narrative without their guidance. My dogged and gifted copy editor, friend, and longtime pen pal Laura Rood Kao. My insightful reader, editor, friend, and personal librarian, Marcia Russo. My oldest friend who happens to be an excellent English teacher, Kevin Williams, whose attention to detail definitely raised my grade on this writing project. My brother, Roger Crum, whose professorial scrutiny of the manuscript kept me humble and kept me laughing. His reward for his efforts was getting to the end of the manuscript to find that he was the inspiration for the character "Professor Hoover."

Everlasting thanks to my father, Howard Crum, who always showed his love for me by putting a special book in my hands. My mother, Irene Crum, who believed that I could do anything.

Finally, my love and deep gratitude to my immediate family. Brian Scholtens, who never fails to listen to me, love me and support me in pursuing my passions. Luci, Michael and Vanessa Scholtens, who call me Mom and cheer me on. It is *their* lives that provide me with my favorite stories to share.